Prize Stories 1971:
THE O. HENRY AWARDS

Prize Stories 1971:

THE O. HENRY AWARDS

Edited and with an Introduction by

WILLIAM ABRAHAMS

Doubleday & Company, Inc., Garden City, New York
1971

CONTENTS

PUBLISHER'S NOTE

This volume is the fifty-first in the O. Henry Memorial Award series.

In 1918, the Society of Arts and Sciences met to vote upon a monument to the master of the short story, O. Henry. They decided that this memorial should be in the form of two prizes for the best short stories published by American authors in American magazines during the year 1919. From this beginning, the memorial developed into an annual anthology of outstanding short stories by American authors published, with the exception of the years 1952 and 1953, by Doubleday & Company, Inc.

Blanche Colton Williams, one of the founders of the awards, was editor from 1919 to 1932; Harry Hansen from 1933 to 1940; Herschel Brickell from 1941 to 1951. The annual collection did not appear in 1952 and 1953, when the continuity of the series was interrupted by the death of Herschel Brickell, who had been the editor for ten years. Paul Engle was editor from 1954 to 1959 with Hanson Martin co-editor in the years 1954 to 1956; Mary Stegner in 1960; Richard Poirier from 1961 to 1966, with assistance from and co-editorship with William Abrahams from 1964 to 1966. William Abrahams became editor of the series in 1967.

Doubleday also publishes *First-Prize Stories from the O. Henry Memorial Awards* in editions which are brought up to date at intervals. In 1970 Doubleday also published under Mr. Abrahams' editorship, *Fifty Years of the American Short Story*, a collection of stories selected from the series.

The stories chosen for this volume were published in the period from the summer of 1969 to the summer of 1970. A list of the magazines consulted appears at the back of the book. The choice of stories and the selection of prize winners are exclusively the responsibility of the editor. Biographical material is based on information provided by the contributors.

INTRODUCTION: PRIZE STORIES 1971

In the long view, it is the story, and not the circumstances or place of its publication, that matters. Properly so. It is of no concern, save to a handful of literary scholars and specialists, in what magazines or newspapers the stories of Chekhov, for example, were first published. But in the short view—the view necessarily of an annual collection such as this, whose aim is to bring together a group of outstanding stories that have been published in magazines during the preceding year—the concern is inevitable and legitimate. Once the story has been written, and granted that it has been written not as a form of private therapy (usually called "self-expression") but with the expectation of presently being read, there follows a set of essential transactions: between writer and magazine, and between magazine and reader. In the early life of the story the role of the magazine is central. Later, should the story survive, escaping from the ephemeral into the permanent (from the magazine to the book), the significant transaction is between the story and its readers; the role of the magazine becomes vestigial, consigned to a footnote in literary history.

I emphasize the point, not simply because there is no place for it in aesthetic considerations, but because any attempt to describe the state of the contemporary American story can't be separated from the state of the contemporary American magazine. For it is the magazines, grudgingly or generously, that publish the stories and provide the first audiences for them. I believe it was Whitman who once remarked, a shade grandiloquently, that to have great poets there must be great audiences —might one not hope, then, with equal grandiloquence, that someday there will be great magazines dedicated to the short story?

Meanwhile we should be grateful for what we have: a number of magazines—some, like *The New Yorker,* with an audience in the hundreds of thousands; some, like *Shenandoah,* with an audience in the hundreds—which include in their contents stories of authentic literary merit and which (it would seem) impose a minimum of editorial restriction upon subject matter and length. The importance of these magazines as they encourage, stimulate and, on occasion, introduce gifted writers of stories is not to be underestimated. But their number is steadily diminishing. In my Introduction to the collection last year I reported the end of one of the oldest and most famous of mass magazines, *The Saturday Evening Post.* This year it is the turn of one of the most distinguished of the literary quarterlies, *The Kenyon Review.* In almost every other respect the two were poles apart, but they were alike in their readiness to publish fiction of superior quality, and indeed a number of authors published stories in both magazines without doing violence either to their principles or their style. (A reminder that the past decade has seen the line of demarcation between the stories in certain of the magazines of large circulation and the little magazines gradually blur, so that, on the whole, it has become difficult to say what a typical "little magazine" story is.)

The *Post,* we have been told in perhaps excessive detail, was the victim of corporate intrigue at the level of high finance in which matters of literary principle figured not at all. The *Kenyon,* simply and sadly, was the victim of rising costs. To the very end it was unwavering in its devotion to the short story, and its final numbers, in addition to some splendid examples of the form, included a fascinating if contradictory "International Symposium on the Short Story" that proved as much an inquest into the story as a job of work by which a writer could earn his living as a celebration of the story as a work of art.

So the name of *The Saturday Evening Post* no longer appears in the "List of Magazines Consulted" for this collection, and the name of *The Kenyon Review* appears there for a final time this year. It is not unreasonable to predict that other magazines, mammoths and minuscules alike, will share their fate. Still, new ones are being founded, and altogether there are some eighty magazines still listed as publishing short stories. To the casual observer this might seem cause for congratulation rather than apprehension. But in too many of these magazines the story is tolerated rather than welcomed, and the proportionate amount of space allowed to fiction is minimal. The preference among editors, as I have remarked in earlier Introductions, is still for the article; and one can only conclude from this that the passion for fact (or what at a given moment passes for fact) is insatiable among readers. Ironically enough, if the passion is as passionate as editors apparently believe it to be, it may lead to their own undoing. For just as the picture magazines appear to be entering into an age of obsolescence—why look at pictures in a magazine when one can watch them, and watch them move, on television?—so one can foresee the end of the article in the rise of the audio-visual cassette for home use.

In the "sifting process"—a continual reading and rereading—that had to be made from among the nine hundred or so stories available for this year's collection, the next-to-final choice consisted of thirty-five stories from nineteen magazines.[1] The interesting thing here, and again in the final choice of seventeen stories from fifteen magazines—arrived at with a full awareness of possible omissions, oversights and one's own fallibility—is that the greater number of stories came from the little magazines and literary quarterlies. This is not the consequence of any editorial prejudice in their favor; it simply reflects the fact that they are more hospitable to fiction, to the story as work of art, than are most of the larger magazines. And those of the larger magazines that publish fiction of genuine merit—several are represented here—can't begin to make room in their pages for the number of worthwhile manuscripts they receive.

There is one further group (many of them enjoying an enormous circulation) that might be singled out for comment: the so-called women's service magazines. None are represented here this year, not because they give no place to fiction, but because the level of fiction they give place to is, too often, inexcusably low. There are exceptions, of course—celebrated writers are welcomed, celebrated and sometimes even gifted writers, and their stories reveal, as one would expect, a practiced talent.

[1] Five stories from *The New Yorker;* five from *Esquire;* three from *The Atlantic Monthly;* two each from *Harper's, Partisan Review, Southwest Review, Transatlantic Review, Shenandoah,* and *Virginia Quarterly Review;* one each from *Southern Review, The Sewanee Review, Kenyon Review, Playboy, Denver Quarterly, Epoch, Perspective, Quarterly Review of Literature, Carleton Miscellany* and *Antioch Review.*

And there are differences, too, among the magazines themselves: some are less offensive in this respect than others. But here, I suggest, is a prime target for the Women's Liberation movement, for these magazines would seem alike in their conviction that while women are qualified to read excellent recipes and excellent advice on interior decoration or child raising, the only stories they are qualified to read are those that trivialize, sentimentalize and falsify the aspects of life with which they pretend to deal. Indeed, it is precisely because their concern is with "life" (but always at a safe remove from the real thing) rather than, as in the shameless past, with "fantasy" that these stories seem so peculiarly deplorable. It is the price we must pay, now that the women's service magazines have "grown up" into a kind of bogus knowingness and sophistication. No longer will we read, say, of the shop girl who by some magical whim of fate marries a millionaire. Instead, we are brought to grips— in a white-gloved and platitudinous way—with the plight of a pretty young widow whose soldier husband has been killed a year ago in Vietnam. (The war is only a name, of course; and although we are given a good deal of "atmospheric" description, the circumstances of his death are passed over in tactful silence.) She has been left with a nine-year-old son to raise on her own, and one day she takes him to the park. There, while he is off playing with his friends, she meets a handsome young man (why is *he* not in Vietnam? but no matter) who engages her in conversation. It turns out that he has lost his wife (divorced? a nurse killed in Vietnam?) and has a daughter to raise on his own. As they talk, her eyes linger on his full, handsome thighs—how's that for sophistication?—and she thinks how long it has been *since* . . . I hasten to add that this example is not an invention of my own, but a fair reproduction of a story published during the past year in a women's service magazine that prides itself on its respectability. I would argue that the contempt for women implicit in the publication of stories of this sort—the unstated conviction that this is all that women want, or deserve, in the way of fiction—is indefensible.

The paradox, of course, is that many of our best writers of short stories happen to be women. A number of them are represented in the present collection; and it is fascinating to see how many of their themes and concerns—marriage, the relation of parents and children, growing old alone—are the themes and concerns that are offered, like counterfeit currency, in those magazines that women, we are told, prefer. The difference, as we are made aware reading Florence M. Hecht or Alice Adams or Evelyn Harter or Josephine Jacobsen or Eleanor Ross Taylor or Joyce Carol Oates, is that their stories have been written, as the stories we value (whether by men or women) must be written, at the level of art.

—*William Abrahams*

Prize Stories 1971:
THE O. HENRY AWARDS

FLORENCE M. HECHT was born and raised in New York City, where she attended City College and the New School for Social Research. Her short stories have been published in *Redbook, Esquire, The New Orleans Review,* the *Denver Quarterly,* and *The Atlantic Monthly.* Mrs. Hecht was a Breadloaf Scholar in Fiction in 1966. She presently lives in Queens, New York, with her husband, two teen-age sons, and her Siamese cat.

Twin Bed Bridge

Later, when it was all over and friends began to visit her again—bringing sympathy, curiosity, opinions—asking as they always did: "What really happened, Syd?", she smiled, and explained: "It all started with Mr. Clean." Laughing, titillated by such impudence from a woman who had so recently flirted with death and nearly succumbed, they'd say: "She's putting us on again . . ." "Come on, Syd, quit clowning and tell us how it happened!" And because she was cured now, able to appreciate the loving attention of men and women who attached real significance to her presence in their midst, her smile was a glowing arc that took them in entirely as she repeated "But it's true. Mr. Clean."

Sitting in a cozy corner of her Danish-modern living room, a cigarette in one hand, a bourbon on the rocks in the other, she felt so relaxed, objective, lucid that it might have been someone else's story. In the easy grace with which she crossed her still admirable legs, in the calculated pauses framing those ludicrous nightmare images, in her awareness that implicit in the first four words there existed for everyone a darkly intriguing realm of possibilities, she was in full command of her past. "Very late that night," she began, "about twelve thirty, I think—the children sleeping and Shephard still at his rally—his *third* teach-in that month—well, I was sitting right here watching television. And there was Zsa Zsa Gabor, obscenely beautiful in sequins, expounding this endless goulash on *love* to an overpowered Johnny Carson. An aging, pampered darling's monologue . . . vanity's last shrill cry. It was so desperate, and sad—"

"You mean you took it seriously?" "How awful for you, Syd!" "Go on, go on! What then?"

"She was finally cut off by a commercial. A giant genie wearing one earring metamorphosized from a detergent bottle—muscled arms crossed over his powerful chest, he grinned heroically coast-to-coast and promised total war on dirt. Yes, all over America women would soon depend on his miraculous capacities and surely love him. Were women stuck with the deficiencies of well-meaning but ineffectual hubbies? Mr. Clean to the rescue! Virile, sterile, vanishing, ubiquitous—here at last, the secret ravisher every woman craved in her dull, dirty kitchen—anthropomorphic, MR. CLEAN was here to make the scene; and outraged, helpless, I found myself overwhelmed by some awful sense of loss. Is this possible?, I kept asking, is this possible?

"And then, Mr. Clean disappeared into the bottle. Zsa Zsa Gabor came back—giggling, dimpling, pouting; 'vot dahling, vot . . . but ahf coorz dees ees vot I mean! Ah vooman veedouht lahv ees no vooman attall!' The camera dollied in on the heaving Gabor bosom, Carson's pygmy eyes large with boyish obscenities, and the audience roaring approval . . . oh, my America, I moaned . . . my America. And then something terrible happened to me, my friends. Inside my head, something slipped. I nearly fainted, but I forced myself to walk to the bathroom . . . I can remember letting the tap run on my head until my brain went numb. When Shephard came home, he found me on the floor. The rest, of course, you know . . ."

What they didn't know was that when she came to at nearly 2 A.M., she said to Shephard: "Why so late?" When he answered: "A bunch of kids hung around after the rally . . . you know, all excited about my speech . . . the leaders of the sit-in . . . we got to talking," what she said was: "Ah, formidable, Monsieur Babble-Babble, formidable! Listen here, my Herr Professor of Very Political Science, it's after hours, and very late in the day."

Then she took a blanket, rolled herself up on the living room carpet, and dropped into an odyssey of dreams.

Later that morning, her two sons were kneeling on either side of her, shaking her awake. Their golden heads rose from the green carpet like tender daffodils, but they spoke with the shrill voices of hungry children demanding breakfast. "How old are you?" she said. "Eight and a half," said Kenneth. "Eleven," said Ivan. "Exactly," she said. "Old enough to feed yourselves. Look—ten kinds of energy cereals open. Delicious. Snap, crackle, pop. Go ahead. Then get dressed and go to school." And as she covered her head with the blanket, their muffled voices disappeared.

Someone pulled down an edge of the blanket and put a hand on her forehead. His voice seemed to rise from a distant glass funnel: "Oh, shit. Come off it, you faker, there's nothing wrong with you. Syd—Sydelle! Do you hear me? You better cut this out, you hear? Are you trying to drive me crazy? Haven't I got enough on my mind? Listen, I'm going. I've got an early class. I'll call you later." The tip of a beard brushed her closed eyes and she trembled, pulled the blanket over her head again, and sank back into dreams. Clouds of lilac wool descended, enclosed her, kept her safe in an endurable world of sleep.

At ten after twelve, the children came home for lunch. Kenneth roused her with kisses, but Ivan stared accusingly at her uncombed hair, rumpled pajamas, pasty face. There it was: Shephard's face in his firstborn, repeated for posterity. The eyes blue and hard in that still-unbearded face, the line of the jaw firmly drawn, the forehead high with purpose—a wall too high to climb over, she could see it separating her from Ivan now and in all the years to come.

So she clung to Kenny's soft baby cheeks, his kisses, the open innocence of him, absurdly moved to tears when he said: "Yuh got any baloney, Ma?" But she couldn't help watching Ivan at the stove, his breakfast lesson in self-sufficiency already enough to give him the outer edges of style as he neatly poured a can of Campbell's chicken soup into a pot and coolly announced: "I'll take my own, thanks." Oh, such civil disobedience. Even the tightassed tone of his father's pompous platform voice. And his eyes all blue contempt on her bare feet . . . three days of

undusted floors between her toes . . . well, like the fella once
said: the apple doesn't fall far . . . still, with a little coaxing, a
gal might remember the resilience of that stolid tree . . . the
juices running wild . . .

because once, long ago, Shephard really tried—made a stretch
of the Atlantic his Aegean, at eighteen already middle-aged
with melancholy, shivering in the gooseflesh of his naked heart
and the plea almost comic, so fractured was his voice with
change, with love, with fear—ah, love, let us be true to one
another, he croaked—and she wanted to kiss him until the
misery reflected in his eyes vanished from the planet

and she did, she stayed in his arms kissing him until the
sun set, the tide went out, and the beach now empty of people
was open to great flocks of birds scavenging in the strewn
garbage on the shore. But Shephard saw only their white fragile
wings, the pure grace of their flight, envying the perfect
solitude of each gull, separate though it flew with thousands

"They really aren't joiners, you know," she told Kenny, watching him munch a baloney hero sandwich. He turned a page of
his Superman comic, said, "Hmm-mm." "*Seagulls, I mean.*"

Surely the backs of their necks had never looked so thin, so
vulnerable before. She poured two extra heaping spoons of chocolate in their milk. "Drink your milk, Ivan." Engrossed in the
final chapters of *1984*, Ivan slurped noodles, hearing nothing but
the voice of Orwellian doom. He looked at his watch, put a
brown leather marker in his book, a souvenir from one of
Shephard's fund-raising dinners. In raised gilt letters, it said: Ban
The Bomb. "Ivan, eat a banana, why don't you . . . that's not
enough for a bird."

"No, thanks," he said, his jacket on, already halfway to the
door.

"Do you have your key? Make sure you take your key!"

He turned around, answered the dull tangle of her hair.
"Why?" he said. "Are you going somewhere?" The door slammed
behind him.

"They'll be rotten in a day or two." Already flecked with
black, the bunch of five bananas in the bowl was a monstrous
yellow hand. Diseased. Disgusting. As she threw them in the
garbage pail, Kenny came to kiss her good-bye. Her soft-
cheeked baby, never noticing her bare dirty feet, reaching up

with his wet chocolate mouth on her chin, blind with acceptance, child-sweet, Siegel-sweet . . . Shephard's mouth after all. She squatted beside him, murmured in his ear, "Oh, sweet, so sweet, my Kenny Siegel—born to make my heart's joy legal."

"Oh, Ma," he groaned, while she checked the string-tied key around his neck. "Remember not to forget, willya—I'm going to Robert's house after school."

"All right," she said. "Watch yourself on that bad crossing. There's no guard"—the door shut between them—"at the bad crossing."

I will take a long hot bath now, she told herself. I will soak for a very long time. My Aegean, my Atlantic, my Black sometimes Red Sea. Sydelle Siegel, what's happened to you? Mismatched sibilants? Symbols of disorder must stand for something. Sydelle Freed never had this trouble. Miss Freed flew with the flock, freer than any Siegel. I am not now and never have been a Seagull. Listen, gentlemen, I protest. On the grounds that it may incriminate my husband, Dr. Shephard Seagull, under whose wings fly flocks and flocks of fledgling seagulls, I resign. My escape clause was announced twenty years ago, 7:45 at Jones Beach

oh, I told him, I warned him—honey, it's not euphonious at all—Sydelle Siegel? And I could see him shiver, waiting, refusing me smiles, trivia, waiting for my yes as if this alone could turn the tide, restore the missing fragments of the world . . . how cruel with power I was, but terrified to see that noble reason melting so unreasonably, the very word love synonymous with prisons for the heart . . . and I trembled too, packing my heart in dry ice. When the birds came, I was laughing, laughing in those arms which wouldn't release me till I'd answered and I said, Shephard, just look at those silly, god-awful creatures! And you want me to marry you? Oh, Shephard, don't you know what a seagull is? A seagull is a Jewish bird! And me, I'll be Mrs. Seagull . . . oh, oh, how funny . . . And he said, shut up, shut up, why don't you, and closed my mouth with his. Say it, he said, please! So I said, I do, Shep, honest I do . . . Do what? Say it all of it. I do, I love you, Shep, and yes I'll marry you . . . yes, yes, yes

far too many yeses. The Garden of Eden repeated ad nauseam. How can it always be The First Time? oh, not only survived but prevailed the man said. Obligatory beach scene. Nature in the raw. Paradoxical head of my beloved so heavy with light-headed love—black black black was the color of my true love's hair—there where it lay salty wet with sweat and the sea of that last murderous crest over my breast—his face so smooth, a boy's, the voice amalgam of all poets' voices, despising all science but the natural, everything politic but the body, vanquishing governments, kingdoms, empires, with anarchies of bony knees. And I, lacking history, myth, educated guesses, I spoke my yeses, embracing the contract of our flesh, wrote my x in blood . . . all because I liked the way he smelled and my flesh becoming hotly as the Bible tells us One with his, and therefore ignorant of banal metaphor, assumed that never before had satin lain so lovely against velvet . . . and loving him, God, and country—in that order—later, later, dared to think beyond his bony knees—how patriotic after all to have celebrated the Fourth with a rocketing of roman candles in our veins—hardly a joke I admit even now—though we did not then or ever allow such levity to make a sacrilege of sacred screwing, any fool can see that gravity is what gets you in the end

because there it is—his struggle with gravity, plain as the beard on his face. Since he let the beard grow. It weighs down his chin, drags down the corners of his eyes, his mouth . . . the dark corruption of academia . . . in every little curl, a cause, a protest . . . he owes me I think one small protest, this professor of the body politic, the science political—owes me this dreary sentiment if only because there lies beneath that fusty beard a girl's first wet and lusty kisses. Yes, the truth is always trite, professor. I knew you when is all . . . I knew you when. And I too heard America singing

and I've told them all—I will not join, I will not sign, I will not speak or march. I will not fight the War-on-Poverty. I am myself a barefoot beggar in the world . . . my brains drained out, I shall invert my empty head and pass the hat—you're a proud land, a proud people, be generous again . . . allow me to do nothing for my country . . . gentlemen, take a good look—I am your tired, your poor. Did Emma Lazarus live in vain? People used to say, where does an alien go to register? No one asks that anymore. But what if someone asked it again and consented to a century of patience?

here in my white American Standard cradle I'll wait . . . let the waters come and join me . . . I will join nothing nothing

It was 4 o'clock when Shephard found her in the tub, her long black hair floating like snakes on the water, her eyes closed, the level of water just teasing her chin. Shouting her name, he pulled her up by the hair and she opened her eyes. A flicker of dull recognition, and she closed them again, saying, "Go away."

He lifted her out of the tub, wrapped her in a towel, and as he carried her to the bed, her small thin body seemed lighter than ever. "I'm calling the doctor," he said.

She was shivering, and he brought her a little cognac, covered her with two blankets, and soon she was sleeping again. The towel he had wound around her wet head seemed the thick white bandages of someone with a head injury; before he dismissed it as only the image of his own anxiety, he saw in her pale, lifeless face the coma of brain damage.

Deaf and blind she lay there on her bed, its twin standing where a month ago she had pushed it to the far side of the room, the northern exposure—*his* bed, in monklike solitude under the window, the very symbol and act of her revenge on him. Of his banishment to Siberia, he thought, I may have deserved that. But not this, not this total desertion. It's not my politics, you're punishing, not my "fidelity to causes," but the other—the betrayal—the sins of what you called my cursed "Judas organ" . . . will you never see the connection, the whole picture . . . there was a time when you saw all the links in everything —at sixteen you were twice the woman you are now . . .

The doctor was out. Shephard had to satisfy himself with leaving a message of "urgent," "emergency"; though he told himself you always had to exaggerate to get a doctor to come, his heart pounded this same message of disaster as he sat staring at her.

He hadn't thought of it in years. But seeing the drowned white look of her, he remembered the breaker catching her off guard, the way she'd disappeared for thirty frantic seconds, and he fished her up by the hair, scared blue, spluttering: I told you we should have gone to Zachs Bay . . . and beside him on the army blanket, her head wrapped in a white towel, wide blue eyes receiving, returning the sunset sky over Jones Beach . . .

She traced his portrait in the sand with a popsicle stick—the forehead doubled, the eyes tripled, grotesquely exaggerated. You've got no sense of proportion, he told her, you'll never be an artist. But it made him laugh all the same. And she explained that it was how she saw him—from the inside out—the high forehead bulging with erudition, the large round eyes ready to take in the whole earth and see it from all sides at once . . . you can tell me, he whispered in her ear—you always said you could trust me with anything. Besides, I just saved your life, you owe it to me; so tell me, what do you really want to be when you grow up? And she answered at once, as if it were something she'd thought about long ago or known all her life: a genius, she said—by the time I'm thirty-six, I intend to be a recognized genius. And he gasped, mock-strangling her for such gross impertinence. And you, Shep? What do you want? To make the world safe for geniuses, he said . . . loving her, oh, loving her till they'd be very old and looking back on this day together . . . for she had thrown her arms around his neck, drawn him inside the blanket, and kissed him so hard the breath sailed out of him and he only caught it again when she bit him playfully on the shoulder, but hard enough to leave her teeth marks for two weeks, turning the skin blue and green and purple and yellow, all the colors of her ferocious love . . . you little beast, he said, stroking the spot, they should lock you in a cage away from everyone . . . alone . . . with me . . .

She moaned something he couldn't catch. "Syd, are you in pain? Is it the kids you want? They've gone next door." Her hand in his was icy, her expression unchanged—it was impossible to tell if she'd heard him. When he started to shake her, her eyes opened for a second, and he shouted in her ear, slapped her cheeks, but she fell back on the pillow, the only sign of life the quiet, even breathing contradicting the mask of her face.

While he waited for the doctor, he searched for some clue, some tangible answer which might turn his terror into understanding. And finally, slipped under her mattress, he found a

large spiral notebook recorded in her black-inked loping scrawl—
the block-printed words on the front page: MY DIARRHEA.

A twisted chronology of events unreeled and interpreted in a
self-created cycle of time, they were visions which sometimes
seemed truer than the lunatic facts at their source. There were
titles over those visions, there were dramas made of them, and
the sound of a mind wrenched in anguish from its moorings.
Stung in a thousand places by the time he finished reading it
and the doctor's car finally entered the driveway, he was shot
through with enough venom to have killed him ten times over.
And with the peculiar irony which she, more than anyone,
would have relished, the only words now left to him were the
same ones with which she began—what can I do? . . . what can
I do?

What can I do? I never wanted to keep a diary, but there is no
one to talk to anymore. I am on the wrong side of everything.
What I need is an anonymous, Miss Lonelyhearts type of person who will care about my problem, let me pour it all out freely,
and dispense that generous, impersonal mercy for the sinned-
against and sinning which takes the same out of confession. I too
would like such anonymity; but I am revealed completely by
the company I keep.

My dear Miss Blake-Franzblau: I trust you to understand that
any lack of discretion on your part will fall like a stone in a
vast political pond, the ripples spreading far beyond my bedroom door. Yet I would not be writing to you if my problem
was not about love. I have told myself repeatedly that women
have lost their men to other women, in love; and in war, to
other men; women have been sacrificial offerings to feed art's
greater life; and in the name of science, been roasted medium
rare over slow kerosene flames. Accepted, understood. Explain
then how only today in the dead and deadly sixties can a
woman lose her man to Martin Luther King? Ah, naturally, you
know now who I am. Professor Siegel's wife becomes relevant
in this context. Need I list his credits? Governors groan, sen-

ators simper, the President pouts at mere mention of his name
—a world-saver, a cause-finder, humanity's redeemer! Oh Miss
B-F—let me confess it at once and get it over with. I am a bad
wife. I will not go whither he goest, and I stopped cleaving
unto him when the voice of the turtle was heard in the land. I
never obeyed him. I have ceased honoring him. And with true
hatred for every vow of love, ten days ago I separated our
twin beds. In all fairness, let me omit nothing: in the decade
before this decade, he gave me two babies; I gave him an
ulcer. We take care of our own—all three are well fed and
flourishing. My children now cook as well as I ever did. More-
over they have TV dinners, TV mothers, Bond and Batman to
see them through. I am the only one who still needs me. But
I'm not committed to that either. Cordially yours.

THE BIG SCAR SCENE

Tonight Professor and Mrs. Siegel have had the sort of argument
which makes him wave his arms and turns his neck into a tangle
of taut ropes. Mrs. Siegel, who believes in neutralizing energy,
responds with hands clasped in her lap and the monotonous
patience of her sex. He accuses her of having glazed eyes, and
she is surprised that the ceramic feel of her head is so aptly
communicated. Her glazed eyes, he claims, are hastening the
imminent holocaust or, at the very least, causing the bombing
raids to continue. "I'm sorry, Shephard, but I can't go with
you," she says. "A lousy citizen is such a drag. I only embarrass
you at these things. And who knows, you might hit on just the
right platitude and save the world tonight. So go on, dear. Enjoy."

"Syd, I'm thinking of you! Not what I want *of* you, but what I
want *for* you! You're not *involved*, dammit—you don't care
about anything, do you? You're just *rotting* with apathy! Tell
me, just tell me—and if you mention the house, the children,
me, I'll strangle you—what do you *do* all day? Up here, I mean,"
he says, tapping his head, "in *here*," fist pounding his heart—
"*what?*"

"I read, I listen to music, I listen to you, I have my painting."

"You call that painting! Look at it!" he yells, turns the easel to the wall. "Shame on you! Syd, you know what it is? The thing that keeps you from being a vital, creative personality? Scars. Open wounds leave scars. And you don't have one single fucking scar! My students may soon be dying like flies, and you're painting butterflies. Mrs. Siegel, you have *sons!*"

Ah. The coup de grace. Monster, *you* have sons.

They arrive now at the same impasse. He deserves this decisive, solemn question: "Shep, I'm asking you again, and answer me straight—do you want out?"

"No, dammit, no! I want you to come *in!* The world is going straight to hell, and you're busy painting lepidoptera!"

Though she might pay with her life, Mrs. Siegel giggles wildly. But regains her self-control: "I told you, didn't I, why I never went back to those P.T.A. meetings—how they asked us to go down to the Board of Estimate in a Body and scream like Mothers—and how the Body was divided between the Mothers who wanted the new school on the corner of Loveless Lane and the Mothers who were opting for the end of Nitwit Drive? . . . lunacies parading as commitments, all of it. Shephard, get it through your head—I don't want *in* . . . there is nothing, nothing to *be* in."

"Then rot in hell with your butterflies," he says, marching on, and out.

Mrs. Siegel, a silent screamer, screams: go to your goddam meeting. Just what'll you do after you've made the universe safe for democracy? You and your lackeys—those dime-a-dozen messiahs looking for a piece of the action—did you ever ponder the fate of unemployed crusaders? Even *God's* beard didn't help Him when the chips were finally down. Besides, only God can make a beard.

THE DAILY PRESS

In this morning's editorial the following paragraph appeared: "Professor Siegel is one of the few sane leaders of the New Middle Left and, in our opinion, one of the few political experts in the entire country who can be counted on for a dispassionate evaluation of our situation. Though yesterday's March-For-Peace attracted the usual number of fringe fanatics, it is to the credit of the enlightened man who led it that even his enemies are forced to answer him on his own moral and ethical terms."

To the Editor: I speak in my dual roles of wife and enemy. Until the moment I read your inane editorial, I had always been in favor of a free press. The man you admire for his sanity, morals, and ethics could profitably moonlight as a Bible Belt Holy Roller. It might interest you to know that despite the influence of M. L. King, Professor Siegel's integration activities down South last month ended in violence. Professor Siegel's admirable broad-spectrum view of integration wound up with North fornicating South and he barely escaped death-by-shotgun. Sincerely yours.

Dear Miss Blake-Franzblau: Your editor, I'm sorry to say, cares nothing about Dr. Siegel's love life, or mine, mutually exclusive though they are and therefore eminently newsworthy. Your boss is making a big mistake. To understand Dr. Siegel's platform performance, you must first consider his bedroom performance. And even before that, you must know that nothing sickens him more than good health; it is the broken and maimed and unlovable who inspire his soul, as well as a variety of noble bedroom charities. I want to impress you with the necessity of remembering this if you are ever to help me forgive him for what happened in Alabama.

This was his confession when he returned: She was a lonely, sensitive kid. We stayed up talking half the night. I found her story moving. I slept with her, yes. Once. It meant nothing. My only regret is that her boyfriend was a nut and you've been hurt.

Bear with me, Miss B-F. If we are to view this with any compassion at all, I must fancify the facts a little—only because the facts seem to *require* a poetic rendering of what might otherwise be construed as plain depravity.

RECONSTRUCTED SOUTHERN INCIDENT

The girl was a young Southern writer, a poet, who every day had marched two Negro children to a newly integrated school. The scar, zigzagged across her cheek, had been knifed there by the Klan, who left her alive to remember her folly. He loved her scar more than the slim young body which had escaped their violation. Later, it was the only thing he remembered of a night that seemed to sing with dark purposes soaring past the singing of their flesh. "I love you," he said, kissing the still-raw wound of her cheek. And she cried, "No, you don't . . . you can't . . . you don't know anything about me." "I know everything about you," he said; "we touch, we touch—the same things matter to us both." "Maybe," she said, "but tomorrow you'll remember that we only touched through veils of flowers."

She was engaged to a hotheaded young politician who was running for state assemblyman but had already won the National Riflery Association's highest award. When tomorrow came, she told her boyfriend that she'd fallen in love with the man of her dreams, a professor from New York. "Filthy Yankee!" he said, and called the professor's wife in New York. "Get your dirty old man to come home," he told her, "or I'll blow his fool head off!"

The professor's wife sent a special delivery to his hotel: "Come home, you filthy Yankee. Do you want your fool head blown off? Dirty old men should not spearhead revolutions. A man could get an assful of buckshot from such shenanigans. Come home, professor, your public awaits you. Me too."

When Dr. Siegel returned, he did not speak of "the significant dichotomy of our lives; inertia vs. action"; he did not repeat his oft-repeated question: "How long do you plan to go around like that, dragging your ass through the greatest revolution in history?" Our true Dialogue of Dialectics speaks for itself:

"Syd," he said, "I've really hurt you this time, haven't I?"

"Yes, you have, you bastard. I'm getting too old to take it with a little maternal smile, forgiving my bad boy another transgression, one more new experience he simply had to have in order to grow up."

"Old? You're not old, Syd! Thirty-five? four? three? whatever—why should you feel?—"

"Another line on my forehead, two around my eyes, the breasts no longer rising to the Playboy standards—you've noticed, of course."

"No, I can't say that I have."

"There, you see?"

"Oh, please! Stop with the dramatics! What are you trying to do—get me to feel so guilty I'll dive out the window?—"

"No darling . . . it's just that I'm getting very tired of living at the foothills of all your peaks . . . so very tired that if *I've* been toying with the idea, it's not altogether improbable. The thing is, none of it really means anything to me anymore . . . don't you see? I'm really in competition with your revolution, not some Southern sugar-pie you took to bed. So go on, go to your meeting, go wherever you're going . . . just leave me in peace."

"Oh, brilliant, a brilliant tactic! Go to your meeting, she tells me, leave me to quietly, peacefully commit suicide—insidious, my God, but you're insidious!"

"Believe me, you needn't worry. I simply haven't the energy or the ambition for it. So go on, please . . . and take an umbrella—it looks like rain in Cherry Blossom Lane."

PORTABLE PLASTIC SAINTS
(with battery), STOP & GO MISTLETOE,
POLY-PASTORELLE

This morning I received one of those mail-order gadget catalogues I never sent for and never know what to do with when they arrive. Compulsively, I always read the description of every item listed, right to the lunatic end of it. I think that if I could understand not so much the product but the advertising of the product, I would know everything there is to know about anything. For instance, this extraordinary invention which can turn two ordinary twin beds into "a modern, single, king-size unit, with no lump or gap in the middle." Called a Twin Bed Bridge, made of polyurethane foam, its quick and easy insertion is so invisible under the sheets that "you won't even know it's there . . ." it's such a temptation to try and confound Shephard with this ultrasimple gap-closer—but could I trust him not to free-associate, not to start blustering about those painfully deeper credibility gaps, passionately cursing the Pentagon while absently fondling my breast . . . besides, I'll have to wait for the bridge to arrive, and I'm running out of patience, faith, aware of the energy it takes to release one breath after another into the

world . . . only to breathe it all back again—noxious, soporific
. . . bridges of breathing collapsing over the junkyard . . . all
fall down allfalldownallfall.

Catatonic schizophrenia, Dr. Fletcher said. All the classic symptoms: the mutism, the suspended animation—her body lying on
the hospital bed like a life-size doll, limbs wired to hold any
position they were placed in, grotesquely immune to fatigue.
But he was not to worry, the doctor assured him. The catatonic
episode, though of indeterminate duration, would certainly end;
it frequently disappeared as spontaneously as it began, and the
patient would suffer no loss of intellect.

Though Shephard found it hard to believe, the doctor further
assured him that she could hear everything and would later
remember it all. And so he came to see her every day during
those first six weeks—spoke of the children, told her anecdotes
of home, hoping for magic, an abracadabra of remembered love
to woo her back to the living. But she never once spoke or
reacted. Her eyes, in that blue impenetrable stare, sometimes
fixed on him with the same unblinking vacuity given the ceiling,
the wall, the chair that held him suffering in every muscle the
paralysis of hers.

It was decided to back up the drugs with more radical
treatment. Though he couldn't bear the idea of electroshock
therapy, he finally acknowledged the tenacious monsters behind
her pale brow, and grimly agreed to this violent exorcism.

She could walk, she could run a mile if she wanted to, the
doctors told him; but it wasn't until the following week that she
even sat up in bed during his visit. As soon as he came into
the room—drenched with the first heavy spring shower of the
year and so busy getting out of his wet coat that he didn't
even notice her sitting up—she spoke her first firmly articulate
sentence. Her voice completely without inflection, she said,
"Bring me a notebook and a sketch pad."

He rushed to the bed, embraced her. "How wonderful, honey!
Sure, I'll get if for you right away, tonight . . . the shop in the
lobby might be open—no, they wouldn't have a sketch pad—
tomorrow then, OK?" The raindrops falling from his hair onto

hers, his beard wet against her cheek, he hiccuped with laughter, finally pausing as he searched for some echo of that laughter in her eyes. Horror closed his throat, and he wondered if he too had slipped over the border, in his sleep perhaps, and was living in his own hallucinated, nightmare world—a place where he could have moments before heard a perfectly lucid request, only to find the lips that framed it sealed, inanimate as rubber to the touch; the body in his arms, balsa wood in light blue nylon; and the raindrops rolling down her cheeks like the mechanical tears of a plastic doll.

He stood up; with tissues from a box on the night table wiped her face, his own; said calmly, reasonably: "Did I hear you right, Syd? Did you say you wanted me to bring you a notebook and a sketch pad?"

"Bring me a notebook and a sketch pad," she said, exactly as before, and he sank into the armchair by the window, watching April beating wet and dark against the glass. "Tomorrow, I'll bring them tomorrow . . ."

He found her sitting by the window, watching the rain. Her back to him, he could hardly believe that the spot of color tied in a bow around her ponytail was a red ribbon. And she was wearing, at last, her favorite green silk robe—worn through two confinements and happier days, it was almost a familiar, natural picture she made. "And it rained forty days and forty nights without stopping," he said softly, coming up behind her. "Hello—how are you?"

"Did you bring the notebook? Did you bring a pen?"

"Right here. See? I kept it dry inside my raincoat. Brand-new, king-size, spiral. And your own pen, two new ball-points for spares, a sketch pad, a box of charcoals, pastels, and soft pencils. I'll just leave it on the dresser here . . . Syd—Syd, you've got a ribbon in your hair. Turn around, let me look at you—please."

When she finally whirled around, her back like some rigid axis, it seemed—horribly, admirably—the panic-transcended determination of someone escaping a burning building by way of flaming rooms. She was wearing lipstick. A carefully reddened mouth. A bit of pencil lengthening her eyebrows, the corners of her eyes. "You look wonderful," he said. "Really, you look great!"

Something was happening to the edges of her mouth: a flicker that was almost a tremor, almost an upward curving—but whatever signals had briefly set off some sort of struggle in her went dead. She turned back to the window.

He took the package and placed it gently on her lap—little enough to bring to that green silk altar where in another century, another world, many a wish of his had been granted. "Syd," he heard himself saying, "I always loved you, Syd . . ." and recoiled in shame from the shivering nakedness of it, began, "I always loved you . . . in that green silk robe."

He didn't expect her to answer, he didn't expect her to turn to him again—it was too soon to feel even minor disappointment. Certainly there was hope in the vanity of that red ribbon, the lipstick—and in the package on her lap, the makings of survival.

The sketch pad and notebook lay unused on her table for nearly a week. On the evening of May 1, he saw, carefully block-lettered on the bright yellow cover of the notebook, the first real evidence of her struggle to make contact again, her rueful awareness that she could not stay separated forever on her sealed-off, desolate island: THE S.S. SINK-OR-SWIM. And it was not impossible that she had deliberately left it there for him to read . . . it seemed almost—offered.

He remembered how earlier that year she had smiled cryptically and announced that her body was only a vehicle which moved her mind from place to place. And now, the vehicle—debilitated, stationary; the mind—deranged, without geography; it was all the more shocking to find that there was in her attempt to group the surface trivia and hidden terrors of his daily monologues a desperate new logic: FACTS—Ivan Siegel needs new sneakers./ Kenneth Siegel tore his sweater when he fell off his bicycle./ At S. Siegel residence, 36–24 Marcy Blvd., the dishwasher is broken./ They have still not bombed Hanoi./ S. Siegel has shaved off his beard./ The nurse who tried to poison me was fired for copulating with two patients./ They have ordered me to eat in the dining room./ I refuse all orders./ S. Siegel is writing article for *Partisan*. His answer to LeRoi Jones. The title is: Uncle Tom's Outhouse./

"Syd," he said. "You haven't told me yet—how do you like it?

I mean, do I look better without the beard? I can't get used to it."

She didn't look at him. She sat as before, her back to him, and began drawing on the sketch pad. Looking over her shoulder, he saw a large box, and another inside that, and still another, until it was a box inside a box inside a box ad infinitum, ending in the center one, no bigger than a dot. And because it represented for him too a fixed infinity of solitude, he could barely resist the impulse to flesh it out, give it nerve ends, enact the here-and-now of his despair—and he wanted to weep on her breast like a fool or a child or a husband lonely beyond pride.

A few days later, the notebook's second entry was her version of what might be called their first "conversation" the night before. But unlike his own recollection of a painfully jumbled dialogue, hers evoked the simple, the terrible language of the pauses: S. Siegel comes to see me every day. How do you feel? he says. The same, I say. They are going to bomb Hanoi, he says. Oh, I say. You don't care? he says. No. The children miss you. In what way? They want you to come home. Is the TV broken? No. Then what do they want? They want you, he shouts. So does Uncle Sam. I want you, he shouts. You've got Uncle Sam. Good-bye, he says. Good-bye, I say. Do call again. I'm always in.

She sat in the corner of the room at a small table, sketching a vase of half-dead roses. "Syd," he said, "Carter was wounded in the riots last night, in California."

"Who?"

"He was attacked by a mob as soon as he left the platform— the Mothers of Soldiers in Vietnam. They wanted to kill him . . . he was nearly blinded by the time the police got to him . . . Syd, do you hear me? I'm telling you that Carter nearly had his eye gouged out last night! You always liked Carter."

"I don't know anyone named Carter."

"Dammit, Syd, you were once in love with him!"

"If all those mothers wanted to kill him, he can't be a nice person."

"Syd!"

"I never heard of him."

Entry #3 from the S.S. Sink-or-Swim:
Professor Siegel is letting his beard grow again. He says he feels
naked without it. Kenneth Siegel has chicken pox. Half the
children in his class have chicken pox. Grandma Siegel had a
heart attack and is in the hospital. They have replaced her
with an elderly housekeeper from the Sunshine Agency who will
be a substitute grandmother. Though they guaranteed grand-
motherliness, Kenneth Siegel hates her. Ivan Siegel hid her false
teeth. She is threatening to leave. Professor Siegel's voice is getting louder. He told me three times in a loud voice that his friend
Carter has a concussion and a damaged eye. I ate in the dining
room today, but nobody knew it. And they have not bombed
Hanoi.

Head back on the chair, eyes closed, he sat for a long time,
too tired to speak. At last he told her, "My mother came home
this morning. She's weak but better. She says she'll stay."
The sketch pad lay open in her lap; she was doing a head
in charcoal. Nearly asleep, he thought he dreamed her question: "How's Carter?"
"What?" he said. "What?" "How's Carter?" she repeated.
He took his time; evaluated her voice, still lacking in inflection;
examined her face, turned to him now and waiting it seemed,
though her eyes focused somewhere left of his nose . . . it was
probably rash to celebrate this with a skipped heartbeat or two.
"He's much better, Syd. They're releasing him from the hospital
next week. It needs a lot of treatment, but the doctors say his
eye won't be permanently damaged."
She turned away from him, went back to the drawing, lapsed
into silence again, as though this burden of information was all
she could absorb. Still, something had flickered over her face
as he spoke, and he almost believed that her nerves had sur-
faced, trembled with some memory of related anguish or human, normal relief.
A charcoal head of her doctor on the pad, recognizably Dr.
Fletcher—his regal features emerging benignly from behind
a web of eerie shadows. She laid it on the table, her shoulders
drooping wearily as if to say it was finished only because she
was too tired to do any more. "It's good, Syd—very good indeed.
Show it to the doctor, will you? . . . you know, the more I

look at it . . . well, I'll be damned if this isn't the best thing
you've ever done."

And it was too! Astonishing, that projection of intensity, of a
real engagement with her subject . . . miraculous . . . as if . . .
as if this three-month nightmare had been *intended, aimed*
toward this higher purpose—one more blessing shrewdly with-
held—a blessing in disguise, dear, his mother used to say . . . the
benediction praising poxes, fevers, fractures . . . and he wanted
to laugh till his guts knotted when he thought of how those
words might easily be spoken someday over the broken bones of
their lives. Christ Almighty, what a happy vision! It deserved at
least one mended smile. He could see it, hear it—but the ways of
the Lord *are* mysterious, dear, and peculiar . . . oh mother,
mother, pin a rose on me, I'm home.

Even before the doctor told him the good news, he sensed
it as soon as he entered the room—if only in the way the afternoon sun poured through the open window, spotlighting the
empty bed, the empty chair.

The month of May wrapped itself around her, a silk print
dress of pink and fuchsia flowers spilled gaily over shadowed
grass-green. In high-heeled black patent shoes, she pivoted
around, stuck a last bobby pin in a shining upswept hairdo, and
smiled. "Your mother sent it to me. A present. Tomorrow's my
birthday. You like it?"

"I love it! It's, it's kind of—"

"Wild? Gorgeous? Yes, gorgeous. From Bonwit Teller's. With
the sweetest note. Go on, read it."

His mother's large, childishly round handwriting all right, and
one of her many large, childish inspirations: "How I'd love to
see this on you, Syd dear. We would make a party and celebrate
your birthday. So why don't you just come on home? Honest, if
I knew you were coming, I would bake a cake. Love, Mother."

"She didn't tell me," Shephard said.

"I know. She always did love surprises. Don't you?"

"Today? Will it be today?"

"Now. In ten minutes, Dr. Fletcher's coming to say good-bye.
My Svengali. I suppose I'll miss him, but he swears I won't. He
wanted me to leave a week ago."

"You never let on."

"I didn't know I'd be ready. I didn't want to disappoint you. What if I said I would and then—"

"Yes, all right. It's all right. I understand. What happened this morning? To make you decide, I mean."

"Well, the dress arrived, and I fit it on."

"That's all?"

"No, it reminded me of something . . . a dress I once had . . . something I wore when I was happy. And I began thinking about Italy. Do you remember, years ago, in Rome—in the museum of the Villa Borghese—those magnificent paintings, and how we fell in love with Caravaggio?"

"It was a long time ago. I can't—"

"Oh, Shephard, remember the one we liked best—the *David and Goliath?* Well, this morning, it came to me again . . . what you said about it" (she walked toward him slowly, reached up, and gently rested her hands on his shoulders) "Shephard, I do wish you could remember it without my telling you!" (and for the first time since her breakdown, her eyes focused straight into his) "We preferred it to the innocence on that lovely *Sick Bacchus*" (and it might have been the deep shadows under her eyes—those dark smears telling nothing, and everything, of her passage back to sanity—accentuating the too-blue irises, the too-clear whites, and the pupils too brightly black, refracting, it seemed, all the sunlight in the room) "and how moved we were!" (surely he could never *imagine* them as bright as they actually were this moment, so that he almost felt the room itself grow darker, as if she had absorbed into those shining pupils an energy, a brilliance which had moments ago shone arbitrarily on bed, chair, walls, mirror—taken it, channeled it somewhere behind her pale wide lids, straight thick lashes, and stored it like gold or uranium in underground shelters) "Imagine, Shep, the sheer genius of that unique perspective on guilt" (and he felt her fingers tighten on his shoulders, her face a little closer now, so that her breath as she spoke drifted upward—shallow, minty, dry, and cool as phantom kisses dusting his face) "achieving the most difficult thing of all; the victor's sorrow and compassion for his victim" (though he trembled only once, the tremor seemed to pass into her fingertips, because she smiled with what appeared to be genuine delight . . . although, whatever it was . . . the line of her jaw, her lips open, parted,

curving upward, but a fraction awry—from what? . . . a mirror
image of delight perhaps, but not that either—unless—and he,
would have torn the word from his mind if he could, but it
stayed—a Steeplechase mirror, that was it) "Oh, darling, you
do remember, don't you? I can see you do!" (and he nodded,
his eyes shutting tight, shutting her out, only to pick up her
image again as it was then . . . no, not the paintings, not
whatever it was he said, winding serpentine around his heart,
but the gardens of the Villa Borghese—formal, lush, their foot-
steps on the stone path, some ancient resonance recaptured,
nature elegantly rearranged by fine Italian hands, and her smile
like a grand opera—the happy waltz-and-champagne scenes—
Traviata framed in roses, roses on the path bursting all around
her . . . catching the fever of Italian drama staged at seashores,
sung in streets and gardens, more real than in the theaters
. . . a tanned little bird in a flowered dress, extravagant with
songs, quivering with prima donna passions, her arms quick,
strong with love, flung around his neck: oh, darling! how wonderful! I'll always remember that. I thank you, Signor Caravaggio
thanks you, and the very stones of Rome have shifted slightly,
moved by admiration . . . *fortissimo, signora . . . fortissimo . . .*
her laughter—child, woman, angel . . . ah, madonna of the Gardens Borghese, I've forgotten already what I did to deserve this)
"I can remember exactly what you said" (phantom kisses on
his cheek, her voice sharp with excitement, prying his eyes
open) "observe, you said, the gruesome bloody head of the
dead Goliath—Caravaggio's self-portrait . . . David too is looking at him, his eyes alive with pity—that's where his real
heroism lies—because who would regret the blood of a villain,
but a soul in league with the angels? It's all there—luminous
in his beautiful face: no exquisite triumph over enemies, but a
passion of remorse that seems to cry aloud to his victim and to
God in his heaven—Forgive me!"

Gratitude was what he felt for the stunning accuracy of her
memory, for the high tide of her rhetoric, which literally swept
him off his feet into the nearest chair . . . dizzy, floating light
as driftwood on those lyric crests . . . surely the leaden memories of this room would someday sink forever—leaving him with
this hour, this knock on the door, her buoyant voice: "It must
be Dr. Fletcher, darling, come to say good-bye."

"Well, today's the day," the doctor said, grinning, squeezing his hand, "What do you say? Isn't she wonderful?" Ceiling, walls, floor, the entire box containing them, shifted, a fraction awry, no more perhaps than her smile before, and her smile now again, expressing quiet pleasure. "You're speechless, eh? Surprising, wasn't it? Not quite as spontaneous as I predicted, but still—Well, anyhow, you're pleased, I think?"

"Yes," Shephard finally said, "Yes, of course. Why wouldn't I be? I don't know how to thank you. She looks so different . . . she's so different, I hardly recognize her."

"So do you, dear," she said. "Doesn't he, doctor? Tell me, how do you like Professor Siegel without a beard? It's the second time in a month he's gotten rid of it. It seems he just can't make a decision about it! So be honest—what do you think?"

"It's fine, fine," the doctor laughed; "pass him on the street and wouldn't know him. Looks ten years younger. Ten years younger, the both of you—you're going to be fine now, the pack of you. Good-bye, good luck! Call me next week, my dear, will you—let me know how you're getting on." And kissing her affectionately on the cheek, he shoved her playfully toward Shephard, "Go on, get out of here—take her home," and waved them off.

She leaned back against him, the top of her head level with his nose, her hair caressing the tip of it. So that he smiled at last, on the two of them alone. Free? Released? In each other's custody? He could not decide. But with her silken-clad body still leaning back on him, gay pink and fuchsia flowers spilling over his dull gray trousers, his arms encircled her waist. She'd become so pitifully thin that he cursed himself for the bloody fool he was not to have noticed it sooner; and he would have gladly transplanted his own flesh, pound by pound, to cover the bones of her suffering. But he felt drained of even the right words, wondering what it was he had left to give her after all—could he make her a gift of his exhaustion? There should have been something profound to be said at this moment, but all he could say was: "My God, Syd, you've never been so thin! A skeleton, that's what—my mother will faint when she sees you! Come on, let's go. I've got to get you home and start fattening you up a little—"

"For the kill?" she said, lightly, pleasantly.

But if she was smiling her fun-house-mirror smile, he couldn't see it, facing forward as she was, and him with his nose buried in the perfume of her hair, deliberately allowing his mind to go reeling in the scent, remembering only that his reason depended on how well he was able to do that. "Come on," he said, "get your things."

The rich dark green leather, the gold tooling, a cover that conveyed a sense of permanence—a ledger rather than a notebook, it demanded a serious attitude, a title that also implied permanence. And the elegant paper, satin-smooth and creamy white, just seemed to *ask* for India ink, careful Gothic lettering on the title page, and the word: JOURNAL. Yes, it belonged here on the new desk in her new studio where she spent so many hours of her new life. The renovated attic, now equipped with a door that locked, the finest art supplies, and guarantees of privacy, was all Shephard's doing. Recalling how she warned him that he might someday regret it, she smiled, amused, and wrote:

It is four months to the day since I left the hospital. The painting is finished at last. Shephard has never loved me the way he does now. He loves every scar on my psyche. He says the memory of the pain I experienced has revitalized my mind, given me a soul, and turned me from a mediocrity into a genius.

I have painted a wonderful Picasso-type picture, like *Guernica*, only smaller, and in all the colors Picasso avoided. Death is not full of dull blacks and grays, the way he has it. But flowing reds, reds spilling over grass-greens—blood, you might say, irrigating a Nature that is parched for it. And golden heads, bright blue eyes weeping blue iridescent tears, and rich whites and browns, skin bleeding on skin. I call it VIETNAM. Shephard says it's a masterpiece and is putting it up for auction at the fund-raising rally next week—together with my series of black-and-white sketches of THE SOUTHLAND REVISITED. Yesterday he told me that when the history of this revolution is written, my name will be forever inscribed next to his.

The children's behavior continues to be incredibly good. Ivan kissed me twice this week. But Kenny, I'm sorry to say, doesn't kiss me anymore. I'm sure that he still hasn't forgiven me for "going away," a reason he tries to conceal with silly statements like: you're not really my mother. And when I assure him that I am, he says: well, if you are, why don't you look like her? It seems probable that Ivan and I have the deeper rapport after all. I just never realized it before.

As for staring into abysses which stare right back, I have lately recommended to all my married friends, especially those on the verge of separation or divorce, that extraordinary Twin Bed Bridge. If the T.B.B. people were to ask me for an endorsement, I would state sincerely that since we've been using it, we have bridged the chasm as efficiently as possible. Which is why I can't understand Shephard's frequently odd moods these days. Where is the exhilaration he used to bring home from the peace marches, the rallies—and especially his pet project, the Harlem Youth Movement? Very often now, by the time we get back from one of these things, he seems past the strength to say another word and his face looks ashen gray. Anemia? It's possible. Tomorrow I must speak to him about seeing a doctor.

Shephard wished he could feel proud of himself in his new clean-living, clean-shaven approach to life. He had at last firmly decided that there was no need to go on with that farce of a beard. It would seem little more than following a fad, now that so many of his students and colleagues had begun to make it the symbol of their maleness, their independence. Besides, it had always itched in the summer, gathered icicles in winter storms, and every night at dinner collected bread crumbs, which Sydelle used to remove as if she were picking nits.

As for his new espousal of virtue, there seemed to be simply no necessity anymore for him to seek warm understanding in the arms of sweet, sensitive women. His days and nights were lived now in the orbit of Sydelle's loving approval and assistance —like a fortune suddenly inherited, he hardly knew what to do with it all.

No, there was no sensible cause for complaint now. At fund-raising dinners, rallies, he stood—taller than ever in her esteem—making his pitch for peace and equality, certain that she would be sitting there in the front row, her eyes burning with pride, her enthusiastic applause lasting one embarrassing second too long.

And her talent, so many years buried in indifferent dabblings, grew deeper, larger every day. He even smiled a little when he remembered that brash adolescent prophecy of hers. Still in her thirty-sixth year, it was not impossible that before her next birthday, the very people who accused him of "husbandly pride" in her work might join him in risking the word "genius" on her.

And so, with everything he had wished for and worked toward granted, his miseries seemed all the more inexplicable. There was, of course, one obvious reason: while the world was the poor, racked, bloody thing it was, how could he help feeling a guilt at least equal to his new wealth of blessings? Nouveau riche, uneasy in the role, no doubt undeserving . . . What else then would account for the nagging persistence of certain notions haunting him throughout the day, and the nights when he didn't sleep at all?

Hallucinated, he told himself: a perverse mirage of surfeit. Because it would have been sheer madness, he knew, to have asked anyone: when you're with Sydelle, have you ever noticed that there's something wrong with her smile? And the pupils of her eyes—have you noticed . . . how strange—too strange to describe in terms of *things known*—but as if a steady beam of light were shining on the mouths of twin tunnels dropping dark and endless into the bowels of her brain. And when she speaks —her words intoxicating, anesthetizing, a flow of 100 proof brandy—so that it seems impossible for the crystal sharpness of her voice, its brilliant finehoned edge, to cause the slightest pain as it slices into the ear.

There was really no one who seemed to sense any of this. Their friends and relatives formed a solidly admiring circle around her; as if they could and would protect her with love from whatever devils had once done their mischief with her.

And, certainly, this was not something you entrusted to a child. Not even the child himself could have confided it in him. Because if one awful confirmation did exist, he felt it was there, in Kenny. Watching the boy's face when he was with her, Shephard sometimes saw an expression so strange and fleeting that he could never be sure he saw it at all—as though the child's blood had run cold and he were rigidly keeping in check some inexpressible terror. Still, just as possible, it was beyond credibility. I am imagining that look, he told himself—because isn't he sitting there no more than a minute later playing cards with Ivan, or putting a record on his phonograph—his face cherubic, open, happy?

Besides, her cheerfulness alone should have thoroughly squelched all of these wild ideas. Serious when she should be, she was otherwise full of jokes, inventive word-plays, and sharp little insights with just enough bite to be painlessly funny. That silly foam-rubber gadget, for instance—the fuss she made with it—the ceremony of installing it, a production replete with TV catchwords, a string of adjectives with suggestive bleeps—what she called a "truly pornographic commercial" as distinguished from the phony ones . . . and the flourishes, the fanfare of bed sheets flying over the damned thing, and what she said would be her last words on the subject—"*Violà, chéri! finis!* our bridge to love!"

And it was true, as she said, that it was invisible: it did adequately take the curse off that ball-breaking crack between the beds; he couldn't blame it on that. And Sydelle—fattened up in the right places, warm, smooth, perfumed, desirable to any man in his right mind—how could he blame her for that most terrifying of all his fantasies? He could only try to ignore, as best he could, the harsh metallic ring of her arms locking around him; the glow in the darkness of the tiny red "on" light burning in her forehead; and the loud, steady ticking from the hollow tin of her heart.

GUY A. CARDWELL born in Savannah, Georgia, received degrees from the University of North Carolina and Harvard and has taught at a number of universities both in this country and abroad. His numerous stories, poems, and essays have appeared in magazines such as *Saturday Review, Epoch,* the *Carleton Miscellany* and the *Yale Review.* He is currently working on a volume of short stories and a novel.

Did You Once See Shelley?

My initial conversation with Dell after thirty-five years was an odd one. My wife and I were in Chapel Hill for the funeral of her father and had just decided to move there from Milwaukee, taking over her father's house. Dell called from Pinehurst. "Hello," he said, when someone got me to the telephone, "this is M. Delacorte Brown. Do you remember me?" Neither the name nor that drawling, insistent North Carolina voice meant anything to me for a moment, partly because of the stilted way he gave his name, as though it were on a calling card or he were being introduced at a court function, and partly because he called from Pinehurst rather than from Essex. I had always known his name—the M stood for *Mumford*—but I had never heard him called anything but Dell. And he had never been a close friend of mine, not really, except for that one summer when I saw a good deal of him. Other than reading in the sports pages a few times shortly afterwards that he had scored well in regional golf tournaments, I have hardly heard of him since. But I answered without hesitation that of course I remembered him and appreciated his calling. My wife's father had been honored and well loved, and I had already said the same thing that morning to half-a-dozen people on the telephone and to many more who had come by the house to pay their respects to the dead.

"Did You Once See Shelley?"—Guy A. Cardwell, *The Carleton Miscellany,* Copyright © 1969 by Carleton College.

The fact is Dell didn't know my wife and hadn't known her father. He had seen my name in a story about the death and the funeral arrangements. He wanted to see me, and his tone changed from one of crude formality to extreme intimacy as soon as I expressed pleasure at hearing from him. At that time this tone was somehow gratifying, suggesting to me as it did a pleasing openness in him and a slightly pathetic confidence that he would again find a friend in me. It demanded a sympathetic response in that he seemed to be lowering the usual social defenses, throwing himself on my mercy as the weaker wolf does when he shows his vulnerable neck to his master in combat. Later on I came to resent this air, reading in it a mingling of surface humility—almost fawning—as he flattered me on my achievements and of underlying arrogance in the way he assumed that I was always at his disposal and had nothing better to do than to listen to his voice—droning, interminable, like the low humming of swamp noises on a brassy, never-ending summer's day. I learned, too, that he was not always so candid as he seemed. In a rather simple-minded way he tended to be secretive as well as intimate, cagey as a salesman is often cagey, intentionally vague, given to a kind of furtive misdirection, like a broody old hen.

"I want to come to see you," he said that first morning, "but I can't get up to Chapel Hill today." By this time I had placed him and remembered even the quality of his voice—the slightly rasping dipthongization of the *a* in *can't* and of the *i* in *Hill*, for example—and had begun to arrange in my mind the scattered fragments of what I could recall of him and his family. I explained that we would return to Chapel Hill in a few weeks to live there permanently. "I'll come as soon as you are back," he promised. "I'll keep telephoning to find out when you are there. You'll be surprised to hear that I am married. I married very late in life. I would like for you to meet my wife. She is an intellectual like you, a well-educated woman, took a degree in biology at Hunter College in New York. I think you would find her attractive."

I said that I would be pleased to meet his wife. Dell gave a nervous little laugh, as he often did, and explained that he couldn't introduce her right now—perhaps not for a long time. She was giving him a great deal of trouble—she was an alcoholic, and he had recently placed her in a sanitorium near Pinehurst. She had in the past been in several different sanitoriums and in the state hospital in Raleigh. He added something I didn't quite get that sounded as though he were saying indirectly that he had also undergone treatment of some kind. I dimly remembered that I had heard during one of my rare visits to Essex something about Dell's having had one or more mental breakdowns.

The intimacy with which Dell spoke to me of his wife during this first conversation and in subsequent ones was embarrassing. He expressed pride in her, saying that she was much brighter and better educated than he, a woman who could do many things well; at the same time he appeared to hint that although his own interest in her was more objective and remote than that interest heavily tinged with sexuality which is usual in a husband or lover—so irritating and off-putting had been her many alcoholic lapses—I would surely be pleased with her, that is, provided her could ever dry her out enough to present her to me. Several times when he was talking to me about her I thought that he was like an unusually sensitive and thoughtful Esquimau, happy because he was sure that the wife whose favors he was offering to a guest was exactly the woman to give the guest pleasure.

Something like this, certainly, was the awkward effect of his tone and of the closeness between us implied by the details he went into when telling me about having to keep money out of her hands, of stopping all credit accounts, of finding pint bottles under her pillow while she was in the very process of swearing she hadn't touched a drink for days, of her intense vitality, and even about how once in a rage at his well justified suspicions she had torn her clothes off and run out of the house screaming "Now search me! Now search me!" He suggested that her powers were so extraordinary that if she could have channeled her bounteous talents she could have had a career, might possibly have become famous.

Dell had never, he told me, owned a house of his own but had lived in his mother's home in Essex or in rented apartments when away from Essex. He enjoyed being nomadic, he said. Now he had a room in a motel in Pinehurst. Thus he was near his wife—though I gathered that this was not the prime consideration—and could amuse himself by watching the golf. He didn't play any more himself. Five years earlier he had nearly died in an automobile accident—cracked neck, cracked pelvis, broken shoulder, and broken foot. Several times he told me in complete detail about his injuries, his state of shock, what he said to bystanders and doctors, and his complex legal difficulties in a small courthouse town.

He was between jobs, he told me almost at once, and there were a surprising number of occasions on which it was convenient for him to stop by Chapel Hill to see me as he drove to or from other places where he was trying to collect money owed him or was talking, so he said, to prospective employers. At first he gave me to understand that jobs were plentiful; companies were hard put to it to find people willing to work; he himself would accept a job when he found just what he was looking for. Later it seemed that he was making the rounds of employment offices in towns in the eastern and piedmont sections of the state. Apparently he had no friend other than me, or no convenient friend. I could understand this, for I quickly discovered that his friendship was a burden. Who wants a friend who has nothing to do and who assumes the privilege of dropping in at any hour of the day? And who stays until one tells him politely to leave?

That my wife and I were settling in Chapel Hill was a result of bad news from my doctor. He had advised me to give up my job at once, to live in a leisurely fashion for at least a year—preferably in a milder climate than that of Milwaukee—and then to see about working again, if I wished, but only in an easier situation or on a part-time basis. He said that if I took his advice and if all went well he would set no definite term to my life expectancy. That at just this juncture my wife could buy her father's house in Chapel Hill from his estate was fortuitous. It stimulated in me a good many thoughts about the replicative nature of existence, the dominance of the past, generations succeeding each other in a *"Le roi est mort!"* way, and, more gloomily, about the possibility that the remnants of the funeral baked meats might be used for *my* obsequies if the doctor in Milwaukee were being overly optimistic about my chances.

Chapel Hill—a pleasantly green provincial village which inclined to luxuriate in memories of dead and gone mediocrities whom the villagers, that is, the academic villagers and their hangers-on, took to be great men—had for me the advantage of being the home of the state university. It was also close to Duke University and to a developing "Research Triangle" park which was intended to do in a small way what the installations on Route 128 do for Boston. I had never taught, but I had been offered professorships several times, and I thought that after I took a year of rest it might be a good thing for me to subside into teaching if I didn't find suitable part-time work at the Research Triangle.

Until I received the bad news about my health I had never stopped to think in more than the most passing way about not having lived up to my early promise. I now confessed to myself that I had not accomplished anything significant in the way of research, and suddenly this became an urgent matter. Time was no longer an unending procession of open, sun-lit days; it was forebodingly of the essence.

I chided myself for having neglected my research talents and opportunities. I had occupied responsible positions; I have even been in charge of research divisions with good companies— Rohm and Haas, Monsanto, and Hercules—and I took some comfort from this, but I definitely had not been a creative chemist. There was no getting around that. My teachers in high school had assured me that I was brilliant. When I was a senior in college I was urged to apply for a Rhodes scholarship, and I was in fact made alternate to a winner who played less good tennis than I but who had been president of the campus YMCA. So I continued for my doctorate at the University and met my wife at a graduate student party shortly before I turned in my dissertation. Corporations bid for me in a period when few of them sent talent scouts to campuses. But the hard truth was that I had spent myself too much on routine projects. I had written at least a hundred group reports and had checked on the economic feasibility of as many proposals for research submitted by other chemists, but I didn't have an original chemical discovery to my name. I told myself ironically that on the negative side I had prevented the corporations I worked for from wasting several millions of dollars on projects without clear practical applications; on the positive side I had shared in winning the doubles title for senior men for two years in a row in Milwaukee. How many of my friends could say as much? But irony didn't assuage the sting of the nagging question: What had I done to justify that early presumption of brilliance? I don't mean to say that I lost my sense of humor. There was never a time when I could not tell myself that the situation was if desperate not serious. I certainly did not think about the matter constantly; assuming that the doctor was right, time remained.

Settling down in Chapel Hill was not a quick or easy affair. The house and yard had been let go for years while my father-in-law was in a nursing home, and for years before that they had not been attended to properly. Talk about Austrian *Schlamperei!* Before the Civil War travelers from the North used to say that they could tell when they entered the slave-holding states by the immedite change from well-kept, prosperous farms to down-at-heels, slatternly plantations. Slave days were gone, but I saw our property as a legitimate though shrunken village descendant of some tumble-down plantation type. The paint inside the house and out was in dreadful condition, the asbestos shingles on the roof were worn in places to the felt beneath, the oversized lot back of the house was a jungle of trees, saplings, and vines—wistaria, of course, and sharply thorned varieties, and some throttling vines, arm-big, that wound like anacondas around tall pines, gums, and oaks and climbed to stifle them at their very tops. My late father-in-law had always intended to do something about that back lot; the attorney who was in charge of the property for some years never gave the matter a thought.

To me it was mildly depressing just to look into the basement or the attic, stuffed as they were with the rather horrible detritus of generations—broken chairs, blackened souvenir spoons from Berlin and Geneva and Florence, a hundred keys that no longer opened anything, disintegrating books riddled by silver fish, crazed mirrors. . . . I estimated there must have been two thousand yellowed, crumbling, unsorted family letters for my wife and me to look at and throw away or to present to the University Library. We were in constant rebellion against all these evidences of past carelessness, inefficiency, and sloth. The mornings of the first three weeks of my temporary retirement I spent on a stepladder washing dirty, marred walls and ceilings. My afternoons I gave up to resting and dozing. I rejoiced in the ocular evidence of my domestic accomplishments. What with one occupation or another and because actually in view of my doctor's orders there was no need for haste, I delayed several months before I talked with people at the Research Triangle.

What I learned there was discouraging. Companies were coming in slowly. The director of the local project for one corporation that was starting up a laboratory thought he just might need me in eight or ten months, which would have been about right for me, but then he took me to lunch with his chief chemist on the grounds, a man there to advise with architects and contractors about laboratory details and equipment, and I knew that my prospects were dead. The chemist was a young fellow I had turned in an adverse report on when I was his superior at Monsanto. He was bright but much too wild-eyed an individualist to play on our team. I could imagine what he would tell the director about me—dictatorial, unimaginative, fossilized—and I didn't bother to write a follow-up letter or to send in my Vita.

Later I got around to making discreet inquiries through friends about openings at the two universities. Throughout my earlier career I had been sought after, a person of value. Now I began to get inklings that I was suspect because I had retired early or that I was considered obsolete, that is, too old to take hold in a new place. Word came back that the two departments were over-staffed in my particular field, that their research projects for NASA or God knows what other gravy trains they were riding weren't precisely my kind of thing, and that they would never think of insulting me by offering me a simple teaching position at an associate professor's pay to handle undergraduates.

On reflection I decided that the rebuffs I received from those idiot academics were a good thing, no matter how wounding to the ego. My wife and I could live well enough on our income—we had no children. Furthermore, the kind of research I really wanted to do would not take impossibly expensive equipment or materials. This, in fact, was my chance to go whole-heartedly to work on my own. We were constantly busy with our house and had started going to and giving a good many small parties, so I didn't take active steps immediately. Nearly a year after arriving in Chapel Hill I began seriously to plan a laboratory that I would install in our large and at last immaculate basement.

All of this time my poor, grey, shambling, moribund friend Dell was the person I saw most of. I suggested repeatedly that he telephone before coming by, and sometimes he would, but as often as not he would simply appear at the door, a small, deprecatory smile wrinkling his face. He would apologize, then, and say that he had just happened to be near Chapel Hill and stopped by on the chance that we weren't busy. We were always busy, but unless we were going out or had people coming in, we never had the heart to turn him away. Though we didn't turn him off we were irritated by him, for as soon as we let him over the threshold he would settle down as though he owned the place. If he came at lunch time he would linger until late afternoon. If he came in the afternoon he would stay on for dinner and leave only when I yawned and muttered that I had better get some rest—doctor's orders. I will say for him that he never drank much, no more than one martini before lunch and two bourbons before dinner. If he had ever been an alcoholic, he was no longer one; he was temperate, except in conversation. He talked. He talked incessantly.

At first I didn't find Dell boring. He was interested in and had some of the jargon of medicine, politics, agriculture, and industry. With a strange kind of modest pride he produced information larded with misinformation on almost any subject, including chemistry. He frequently misused, mispronounced, or somehow distorted language. Out of a thousand examples I remember only a few, and those not of the most choice: a friend was a better than merely comparable golfer; he had read a portentious statement; although his tastes were simple, he liked good coosine; poverty would be with us for time on and on; he regretted having no posteriority. I could remember no such eccentricities in the language of his youth.

For the most part Dell talked about things he had done and seen, about Essex people I was supposed to recall, and about that long-gone summer when we loafed and dreamed in town and on the beach near town. He spoke often of his work as a salesman, telling me with pride that he had practiced what one of his college textbooks called missionary salesmanship. He introduced new products; he didn't just go around with an order book and a pencil to make sure that the same old items were periodically restocked. His pride in creativity, in doing missionary selling, was in the beginning tempered by apologetic remarks suggesting that his life and accomplishments were cast at a regrettably lower level than mine. He expressed an exaggerated respect for my supposed achievements as a research chemist employed by great corporations. If I said that I had done relatively little, he indicated that I was excessively modest. He suggested that although he himself had on an inferior level enjoyed a not entirely uninteresting life, I had enjoyed a distinguished career.

Exactly why Dell thought his salesmanship creative was never entirely clear to me. It sounded comparatively humdrum except for the setting. He talked of peddling roofing materials in the backwoods, of selling freezers to country stores, about small adventures in the Cherokee or Croatan Indian counties (if there is a difference between the two) and about quitting jobs because he could not put up with the dishonesty of employers. In more recent years he had been his own boss, selling clothing —work clothes for men for the most part I gathered—to crossroads stores. Sometimes he bought seconds direct from the mills and peddled them throughout the south-eastern part of the state. But this business had played out, he said. Not many people knew what was happening to the small business man in this country, he added, and it was a national disgrace. So many people have so much money that they had rather climb in their automobiles and drive twenty or thirty miles to the nearest town to buy a shirt or a pair of pants from a chain store than to pay twenty cents more for the same article from the country store half a mile from home. In addition, the textile mills were making so much on government contracts that they had no time for people like Dell.

So Dell had given up and was living on dividend checks from a family-owned textile mill near Erwin and on what he could collect from storekeepers who still were on his books for large sums, or so he intimated. He went on periodic collecting trips, which brought in a little, although he said he hated to collect and was considering turning everything over to an agency or putting his major accounts into the hands of the sheriffs of the appropriate counties. As soon as he took a job again he wouldn't have much time for collecting, anyhow. Nothing precisely right for him was available quite yet, and he simply would not accept a routine job, no matter what pay was offered him, especially not a routine desk job.

Until Dell reentered my life I had forgotten all about that happy, lazy, talkative summer when we spent much of our time together. I had just completed my comprehensives for the doctorate and was recovering from a case of pneumonia. Dell had finished college and was trying to decide whether to go on to a graduate school, work for one of his rich uncles, or look around for a job on his own. We played a lot of leisurely golf and tennis —golf was his game, tennis was mine—and I encouraged Dell to read books about the history of science and to contemplate the glories of research. I intended to make a name for myself as a chemist, and I thought he should at very least go on to the Harvard Business School.

It was flattering to have Dell remind me of things I had said and done. He remembered the books I put into his hands, how I had labored to improve his erratic overhead, and the seriocomic story of how I saved our lives. He remembered every detail of the life-saving episode. A flamboyant, enterpreneurial cousin of mine had acquired—as part payment for a bad debt, I believe—a small houseboat floated on oil drums and languidly propelled by a sputtering outboard motor. He kept the boat that summer in the channel on the shore side of the well populated white sand island which lay about ten miles from Essex. The island was reached by means of a streetcar that made the last leg of its journey over a long trestle.

After a few days of playing with the houseboat, my cousin, an already successful if not a settled man, decided that it was too sedate for him and turned back to a speedboat he owned. The houseboat he put at the disposal of various friends and relatives, which was how I happened to have it for approximately two weeks. My family believed that I would benefit from the healing effects of sunshine and ocean bathing, and as the cabin contained two bunks I took Dell along.

On a Sunday afternoon we had the boat dangling from a small anchor about fifty yards from shore, not tied up at its regular moorings near a relative's gangway. We had bought a bottle of bourbon and were attempting with conspicuous unsuccess to seduce two giggling young ladies of our acquaintance whom we had lured on board under the pretext of giving them a ride up and down the channel. I think we hoped that the bourbon would have sedative or aphrodisiac properties or would at least be conducive to an atmosphere of libertinage, but the girls preferred Coca Colas. Aside from the fact that the girls were fixed in their intention to tease and circumvent us, our efforts were negated by our being inexperienced, timorous, and possibly deficient in genuine ardor.

Neither Dell nor I was aware of an approaching squall until I heard wind rising, pulled a curtain aside from a cabin window, and saw that we were moving. After that the squall pounced so rapidly that we were in the middle of the channel by the time I got on deck. Our inadequate anchor slid over the bottom as though I had dropped it on a well-waxed dance floor. Choppy seas half-filled our tender, and the driving rain drowned out the motor. When the girls saw me tug fruitlessly at the starting cord of the motor, their gay shrieks changed to real panic, and they scurried about the little stern deck like frightened quail. As Dell recalled it, I took charge in masterly fashion. I dropped the starting cord—Dell supposed that the motor would have been of little or no use if I could have started it—and ordered the girls to get in the cabin and shut up. Surprisingly, they did. Even with the rain striking our faces like pellets, we could see that we were bearing down on the trestle at alarming speed—like a runaway freight train, Dell said. At the time he was positive that the jerry-built houseboat would crack like a dropped egg when we hit the trestle and that we would all be drowned. He had a vision of his own body, bleeding from gashes suffered when he tried to grasp pilings of the trestle and was raked by the seas across the barnacles that encrusted them. He remembered just standing there for two or three minutes, frozen, thinking "This is the way I am going to die." "But *you* weren't paralyzed," he told me proudly; "*you* were thinking."

We had two small oars aboard, used mainly for holding the boat off docks or for pushing it out from shore. Dell said that I grabbed one, handed him the other, and told him to go forward and use the oar to scull the boat as much toward shore as possible. Extending out from shore for twenty or thirty yards along the trestle was a dock, and tied with their sterns to the dock were eight or nine fishing boats. Lines ran from their bows to big anchors, and their anchors were holding. My idea was to try to maneuver the houseboat close enough to shore to run up on one of these ropes. I thought the rope might slow us enough to let us get the girls and ourselves onto a fishing boat or onto the dock before the houseboat went down. Dell said he complained that we might sink one of the fishing boats and I yelled, Farragut-like, "Damn the fishing boats!"

We labored like fiends, and my tactic worked to perfection. By great good luck we came broadside up to the bows of the first two fishing boats, ran up on both of their lines at once, and didn't even mar their paint. The cursing captains and crews first held us off then eased us into the dock.

In ten minutes the squall was past, the girls went home, the sun came out, and up came my cousin with a pair of friends in his speedboat. He had been summoned from his cottage by an acquaintance who had told him to hurry if he wanted to get to the trestle in time to see his houseboat sink. My cousin came aboard, we bailed out the pram, started the motor, and headed back up the channel toward the houseboat's moorings. Dell remembered that we got our comic relief at this point. My cousin had taken a nervously hectoring attitude—he wondered repeatedly how the hell we could have been so stupid as to have dropped that little anchor in mid-channel. As we approached the moorings, he said, "Here, I'll show you how to handle her; I want to get off at the gangway," and took over the steering from me. Not counting on the fact that the tide had turned, he brought the boat smack up into the gangway, knocked down some steps hanging out over the water, nearly yanked Dell's arms and my arms from their shoulder sockets as we tried to hold it, and stuck a two-by-six that projected from the little pavilion at the end of the gangway straight through one of the cabin windows. As the boat bumped and heaved, the jutting two-by-six ground out lights, transoms, and mullions and nearly scraped the window-frame loose.

"Do you remember what he said then?" Dell asked.

"No," I said, "I don't remember that part of it at all."

"He said, 'Well, I guess you boys can handle her now,' and you smiled and said, 'We'll try to be careful, Cousin Nate.' It was funny as hell. When Nate left we tied the boat up and sat down and laughed for at least half-an-hour."

We both laughed again, if only for a moment. "Good Lord," I said, "you turn the clock back. That was a heroic occasion. An age of heroes."

"Part of it wasn't funny," Dell said. "You really saved our lives, the lives of all four of us. You were up to anything."

"We were lucky," I said. "Maybe the boat wouldn't have cracked up. Maybe they could have thrown lines to us from the trestle and gotten us off. Whatever happened to that little blonde? She was gorgeous, even with her hair done cootie-garage style. Even half-drowned. A nice girl, too, as I remember it."

"She killed herself," Dell said.

"My God," I said, "how did that happen?"

"I never really knew," Dell said. "A couple of years later she married a boy from up-state. People said she started using dope. Anyhow, about three years after she was married she jumped out of a window of the King Cotton hotel in Greensboro. Some said she didn't take dope but that she had something wrong with her mind. Others said she got syphilis from her husband. A beautiful girl."

As often as not Dell's stories about people I had grown up with ended somberly. His prodigious knowledge of Essex was much less clouded, I thought, than his knowledge of science, literature, business, and technology. Part of what he knew came from the newspapers, of which he was an assiduous reader, part from gossip passed on by relatives or friends, and part from what he heard and saw, especially during the long hours when he served for several years as night manager of an all-night drug store. "What ever happened to George Davison?" I asked once, for example.

"George was an alcoholic—real bad—you must have known that," Dell answered. "He married a girl from Illinois. She had more than a million dollars, and George never went back to work at the Atlantic Coast Line after the honeymoon. He was a fine fellow, but he just couldn't stop drinking. Bourbon, Scotch, vanilla extract, cough medicine, anything. One winter night about fifteen years ago he slipped out of the house and came to my drugstore with nothing on but his pajamas. He was supposed to be in bed with pneumonia, and they were trying to keep him off alcohol, too. I wouldn't give him any liquor and he went on off. A few days later he was dead. Did you hear about his brothers, Ennis and Rees?"

"No," I said. "They were younger than I. I remember that Ennis was one of the most beautiful young boys I've ever seen."

"I'm not sure about Rees," Dell said. "He quit college in his sophomore year, though they had thought he would make the best pass-catching end in Duke's history. The story was that he had knocked up the daughter of one of the professors and didn't want to marry her. His father and mother were on his back—they wanted him to act like a gentleman—so he ran off to Texas. He died in Houston, but not until about ten years ago. Acute alcoholism, they said. Ennis died a long time ago. That was another funny story. He was found stabbed to death in a motel room near Richmond. No one ever said exactly how it happened, but as I heard it Ennis had a fellow in his room with him and they quarreled. Trouble with Ennis was, he was a fag and he like to drink, too."

That was the way it went. Eloise, a girl I had been in love with when I was in high school, had had two operations for cancer but was still alive and did nothing but stay home and drink and scream at her Negro maid. Everyone had thought that two attorneys—high school foes of mine—would drink themselves to death before they were forty, but they didn't. Billy had a stroke before he was forty, though, was badly paralyzed, and could hardly say an understandable word. He sat in a wheel chair all day and had himself pushed around by a Negro man. Fortunately for him, he was married to one of the rich Ballou girls. His favorite occupation was attending funerals. Every funeral that took place in Essex, he had his man push him to a corner where the automobiles would pass, and he would watch with saliva trickling down from the corners of his mouth. He could just manage a half-smile, Dell said, and one of Billy's friends told Dell he sat there saying to himself all the time, "I outlived you, you bastard." Or "you bitch," as the case might be. The other attorney, Hugh, was divorced by his first wife; she couldn't take his meanness when he was drinking, which he nearly always was. Hugh married a nurse he had started going out with before his wife divorced him. But the nurse was a

hard sister; she liked to take his automobile and go out and
drink with other men. She was good at spending Hugh's money,
too, some of it on the other men she went with—Hugh was
usually too drunk to be much good to her. One night Hugh left
the house to get away from her after they had a fight and
called Palmer McGee, a fellow who had been in Dell's class in
high school, and they took a room at the Tar Heel hotel and
sat down to drink together. After a while Palmer decided he
had better go on home, and Hugh said he was going to bed.
Hugh's wife telephoned Palmer after he got home. She made
Palmer tell her where Hugh was, but she promised not to
bother him. She went down to the hotel, anyway, and stayed a
little while. Next morning they found Hugh stretched out on
the floor, dead as a mackerel. The doctor thought he had taken
maybe fifteen or twenty sleeping pills. There was good reason
to believe his wife had carried those pills down to the hotel and
fed them to Hugh, but they couldn't do anything about it, and
she inherited his house and automobile and a few thousand
dollars. That was all he had left, although he had been a federal
judge. A very popular fellow and set records for the hundred-
and the two-twenty that lasted for about ten years in the Southern Conference.

I didn't have to believe the part about Hugh's widow, Dell
said, but he had the story straight from Palmer. Speaking of
Palmer, did I remember Dr. Ed Stoner, son of old Doc
Stoner? Palmer was the lover for a time of Ed's wife and Ed
took up, though not for long, with Hugh's widow. Ed was a
miserable man, now. He had emphysema real bad, and his
only daughter, the apple of his eye, had a bastard child by
Nelson Horney, son of the owner of the best ice cream plant
in town. Nelson said he didn't love the girl but would marry
her. She said she wouldn't marry him, and off she went, just
sixteen years old, to stay for a time with Ed's sister in Connecticut and have her baby there.

There were more stories every time Dell came to see me.
"Unbelievable! Insane!" I said to my wife after one of my
sessions with him. "Positively psychedelic. Essex must be the
craziest place on earth. I'm lucky to have gotten out of there."
But I couldn't get altogether out of Essex, not with Dell around.
He telephoned or dropped in so frequently that my wife started

saying "Here's your voice from the past, again," before one of us picked up the receiver or before we actually saw who was pulling up in our driveway.

I didn't spend all of my time talking with Dell, of course. We did gradually get a good many things in shape around the house and yard. The trouble was that we insisted on lapidary precision or thought of new things to attend to or new improvements to make and before long some of the things we first attended to needed working on all over again. There is something dreadfully seasonal, cyclic, and unending about keeping up a house; one never really manages to get ahead. And Dell actually did consume more and more of my time. By the time we had been in Chapel Hill eight or nine months, he had given up collecting and was free to turn up at our place every three or four days. My wife said that pretty soon he would be living with us. Sometimes he was amusing, to be sure, even if his stories had no particular point, like so many of his golf stories.

There was one golf story he told about himself and Tommy Armour that I thought was good. He had known Armour very slightly years earlier, when the Silver Scot was a regular winner. Dell had played poker with him and some of the other pros. "Those fellows knew how to gamble," he chuckled; "now, as I understand it, there are not many high-flyers left. They are more like business men." The amusing part of his Armour story took place when the Scot was no longer an active tournament player. One day when Dell happened to be in Pinehurst and was killing time on a practice green, Armour walked up and said he wanted Dell to accept a set of matched irons as a gift. "Why me?" Dell asked him. "No secret, no strings," Armour said, "the company I represent has asked me to give ten sets to people I know who know golf. All you have to do is use the clubs and if you like them say so." So Dell grabbed the clubs.

"I'll ask your question," I said. "Why you?"

"I figured it out later," Dell said. "It was just a mistake. Armour had forgotten me, but I looked a lot like one of the Tufts, a family that owned most of Pinehurst—wonderful people they were."

The possible job Dell talked about most—like all the other jobs—never materialized. According to him, this was just the kind of thing he wanted, and he kept hinting at offers he turned down while waiting for it. It would pay well—$800 a month, an automobile, and commissions on sales above a certain figure. It would keep him in the open air and give him a chance to travel. It had dignity and, best of all, called for imagination in presenting the product. He would be selling Belgian steel and steel products in several southern states as soon as they got rid of an unsatisfactory salesman, or so Dell first told me. This yahoo sat on his ass in a motel and tried to sell by telephone instead of getting on the road and seeing people. The son of one of Dell's friends was managing sales, and the yahoo's territory as good as belonged to Dell. But complications developed. The owner of the importing company—an old bastard worth millions operating out of Atlanta—wanted to give the derelict salesman one more chance. Then it was a question of waiting until the salesman turned his automobile in. Next it seemed that steel was over-ordered—the firm couldn't deliver stuff it had already promised. For a long time it was a question of the use of dock facilities. The North Carolina Maritime Commission had to make a decision, and the whole thing was mixed up in politics. Meanwhile Dell lived on in his motel room in Pinehurst and found it easier and easier to come to see me in Chapel Hill.

It wasn't even as though he could help me with my Herculean labors in and around the house. He knew or thought he knew how I should do whatever it was I was working at, but I soon discovered that his knowledge wasn't to be trusted, whether I was taking off blistered paint or replacing old caulking or pruning shrubs or killing poison oak. I couldn't ask him to do any physical work. His automobile accident had left him in bad shape, and now he was plagued by gout, degenerative arthritis of the spine, a perpetual cough, and God knows what else. The first time he came up our front walk I wouldn't have known him from Adam if I hadn't been expecting him. He was bald, his walk was shambling and stiff at the same time (he suffered from extreme lordosis), his narrow eyes were closed to slits, as though he had spent a lifetime in tropical sun, and his whole body, except for a grotesque paunch, had diminished. Gradually I discovered something of the old Dell in him. He had the same big hands and wrists, the same voice, and deep inside was something like the same innocence. At least, the more I saw of him the more he seemed to me to be a child or at best an adolescent who had lived for a long time. Getting down to these essentials, if they were essentials, was like peeling an onion—stripping off the baldness, the wattled neck, the slitted eyes, the crooked feet, the logomania.

I came to dread that voice—the almost mocking respect for me, the covert egotism, the misused polysyllabics, the combination of whine and drawl. I hated myself when, influenced by him, I started to drop into the speech patterns of my youth.

As Dell talked less about jobs he might take he started talking more, though in a casual way at first, about some scribbling he was doing. But soon he abandoned the casual pose and spoke as though it were agreed between us that he was going to become an important writer. He was setting down oddities in the lives and personalities of backwoods characters he had known. For a month or more he talked of a sketch he was writing of an eccentric storekeeper in Cherokee country. He thought he could sell it to the *Reader's Digest*. At last he brought it to me and asked me to criticize it for him. I read it and said I was a chemist, not a literary critic, but that it seemed to me to have points of interest. In fact, it was almost unbelievably bad, full of misspellings and faulty diction, lacking in coherence, of some slight interest only because somewhere floating around the edges of it was a conception of an old rustic loaded with prejudices. Then I found he had already submitted it to the *Digest* before he showed it to me. He had brought it to me for praise, not criticism.

After that he insisted on talking a lot about pieces he was writing, and although he often referred to them as amateurish jottings, it became clearer and clearer that he thought of himself as an unrecognized Faulkner and of me as an always available ear. Voice and Ear! It was really too much.

It wasn't as though I encouraged Dell in his increasing smugness in any way. He wasn't countering any stories I told about my achievements as a chemist, such as they were, for I never told any. A curious thing about my knowledge as a chemist—Dell seemed to take that for granted. When I gave him answers to difficult questions in my field he was unimpressed. On the other hand he misconstrued shallowly based bits of lore as great erudition, as when I told him a little bit about guaiacum. He had mentioned it in a sketch he was writing.

"Gum wacky balls" were used to cure nearly anything in one of the backwoods districts he had traveled, he told me. Usually taken dissolved in bootleg whiskey, they were considered good for swollen feet, backache, headache, upset stomach, and loss of virility. "That stuff sure does give you courage," an old Indian told Dell. He tried it once himself, dissolved in bourbon, but it didn't heighten his virility—it just made him sick, sick as a dog, and his wife laughed at him for being naive.

As it happened, I had read an article only a few days before on osteoarthritis, and I identified gum wacky as guaiacum, a resin taken from trees found in the West Indies and along the Caribbean, good for generating a sweat and used for inflammation of tonsils or larynx. I could throw in such inane esoterica as that in the nineteenth century guaiacum, Dover's powder being added, was prescribed for pain. Compounded with rhubarb and sulphur as a nauseous treacle—the Chelsea Pensioner Electuary it was called—it was supposed to be beneficial to sufferers from osteoarthritis. Impressed though he was by this recondite knowledge of mine, Dell's self-satisfaction continued to mount. In his own eyes he had become my peer, perhaps my superior, and I was there to be used.

Finally he did something that forced me to make plain what his position was. He was pitiable, but no matter how often my wife said he was my problem, meaning not hers, I had no intention of making him my responsibility. The crisis came after he had visited us three times in ten days without ever bothering to telephone in advance. My wife was furious. She had wanted me to go out with her on one of those days. She announced that he was a supreme egotist, a nuisance to her, and a serious interruption to my work. On a Friday I suggested to Dell once more that he telephone in advance the next time to make sure that we were not busy. "Of course," he said. He wouldn't inconvenience us for the world. And he did telephone on Monday morning. He was making a little trip to Raleigh; could he drop by that evening? We weren't going anywhere, but I meanly told him that we were engaged. In that case, he said, he could put off his trip to Raleigh until Tuesday. I felt bad about having lied to him; so I called to my wife, who said despairingly that it would be all right to invite him to dinner for Tuesday night. "Very good," I told Dell. "Come about five-thirty tomorrow for a drink and dinner."

On Tuesday morning I went promptly to work after breakfast stripping paint on a side porch. All morning I applied paint remover, scraped, rubbed with steel wool, and sanded. After lunch I was more than agreeably tired, but I decided to work for another twenty minutes before putting my equipment away for the day and taking a rest. At one-thirty, just as I was preparing to stop, Dell's big Mercury station wagon, looking a good deal like him, battered and stringhalt, rolled up and, as usual, parked in our driveway. Dell came in as cheerfully unconcerned as though he were expected. He had finished what he had to do in Raleigh very quickly, and he had decided not to call on a large hardware supply house in Fayetteville that had a job for him if he wanted it—he was sure the work would be too routine to suit him. He thought he would come over and chat instead. He seated himself on the porch and asked me not to mind him—just go on with my work. My wife put together a cold lunch for him—he hadn't eaten, of course—and I gritted my teeth and spread more paint remover.

His visit to Raleigh had been slightly unfortunate, I understood from his opening remarks. As he often did, Dell juggled two subjects at once; this time it was his day and what I should be doing about removing paint. The effect—deliberately aimed at I was sure in this instance—was to make vague what he was saying about his trip to Raleigh. From time to time he opened his lidded tortoise eyes to peep at me. I had almost immediately the feeling that he was somehow attempting to manipulate me, and I was annoyed by his childish presumption.

He had gone to Raleigh, he said, because his wife owed a debt to her sister, who lived there. His wife was meticulous about such things, inflexibly honest; it upset her to owe anyone. He had found the sister-in-law at home, sober for a change and not on marijuana, either. The debt was for a small amount, but he handed her a twenty-dollar bill. She put the bill in her purse, went on talking, and didn't offer him any change. "She's like that," Dell said, "careless." Then the telephone rang and it seemed she would never stop talking; so Dell got tired and left. When he reached his automobile he felt in his wallet and discovered that he had not put in it the three or four twenties he had meant to carry with him. He had only a couple of dollars. So it looked as though he might have to borrow ten dollars from me to make sure he had enough to get back to Pinehurst. I didn't say anything; I doggedly scraped paint as though I hadn't heard. Now he stopped to think about it, Dell added, he supposed he should have gone right back and insisted on getting his change, but then he hadn't wanted to bother with it. He could go back now, but probably the sister-in-law would deny he had given her a twenty or would have gone out and bought whiskey with it. I still didn't say anything, and Dell turned to other topics.

By five o'clock I was exhausted and out of patience. Speaking with extreme restraint, I told Dell that I was very tired and had to take a bath and a short rest before joining him for a drink. He stirred the air with a gracious movement of his hand, and I picked up my tools and went in the house.

Before I took drinks out and rejoined Dell on the porch, I had decided what I would say if he brought up the matter of a loan again. He did, shortly before my wife joined us, adding a few new details to his previous story, saying confusedly that he had given his sister-in-law a five-dollar bill and a twenty-dollar bill, and alleging that to his surprise on leaving Raleigh he had found only sixty-three cents in his pocket. He really should have gone back for his change.

"Yes, you should have, Dell," I said. "I hated to tell you when you mentioned it earlier, but as a matter of principle I do not make loans, not to anyone or for any amount."

"Oh, that's all right," said Dell, "I really shouldn't have mentioned it. You see I thought I had several twenties in my wallet, and I wouldn't have mentioned it except that you never know when something will happen when you are on the road and you'll need a few dollars."

I cut in ruthlessly. "I understand entirely, Dell," I said, "and it embarrasses me to have to tell you that I don't make loans. I realize, though, that you need a little something to make sure of getting back to Pinehurst. How much gas do you have in your car?"

Dell accepted the question. "It's about quarter full, but I never trust one of those gauges," he said.

"At least you should make it back to Pinehurst without any trouble," I said, "but just in case some small thing goes wrong, I want to give you three dollars."

"Thank you," Dell said. "I'll probably return it when I drop by toward the end of the week."

"You don't understand, Dell," I said. "This isn't a loan. It's a gift. I don't make loans."

At that point my wife came out to say that dinner would be ready shortly. It was a good dinner, too. My wife had planned it that way because she had been thinking wicked thoughts about Dell and wanted to salve her conscience. She had chilled garbanzo soup, a rib roast, baked potatoes, eggplant, and a green salad. For dessert she had ice cream with brandied peaches. Dell liked everything. After dinner my wife obviously felt that she had done her Christian duty; she washed the dishes, excused herself, and went up to read in bed. This was consistent with her general attitude that Dell was my problem; I was the one who had to listen to his reminiscences. So we sat, and Dell didn't pull himself to his feet until after ten—he didn't like to be too late getting to bed, and he planned to do some writing in the morning.

At the door Dell paused and shuffled his feet. "I expect I'll be back up this way in a few days. I'll keep your loan in mind."

"Don't think of it, Dell," I said. "I'm glad to have been able to help you this time. It isn't a loan. It's a gift."

It was clear that Dell was nervous; things hadn't turned out the way he had planned them. "Then let's call it an Indian gift," he said. "I should like to return it."

"I'm sorry, Dell," I said. "It's a real gift. I don't make loans even under some other name. Now don't forget; call us again when you are coming up this way." I shut the door, waited until I saw his headlights go on, and turned off the porch and yard lights.

My wife put her book aside when I got upstairs. "I thought he would never go," she said; "You must be worn out."

"I'm exhausted," I said. "I put in a full eight-hour day with him. But I think he may stay away for a while."

"Why are you so optimistic?" my wife asked.

"I've insulted him," I said. "This time he went altogether too far. Coming for lunch when invited for dinner and trying to slip the entering wedge in for a series of loans. In all the time he has been visiting us he has never brought so much as a bouquet of flowers with him. Now he asks me for ten dollars, which isn't a lot, but I'm sure he was measuring me for a lot more, and I wouldn't let him set me up—I stopped him cold. He hasn't been making any collections recently, but he gets money from his stock in the family mill and his sisters are married to successful men. I won't be his patsy."

"What did you do?"

"I told him I never make loans. Then I made him a *gift* of three dollars and told him I wouldn't let him owe me."

My wife gasped. "How could you?" she said. "That was cruel."

"You are the one who has been telling me to keep him from coming here so often," I said.

"That's different," she said. "Besides, he's not *my* friend. He's *your* friend. You are probably the only friend he has in the world, and you have humiliated him."

Tired as I was, we argued about it for an hour. I reviewed several times the wretched, childish lies Dell had told me. Finally my wife said I might be right; anyway Dell was my problem and she was going to stop worrying about him. "All right," I said, "and I'm going to stop worrying about him, too. If he calls again and you answer the telephone . . ."

"He won't call again," she said.

"I think he will," I said. "If he does, tell him I'm busy planning my laboratory and have asked not to be disturbed by anyone. He thinks his scribbling is important—he has to realize that I am a research chemist. I agree that we must be kind, though. Say that I may want to come up for air in a week or ten days and he should call back—you are sure I'll want to talk with him when I'm not so busy."

Dell did telephone the following Sunday night, and as it happened my wife answered the call. "What did you tell him?" I asked.

"Just what you told me to tell him," she said.

"What did he say?"

"Well, he seemed sad about it. He said he had hoped to have another chat tomorrow or next day. I know his feelings were hurt. He hoped you might call *him* sometime when you weren't too busy."

That was the end of it for three weeks. Then on a bright, warm Monday in late October, an Indian summer day it turned out to be, the telephone rang while I was shaving. I was more pleased to hear it than not. Waiting for Dell to call had made me uneasily expectant, and I thought that no one but Dell would call so early. It was the sandhills voice of Mrs. Pridgen, the woman who operated the motel Dell stayed in. "I imagine you know who I am," she said; "Mr. Brown has been a guest of ours for so long and he speaks of you so often. I'm sorry to be the one to tell you he is dead." Then she tumbled it all out. It was the worst thing that had ever happened in her motel. Dell had asked the night before to be awakened at six-thirty. This morning he didn't answer. The night clerk went to his room. There Dell was in a bathtub half-filled with water and blood. The doctor that Mrs. Pridgen called said he had been dead for six or eight hours. He had used a straight razor, one of a set he had. On his dressing table were several messages, one telling Mrs. Pridgen to ask me to come and make the necessary arrangements.

I calculated as rapidly as I could. "Thank you, Mrs. Pridgen," I said, "I'll have to do some telephoning, but I think I can be there or have someone there before noon." It seemed outrageous to me that Dell had not left word for his wife or the sister who lived in Morganton or one of his relatives in Essex to take care of things. But they didn't see it that way. His sister had a sick child and couldn't possibly leave Morganton. A doctor at the sanitorium said that Mrs. Brown was well enough to be working there—she wasn't just a patient any-more—but the most he would recommend was that she meet me at the motel. When Mrs. Brown came to the telephone she advised me to notify Dell's cousin Sanford Brown in Essex. Probably he would know what to do about the funeral. "The Browns have a big lot in the cemetery," she said. "Or do I say 'a big plot'? Sounds funny either way, doesn't it?" As nearly as

I could judge, she was not at all shaken by Dell's suicide; she said something about his having died a long time ago, and she agreed to meet me at the motel at noon.

Sanford Brown was cooperative and business-like, but he did ask me to call the funeral home in Essex so that I would know when to expect men to pick up the body. He would see to everything else. The director of the funeral home was professionally consoling and knowledgeable. He had buried my father and mother, he told me, also Dell's parents. One would have thought that suicide was the most normal thing in the world.

I wondered whether the coroner of Moore County would let him have the body or would want to hold it for an autopsy and inquest. "No problem," the director said, "not with slit wrists. He wouldn't want an autopsy, anyhow. Couldn't afford it. A full autopsy costs about five hundred dollars, nowadays, and that coroner's total budget is probably less than ten thousand for the year." The director would himself handle doctor, coroner, official papers, everything. All I had to do was meet him and his driver at the motel at one o'clock. He would be there himself.

I rang several times at the motel office before Mrs. Pridgen came bustling in. It was a slack time of day, and she had been in the back seeing about linens and hadn't at first heard the "baa-yul." Mr. Brown had been a lonely guest, a good talker, and never gave her any trouble, she told me. But she had all the responsibilities she wanted, she was short of "he'p," and besides she had to go to Charlotte in about an hour and wouldn't get back until the next morning, so she was glad I had come. Then she gave me, repetitiously, the entire account of the early morning. Twice she asked me, "Have you ever looked into a tub that was half-full of blood?" I could see that this would become a stock line in future renditions.

While Mrs. Pridgen was talking, an erect, deeply tanned woman walked in. She looked twenty years younger than Dell or I, still strikingly handsome in an Indian kind of way—black hair, black eyes, straight nose, wide mouth. Hard as nails, I though, a barbarian, a regular Scythian. Aloud I said, "Mrs. Brown?"

"Yes," she said, and then as though she were answering my

thoughts; "We have a pool at the hospital. I'll miss my swim today. Have they taken Dell?"

"Not yet," said Mrs. Pridgen briskly; "I'm pleased to meet you. We can have lunch out on the patio and I'll give you Your Message. Then I must go." Mrs. Pridgen sent a Negro girl for sandwiches and Coca Colas, and we moved to a patio.

"Now here," Mrs. Pridgen said, her voice temporarily taking on pulpit tones, "is Your Message." She handed Mrs. Brown a large envelope. "Just as it was when I got it," she added, "and except for cleaning the tub out, we haven't touched a thing in that room."

"Thank you," Mrs. Brown said. "Let me see if he says anything you may want to hear." The envelope had printed in the upper left corner the legend, "M. Delacorte Brown, Broker, P. O. Box 321, Essex, N.C." "Yes," she said, "he wants you and Mr. Pridgen to have his portable typewriter, for me to take his clothes, already packed in his two suitcases, to give to people at the hospital, and," turning to me, "for you to have his golf clubs."

"Really," I said, "I don't expect to play golf any more. Wouldn't you have some use for them?"

Mrs. Brown shrugged. "He valued his clubs very highly," she said, "perhaps more than anything else. He says, too, that you needn't search for his manuscripts. For good and sufficient reasons he has destroyed them."

"I must be going, folks," Mrs. Pridgen said, "and I hate to bring it up at a time like this, but . . ."

"His bill?" asked Mrs. Brown.

"He owes for a whole month, as of yesterday," Mrs. Pridgen said, looking at Mrs. Brown.

"The bookkeeper at the hospital gives me only five dollars at a time," Mrs. Brown said, looking at me. I took out my check book.

"Just a minute," Mrs. Pridgen said; "let me give you a re-ceipted statement." When I glanced at the bill without really seeing it, she said, "I added in the cost of one used sheet, the one the doctor has him wrapped in. Even if the undertaker brings his own coverings, I don't think it would be nice to use that sheet again."

A maid came to tell us that the hearse had come, and we went to Dell's room with the undertaker. Mrs. Pridgen picked up the portable typewriter and said good-bye. "I'm not charging anyone with the rent for today," she said, "and take your time. I'll not send a maid in to clean 'til tomorrow." When the undertaker had gone I went back into Dell's room and closed the door. It was a small room, and for a moment I thought that Mrs. Brown had gone out. Then the bathroom door opened, and she stepped into the room. She had already begun to take her clothes off—that is, she had kicked off her shoes and slipped out of her dress. In her right hand, near her throat, was one of Dell's straightedge razors.

"What's the matter," I said stupidly. I had started to say, "Are you crazy?"

"Don't be frightened," she said quietly; "I'm not going to hurt you." More dramatically, she added, "Do just as I say, or you'll see real blood all over this room." She touched the edge of the razor to her throat, and I never doubted for a moment that she was serious. "Now start taking your clothes off," she said. "I want once more the experience of loving."

The scene was very familial, like an at-home strip-tease, or the awkward mating dance of arctic birds that happen to be shedding, or, in commoner terms, as though a couple had left home in the morning, driven all day, and were slowly, stiffly, bemusedly getting ready for bed in a strange motel. "You put your things on that chair," she said, "and I'll use this. Don't throw your shirt on that radiator—it's dirty." All very familial except for the razor. At last neither of us had anything on.

"Look at me," she said. I looked at her hard, dark body, the high breasts, and the firm, small belly. But I still had nothing on my mind but that razor.

"I don't think I can help you, Mrs. Brown," I said. "I'm not a young man anymore, and I'm afraid I'm too upset to be of any service."

Mrs. Brown smiled. "Do you like me?" she asked, and I said that I did. "Now I'm going to put the razor away," she said, "but I can get one any time and you would know it was your fault." She looked at me. "Poor little limp fellow," she said, and came over and moved slowly against me. I was the taller by several inches, but she did the embracing. It was like being embraced by rock-hard, dangerous nature in one of her softer moments. The woman was strong as a panther, smoothly muscled in legs, buttocks, and back. She went on rubbing delicately against me, and as she did she murmured something.

"What's that you say?" I asked.

She laughed. "I said that human hair is wonderful, useful for one thing as a sensing element in humidity controllers." I tried to laugh too. "Poor little thing," she said tenderly. "You will be able to help me, because I'm sure now that I can help you." She was right; she was exciting.

When we were altogether through we just lay there on Dell's bed for a few minutes. She spoke first. "That was very fine," she said; "just what I wanted."

"Thank you," I said. For the moment I felt good about myself.

She gave a small smile. "Thirty years ago you might have been magnificent."

"I thought I was still pretty heroic," I said, not exactly joking.

"It's nice for you that you can think so," she said. "You'd better get up and go now. I'll leave in a few minutes."

I went in the bathroom and washed. When I came out she was still lying on the bed, one tanned leg raised above her head, the toes pointed, inscribing a small circle in the air. "I bet your wife is big in the AAUW," she said.

"No," I said, as though she were accusing my wife of something reprehensible, "she's not." Mrs. Brown rolled her body toward me, pointed at my head with that implacable aggregate of minatory toes, and waited. "She likes cats and gives them cute names," I said.

"Like?"

"Like Jezebel Jingle and Beelzebub Bickerstaff." As soon as I had said it I was annoyed with myself. Under the circumstances this kind of disloyalty seemed more contemptible than merely being adulterous.

"Don't worry," Mrs. Brown said, "I don't expect to meet your wife, not ever, and this is good-bye for us." I nodded and turned to the door. "Take the razors with you," she said, "and don't forget the golf things."

With the box of razors in one hand and the golf bag in the other I worked myself part-way through the door. All at once I found myself as ill at ease as I had been when she held the razor at her throat. "Good-bye," I said; "it's been nice to have had this chance to meet you."

Mrs. Brown again pointed that aspiring muscular column at the ceiling and watched her circling toes. "Feel secure," she said. "You were great. Like Gang Busters. *Per aspera.*"

I pushed the door to and walked around to my car and got in with my razors and my golf clubs. It was still early on a beautiful Indian summer afternoon. Pale sun filtered through the pines. Camellias, azaleas, and magnolias were glossy and healthy looking—it had been a good summer for them, and their blooms would probably make a show. I had plenty of time to get back to Chapel Hill and have a couple of relaxing drinks before dinner.

As I drove I decided it would be best to say very little about Dell's widow—that crazy high school gymnast—to my wife. Had Dell somehow set that sex maniac on me? The woman was probably still lying there exercising and thinking about the Freudian implications of my golf clubs. There was no reason for me to shed tears over Dell. I was sorry about what he did, but at most I could feel nothing more for him than reluctant compassion. As Mrs. Brown herself had said on the telephone, he had died years earlier. Those stories of his—galvanic responses. He had destroyed his manuscripts for good and sufficient reasons! The poor, shrunken, broken down ex-salesman! Given his megalomania, it would have been like him to have appointed me his literary executor. Ah, did I once see Shelley plain, and did he stop and speak to me! As it was, he had managed to go on making a nuisance of himself and to get into me for a month's rent. Which in itself was ridiculous, when you consider that we really never, not even during that lazy summer, had anything in common.

Long before I reached Chapel Hill I found myself turning to other matters. The whole day's business had been so fantastic, so out of this world, that I could hardly think of it as real. Why dwell on the murky, the unfathomed, the unfathomable? My mind slipped off to topics that were less melodramatic and more probable. I had several projects lined up for myself. A few weeks earlier some equipment had come in for my laboratory; it was high time I set it up. My wife was eager for me to paint the living room—one of the inside jobs we hadn't gotten around to. And lunch at the motel had convinced me that I wanted to lay a brick patio in our side yard, a cozy place where we could have drinks and snacks in good weather, even on mild winter days. I considered things and decided to start on the patio. The living room and the laboratory could be attended to after the weather turned colder.

ALICE ADAMS grew up in Chapel Hill, North Carolina, went to Radcliffe, and for the last twenty-odd years has lived in San Francisco. The author of *Careless Love*, a novel, and many short stories, she is completing a second novel, to be called *Mothering*.

Gift of Grass

"But what's so great about money—or marriages and houses, for that matter?" Strengthened perhaps by two recent cups of tea (rose hips, brewed with honey and a few grass seeds), Cathy had raised herself on one elbow and turned to face the doctor. "Couldn't there be other ways to live?" she asked, consciously childish and pleading.

"Have you thought of one?" Oppressed by weariness and annoyance, Dr. Fredericks was unaware that both these emotions sounded in his soft, controlled voice. Once, in a burst of confidence, Cathy had said to him accusingly, "You speak so softly just to make me listen." Now she said nothing. Believing himself to be in command, Dr. Fredericks also believed his patient to be overcome by what he saw as her transference. She saw her feelings toward him as simple dislike and a more complicated distrust.

She lay back down, giving up, and reconsidered the large space that served as both the doctor's office and his living room. It was coolly blue and green—olive walls and ceiling, royal-blue carpet, navy silk chair and sofa, pale-blue linen lampshades on green pottery lamps. Only the couch on which Cathy lay was neither green nor blue; it was upholstered with a worn Oriental rug, as though that might disguise its function. Like most children—she was sixteen—Cathy knew more than her elders thought she did. She knew that at one time her

mother had been a patient of Dr. Fredericks', and she recognized her mother's touch in that room. Her mother, who was
an interior decorator, had evidently "done" it. As payment for
her hours of lying there? It would have been an expensive job;
Cathy saw that, too. God knows how many hours it would
have taken to pay for all that silk.

All her mother had ever said, in a tearful voice that was
supposed to extract similar sincerity from Cathy, was "At one
time when I was very troubled about my life a psychiatrist
really helped me a great deal. In fact, you might say that he
saved our marriage. Bill's and mine." Not wanting Cathy to
sense a conspiracy, she had not told Cathy that she was sending
her to her own psychiatrist. This was when, in August, Cathy had
said she was not going back to school in the fall, and her
mother and Bill—her stepfather for the past ten years—had
told her that in that case she must go to Dr. Fredericks.

"But I'm not troubled," Cathy had lied. Then she had giggled
in her unrelated, unnerving way. "Or married. I just don't want
to go to school for a while," she had said.

"But I hope you will be married," her mother had said. She
had sighed, frowned, and then smiled, attempting reassurance.
"Dr. James helped me a great deal," she said. "He's one of the
best doctors in San Francisco." She used the first name of
Dr. Fredericks—Dr. James Fredericks—which Cathy did not think
was a very smart disguise.

While the long pause after his question lasted, Dr. Fredericks
struggled with his counter-transference. He stared down at
Cathy's rather squat, short body in its jeans and black turtle-
neck sweater, at the long, limp brown hair that fell from the
edge of the couch and the perfectly round, brown eyes in
a pale, round face. He had to admit it. He couldn't stand
the little girl. Injecting kindliness into his voice, he said, "Isn't
there anything on your mind that you'd like to tell me about?"

At this, Cathy burst into tears. A quick, noisy storm of sobs
shook her shoulders and her chest, then stopped, and she said,
"You dumb fink."

He leaned back comfortably in his raw-silk chair that did
not creak. Seductively, he said, "I suppose by your standards
I am in some ways rather dumb." He did not say, "Such as
they are."

"Such as they are," she said. "I'm not interested in standards, or school or earning money or getting married."

"I wish I knew what you were interested in," he said.

This seemed to Cathy his most heartfelt and least contrived remark of the hour, and she answered him. "Clouds," she said. "And foghorns. I wonder where they all are."

"If you really wonder, you could go to the library and get a book."

"I'd rather wonder." She giggled.

"The 'trip' is more important than the destination, is that what you mean?" Despite himself, he had underlined "trip."

"I don't drop acid, I've told you that," she said, deadpan. "I'm afraid to."

"Well," he said, warming to his task, "that's a reasonable enough fear. But perhaps you have some other less reasonable fears."

"Deer-hunters. God, they have the worst faces I ever saw," she suddenly brought out, forgetting him and remembering the weekend just past. She and her mother and Bill had driven up to Lake Tahoe—a jaunt intended to prove that they were not really angry with Cathy, that they loved her nevertheless. By an unfortunate coincidence, this was also the first weekend of the deer season. On the other side of Sacramento, winding up past Auburn through beautiful mountain rocks and trees, Highway 80 had been lined with white camper trucks bearing hunters. The men wore ugly red caps and red plaid shirts. They had looked remarkably alike, at least to Cathy—as alike as their campers. Fathers and sons and friends, their faces had been coarse and unintelligent, excited, jovial, and greedy. Cathy shuddered. "God, I hope they all shoot each other," she said to Dr. Fredericks.

"Well," he said hopefully. "Let's see if we can find out what deer-hunters mean to you. I doubt somehow that it's sheer dislike of killing. For instance, you don't seem to be upset about the war in Vietnam."

"That's so bad I can't think about it at all," said Cathy with total candor.

"Well, let's see." Dr. Fredericks, almost alone among his colleagues, was more opposed to protesters than to the war, but bringing up Vietnam had been a ploy. He now thrust his real point home. "I do seem to remember that your stepfather is something of a hunter," he said.

Cathy heard the light note of triumph in his voice, to which she reacted with rage and despair and a prolonged silence. Why bother to tell him that Bill had only hunted ducks—and only with his father, before that awful old man had died? During the silence, she listened to the leisurely sounds of outlying San Francisco traffic and the faint, distant foghorns from the Bay. Concentrating on these, she was able to stop the echo of Dr. Fredericks' voice in her mind. Their voices were what she could stand least about adults: Dr. Fredericks' bored hostility; her teachers' voices, loud and smug; the alternately anxious and preening, knowing voice of her mother. The only thing that she could remember about her natural father, who had divorced her mother when Cathy was two, was his voice. It was high-pitched, almost a whine—nothing much to miss. Actually, Bill had a nice, warm, deep voice, until he drank too much and it blurred.

A heavy truck went by, creaking and lumbering as though weighted with old furniture or barrels of china and glass. Brakes screeched several blocks away. Then the traffic sounds continued as before. For a few minutes, there were no foghorns and then there they were again, discordant, with no rhythm.

Both Cathy and Dr. Fredericks glanced over at the clock on his desk. Five minutes to go. He sighed softly and pleasurably. He had recently stopped smoking and he enjoyed the air in his expanded chest. Although he was nearing sixty, he was well preserved. Squash and swimming at his club kept him in shape; he felt a certain snobbery toward many of his colleagues who were running to fat. He and his wife, who owned and ran an extremely successful chain of gift shops, spent vacations at health spas, playing tennis and dieting together. A blue-eyed Southerner, from West Virginia, Dr. Fredericks liked to view himself as a maverick among psychoanalysts—another breed, one might say.

Cathy swung her short legs off the couch and sat up. She clutched her knees and faced him. "Look," she said. "It's hopeless. You and mother think it's important to get married and save marriages and get money and save that, and I don't."

"We're trying to find out what you do think is important," he said. He did not bother to conceal his impatience.

Neither did she. "So am I."

"Next week?" They both stood up.

Out of context (he felt), she giggled. "Maybe."

Cathy's parents lived about ten blocks from Dr. Fredericks in the same expensive and fog-ridden San Francisco neighborhood, but instead of going home Cathy walked to the park she often went to, along the broad streets and down the hill leading toward the Bay. Here the sun was shining. She pulled a small box of raisins from her pocket and began to eat them as she walked.

The park was surrounded by rolling woods of pine and fir, cypress and eucalyptus, through which on clear days one could catch blue views of the Bay, red glimpses of the Golden Gate Bridge. Cathy walked past creaking swings and a slide crowded with small children. Out on a playing field, lounging about on the beaten grass, there were some kids her own age whom she thought she knew, so she hurried on toward the woods.

Off the path, she came to a place where there was a large sloping patch of sand. She sat down and reached into the back pocket of her jeans, where there was a very mashed joint, which she lit. She lay back, her left arm protecting her hair from the sand. She sucked in and waited for the melting of her despair.

The air smelled alternately of the sea, of lemon-scented eucalyptus, of pine, and of the dank, dark earth. It was nearly a clear day, but the foghorns sounded more strongly to her from the water. Soon the fog would come in, gigantically billowing through the Golden Gate. Now, in the visible sky above the dark, thatched cypresses, there were only a few large clouds; they were as heavy and slow and lumbering as bulls, a slow-motion lumbering of bulls across the sky. Cathy concentrated on their changes, their slow and formal shifts in shape and pattern. Then, in the peace, in the warm silence, she fell asleep.

Bill, Cathy's stepfather, had at moments a few of the reactions to Cathy that she evoked in Dr. Fredericks. At worst, he despaired of reaching her. But he was exceptionally sensitive to the feelings of women. He could often feel what Cathy felt, and could bear it no better than she. It was his sensitivity, in fact, that had kept him from leaving Cathy's mother, Barbara, who was his second wife. The extent of Barbara's anxiety and despair when they first spoke of separation had got through to him. They had seen Dr. Fredericks, together and separately, for more than a year. But before their meetings with him began Bill had already decided not, after all, to leave Barbara for Ruth, his girl friend. (Ruth had been unhappy, too, but she was younger and more resilient; her despair hit Bill with lesser force.)

Perhaps to avoid a discussion of Ruth, Bill had talked about his inheritance from his father, and Dr. Fredericks had given Bill good advice about investing it. Bill gave him credit for that. Actually, investments were Fredericks' real but unacknowledged field of expertise. Bill was a commercial artist, and not a terribly successful one. The investment had brought his income well within range of his wife's, so it may have been Dr. Fredericks, after all, who saved the marriage.

It was nearly dinnertime when Cathy came home from the park, and Bill and her mother were sitting in the living room having drinks. Barbara had done their living room, like Dr. Fredericks', in cool blues and greens, except for the brown leather sofa—a kind of tribute to Bill's masculine presence; ordinarily, she did not use leather. Bill almost never sat on it. He would sit instead, as he did now, on a small Victorian dark-blue silk chair that must have been intended for Cathy. Fortunately, he was light—a very thin, narrowly built man with delicate bones and sparse blondish hair. Barbara, wearing a smart gray wool dress, was sitting on the leather sofa, and Cathy joined her there. During the cocktail hour, they would sit that way, at opposite ends of the sofa, facing Bill rather than each other.

Mother and daughter appeared to Bill remarkably alike. Barbara's eyes, too, were round and often opaque; her body tended to be squat. Its shape was childlike, which at times Bill found quite touching. At other times, it turned him off, and on to voluptuous Ruth. In Cathy, naturally enough, the sexlessness was more marked. Bill sometimes wondered how he would have felt with a voluptuous daughter, a swinging chick. Would it have made him more uncomfortable?

"I told Dr. Fredericks how much I hated deer-hunters," proffered Cathy. Since Barbara, on principle, would never ask what went on during "her hour," Cathy would throw out indecipherable and tantalizing tidbits.

Feeling his second drink, Bill said, "God, I hate them, too. They all remind me of my father." Bill's father had been a mighty hunter, out of the great Northwest, with rather Bunyanesque notions of manhood, so that Bill had trouble from time to time believing in himself as a man, feeling that if those coarse, red-faced, hunting cretins were men he was not one. Indeed, he had been told by several women, including Barbara, that he played around only in order to prove his manhood to himself. At times, he thought that might be true. At other times, he thought it was simply because he very much liked women, lots of them.

But he was not supposed to voice as strong an emotion as hatred in the presence of Cathy, and he sensed reproof in Barbara's slightly stiffened posture. She was an extremely nice woman who wanted things to be perfect—her house, her husband, her daughter, and especially herself. Now, instead of reproving Bill, she smiled at him, sighed, and said, "God, I'm tired. I really did have a day."

"You didn't like your father?" Cathy asked in a neutral voice that bore, for Bill, an unnerving resemblance to Dr. Fredericks' therapeutic blandness. But it was almost the first personal question that he could remember Cathy's ever asking him, and he found that his chest warmed and expanded with pleasure. "To tell you the truth," he said, "I was very much afraid of him. The way I find hunters frightening."

"Oh," said Cathy, and then for no reason she giggled.

"We're having a really wicked dinner," Barbara said. "Prawns with that sour-cream sauce. I absolutely couldn't resist them in the Grant Market, so big and pink and perfect. And, of course, rice."

"You are wicked," Bill responded, since this was how they talked to each other, but he was hearing them both with Cathy's ears, and he wondered how she could bear their middle-aged fatuity. She was staring at a small porcelain vase of tiny blue strawflowers as though she had never seen it before. Bill asked Barbara if she wanted another drink.

He made them strong, and by the end of dinner, during which he and Barbara drank wine and told Cathy illuminating vignettes from their own histories, stressing education and travel and friendship, reminding her that they had once been young—by the time all that was over, Bill was almost drunk and Barbara had a headache. But he was still aware of the troubled depths of tenderness in her round brown eyes as she said good night to them both—quite out of character, she had decided to give in to her headache and go to bed.

"Cathy and I will clear up," said Bill decisively.

The truth was that he liked to wash dishes, which his father had seen to it that he was not allowed to do. He liked all that warm, foamy water around his hands and the essential and marvellous simplicity of the task. He handed each hot, clean dish to Cathy, who dried it with a sparklingly clean white towel in the blue-and-white-tiled, Philippine-mahogany room.

For no real reason, a picture of Cathy the first time he had ever seen her came to Bill's mind—a small, square girl with chocolate cake and frosting all over her face and hands. It was during what he and Barbara ironically referred to as their courtship, a protracted and difficult period during which they had both been concerned with Bill's shedding his wife—and with the difficulty of seeing each other privately, what with Barbara's child and his wife. Barbara's first husband had moved to Dallas and had not seen Cathy since the divorce, but Barbara had felt that Bill and her daughter should not meet until Bill was actually free. So it was quite a while before Barbara could invite Bill for dinner. And on the occasion Cathy found the perfect, beautiful chocolate cake that Barbara had made and plunged her hands into its dark, moist depths, then smeared her face. Barbara had chosen to laugh rather than scold, and Bill had liked her for that. Now the remembered sight of small, smeared Cathy moved him. He wanted to tell her about it, but he knew she would not understand; nor could she know that simply watching someone grow can make you care for them. So instead of any of that he said, "As a matter of fact, I think James Fredericks is a jackass," and handed her a wet wineglass.

Carefully polishing, as she had been taught by her mother, Cathy asked, "Is he? I don't know."

"God, yes. All he can talk about is what he likes to call

'finances.' He can't say 'money.' Besides, you don't see his name on any anti-war petitions of doctors, do you? He probably owns stock in Dow Chemical."

Plunging his hands back into the sink, Bill realized that he had wanted to say this for a long time. He had forgotten that Cathy was not supposed to know that he and Barbara had gone to Fredericks, and he wanted to reassure her, to tell her that if she didn't dig Fredericks it was certainly O.K. with him. But then he felt her mind float off to some clouded private distance of her own, and suddenly he couldn't stand it, and he turned furiously to confront her. "Listen," he said loudly, "you think you're confused, and that the world is difficult. Christ, what do you think it's like to be forty-one? Christ, talk about confused and difficult. Do you think I like getting outside myself and seeing a fatuous drunk whose scalp is beginning to show through? Christ! And believe me, being married is a hell of a lot more difficult than not being married, let me tell you. Your mother has to diet or she'd be fat, and she can't stand fat. And it's very hard to live without a lot of money and booze. You give it a little thought—just try."

Cathy's round eyes did not blink and she went on polishing the second wineglass. Then she glanced quickly at Bill and said, "O.K." Then she said, "I think I'll go to bed now," and Bill was left alone to clean the sink and wipe off the unvarnished wooden chopping table.

After he had finished that, he went into the small room off the living room that was known as his study; his books were there, and some portfolios of old drawings, and a collection of dirty pipes that he would have smoked only in that room. Now as he entered he found placed squarely in the middle of his desk a white sheet of paper, and on it were what he recognized as two joints.

He sat down in the comfortable green wool upholstered chair that Barbara had provided him, presumably for meditation, and he meditated, seeking a variety of explanations for Cathy's present, or gesture—whatever it was. However, nothing rational came to his mind. Or, rather, reasonable explanations approached but then as quickly dissolved, like clouds or shadows. Instead, salty and unmasculine tears stung at his eyes, and then he fell asleep in his chair, having just decided not to think at all.

REYNOLDS PRICE is the author of three novels, *A long and Happy Life*, *A Generous Man*, and *Love and Work*, and two collections of stories, *The Names and Faces of Heroes* and *Permanent Errors*. He lives in the country in North Carolina, and teaches at Duke University. "Waiting at Dachau" is his third story to appear in the O. Henry collections.

Waiting at Dachau

The camp itself—its active life—only lasted twelve years ('33–'45). Twelve years after that, we parked by its gates. Now, twelve years after that, I still don't know; the question has gathered force with every year's distance—why did you balk and refuse to enter Dachau, letting me, forcing me to go in alone? I need to know several things—my version, your version, then the truth.

Is the answer simple?—You were sick or tired or fed-up with sights after six-weeks' traveling? Or were you miffed about the night before, or—being a little younger—you may not have seen my urgent need, as a radio-and-newsreel child of the Forties, to test my memories against the source? (Dachau and I are almost exact contemporaries; I'm one month older than it and still running.) For months in advance, I'd braced for the prospect. Me at the Abyss—*us*, don't you see?—the heart of darkness head-on, between the eyes. (What did I expect?—to stagger? vomit? No, I knew all wounds would be internal, all effects delayed.) Or maybe you understood quite well—you and your Imagination of Disaster—and were only invoking your famous policy of kindness-to-self. Surely, though, your chances of bearing up were as good as mine—we'd been told the camp was hip-deep in flowers! Couldn't you have entered as a simple gift to me?

Well, you didn't. You waited. The last time you waited—for
me, at least—and I still wonder why.

My version is this: we'd planned it from the first. Christmas
of my first Oxford winter you'd flown from Paris and we'd
stretched out on the frigid floor of my digs, maps and budgets
around us, and plotted the summer (should it ever come: your
nosedrops had frozen on my bureau Christmas Evel)—a slowly
warming arc. You would join me again in mid-July. We would
ship my new Volkswagen-Newcastle to Bergen. Then we'd push
slowly on—a week each for Oslo, Stockholm, Copenhagen; then
a nonstop plunge through Germany to Munich, Dachau.

Why Dachau at all? We passed within twenty miles of Belsen,
Nordhausen, Dora, Buchenwald, Ohrdruf, Flossenbürg. Dachau was never a major death camp. Only a third of its inmates
died. Yet I never considered another camp. Three reasons, I
think: I knew it was there (most others were razed); the name
itself was the perfect emblem, as it was for the Germans
themselves, it seems—anyone who disappeared was assumed
"to be in *Dachau*." (Something inheres in the name, the sound—
pronounced correctly it contains an unstopped *howl*. So does
Auschwitz but Auschwitz could be—for Americans born after
1950—a brand of beer; *Buchenwald* could be a national park;
Belsen a chocolate factory. *Dachau* seemed to me then—and
seems now—only a terminus; last-stop, as Auden knew in '38—
". . . the map can point to places/ Which are really evil now—
Nanking. Dachau.") And then nearby was Salzburg, as antidote—
Figaro with Schwarzkopf, Fischer-Dieskau, Seefried, Karl Böhm.
Then we could slowly climb the Rhine to Cologne (still without
a whole building), The Hague and Vermeer, Amsterdam and
Rembrandt; then (healed by now, stronger for the burns), we
would ship back to Oxford, take a look at our gains, our chances,
maybe marry. You'd pack up your chaste tight paintings in Paris
(adjectives yours—triangles, oblate spheroids, cubes, all aching
with loneliness in empty space) and join me for a last Oxford
year on my thesis; then we'd sail home to all the books I'd
write (my dreams of extracting love from my past, the bone-
yard of my childhood)—having already, well before we were

thirty, faced the worst life had ever offered any human pair, the final solution.

We made it to Munich precisely on schedule, only slightly in the red and apparently in love after four weeks of cold-water hosteling, cold roadside meals—canned potato salad, canned corned beef; we had bought a case of each and would only need bread every day at noon. I keep a photograph of one of those lunches—even without it, I'd have it in my head. We have stopped for lunch by a lake somewhere between Geilo and Oslo. Clear sky, the light a lemon yellow. You sit on a large stone, ten yards from the water, surrounded by smaller stones round and large as baseballs. The sounds are: our feet in those stones, water stroking, your opening of cans. I squat watching you warmed to fragrance in the light, adding to my luck only one more sound—in my head, the voice of Flagstad. She is still alive, a hundred-odd miles from here in retirement, playing solitaire and knitting—and that voice like a new lion in a zoo, *intact!* If she'd sing now we'd hear it across valleys, through pines! (She will of course return to make those last recordings which calmly eliminate all future need for Wagnerian sopranos.) You speak—"Sir, your lunch." You are holding out your hand with a plate of food, but you have not risen. I must come to you. Halfway is halfway. I rise and go. *The happiest day in all my life*—I say that silently, moving toward you. Now, twelve years later, it is still unassailed. There hasn't been a happier day. Yet, how do I have this photograph of it, in which your hand and the plate of food are blurred, moving toward me? Did I force you to offer it again for the camera or had I waited, shutter cocked, for the moment? Why did you let me complicate your simple service? You smile in the picture but you have at least the grace to refuse to meet my eyes. Your refusal has begun; your heels are digging in. I am drowned, though, in what tastes to me like good fortune; so I fail to notice for weeks, days or nights.

In the days I could see you—walking gravely past acres of Norwegian painting (every painting since the war in shades of pink and yellow) to smile and say at last, "A nation of fairies!" Or sitting in a Stockholm park, eavesdropping on a Swedish girl and her compact, rapidly heating French boyfriend

(the girl so liberated that I all but expected a taut diaphragm
to pop out and roll to rest at our feet when she uncrossed
her legs), you said, "Knock her up and she'll wail like Queen
Victoria!" Or stopping in the midst of tons of bland Thor-
waldsen marbles in Copenhagen (all like variations on the head
of Mendelssohn)—"Well, I like the *Danes*. They're crooks."
Setting those down makes you sound studied, tough; a big
reader of Salinger and Mary McCarthy. But I *saw* you. You
were then, every minute of those long summer days, the perfect customized answer to all my optical needs. You seemed
—you threatened!—to lack outer boundaries, integument; to vi-
brate within only vaguely held limits which, each night, permitted—welcomed!—me in to form a perfect compound.

Was I wrong, self-deceived, about that as well? I could even
see you then—by the Midnight Sun; the birds never slept.
Were you merely drumming time through all my happy hours
of artful plunging? (the years spent studying van de Velde,
Eustace Chesser)? It's accurate, I know, to say you never
turned to *me*. I was the one to initiate action. But once I
had laid a hand on your hip, you would rock over toward
me and open like—gates! Very earnest, weighty gates that not
every man could move. And you'd smile and *thank me!* Always
at the end—and you almost always made it or threw Oscar-
winning acts—you would say (not whisper; have you still never
whispered a word in your life?) *"Thank you"* as though I had
zipped the back of your dress or made you a small expensive
gift (when there stood my donor capped with high-smelling
rubber, reservoir tipped to *block* small expensive gifts). And
that in the Fifties before the Revolution, when ninety-eight percent of the girls I'd had still shuddered at the end and asked
forgiveness—asked me, Count Vronsky! I would lie some nights
for hours, too grateful to sleep. You'd be gone in ten seconds.

Was I really wrong? Wasn't the only bad night the one in
Munich? Where did we sleep there? Some station hotel or
with one of our specialty, war widows with lace-curtained
bedrooms to rent and permanent frozen killing smiles propped
round government-issue teeth? I can't see the room but I hear
the silence—that I took you, really *had* you, against your will
for the first time ever. You were tireder than I; but even then
you laughed when I'd hacked to my reward, all huffs and

puffs, and questioned your stillness. You said—*said!* surely our *witwe* heard you—"Riding shotgun in a Volkswagen daily leaves a body badly tuckered." Well, pardon me, Sara—twelve years too late, if you even remember. Hadn't all the other sex till then though been mutual? Wasn't it *love?* We had known each other for ten years exactly, grown up together. We knew all the ways—more than half of them hidden—to protect each other; and any damage was a slip, inadvertent. We could have lived together as easily as dogs; and I'd thought—till that day at Dachau—we meant to. If we didn't love each other, who ever has?

—The de Wieks anyhow, if nobody else. You won't have heard of them. I hadn't till two years after we parted—in Ernst Schnabel's book on Anne Frank. A Dutch Jewish husband and wife flushed from hiding in 1943 and shipped to Auschwitz, where the husband died and the wife survived to remember Anne Frank's death. But this is the thing I want you to know —Mrs. de Wiek's memory thirteen years later of a moment on the packed train threading toward Auschwitz:

I sat beside my husband on a small box. The box swayed every time the wheels jolted against the tracks. When the third day came and we had not arrived, my husband took my hand and suddenly said: "I want to thank you for the wonderful life we have had together."

I snatched my hand away from him, crying: "What are you thinking of? It's not over!"

But he calmly reached for my hand again, and took it, and repeated several times: "I thank you. Thank you for the life we have had."

Then I left my hand in his and did not try to draw it away. . . .

There is no photograph in the book of him or her; but they've walked, since I read that, as clearly in my head, as in *Daniel* three just Jews walk safe through the flames of Nebuchadnezzar's furnace. Shadrach, Meshach, Abednego—and a fourth, their angel. The de Wieks walk alone, two stripped Dutch Jews, dark-eyed, grinning, safe in my head; to Hell with *my* head, safe through all time should *no* one know of them, sealed in the only knowledge that turns fire—to have loved

one another through to the last available instant, to have *known*
and then had the grace to say thanks.

Were you just not that good—that strong and pure—or did
you choose not to be that good *for me?*

I see them in their flames (or you by your lake) much more
clearly than I see Dachau. My world-famous total recall deserts
me. Or does it? Can it have been the way I remember?
(I've never gone again.) The latest *Britannica* gives this much—
that Dachau is a town eleven miles northwest of Munich,
population ('61) 29,086, first mentioned as a market village
805 A.D. and continued as a village till 1917 when an ammunition factory was built there—the site in March 1933 of the
first Nazi concentration camp; that the town stands on a hill
at the summit of which is the castle of the Wittelsbacher and
that the other sight is a parish church (1625).

What *I* remember is driving through sunny fields of potatoes
and grain, you watching for road signs and calling the turns
(German roads then were still under heavy reconstruction; and
one of your frequent bursts of song was *"Umleitung*—there's
a muddy road ahead!"). Wasn't my right hand holding your
thigh, except when a farmer waved from a yard? Wasn't the
town still a village after all, merely houses (no business street
that I remember)?—low white houses with small sandy yards,
green gardens in front? Don't I remember screened porches,
green rockers, dusty ferns in cans, geraniums in boxes? A grey
frame railway depot and platform? Didn't I ask to stop and
walk a while or to drive slow and aimless (we had hours till
the camp closed) through the loose grid of streets that seemed
home at last (Were they really unpaved, ankle-deep in white
dust)? But you led us on—"Turn right; here, here." Your un-
failing sense of where we were, where we must go. I was
ready to wait, stop short of the camp. The village itself,
your warm proximity, had eased my urgency for confrontation.
What we had—there and then—seemed tested enough by time
and chance, to require no further *pro forma* buffeting. It was
you—I'm sure of this—who forced us on. An Ariadne who—
calm in her beauty, perfectly aware of the course she's set—
calmly leads dumb Theseus back into the lethal heart of the

maze, its small tidy utterly efficient death chamber, the patient minotaur who has only played possum and waits now, famished.

From the parking lot (!) on—in my memory—it does seem a room, not ample but sufficient and sturdily enclosed. The new small gates (where are the old ones?—*Arbeit Macht Frei*), the cyclone fence thickly threaded with vines, the no-nonsense sign (*Maintained by the Corps of Engineers, U. S. Army*), the clear sky, the light—seemed interior, roofed, sheltered, shrunk or a model scaled precisely to a larger form. Is that why I didn't lock the car—after weeks of paranoia, left our luggage available to any passer? Or had I started guessing you would stay behind—guessing and hoping?

You had got yourself out ("Chivalry ends here," you had told me in Stockholm) and stood in sun that suddenly had the weight of sun at home, that seemed each second to be loading you with burdens. Also the color—you were bleaching as I watched. Yet you took off your sunglasses and stood by your shut door, hands at your sides, squinting straight at me.

I came round to you and extended my hand. You accepted. I took a step onward and engaged your weight, gently.

You said "No." You were planted. Your hand stayed in mine but your face refused.

I said, "No, *what?*" and laughed.

"Not going," you said.

I didn't ask why but said what my father always said when I balked—"Are you sick?"

"No," you said.

"Then you promised," I said.

You had not; you should have laughed. But you shook your head.

"If I ordered you?" I said.

"You wouldn't."

"If I did?"

"I wouldn't go."

I said "*Wouldn't* or *couldn't?*"

"Wouldn't," you said.

We had not smiled once!

You took back your hand.

I said "Will you wait?"

You nodded yes.

"Where?"

"I'll *wait*," you said. You half-waved behind you, a cluster of trees, shady grass beneath.

So I moved again to go—to leave in fact—not looking back, and entered the camp. Dachau. Left you waiting as you chose. Are you waiting still?

You have never seen it and, as I've said, my otherwise sharp pictorial memory is dim on Dachau; so to write this, I've spent three days trailing information through volumes of war-crimes trials, memoirs, histories of the S.S., photographs (forty Jewish women—nude, mostly potbellied, three of them holding children—queue up for a massacre in some Polish ditch: two of them are smiling toward the camera). Guess what a good three days I've had—to learn very little more than this (the memoirs on Dachau specifically are in Polish and German, shut to me): Dachau was opened in March 1933, a pet project of Goering and Himmler. The site, a mile square, was equipped for 8000 inmates. At its liberation in April '45, it contained 33,000—ninety percent civilians, ten percent war prisoners. The civilians, from the first, fell into four groups—political opponents, "inferior races" (Jews and Gypsies), criminals, "asocial elements" (vagrants, pimps, alcoholics, etc.). Further divisions were recognized by the colored patches on prison clothing (selected with a grinning irony)—black for "shiftless elements," yellow for Jews, pink for homosexuals, purple for Jehovah's Witnesses. Though the oldest camp and the popular symbol for all, it was classified in the S.S. scale as a class-I camp —the mildest rating (Auschwitz was III). Only 70,000-odd inmates are estimated to have died there (4,000,000 at Auschwitz). The existing gas chamber was used only experimentally. Indeed, experiment was among the camp's functions—the famous experiments of Dr. Sigmund Rascher in chilling prisoners to 19° C., then attempting to thaw them with live whores stretched on their bodies (Himmler regretted that the chosen whores were Aryan). Or locking prisoners in mock altitude chambers to observe when they'd die of oxygen starvation. Or the study of asepsis by inducing infections which were left to gangrene.

—You know most of that. Everybody over thirty does (though

to anyone not there, as prisoner or liberator, it had never seemed credible). What I'd like to tell you is what I saw, twelve years after its liberation. I have the four photographs I took that day. I can build it round them.

The gates were unguarded. I walked through them onto a central road wide enough for trucks but closed now to all but lookers like me—there were maybe a dozen in the hour I was there. To my left, one compound (the only one or the only one saved?)—a four-acre piece of flat tan dirt enclosed by stretches of concrete wall (seven-feet high, electrified on top), relays of barbed wire and, in each corner, an all-weather guardhouse (twenty feet high, *all* empty now). No trace of barracks, no sign of shelter. Where were the famous "dog cells" in which prisoners could only lie on their sides and were forced to bark to earn their food? Razed apparently (on a partial diagram I count thirty barracks). A few weeds grow and, in my picture of a stretch of wall and guardhouse, a leafy branch decks the upper right sky. (Good composition. But how old is the tree?) No entrance there, no gate in the wire. To the right, though, free access—trees, grass, flowers, buildings.

All the people were there. I remember them as old and all of them women; but my photographs show one man (late forties, his suit and tie American—was he a prisoner here?) and two children under ten (a boy in *lederhosen,* a girl hid behind him)—otherwise, old women in long cheap summer dresses, stout shoes. All in clusters of two or three, simply standing akimbo or reading, their lips moving dryly at the effort. There are no talking guides, no sign of a staff to question, only scattered plaques and inscriptions in German—the single attempt at a monument, modest, dignified, undistinguished, a three-quarters life-size gaunt bronze prisoner gazing across the road to the compound, head shaved, hands in his scarecrow overcoat, feet in wooden shoes, on his marble base DEN TOTEN ZUR EHR', DEN LEBENDEN ZUR MAHNUNG ("To Honor the Dead, To Warn the Living"), and an urn of red geraniums. Granite markers maybe twelve inches square set in beds of geraniums —GRAB HUNDERTEN NAMENLOSEN (that's from memory—"Grave of Hundreds Nameless"; was it *hundreds* or *thousands?*). Then twenty feet onwards—it is all so small—six or eight women wait beside a building. It is one-story, cheap brick, green tile roof, straight as a boxcar and only twice as long. At the pitch of the roof there are turret windows; in the end near me, one large brick chimney eighteen feet tall. Along the side, frequent windows and doors. The only sign was a single black arrow aimed toward the far end (the end farthest from the compound and hidden). I followed, past a postwar willow tree, and found at the end a door—normal size, no wider than the door to my own bedroom.

From here I am on my own—no pictures. I think I remember the logic of progression, each small room labeled in German and English, giving into the next like a railroad apartment—*Disrobing Room, Disinfecting Room* (roughly ten feet by twelve, nine-foot ceilings, unpainted plaster walls scratched now with the names and hometowns of G.I.'s). Then another normal-sized wooden door opening into a larger room—maybe fifteen by twenty, shower spigots, soap dishes, floor drains, a ceiling window.

—I've built that effect outrageously—I'm sorry—to the oldest surprise of the twentieth century. The shower was gas, Cyklon B; the window was a deathwatch; the drains were for hosing down the products of surprise and suffocation. The next room was small again—*Storage Room*. The walls were printed from floor to ceiling with dirty bare feet, all turned neatly up. Corpses stacked like cordwood for the ovens. Next room, the ovens. The largest room and last, *Crematorium*. Four or five brick ovens spaced six feet apart, their iron doors open on seven-foot grill racks. The walls bore sets of black iron tools—tongs, prods, pokers, shovels. Behind the ovens, in the wall, were little doors—ash chutes to outside, for the *namenlosen*.

End of tour. No more sights—oh, an old woman kneeling by the farthest oven, clicking off her rosary. Otherwise nothing else to linger for but sunlight, geraniums. Or to make you wait a while. I thought you were still waiting; and I thought, retracing my way toward you, that I was returning.

You could easily have stood it—have I made you see that? It lacked—now I understand the vagueness of my memories —the mystery of place. There are places, objects, quite literally impasted with the force of past event; places in which one is pulled up short by the pressure of actual atoms of the past. Almost never in America—our shrines being ruthlessly scalded and scoured if not bulldozed—and almost always in sites of suffering or wickedness. The Borgia apartments in the Vatican still are oiled with the presence of Rodrigo Borgia's rotting body; electrons that witnessed, sustained, his life still spin in the plaster; the stones underfoot can be gouged (brown and rank) with a quick fingernail; unaltered atoms of hydrogen and oxygen that occupied his holy dissolving lungs in 1497 rush over one's lips and teeth with each breath. Or the Domus Aurea of Nero, subterranean now and leaking, where I rounded a dark corner on an elderly English gentleman masturbating (English by his clothes). Or the dungeon beneath the Capitol in which Caesar strangled Vercingetorix—45 B.C. Or—another thing entirely—the crystal reliquary in Santa Maria Maggiore which one Christmas Eve mass was borne toward me, immobile in the crowd, its scraps of wormy wood, whether hoax or not (the remains of the Manger) as immanent with promise and threat to my life as a gram of radium bombarding my eyes. Dachau is one month younger than I. It saw—caused— the agonizing unwilling death of tens of thousands while I was still paying half fare at the movies; yet its huddled remains bore me less of a threat, less pressure of the past than Williamsburg, than any plastic Hilton lobby.

—Why? That's *my* question. Why was I unshaken, unmoved? Anger with you? Tourist fatigue? (I who could weep years later in Chillon at the pillar to which Byron's Prisoner was chained?—and that after ten days hiking in the Alps.) What had I expected?—a Piranesi prison with eighty-foot ceilings, thick brown air, torture wheels staffed by malignant dwarfs? No doubt that would have helped. The physical remains of Dachau are so mindlessly disproportioned to the volume of suffering they were asked to contain, the literal volume of agonized breath expelled in that square mile in those twelve years. The slaves who died building pyramids are at least survived by pyramids, not tar-paper shacks and geraniums.

But no—don't you see?—I'd expected *home*. It's taken me these twelve years to understand that even—my curious memory (dead wrong surely) of the town itself as a scene from my childhood (porches, ferns, dust!—eastern North Carolina) and my readiness to dawdle there with you, my near panic at the camp gates when you refused. I had secretly thought through all those months of planning that this would be our home, that if we could enter Dachau together, face and comprehend its threat and still walk out together, then we'd be confirmed—a love not soluble in time or death. *Home* in the sense of birthplace; we'd have been born there, our actual marriage, a perfect weld-job in the ultimate crucible.

Nonsense, you're thinking. Were you thinking it then? Is it why you refused—you would not be a party to soft-brained theatrics?

But surely you're wrong. Sappy as my whole secret plan may have been—so sappy it was even secret to me; a Fiery Consummation!—it was not a fool's plan, not built on lover's lies. I wrote of "comprehending the threat of Dachau"—hadn't I done that already, in advance, by insisting on this visit? Its final horror—and that of all the camps, class I-III—was not the naked fulfillment by a few thousand gangsters of their fear and hatred on impotent objects (that, after all, is everyone's dream), but precisely the threat to human attachment, loyalty. The ghastliest experiment of all was not one of Dr. Rascher's mad-scientist pranks but the high voice that pulsed out its desperate need like a hypertensive vein—and at first uncertain of its power to enforce!—"Let me set you apart. Mothers here, children there. Husbands left, wives right." And millions obeyed, even the de Wieks—the most successful human experiment in history.

No, the horror is not that the camps did not revolt, that Treblinka stood alone—the horror was accomplished, ineradicable, the moment any one man entered Dachau—but that no husbands, wives, parents, children *stood*—by their radios or sofas or milking stools—and said, "No, kill us here in our tracks together." Oh maybe some did—then why are they unknown? Why aren't their statues in every city center, our new saints of love?—so far surpassing Tristan or Abelard or Antony as to burn like constellations over fuming brush fires. We are only left with endless processions of pairs who *agreed*—to abandonment, to separation by other human beings (not death or time). You know that there were mothers who hid from their children on arriving at Auschwitz—buried their own heads in coats or crawled through knees—to escape immediate death. Can they be forgiven that?

Every American over thirty has his favorite obsessive Holocaust story which he's read or, rarely, heard and retails ever after as his version of Hell. An entire sub-study might be done of these stories and their relevance to the teller. I *heard* mine, and after we parted. A colleague of mine—age thirty-eight—is a west-Polish Jew. His mother died of TB early in the war. There were no other children and he lived with his father, a practicing dentist. When the roundup came in '42, my friend was eleven. In warm July weather he rode with his father in the packed train to Sobibor—two days, I think, stopping and starting—and once they were there and unloaded on the siding and a doctor came round to eliminate the sick, my friend's father said that his son was consumptive. It was news to my friend; but, being a child, he only thought, "Of course he's right; they kept it from me." But his father never touched him and my friend was led off, presumably for gassing or a lethal injection. Some balls-up ensued, his death was delayed; he never coughed once, chest sound as a stone. But he never saw his father. He was strong enough to work, my friend—farm the camp potatoes—so he managed to live through two more years and a transfer to Auschwitz. Then one day—age thirteen—he was standing in a compound when a line of new men passed. One man fell out for a moment and came toward him. My friend said, "He thought he was running; he was creeping" (too weak to run). Of course, it was his father. They both knew that. But they didn't speak and, again, didn't touch; and a guard beat his father into line—fifteen seconds. Never met again.

Well, in the immortal words of King Lear—"*Howl.*" My friend thinks the question in his story is *Why?*—why his father did that. I'd never tell him but the question is *how?* There are degrees of offense at which motive is irrelevant. Can he ever be forgiven?—that father (out of Dante) stumbling on his appallingly vital son whom he'd lied to kill? Can any of the millions ever be forgiven?

Can you, Sara, ever? And not just by me. It was you who refused. Only you were not killed. You could have walked into that tamed camp with me; you could have had the guts to settle it *inside*—to have seen it all with me, to have armed it with the threat which without you it lacked and then (if you needed so desperately) have said to me, "No, I will not live for you." Instead, for your own no doubt clear reasons, you lurked outside on the shady rim, half-sadist, half-coward— unwilling to choose, thinking you could wait and that I, having waited for half an hour beyond a wire fence among debris as meaningless as MGM sets, would presently return.

I did and didn't. When I came back through the gates, I didn't look for you but went to the car and sat in its oven-heat. I already knew that I was not waiting and had not returned, not to you at least; but—stopped short of panic or the courage to act my feeling—I was not prepared to abandon you physically, to leave your bags on the empty parking space and drive off for Salzburg with your twenty-dollar *Figaro* ticket in my wallet. So I thought in the heat, "I may go under but I won't go looking."

In three or four minutes you walked up slowly, got in and sat, facing forward. How did I feel to you? What vibrations, what aura? Or were you receiving? Had you ever been?

What I felt was hatred. What's *hatred*, you ask?—the wish that you were absent from my sight, my life, absent from my memory. I had put my hands on the wheel for steadiness, and I thought my hatred was shaking the car. Then I saw, in my head, a Volkswagen jittering away in the sunkist parking lot at Dachau; so I cranked up and moved.

You said, "Where are you going?"

I did not want to stop now and look at you—I must keep my hands busy. I said, "*I?* To Salzburg."

"Am I coming?" you said.

"Unless you jump," I said.

I think you took that to mean you were forgiven. You behaved as though you were. Slowly through our drive to Salzburg you loosened, slowly became the girl I'd thought I needed —smiled at my profile and, then when we'd got in sight of hills, you sang the whole final scene of *Figaro* (from "*Gente, gente, all'armi, all'armi*"), taking all the parts, chorus included. Your text was letter-perfect, your Italian B+; only your baritone plunges failed. Yet I knew your motive far better than you. It had nothing to do with the coming evening. It all bloomed out of your need and wish to sing five lines—

The Count: *Contessa, perdono.*

The Countess: *Più docile io sono, e dico di sì.*

All: *Ah! Tutti contenti saremo così.*

[*Countess, your pardon.—I'm gentler now and I'll say yes.
—Ah! Everybody's happy with that.*]

That, I think, was the climax, though the day (and this
piece) had a good while to run. I took that to mean you
were pardoning *me*—for not having cheerfully granted your
independence back at Dachau, for not having bought the metaphor your refusal offered (we'd be hitched to one load but
in separate yokes). So I thought I would launch a spot of
unforgivability. When you'd sung through the orchestral *tutti*
to the curtain, you faced forward resolutely—no bow in my
direction. That meant I should applaud—right? Well, I drove
a good mile before making a sound; and then I said: "One
question."

"What?"

"Why in all your extensive *reconciliation* repertoire"—can you
still do Cordelia, Marina, Fidelio?—"is it always the *lady*
dispensing largess?"

You'd have bit off your tongue before admitting you hadn't
noticed. You said, in an instant, "It's the way the world's
built."

"Many thanks," I said and by then we were threading the
fringes of Salzburg, its castle as stunned by the day as I.

I said that this would be my version, what I remember and
understand. The rest of the day—what I thought was the day
—is necessary; then tell me yours; I genuinely need it. Yet,
again, my memory of *places* is vague, my grip on surfaces.
You've greased my hands, greased every wall; or is it only
some new lubricant from myself, manufactured now in me—
suddenly—in response to your refusal, to ease me away? Anyhow, it's still produced. Some days it pours.

Mozart's *Geburtshaus*—we saw that together but what do I
recall? Two or three pokey rooms, white walls, dark brown
woodwork, an early piano on which (the guide told us)
Harry Truman had just played. Was there even a *birth*-room?
Were they sure of which room? I couldn't say. It seemed
more like the birthplace of some dry chip—say, Metternich—

82
Reynolds Price

than the Sublime Foul Mouth. And didn't you recognize that? When we'd made our separate rounds and I passed the guest book on my way downstairs, I saw you'd signed with your comic alter-ego—*Veronica F. Pertle and traveling companion.* We were already lethal, in under three hours—we'd agreed to be a team of cut-rate Midases, transmuting all we touched to chalk.

I slept through a good deal of *Figaro*—all that endless nocturnal business at the start of Act III, the confused identities. I've slept through greater performances than that—Melchior's Lohengrin, Welitsch's Salome—though always before from travel fatigue, biting off more grandeur than I could chew, but here I wasn't tired. I'd slept eight hours the night before, driven ten miles to walk maybe five hundred paces round a concentration camp, then eighty miles farther on a good wide road. No, I was retreating. The great death wish, Sleep Mother of Peace—if I couldn't lose you, I could lose myself. You woke me toward the end with a firm elbow—"Don't miss the forgiveness." So I can still hear that (Schwarzkopf's perfect frailty, a bulldozer disguised as a powder puff); thanks for the elbow —the trip was not in vain.

What I think I remember—as clear as the Norwegian day, your offered food—is the rest of the night. Correct me on this—

We had late coffee in some hotel lobby which seems, in memory, entirely upholstered in 1938 Pontiac fabric, and were spared conversation by a pair of purple-haired American ladies drinking *Liebfraumilch* six feet away. They had also heard the opera and debated the performance. One defended it stoutly but the doubter trumped her in the end—remember?—"Ella, all I know is, when I hear great singing something in me swells up. Tonight it didn't swell."

—"Mine neither," you said and stood and we left, heading toward Munich still hungry (no supper). Yet you didn't mention food, barely spoke at all; and what did I feel?—that really I was racing, to end this night, the trip, what we'd had and you'd failed, that I could go without food and sleep for days, an emergency encystment for however long it took to deliver you to whatever door you chose.

Then on the edge of Munich you said, "I'll never sleep without some food."

It was pushing two a.m. So I had to hunt awhile; but we found a place open somewhere in Schwabing, down a flight of stairs thickly cushioned with dirt.

"More dikes than Holland," you said going in; but in what light there was, they seem more like gypsies to me on hindsight.

You wanted fondue but we settled for something merciful and a good deal of wine; and with all the eating, surely we hadn't said fifty words when the two men entered with the lion before them. If they weren't gypsies I'll surrender my license—they laid down about them that heavy metal air of offense and threat I've known all my life (they still roamed the South when I was a boy, telling fortunes and offering odd skilled services no one would accept, though by then in trailers, not painted wagons; and their squat swart women with the Carmen earrings and their men whose hard faces all wore livid scars are high in my childhood pantheon of menace).

They picked you at once. Do you still think I signaled them? I *saw* them see you the moment they entered, even the lion.

He was straining toward you on his red dog-leash—maybe six months old?—and no one held him back, though I swear the rear man—the one with hands free—passed the huge lady-owner a small piece of money in their rush to you. Were they illegal, bribing their way? The lion was smelling your foot before you saw; and of course you didn't flinch—a male lion cub in a Bavarian dive at the end of a day comprising Dachau and Mozart: oh.

They were photographers—take your picture with a lion; best American Polaroid, instant result. I told them No—didn't I? I'm almost sure I did—but the contact man (the one with the leash) held the lion up and said, "See, he *begs*." With his free hand he clasped the cub's front paws together in a mockery of prayer (its high tight testicles were pink as salmon, utterly vulnerable). The man's English seemed more Italian than German, but maybe just basic P.X. English—"He begs you to warm him; four dollars for picture, give to your husband. He lose his mother, he lonely here." The cub's eyes were shut, so lonely he was dozing.

You continued eating but you asked him, "Did you kill her?"

That seemed the terror button. Surely these two oily small-time spivs had not been poaching in Kenya; yet at your question, they both threw grimaces at one another, and the talker said, "Look. No charge for you." He extended the lion, eyes still shut—"He need your help."

"He's asleep," you said.

The man jogged him hard; he looked out, groggily.

"No," you said.

But I said, "Do it" and produced my wallet. I wanted you to do it and I wanted to pay.

Looking at the lion, not me, you said, "Why?"

"I want the picture."

I extended twenty marks to the man and you stood.

"You sit," the man said, "then we take you both."

"I'll stand," you said. "It's me he wants." You stood and reached out. You were in the black dress with narrow shoulder straps—much white skin showed.

He moved close against you and hung the lion on your shoulder like a child. The photographer—the silent man—backed off and raised his camera; the talker said, "Big smile."

You smiled sideways, no teeth. The other diners paused, awaiting the flash. It came. In its light, blood streamed down your arm.

The lady-owner bellowed, came waddling forward. The two men leapt toward you. The lion was clamped into the meat of your shoulder.

I was still in my chair.

"Stay back," you said.

They understood and stopped a foot from the table.

"What's his name?" you said.

The talker said, "Bob."

The lady-owner babbled coldly in German. They must get him out, get out themselves, *die Polizeil*

You were stroking the back of Bob's locked-on neck, simply saying his name again and again—the two of us the only calm people in the room, only still ones at least. Us and the lion—he was motionless, teeth deep in you. What nourishment was he taking?—what pleasure, fulfillment? What did he think you were?

—A lion-tamer, anyhow. You stroked him free; he looked round at his owners. You had never smiled, talked baby-talk to him, given the odor of fear or asked for help; you had saved your day. You handed Bob over to the trembling talker.

He slapped him once across the nose, laid my money by my plate; and they left at a trot—the owner behind them, maledicting.

(*I don't have the picture.* Have you thought of that? Did we ever mention that? Of course, I didn't pay but a picture was taken, at the instant of the bite. Does it still exist in some gypsy's pocket?—an image of a bad night, another close call, image of his *life,* assault and impotence, the helpless witness of another's competence to solve hurtful puzzles? I would give a lot for it. What is on your face?—still, after twelve years? What did I miss in the moment of flash, your moment of sudden unexpected pain? Whom were you blaming? I need that picture badly.)

Before I could stand up to check the damage, you had asked a bystander, "*Wo ist die Damen?*" and loped off to that.

So I sat again and was wondering what next when the owner pounded back with a rusty first-aid kit and stopped at me, aghast.

"*Wo ist ihre Gattin?*"

I said that the *Fräulein* was in the cabinet, washing.

She considered attempting to wither me for negligence but no doubt remembered that in her situation *die Polizei* was a two-edged blade; so she said, "*Nicht toll, nicht toll. Er ist nicht tollwütig*" (not rabid), and headed for the *Damen* to disinfect you.

I ate on and in five minutes she returned to say you were all right, would be back soon and would we, in recompense, have a free dessert? I thought that seemed uniquely German —for a lion-bite, dessert—but I accepted and she quickly produced two enormous wedges of obscenely moist chocolate whipped-cream cake. I thanked her, she assured me again, "*Nicht toll,*" and that you were fine. Then she left.

I waited awhile—thinking what? Most likely, nothing. (I can sit for whole half-hours, thinking nothing, my consciousness a bowl of thick soup, cooling. You'd never accept that; so often, on the road, when we'd ridden in silence, you'd say, "What are you thinking?" and when I'd say, "Nothing," you'd clearly disbelieve me. *Why?* What mutterings filled *your* silence? It is how I understand the life of objects. Keats said that he could inhabit a sparrow and peck in the gravel. I can inhabit, say, a walnut log or the white blind heart of a loaf of bread.) Maybe though I thought a few calm sad thoughts on our imminent split—*past* split, in fact; it was hours old. But I know I wasn't yet asking *why?* I was now an engine geared for one purpose—the expulsion of waste parts, self-starting restored. And when, in five minutes, you hadn't come, I began my cake and called for coffee. In ten more, I'd finished; you were still absent; and the owner walked past me—no word or look— to check you again.

She returned and I managed to understand through her fury that now you had the outer door locked and had spoken to her but would not open.

I couldn't think of how to say "Give her time"; so I must have stared blankly till the owner said in English in a python-hiss (discovering *Ssss* in two *s*-free words)—"Go. *You* go!" She'd have punched me in the breastbone with her short fat finger, but I leaned back and stood and went to the *Damen*.

I knocked and called your name.

You must have been against the door—no sound of steps— but you took a few beats before turning the lock.

When I opened, you were standing three feet away, by a grimy wash basin, your back to me, your head down but silent.

I said, "Are you hurt?"

You turned to show me. Your face was splotched from crying; but you weren't using that—no mercy pleas. You pointed to your shoulder. One single strip of bandage, one inch by two.

I looked from where I was—I'd entered entirely but the door was cracked open (for needy *Damen*). It didn't occur to me to take another step, touch you gently, peel the bandage back and check—was that all my fault? Weren't you throwing off a field of volts that I'd never have pierced, however determined?

"One tooth," you said, "one canine puncture."

"Good," I said. (I knew you'd had tetanus shots and, now from the owner, that Bob was not rabid.)

You said it to my eyes (I grant you that), "*Good?* Well, I guess"—another three beats, no shifting of gaze—"*Yes, marvelous.* Something *in* me finally. And a permanent mark." You pressed the bandage. "I'll carry a little white scar to my grave, the size of a navy bean—a real lion, my summer in Europe. I can show my children." You reached for your purse and, as you came toward me, said, "Chocolate on your teeth." (Was I grinning by then?) Then you said, "I need air. Please wash your mouth and I'll meet you at the car." You went out past me, half-closing the door again.

So since the room was empty I went to the basin. In the mirror I seemed unaltered though my teeth were socketed in chocolate. I was flushing my mouth when (I never told you) I saw your little message—to the side of the mirror and in small printed letters but quite clearly your hand (the only graffito, your color of ink, of course in English). Before I could read it, I knew it was not for me. You'd had no way to know I'd enter the *Damen*—or had you?—did you wait to force me to come and see the two lines? Is it why you wouldn't let the owner in? How could she have minded? She'd have never understood. Who on God's earth would?—

Jesus, will you help me now?
I will. I have.

I thought at once of Salinger's *Franny*—mystical union in the Ladies' Room—but I knew that, even if you'd read the story you'd have thought it unforgivably corny to mimic its action, like quoting Edgar Guest at a family funeral. In any case, Franny only squeezed her little book, *The Way of the Pilgrim;* you addressed Jesus straight and claimed a straight answer. You were surely not drunk, surely not joking. I dreaded facing you. What help had you got? What new fierce power? How much farther could you thrust me?

But I went, paid the bill, thanked the owner for her help and the chocolate cake—she smiled but despised me—and climbed to the street.

The car was parked five steps away—no sign of you. I looked toward both dark ends of the street—nothing, empty. I stood yearning to run—to enter the car silently, crank and drive away. You had your passport and traveler's checks. And I'd taken a step—would I have done it?—when you rounded the nearest corner, stopped in the cone of light. I waited for you to come on to me.

But you pointed behind you down the hidden street and held your place.

So I went to you, more curious now than dreading. You were back in darkness before I reached you—I was both spared and deprived full sight of your face. "You're all right?" I said.

You didn't answer that. You pointed again toward the end of the street—what seemed a small park, a knot of trees.

I said, "Do you want to walk?"

You said, "No, I've got something to show you."

I walked beside you but you were leading.

The park was two concentric rings of sycamores that all but filled the dark space above with limbs, leaves. Only a piece of sky twenty feet square, say, was visible; but despite the glow of Munich and the few park lights, there were stars —oh, a dozen. You took us to the center.

I looked round—alone; all benches empty.

Then you said, "Straight up!"

I looked, half-thinking you had lost a screw; even one-tenth wondering if you'd stab my unprotected gut (you who trapped spiders in my Oxford rooms and conveyed them, live, outside to grass).

Again you were pointing. "See those two stars there?"

"Yes."

"Now shift to the right and down an inch or so."

I did.

"See that blur?"

I waited, straining not to blink; then I saw it—a faint smear, an old chalk fingerprint. "Yes."

You moved closer on me and, there as I was, hands loose at my sides, head back, throat stretched taut, I considered again that you might have plans and means to kill me—a sacrifice to what? Your Jesus-of-the-*Damen?* Some Eastern star god— Ishtar, Ahura Mazda? For that moment, it seemed an acceptable fate—or not to over-dignify it, *acceptable next act*, Tosca and Scarpia, *finalmente mia!* (Is it from this whole full day that my total fearlessness emerges? Death would startle me, granted, but roughly as much as an air-filled bag popped behind my ear. I face all prospects quite nicely, thank you; let Nothing mishear me though and apply misfortunes.)

But you only spoke. "Do you know what it is?"

I said, "Do you?"

"NGC 224."

"Is that a space ship?" I said (no satellites yet, though the Russians were cranking up, a little to our right).

"No, the great spiral galaxy in Andromeda."

I had vague recollections of boyhood astronomy, photographs in *My Weekly Reader* from Mount Palomar; but I certainly made no leap of awe.

You said, "Do you know how far away it is?"

"No."

"One million, five hundred thousand light-years. And what its apparent diameter is?"

"No," I said.

"Sixty thousand light-years." Your hand was still up, no longer quite pointing but in a sort of arrested Boy Scout salute; and your lips were parted—you were just beginning.

Yet my dread, such as it was, was ebbing. The worst possibility now seemed clearly nothing more than a Thornton Wilder sermon on Just-us and the Stars—you *were* drunk, I thought; this was way below standard.

You dropped your hand but continued silently looking up.

So I felt I had to speak. "What am I supposed to do?"

"Forgive me," you said.

That was meant to be worse than a sacrificial knife. It was. I must have wobbled. At some point I said, "For what?" I was facing you now—or your dim profile; you would not look downwards.

"You know," you said.

"For waiting back today at Dachau?"

"More than that," you said.

"Say what then, please."

"For not thinking you were safe to follow."

"Into poor Dachau? It's a national park. There are not even bears."

"Don't joke. *You* know."

I didn't know but I didn't ask—because, just then, I didn't want to know and, after the whole day, couldn't care much. Simple as fatigue.

You apparently knew—had thought through your balking and, in asking for pardon, were asking your way back into my life. I was safe, after all, to follow—was that it? Or safe as you guessed you could hope to find? Or maybe you'd realized after all that you'd led, not followed, all those years in any case?

I wasn't standing there, in silence, asking questions—again I was locked in simple fatigue.

Then you looked at me and said, "You haven't answered."

"What?" I said.

You said again, "Forgive me?"

I should have said Yes. It was surely the instinct, the reflex of my feeling; but with Yes in my mouth, I balked and thought, "I must wait till tomorrow. It would be my tiredness talking, and the wine." It would—I know now—have been my heart but wait I did. I said, "Give me time."

You nodded, gave it and went to the car only slightly before me.

But in two further weeks on the road, I never answered. (Not that I forgot; it was all I thought of—a glaze of scum which I laid across all those Rembrandts and Vermeers that might have saved us if they'd cared enough to fight. They survived it though, my self-surrendered vandalism. You and I didn't, no masterworks.) And you never asked again. You should have. Why not? You had led so much of the way. Your silence and patience only fueled my flight, stoked a natural warmth of sadism in me which let me ride beside—*lie* beside you—for weeks more and still wish that you would vanish, speaking civilly but coolly, touching you only by accident. (If you were awake—and I did wait until you were breathing like sleep—I beg your pardon now that twice in those last weeks I lay beside you, not ten inches away, and took what pleasure my head demanded from my own dry self with my own dry hand: dry to keep the slapping down. Fun, fun.)

Why? You never asked that even. Why, after years of assuming I required you—daily sight of you, daily touch—after gladly embracing the prospect of *life* with you, your one false move in the parking lot at Dachau thrust me from you in a helpless irresistible rush? Worse than helpless, *grinning.* I was glad, I thought, to go. Blessed clear space at hand—empty, free —toward which I flew at stunning speeds like your galaxy.

Well—Jesus—we've uncovered the secret of Dachau, of all the camps, every act of submission, why no one refused, even the de Wieks—they were glad to go! In secret glee, which they could not have borne to face or seek themselves, millions like us were permitted to abandon all human contracts, bonds—*duties!* —to shed all *others* like last year's skin and to stand, if only for a few hours, free; breathing free air (unshared by wives or children) till the air became gas. There were two women smiling in that photograph, remember? holding their children for the last heavy moment before pitching forward, dead in a ditch, but alive maybe one moment longer than the child. After such knowledge, what forgiveness? We should never have acquired it, by chance or intent. Yet you forced it on us—by your simple refusal, twelve years ago at Dachau.

I'm back where I started, Sara—why did you refuse?

Never mind. I won't care now. But one more thing—your astronomy lecture, so unheralded that night in the Munich park, when I thought you'd gone nuts if not homicidal (messages from Jesus and NGC 224)? I've been working on that lately— what you might have intended, short of an open-air homily on the need for love in the drowned depths of space. I've read up on your pet galaxy Andromeda—Fred Hoyle, the *Larousse Astronomie,* even old Sir James Jeans' *Mysterious Universe* with its chilling, exhilarating, unanswerable conclusion—

We discover that the universe shows evidence of a designing or controlling power that has something in common with our own individual minds—not, so far as we have discovered, emotion, morality, or aesthetic appreciation, but the tendency to think in the way which, for want of a better word, we describe as mathematical. And while much in it may be hostile to the material appendages of life, much also is akin to the fundamental activities of life; we are not so much strangers or intruders in

*the universe as we at first thought. Those inert atoms in the
primaeval slime which first began to foreshadow the attributes
of life were putting themselves more, and not less, in accord
with the fundamental nature of the universe.*

Were you making one last try, that night, to accord us with
the universe?

I've bought its picture—your galaxy's. After years of wondering and stumbling across it, badly printed and dingy, in various
books, I ordered its photograph from Mount Palomar. For two
weeks now it's hung above my desk—only just below Jesus, your
other messenger (Rembrandt's Hundred Guilder print, in a first-
class fake). So it watches me this minute (as it watches perpet-
ually, day-sky or night). The picture (through the forty-eight-
inch Schmidt telescope) is in color—the great spiral itself in
white, rose and lilac on a matte brown sky pierced by single
stars. If I didn't know, it could be several things—a Miami
lady-decorator's dream of the ultimate ballroom chandelier. Or
—for me most pleasing—the loveliest toy ever made. It could be
that (sixty thousand light-years across)—a cooling circular platter
of light that whirls round its billowing center in utter silence,
having no final rim but diminishing slowly into thinner clouds
of stars and finally night; my dream of a mobile to hang in my
bedroom to wake to at night; or the sort of gift that God the
Father might have willed for the Infant Christ (trumping the
Magi) in a Milton ode (what if Milton could have seen it?)—

> *And for a sign of My delight in Thee,*
> *I hang this tilted wheel above Thy bed,*
> *Attended at the rim by Hosts who smile*
> *And, smiling, face the axle drowned in light*
> *Whence My eternal love for Thee streams fire.*

Did we really see it that August night? Was that smudge
above Munich really it? Or were you lying? Or did you not
know? I haven't yet found in any of my reading whether or not
the Andromeda galaxy is visible ever to the naked eye—and, if
so, was it visible in Munich that particular night (or early
morning)?

Look. I'm going to assume that you really thought you saw it
and that—calling me and pointing up and reeling off those

almanac-facts as prelude to asking forgiveness—what you meant to say was something like this, another effort at the poem you were always aching to write (your poem, not mine; mine would be better but that's my job, right?)—

There it hangs, a million and a half light-years away, sixty thousand visible light-years across, composed of billions of separate stars all drowned in isolation yet all wheeling round a common center at something like a half million miles per hour, a stroke of radiance on your retina dimmer than the luminous dial of your watch. Or there it hung a million years ago, for the instant it took to launch this present light in its unimaginable outward flight towards the curved walls of space. Flight from what though?—the Big Bang? Maybe. But maybe flight from us, simply you and me, the two repellent objects at the core of space from which all other matter hurtles at speeds increasing till they pass the speed of light (and hurtled for millions of years before us in anticipation of this one day). Or a little less narcissistically—in flight from the blue planet, home of men. For elsewhere, all creatures desire perfect union—desire not require—and each one's desire is silently achieved. Parallels meet. It is how the world is made. Andromeda—the millions of other universes, the billions of planets—is swarmed with pairs who serve each other. Or, barring that, is empty; has the grace to be empty. We will not be forgiven for forcing their flight. Turn. Return.

I'd add only this—it is all no doubt grander, funnier than that. God only watches comedies, can only smile. Waterloo, Dachau. The end is planned. There are no options.

Sara, come back.

JULIAN MAZOR grew up in the Baltimore-Washington area and graduated from Indiana University and the Yale Law School. His collection of short stories, *Washington and Baltimore*, was published in 1968. He presently lives in New York City with his wife and child.

The Skylark

A few weeks ago, on a hot Saturday afternoon in July, I decided to go to the Army Medical Museum at the Smithsonian Institution and just wander around. I felt a little restless and strange and couldn't seem to settle down. My best friends, Ewing and Hal, had afternoon dates with the Margot sisters who were up from Richmond. I probably would have gone out with them, if I'd had a date. Ewing and Hal wanted me to come along, date or not, but I felt that four's company and five's a crowd. I had a date that night with Alice Hammershorn, but that would have been too late to meet up with them, as the Margot sisters would be on the train for Richmond by then.

I certainly didn't want to get any old date for the afternoon merely to be going out. I guess I'm rather particular for sixteen. I only like to take out girls I'm fairly much in love with, or at least infatuated with. Not that I was in love with Alice. She was merely an old friend as far as I was concerned. Though I suppose that she was in love with me, not that I ever encouraged her.

She was one of the best liked girls in school. I mean she wasn't the cheerleader type, but she was very popular, in a way. In the high school yearbook, it said she was the "truest of the true" and "a good friend". She was very intelligent, too.

Actually, I was growing tired of Alice. What bothered me about her was that she was always so eager to please. I wish she could have been more nonchalant. She took everything so

seriously that she got on my nerves. I hated myself for feeling
that way, but there was nothing I could do about it. The more
she looked at me with her large sad eyes, and the more she
tried to please me, the more irritated and unpleasant I became.
I hated it when she went out of her way to be kind and
thoughtful. It was like it took all the fun out of life, though I
can't say why.

I guess I was the most important person in the world to her.
Why, she even kept a scrapbook on my life—not that there was
that much to put in it except for a few clippings from the Washington papers about me as a baseball player in the local amateur
leagues. There was even a picture of me sliding into third base
in a cloud of dust in a game on the Washington Ellipse. It was a
perfect fadeaway slide. It started out as an ordinary hook slide,
but then I threw my leg up and over, going into a kind of roll,
and went by the bag, grabbing it with my hand. I'd faked out
the third baseman, and my hand went right under his glove.
It was really beautiful, even though I was called out. I guess I'm
a fairly good player. Ewing and Hal and I play for a team that's
going to the Johnstown Tournament this year, and we should
do all right.

Anyhow, Alice had these clippings in a scrapbook, and she
had a section called 'Mementoes' as well. In this part, she
pasted on to the page scraps and souvenirs, like the menu and
a book of matches from the restaurant in the Carlton Hotel
where we had dinner with her parents one time, a post card
I'd sent her from the Luray Caverns in Virginia, ticket stubs
from the National Theatre, where we saw a play, and the red
ribbon that went around a flower corsage that I gave her before
I took her to the junior prom, and many other things as well.
Why, if I threw the wrapper of a Baby Ruth candy bar up in
the air, Alice might run and catch it and paste it in her scrapbook,
and write something about me underneath. There was even a
page called 'Important Dates'—like the day she first laid eyes
on me, January 4, 1941; and the time I first said something to
her, April 15, 1942; and when I first smiled at her, later in the
same year. As far as I know, the scrapbook still exists, and the
important dates go right up to 1946, which is the present time.

She was fairly sad lately, and I guess it got on my nerves. Of
course, maybe I was the one who made her sad. I don't know.

Sometimes she'd get this strange expression on her face—a far off look with a sad little smile, and I'd really get upset. I guess she was just rather 'melancholy', as they say in English poetry. She once said to me on a rainy day, "John, I love the rain so," and I said, "Alice, you're just a melancholy girl." I just wanted to use the word, but I guess the way I said it must have hurt her feelings, and perhaps I really meant to hurt her feelings. I don't know. She's certainly easily hurt. Only last spring, sitting in the school library, I read her a poem that was assigned for English—To a Skylark by Shelley. I thought it was a swell poem. It starts off, "Hail to thee, Blithe Spirit, bird thou never wert." I read it through to Alice, and then I said, "Alice, you're certainly no blithe spirit," and she put her hands over her eyes and began to cry. When she wouldn't stop crying, I said to her, "You can cry all you want," and I just got up and left her sitting there. It was getting to be a terrible strain to be with Alice. I was getting a little sad myself.

Not too long ago, Alice told me that she loved me, and that she hoped I felt the same way.

"Well, I like you a lot," I said, but I didn't say that I loved her, which would have been a lie. I was glad I hadn't lied to Alice. I believe in the truth, which is the most important thing in the world. It was hard not to lie to girls though. You just had to tell them what they wanted to hear, particularly where sex was concerned. A few months back, my father said that he wanted to talk to me about my relationship with girls. He said, "John, there are two things that you have to remember. Never give a girl a line, and never seduce a virgin." In a way I agreed with my dad. I hate guys who give a girl a line and aren't honest and straight-forward, though I guess I'm one of them. But I try not to say, "I love you." As for seducing a virgin, I can't see anything wrong with that—as long as the girl is willing. The fact is, I'm still a virgin myself.

The first time I went out with Alice was about four years ago, when I was twelve. It was my first date. Alice asked me to take her to the class picnic which was in Rock Creek Park. Since her parents were friends of my parents, and as I knew her brother, Jack, I felt I had to take her. I'd much rather have gone alone.

It was a warm night in June. Ewing and Hal were there. They

just came by themselves and didn't bring dates. "In that way," Ewing had said, "we don't have to get stuck with any one girl but can take our pick." I knew right away that I'd made a mistake getting stuck with Alice. I'd picked her up at her house at seven o'clock, and I'd said hello to her mother and father and was very polite. As we left, her mother had said, "Now, Johnny, don't bring Alice home too late. I'll be waiting up." We took a bus. The bus brought us to a stop not too far from the picnic site, a little meadow near the creek. There was still some light in the sky but growing dusky. All the boys and girls in my class were there, sitting at picnic tables or toasting hot dogs and marshmallows over the fire, or just running around. It was very pleasant, with the crackle of burning logs and a soft breeze and the good smells of the grass and trees and the food cooking on the fire. Farther off in the meadow, there were some swings. Some girls were sitting on the swings in white summer dresses. Most of the boys were running wild, yelling, throwing paper plates—sailing them into the creek—and the teachers, Miss Craddock and Mrs. DeLong, were yelling for everyone to come and get something to eat. We'd got there just in time.

At first I was very polite and treated Alice with great courtesy, and I'd made sure she had enough potato salad on her paper plate and got her hot dogs from the fire, but as the evening wore on, I got impatient to leave her. I couldn't think of anything to say to Alice, or I didn't want to, and I resented that she wouldn't mingle with the other kids but just wanted to be with me. I wanted to wander off and do as I pleased. Ewing and Hal came over for a while, and we talked and kidded around, but it wasn't the same with Alice looking so sad and everything. She was like an anchor pulling me down to the bottom. But the main reason I wanted to get away from Alice was that I was very much infatuated with a pretty blonde girl named Mary Lou Turner who was sitting on a swing and laughing and kicking her feet. I was so infatuated with her that she made me a little shy and wild at the same time. While I was getting Alice some potato salad, I said to Hal, "Say, why don't you sit with Alice for a while?" Hal liked Alice, so I persuaded him to deliver the potato salad and keep her company for a while. He walked off with the plate, and I went and found Ewing, and we went over to the swings and asked Mary Lou if she wanted to hear an imitation of a sports announcer doing a broadcast of a football game. Ewing and I alternated at the 'mike', and we made it a very exciting game, with the Redskins winning in the last second on a long pass from Baugh to Milner. "That's the stupidest thing I ever heard," Mary Lou said, her eyes smiling. "Would you get me a vanilla dixie cup?" We ran off and got her some ice cream. I ran right by Alice, who was looking sad and hurt, but I pretended I didn't even see her. Hal was sitting there and looking at his hands. I knew he was trying to think of something to say. He was a wonderful friend. But it wasn't my fault that Alice loved me, and I was infatuated with Mary Lou Turner. At about ten o'clock I got into a fight with Martin Denison who told Mary Lou that I was "the biggest fool in the entire class." We fought and rolled on the ground, and I finally managed to twist Denison's arm behind his back. "Now you just take that back," I said, twisting it more, but Martin said that he didn't care if I broke his arm but that he still meant what he said. I couldn't help but admire his courage, and I let him go, hoping that I wasn't too silly in Mary Lou's eyes. When I got to my feet, I noticed that she had moved away and was sitting at a picnic table with some other kids, just laughing and enjoying herself like she didn't even know I was alive. I was furious that she just ignored me, and I was sure that she'd done it on purpose because she knew how much it would hurt me. I was certain I really loved Mary Lou. It was so beautiful in the park, with the dark woods rising up beyond the meadow, and the darting blinking lights of the fireflies. There was a pleasant breeze. The light from the campfire made little flickering shadows. In the sky, there was a slight haze and pale stars and a quarter moon. I suddenly hoped that we'd get to play Spin the Bottle or Postoffice later on, so that Mary Lou would have to pay the postman—me, of course, with a whole lot of kisses. But though Ewing and I tried to organize a game, the teachers put a stop to it. Then I just started running wild, and later on Martin Denison made another remark about what a fool I was, and we had another fight, and I knocked him in the creek. Then I got knocked in the creek by somebody else, and there was a real battle royal with a lot of boys going in the water. The teachers were really mad, but there was nothing they could do. Ewing and Hal and I were laughing so hard we could hardly stand it, and it took us nearly ten minutes just to get to our feet, and then we'd all fall down and laugh some more. We sat on the bank and dried off. Mary Lou was paying a lot of attention to me now, and she kept walking along the creek bank, back and forth, like a cat who wants to be friendly, and she said, "John, I know someone who thinks you're swell." I knew she was the one who thought that, and I guess I'd never been so happy in my whole life. As I was about to talk to her some more, Alice came over and said that she wasn't feeling well and wanted to go home. I was really furious, as I knew there was nothing wrong with her except that she couldn't stand I was having fun. "Oh, what's the matter, Alice?" I said. "I don't feel well," she said. "I have a headache." She looked so sad and resentful, like she'd had a terrible time and it was all my fault. "Oh, come on, damn it all. Let's go," I said. She began to cry, and I grabbed her hand and just pulled her out of the park. I didn't even say goodbye to anyone. I didn't even nod to Ewing and Hal, or Mary Lou. We walked a quarter of a mile to the bus stop, which was a small clearing on the side of the road. We stood there, with the silent woods all around us, and we waited for the bus. Alice leaned against the bus stop pole, with her head slightly forward, her long straight hair on the puffed shoulders of her white dress, and then she looked up and tried to smile. I really hated her then. Far off I could see the trees lighted by the camp fire, and I wished I was back at the picnic. Alice put her hands over her eyes, tried to smile again, and then began to cry. "I'm sorry," she said, sobbing. "But I don't feel well." Her shoulders, which were frail and narrow, began to heave. Suddenly, Alice's face got red and her mouth got very bitter, twisting into an angry little sneer—I'd never seen that expression before—and she said that I was just "too stupid to go around fighting and falling in the creek." And then Alice began to cry harder than ever. What she was really sad about was that I liked Mary Lou Turner. She was jealous. When the bus came, I was a little ashamed to get on with her, the way she looked, and I was afraid everyone'd think I'd done something to her. In the bright light of the bus, I could hardly look at her, with her eyes all red and her face all stained with tears.

As the bus moved up the hill, I noticed my own house come into view, and I don't know why but I was so surprised to see it that I got kind of dazed—it was so sudden—and I was tired, and I felt terribly strange all of a sudden, and I just got up when the bus came to a stop and said, "Well, so long," and then I got off the bus. And before I knew what happened, the door closed and the bus pulled off on the way up the hill to Alice's house, a mile farther on. It was like a dream seeing her face in the window, and I knew I had done something terribly wrong. I'd come out of my daze and realized I was letting Alice go home by herself. She looked so sad, even a little stunned, like she didn't think that even I could do something like that. I tried to catch up with the bus, breaking into a little run, but then I realized that it was no use, and that I'd really done it. I felt sick, kicking the ground; and then I covered my face with my hands for a few moments.

I wasn't even angry anymore. Actually, I'd stopped thinking of Alice half way up the hill. And when I got up from my seat and saw her there, it was almost like I'd seen her for the first time, and after I said, "So long," I could hardly put on the brakes and keep from getting off the bus. In a way, it was like an unseen hand was pushing me.

I tried to explain all this to my dad—Alice's mother had called the next morning, and he wanted an explanation—and I never saw him so mad. He said I was no gentleman, and he called me every name you could imagine, and whipped me with his belt besides. My mother acted like I was a criminal, and she had a look of horror on her face for two days. As for my sister, Carol, who is two years older, she has always rather enjoyed seeing me in the wrong. She said that no girl in her right mind would ever go out with me, even when I got older.

I had to call up Alice and apologize, and I had to apologize to her mother and father, and then I had to write Alice a letter and another one to her parents, saying fairly much what I'd said on the phone.

I didn't see Alice much after that, for about a year and a half. Then every so often I'd walk her home from school, and since she was very good in science, I'd sometimes copy her chemistry experiments, or get some help for some project in physics. When I was about fourteen, I took her to the movies about two times. But I really didn't start taking her out until I

was sixteen. That is, when I wasn't taking out the more exciting girls, I would spend some time with Alice.

I guess my trouble is that I'm fairly 'hard to please', as Ewing
would say. He ought to know. He's the same way. Hal is different. Everything pleases him. He's almost always polite and
pleasant. Ewing and I've never heard him complain. Why, if
Hal was fixed up on a blind date with an orangutan, he'd be the
perfect gentleman. I'm just the opposite of Hal. I get upset if a
girl's speech or tone of voice isn't just right, or if her legs aren't
perfect, or if she's not a good conversationalist. I get almost sick
if her smile is false and insincere, or if she has a stupid laugh.

Anyway, it was really interesting, as I sat on the bus on the
way to the Smithsonian, to think back to when I was twelve. I've
changed quite a lot since then, but not necessarily for the
better.

I walked into the Army Medical Museum about three o'clock
in the afternoon. It was a hot, cloudy, rainy day. I'd got caught
in a sudden shower on my way through the Smithsonian
grounds. Inside the museum, I wiped my face and hands and
hair with a handkerchief, and then I took off my khaki poncho—
it was army surplus—and folded it up. Except for my sneakers,
I was dry, though it wouldn't have mattered if I'd gotten soaked.
The clothes I was wearing were fairly old and torn up—a pair
of blue pants with a rip and a little dried white paint on one
leg, and the shirt top of a baseball uniform of a team I used
to play for, with the lettering Roger's Supply on the front and
number 6 on the back.

I began to wander through the museum, in the part called
the Hall of Pathology. It's a strange place and quite ghastly in
a way, but very interesting, too. There are diseased organs
preserved in formaldehyde, and there are exhibits on how a
child is born, and about yellow fever and typhoid and how these
diseases were brought under control. One of the exhibits was on
venereal disease. It nearly scared the living hell out of me. Then
there were the various examples of battle wounds, with the
preserved organ or bone still holding the bullet or piece of
shrapnel. There was one exhibit on Major General Sickle's leg.
His lower leg bones were preserved in a case. According to the
writeup, he had been a union general in the Civil War, and he
had been wounded at the battle of Gettysburg, where his leg

was amputated by an army surgeon. The amputated leg was sent to the Army Medical Museum in a little coffin, in which there was a little visiting card which said, 'With the compliments of Gen. Sickles'. I thought it was fairly interesting but rather strange.

While I was reading something about Malaria, I heard someone say, "Oh, how disgusting!" in this loud, clear and incredibly confident and musical voice. I turned around, and I saw a girl staring at one of the glass cases. She was alone. She was the most attractive girl I'd ever seen in my whole life, and I was nearly struck dumb with admiration. Standing there in a tan raincoat, with a hand on her chin, staring intently with large blue green eyes, she seemed about eighteen. There was a slight smile on her face, as though she had just had some very interesting and amusing thought. Looking at her, I was nearly turned to stone. She was lovely, about five feet four, with a full mouth you'd just love to kiss, and beautiful, soft auburn hair that was partly under a yellow kerchief. I couldn't take my eyes off of her, and the sound of her voice kept swimming around in my mind. I knew right away she was everything I ever desired in a girl, or ever would for that matter. Fortunately, she hadn't seen me, and I put on my poncho. I didn't want her to see me in my baseball shirt, as it made me look too much like a kid.

I thought maybe she'd appreciate the careless approach, and so I tried to figure out a way to ease into conversation so it would seem as though I was just passing the time of day. I didn't want to scare her and have her call the guard. That was all I needed. I'm easily embarrassed, and I knew I'd never be able to stand that. The more I watched her walk around the Hall of Pathology, the more impressed with her I became. I hate to use the expression, but it really was 'love at first sight'.

It was fairly dim and murky in the room, but there was enough light to see that she had a truly wonderful face. There was a golden glow about her which came right through the shadows. God, I wanted to meet her very badly, and yet I was afraid of making a fool out of myself. It was obvious that she was a sophisticated girl, and this meant naturally that she wasn't from Washington, which made her even more exciting. My heart began to beat very fast, and my palms broke out in a sweat.

I took a deep breath, and began to sidle over to the glass case which she happened to be then observing, until I was standing next to her. She was looking at a model of the large intestine. Watching her out of the corner of my eye, I tried to pretend that I was interested in the model. I've got to do something right now, I thought, or she'll go over to another case, and if I follow her then, it would just seem too obvious. Of course, I thought, I wouldn't have to follow her, but could start circling around her and then pick a better time to make a move. I took another deep breath. What a fragrance! It was probably some rare perfume. I was nearly paralyzed. I couldn't say anything. If she had handed me a revolver and told me to shoot myself, I would have seriously considered it. At least I might have shot myself in the leg. I never felt so great and terrible at the same time.

She turned slightly, with this absent look on her face, and then tucked a few strands of hair under her kerchief, and then she saw me for the first time. She was startled. "Oh, pardon me, I didn't realize anyone was so *close* to me," she said.

I was terribly embarrassed, and I said, "I didn't realize I was so close," in this very strained, unnatural voice. It was a stupid thing to say as well, and I really hated myself.

She ignored me and just looked in the case again; she wasn't even aware that I was alive. I felt like an awful fool, but being rather paralyzed in my mind, I couldn't find the strength just to walk away. If I could only have said, "Look, my name is John Lionel. Why don't we have dinner tonight?" but I could no more have done that than taken a swan dive off the Washington Monument. We were the only two people in the room except for the guard. It must have seemed very strange, the way I was acting. I backed away from the case, trying to think of an approach; I was really upset.

She slowly turned around and saw me standing there. I looked up at the ceiling, as though I were really interested in something. My heart was beating very fast. It was now or never, I thought.

"Excuse me," she said. "Do you have the time?"

I'd half way expected her to tell me to stop bothering her. I looked at my watch.

"It's quarter to four," I said, rather nonchalantly.

"Gosh, I'm late," she said, and then she started out of the museum. I don't know what was wrong with me, but I started right after her; and then I suddenly stopped, as she turned around at the door and said, "Can you tell me the way to Pennsylvania Avenue?"

"I happen to be going there myself," I said, thinking fast.

Outside it had stopped raining. There was a mist in the air, and from time to time the sun came out of the gray clouds and went back in again. We walked across the Mall toward Constitution Avenue. I walked beside her, though slightly to the rear at times, and then slightly to the front. I didn't quite know how I should walk with her—like a guide or as a friend—and so sometimes I'd walk on the grass and then I'd weave back on the sidewalk along side of her. At first I was very quiet, afraid of ruining the good impression I might have made. But then I became a little embarrassed by the silence—I was afraid she might think I was stupid—and I said, finally, "Well, anyway it stopped raining." I didn't like the sound of my voice.

"Yes, it has," she said, without turning her head in the slightest, as we walked through this small grove of trees still dripping from the rain. Her voice was clear as a bell. She seemed to have a kind of British accent.

"I guess you're not from Washington," I said.

"Oh, no," she said, looking straight ahead. "I'm just visiting."

I nodded. She was probably visiting her boyfriend, I thought, hoping I was wrong. "Where are you from, may I ask?" I said.

"New York City," she said.

I knew that must be true.

I nodded, and then I said, "I guess you must be visiting relatives."

She looked at me rather quickly, and then looked away, not saying anything.

"I didn't mean to get personal," I said.

"I'm visiting my father," she said.

I nodded, feeling great. I hoped I hadn't been too obvious. "How is he?" I said, not that I cared.

"Very well, thank you."

We walked along. Since she knew where Pennsylvania Avenue was by now, I wondered if she would suddenly say, "Well, thank you very much. Goodbye," and then speed up her pace. But she continued to walk along beside me, though she was rather aloof.

I tried to think of something interesting to tell her, but I knew I couldn't tell her anything she didn't already know. I took out my handkerchief and wiped my face. I was a little warm in my poncho, but I didn't dare take it off. She suddenly looked at me with this strange little smile on her face.

"Are you in college?" she said.

It really took me by suprise.

"Well, yes," I said. "I mean—"

"I'm sorry. I didn't hear you," she said rather offhandedly.

My face was burning.

"You might say—"

"Are you in *high school?*" she said.

"Not really."

"What do you mean, 'not really'? You're either in or you're out. Now which are you?"

"Well, I'm on my summer vacation—"

"Why can't you answer a simple question?" she said, stopping and looking at me directly in the eyes. She smoothed her hair.

"Well, I'm not in college," I said, feeling sick. I knew it was all over. I should have told her I was in my third year at Yale.

"And you're still in high school," she said, in this rather haughty way.

"Yes."

"Well, that's settled," she said, beginning to walk. "I prefer the truth, don't you?"

I nodded.

"I guess you're in college," I said.

"I'm at Bryn Mawr."

I knew that was really a great school, and I admired her quite a lot for going there. I liked the way she was so frank and open about things. She was a very honest person, I thought, and I was ashamed I wasn't the same way.

We continued to walk without saying much. The clouds were blowing away, and some birds were flying over the monument, which was gleaming in the sunlight. When we reached Constitution Avenue, she said, "Well, I know where I am now. I guess I can make it to the hotel."

"Where are you staying?" I said.

"The Willard."

"I happen to be going that way," I said. "It's not too far from here."

She didn't indicate one way or the other whether she was glad that I was going with her, and we started off for the Willard Hotel. On the way, I introduced myself, and she told me rather half heartedly that her name was Sheilah Lorraine. It was as though she had to tell me her name, as I had told her mine. That was putting pressure on her, and I should have just let her volunteer her name. I really didn't like the way I was acting—so artificial and insincere.

"How long are you going to be in Washington?" I said.

"I'm leaving in the morning."

"Are you meeting your father now?" I said.

"I said goodbye to him this morning out at Walter Reed."

"Is he in the army?"

"He's a general," she said, a little annoyed. "He teaches at the Army War College, and he's in Walter Reed for a checkup." She pushed some stray hairs under her kerchief, then stopped and looked at me in this very cool and slightly haughty way. "Do you have any more questions?" she said. I was a little embarrassed, but I felt very bold at the same time, and I said, "Sure, what are you doing tonight?"

She stopped. There was this glazed look in her eyes.

"I don't know. Why?"

"Well, I thought we'd go out and have dinner or something," I said. I thought I sounded fairly debonair.

"I can't see the point of that," she said, very cool and reserved. Then we began to walk again.

"I could really show you around Washington," I said.

"Well, I'm not sure that's a very good idea."

"Oh, it's a pretty good idea," I said. "And you'd agree, after you got to know me."

She smiled slightly, then stopped and adjusted the collar of her raincoat. We were standing on the corner of Eighth Street and Pennsylvania Avenue.

"Well, why don't you think about it?" I said. I wiped my face with my handkerchief.

"Look, uh—what is your name again?"

"John."

"Well, John, I'm afraid I can't."

"I'll call you at seven thirty," I said.

"Well, I can't stop you from calling," she said, smiling slightly.

We arrived at the Willard Hotel. It's a fine old building really, and my favorite hotel in Washington, not that I've stayed in any, but have been inside of most of them, visiting friends of ours who've come to town, and I've had dinner in a lot of the hotel restaurants. I was glad she was staying at the Willard.

I certainly didn't want to say goodbye, and I just stood near the entrance waiting for her to say something about the evening, but she just said, "Well, thank you again," and she extended her hand. I nearly raised her hand and kissed it the way they do in France, but I wasn't that crazy, and we just shook hands.

"Goodbye, Sheilah," I said. "I'll call you later." And then I felt a little sick and warm. I shouldn't have used her name like that. It was hardly casual or nonchalant, but rather too eager to please. I should have just said, "See you later," or "Seven o'clock then." I was a little disgusted with myself. I hate to be too nice.

I felt like calling up Ewing and Hal and telling them lightning had really struck, but I imagined they were probably still out with the Margot sisters, and I was feeling a little strange anyway.

On the way home on the bus, I felt rather sorry that I wouldn't be able to pick up Sheilah in my father's car. I knew how to drive and had a learner's permit, but I didn't have a license to drive alone. I was going for my test next week. Even if I'd had a regular permit, I doubt that my father would have let me drive his LaSalle. He thinks I'm the kind that takes a curve at eighty and the straightaway at a hundred and ten, and he'll say things like, "All right, Barney Oldfield, cut it down to ninety," when I'm only going sixty-five.

So, I thought, I'd have to come down to the Willard on the bus, and then I'd take her out from there in a taxi. I had fourteen dollars put away, and that was plenty for an evening in Washington. I became a little nervous. What would I talk to her about? Suppose I couldn't think of anything that made sense. I told myself not to worry, that it would work out all right. I'd just be very natural and pleasant and I wouldn't let little things embarrass me. I was rather excited to be going out with a Bryn Mawr girl. It was like I was a college man myself.

Suddenly, I thought of Alice. I was supposed to take her to a movie at Keith's Theatre. She'd been really looking forward to it. Well, I'd just have to disappoint her, I thought.

When I got home, I immediately went into my father's study and closed the door. Nobody was home but our maid, Bessie, and she was in the kitchen. I wanted privacy. I sure as hell didn't want to be overheard. I took off my poncho and laid it across a leather couch, then took off my sneakers and sat down in a chair and placed my feet on my father's desk. I looked at the green backs of a set of Encyclopedia Brittanica on the top bookshelf, and I thought for a few minutes about what I was going to say to Alice. Then I called her up.

When she answered the phone and I heard her sweet little voice, I felt a kind of loathing for her.

"Oh, John, hello," she said. She was so glad to hear from me. It was really very painful. I told Alice that I was very sorry but I couldn't see her that night as a friend of mine from Wheeling, West Va., had suddenly arrived in town with his family, and that they'd invited me out to dinner. It was the only chance I'd have to see him, as they were all in for just one night. Every so often during the telling of the lie, I'd stop and listen to the silence on the other end, and I'd say, "Alice?" and she'd say, "I'm still here." I knew she was, as I could barely hear her breathing. It was obvious that she didn't believe me, and I finally said, "Well, I've got to go," and hung up.

I felt rotten. I took a deep breath, then walked over to the bookshelf, and after removing a book and opening it, I slammed it shut and put it back. I fell into an easy chair and tried to read the morning paper. But I threw the paper on the floor. I lay down on the couch and looked at the ceiling, and then I closed my eyes. Should I call Alice back and tell her the truth? That I was never going to see her again. But what good would it do? I thought. I'd tell her later.

About five-thirty in the afternoon, I went upstairs and took a bath, and began to get ready for the evening. As I lay in the tub, I was fairly confident that Sheilah would go out with me. She wouldn't let me call her at seven thirty for nothing. I took my time getting ready. I put on a white oxford button down shirt, and then I went to my father's closet and borrowed one of his ties—a fairly conservative red and blue stripe. After that, I returned to my room and I sat down on an old leather chair and put on a pair of lightweight charcoal gray socks, and then I put on a pair of dark brown wing tip Bostonians, my best shoes. I was all set except for my suit. And then I put it on. It was my favorite—a gray, summer herringbone. I looked at myself in the full length mirror on the closet door. I looked rather man about town, a little like William Powell as Nick Charles in *The Thin Man*. I gave my shoes a good brushing, and I combed my hair again. After looking in the mirror once more, I went downstairs to see Bessie, our colored maid, before I left for the Willard Hotel. Bessie's been with us since before I was born, and she always looked me over when I went out.

She was in the kitchen, wearing her light blue uniform, her brown arms up to her elbows in soapy dishwater. She was medium brown, and a fairly hefty large-boned woman. When I walked in, she smiled, then frowned.

"Honey, where you going?"

I didn't say anything, but just did a little soft shoe routine on the linoleum.

She wiped her hands with a towel. "John, where you eating? No fooling."

"Not here," I said. I suddenly felt great. "If anybody wants to know, just say I was invited out," I said, doing a little hop and slide.

"You taking out Alice?" Bessie said.

"No. Do I look all right?"

"You looking sharp. You ain't taking out Alice?"

"Not anymore," I said. I felt this little guilty pain, like a twinge, but it was very brief; then I was all right again.

Bessie took a lid off a pot and looked in, then she took a deep breath and smiled. I was waiting for her to say something.

"Oh, what are you smiling at?" I said.

"I just so glad you *invited out*," she said, putting a hand lightly on her cheek. I couldn't help smiling.

"I have a new girl, Bessie."

"I bet she's some girl, the way you acting," Bessie said. She pulled a loose cigarette out of the pocket of her uniform and lit it.

"She's from New York," I said. "She's very sophisticated—you know what that means, don't you?"

"Uh huh," Bessie said, smiling.

"She's been around, Bessie, and she knows what it's all about. She's not like any around here."

"Well, that's good," Bessie said.

"I'm really in love with her," I said.

"How long you known her?"

"Not long, but that doesn't matter," I said.

She smiled.

"Honey, I guess it don't," she said. "You just all hot and bothered."

I gave her a hug, and then I left.

It was a little too early to meet Sheilah. It was six thirty, and the sun was still fairly high. There would be light for another two hours. When I picked her up at the Willard Hotel, the time of day would be perfect—a dusky twilight with just a little orange on the horizon. I got on the bus which was going in the general direction of the hotel. On the way down, it began to worry me that maybe I wouldn't have enough money. I had about fourteen dollars, but that wouldn't go far if she had champagne tastes. If both of us had dinner, and if we knocked around in taxi cabs, it could be quite a problem. And there was always the chance I'd take her dancing later. So I decided I'd better have something to eat first, like a little soup. It would give me a little strength and partly kill my appetite at the same time, and later I could say to Sheilah, as we sat in the restaurant ordering dinner, "I think I'll just have the shrimp cocktail. But you go ahead. The steak is very good here." When I got within walking distance of the Willard, I got off the bus and went into a People's Drug Store and sat down at the counter and ordered a bowl of split pea soup. While I sat there, I tried to recall Sheilah's perfume, but I couldn't bring back the fragrance. It was just as well, as it made me weak in the knees. I wondered if we'd make love in the Willard Hotel. I finished half the pea soup and drank a glass of water, and then I paid the check. I felt very strange. As I left the drug store, I looked in the mirror behind the cigar counter. I seemed to be breaking out in a nervous rash.

I arrived at the hotel at a quarter past seven, fifteen minutes early. I walked right to a house phone and asked the operator to ring Sheilah's room, then suddenly changed my mind and walked out of the hotel. It was too early. It doesn't look good to appear so anxious. So I left the hotel and I walked around the block. It was rather warm and sticky out, and I kept wiping my face with a handkerchief. My eyes were burning from the sweat. At seven thirty sharp, I walked back into the Willard lobby, but I didn't go right to the phone. I waited about seven minutes, and then about seven thirty seven, I had the operator ring her room. I felt being five to ten minutes late was perfect—sort of casual and urbane, but not tragic or anything to get excited about.

"Hello," she said.

"Hello," I said. "This is John Lionel."

There was a pause.

"Oh, yes," she said. "Please excuse me for a second."

Then she covered the mouthpiece of the receiver, and I heard some muffled voices—Sheilah's and another girl's—but their voices weren't too distinct, and I couldn't hear what they said. Then I heard a kind of squealing laughter.

"Oh, yes. Well, how are you?" she said, finally.

"Fine," I said. "I'm all right."

And then suddenly she must have clamped the mouthpiece again. There was more muffled laughter, then a slightly hysterical scream, and the sound of something falling to the floor, then Sheilah's voice coming through again, sort of breaking and unusually high pitched. "Excuse me!" she said, then she covered the mouthpiece briefly again, and then came back on, sounding more in control. "Could you possibly call me back? Uh— Oh, God, Gloria, please! For God's sake!—look, excuse me, what did you have in mind?"

"Well, that we'd go out."

"Oh, I think that might be a little difficult. Tomorrow I have to catch an early train for New York, and really I don't think it would be a good idea—" I heard this scream in the background, and the sound of a thump, like a body hitting the floor. Sheilah laughed, then said, "It was awfully nice of you to call."

"Look, I thought maybe we'd have dinner, or just meet for a little while."

"I'm very sorry," she said.

"Or we don't have to have dinner," I said. "We could just meet and have a cup of coffee. I'm in the lobby."

"The lobby of this hotel?"

"I gathered we'd decided to go out at seven thirty, or that's what it seemed to me."

"I never said we were going out," she said.

"Well, not definitely," I said.

"Oh, what's the difference," she said. "Look, if you're in the lobby, why don't you come up. Room 543. My roommate from college is here."

The door to Sheilah's room was part way open. I knocked just to let them know I was coming, and then pushed the door all the way open. Inside, Sheilah was sitting on one of the twin beds next to a small night table on which there was a bottle of champagne. She wore a blue bathrobe, and held a half filled glass. Her eyes were bright and sparkling. As I entered, she said, "Oh, look at him, Gloria. He's changed. He's nothing like he was this afternoon," and then with a little wave of her hand, she said, "John, meet Gloria Danz."

She was kneeling on the floor in her bare feet, a slightly overweight girl, with short black hair; she wore a green dress with a bow on the back. Her face was fairly pretty, though she had a small pug nose, and she had a squinty, near-sighted look. A pair of high heeled shoes and a champagne glass were on the floor beside her. She looked at me and said, "Oh, for heaven's sake, hello. I've been trying to stand on my head for twenty minutes, but I'm just too *dizzy*—" and then she began to giggle and collapsed on her side, knocking over the glass of champagne.

"Oh, n-o-o-o-o," she said, touching the wet spot on the rug.

"No harm," Sheilah said, getting up from her chair and picking up the bottle from the night table. She walked over to Gloria, who was holding up her glass, and poured her some more champagne. Then she said, "Won't you have some, John? Look, we'll have dinner together. OK? It's a very good idea. Well, please have some champagne, John. I'll get you a glass from the bathroom." She walked off with one hand on her head and holding the bottle with the other. I was really surprised and happy that we were having dinner after all.

I just stood there and looked at Gloria who lay back on her side and sipped champagne from her glass. She kept looking at me in this very serious way, and I felt a little uncomfortable. I put my hands in my pockets and tried to look unconcerned. Then Sheilah came back with the champagne.

"John doesn't like me!" Gloria said, suddenly, making this very exaggerated downcast face. "He hates me!"

I took a sip of champagne, then sat down in a chair. I just ignored the remark, but Sheilah said, "No, John loves you. John, tell Gloria that you love her."

"He does not!" Gloria said, with this downcast face.

"Please tell Gloria that you love her, John," Sheilah said. "She brought the champagne all the way from Philadelphia. Say that you love her, John."

I took another sip of champagne, and I looked over at Gloria. I was terribly embarrassed. I certainly wasn't going to tell her that I loved her. Instead, I tried to think of something fairly witty to say, a clever remark about champagne or even Philadelphia, but I couldn't think of anything, and I felt myself blushing.

Sheilah laughed.

"Now isn't John wonderful?" she said. "Isn't he simply grand?"

"Well, he isn't too bad at all," I said, suddenly, trying to sound superior and casual, but it was all wrong. I hated the sound of my voice. I sipped some more champagne and tried to appear interested in a picture on the wall. I suddenly stood up, and then I sat down again.

"John's bored," Gloria said. "He's very restless." Sheilah smiled at me. It was a wide and winning smile, and her eyes were sparkling. She wasn't at all like she was in the afternoon— all the cool reserve was gone. I didn't know which side of her I liked better. She seemed a little 'under the influence,' but it was all right with me. She suddenly looked at me very seriously, then held up her glass and said, "To friend John." Then she put the glass on the floor, stood up, and very calmly and naturally took off her bathrobe—all she had on underneath was a brassiere and a slip—and she went into a kind of a sexy pose, with one hand on the side of her face and the other on her hip. Gloria began to scream with laughter. I was never so surprised in my life, but I didn't move a muscle, and tried to be very nonchalant, but my heart was beating very fast. Sheilah was beautiful, her skin all copper brown from the sun, with fine shoulders and a really fine looking bosom, not too large or small, but just right; and her legs were fine, too. As far as I was concerned, she was a perfectly well-proportioned girl. I felt a little strange.

The last rays of the late afternoon sunlight were coming in

through the window. I picked up my glass of champagne, and I said, simply, "To beauty," but then I felt so foolish—it was just wrong in every way—that I had to sit down.

"Oh, John is shocked," Gloria said. "He's really shocked."

"Oh, not at all," I said, trying to be matter of fact, but my voice was shaking slightly, and I hated myself.

Sheilah put on her robe and tied the belt. After going to a closet and removing a dress, she said, "Don't go away," and then went into the bathroom. I could hardly believe I was in Washington.

Gloria seemed suddenly a little let down and tired. Putting a hand to her forehead, she stood up and complained of a headache; then, without saying anything further, threw herself across one of the beds and went to sleep.

I sat down and sipped some champagne. I'd hardly drunk half the glass, and I wasn't at all 'high.'

A few minutes later, Sheilah came out in a blue dress that was simple and elegant at the same time. She really knew what it was all about, I thought. I suddenly thought of Alice in her cute little Washington 'girl scout' dresses. It was a sad comparison.

"Get up, Gloria," Sheilah said, going over to the bed and nudging her on the shoulder. "It's time to get the train."

Gloria rolled over on her side, opened one eye, then yawned and stretched. "Oh, God," she said, sitting up. "I'm a virgin again!" They both laughed, then Gloria looked at me with surprise, as though she's seen me for the first time. "Oh, I remember you," she said. "You're John. Well, goodbye, John."

She sounded a little English all of a sudden, like Sheilah; she was fairly interesting and witty in a way, I thought, and sarcastic and amusing. I was almost a little sorry to see her leave.

"Au revoir, Sheilah," Gloria said, giving her a peck on the cheek. "See you soon."

"Thanks for coming," Sheilah said. "I was so sad, and you cheered me up—" She nodded and smiled. "Bless you, dear girl."

They said goodbye a few more times, and then Gloria left, waving and blowing kisses.

Sheilah looked at me without expression. She began to walk around and pick up glasses and stray clothing from the floor. I went over to the window and looked out. There was a dusky light with some orange near the horizon. I could see the old War Department. A pleasant breeze was coming in through the window.

I turned around and looked at her. It was a little strange being alone with her in a hotel room. For a second, I thought of trying to kiss her. After all, we'd been drinking champagne, and perhaps she was expecting me to try. I certainly didn't want to disappoint her. But then, I thought, it wasn't the sort of thing a gentleman would do. It wasn't suave. I sat down in a chair and waited for her to finish cleaning the room. When she was through, she stood with her hands clasped in front of her. There was a look on her face that seemed to say, "I said I'd go out with you when I'd had too much to drink, and now I'm sorry." She seemed a little tired and let down. I was glad I hadn't made a pass.

"Well, shall we go?" she said.

"Fine," I said, trying to smile.

On the way down in the elevator, I tried to think of where I could take her for dinner. I needed the right sort of place for a sophisticated evening. I thought of the restaurants in the Hay Adams and Carlton. They are fine old distinguished places, but then, I thought, they may not be lively enough for Sheilah. For a girl like her, there had to be something rather special. I couldn't think of a place like that in Washington. As we walked through the lobby and out of the main entrance, I began to feel a kind of lightheadedness and panic. She was a girl who was not easily satisfied. God, I thought, if I only had a car. We could drive around and have a pleasant conversation at least. It would be fairly urbane.

The last of the twilight was turning to dusk. There were a few cabs lined up on the curb. While I was thinking about where to go for dinner, the street lamps came on.

"What's wrong?" Sheilah said. "Why are we just standing here?"

"Oh, we're about to go," I said.

"Where are we going?" she said.

"Well, it's rather early. I thought we'd take a walk first, and then go out to dinner," I said, stalling for time.

"Why don't we just go to a restaurant?"

"Sure, if that's what you want to do," I said. I still couldn't think of a restaurant that would be all right. I'd narrowed it down to Fan and Bill's, Harvey's, The Occidental, O'Donnel's, and the restaurants in the Carlton and Hay Adams Hotels. I really didn't want to go to any of them.

"Look, what are we going to do?" she said, slightly irritated. "We can't stand here all night."

I had to do something do it fast, and I found myself hailing a cab. I opened the door for her and helped her in the back, and then I got in and closed the door, and said, "Take us to Harvey's Restaurant, please." I don't know why I picked Harvey's except that it's over a hundred years old, and I always liked the atmosphere there. It's one of the best seafood restaurants in Washington, maybe the whole world.

It was about an eight minute ride in the cab, and all the way over, Sheilah sat smoking on the left hand side of the cab, as far away from me as she could get. I tried not to appear terribly concerned, and I made light conversation with the driver. By the time we reached Harvey's, I was feeling fairly confident again, and I gave the driver a half dollar tip.

Actually, it was the first time I'd ever taken a girl out to dinner. I'd always picked up my dates after they'd eaten, unless they'd invited me over to their house for a meal, like Alice did a number of times. Her parents treated me like a member of the family. The truth is, in Washington you'd never take a girl out to dinner, as it just wasn't the thing at my age. And I never could afford it anyway.

As the Negro headwaiter took us to a table, I said, "This may be the oldest restaurant in Washington."

"Oh, that's interesting," she said, in a faintly sarcastic way.

After we sat down, I looked around the restaurant. It's really a fine old place. All the waiters are rather old Negroes who are rather humorous in a dry way. I was looking for Branlee Hobbs, a dark brown wiry little man who always waits on my family. He saw me and smiled and nodded. He was picking up some menus in the back of the restaurant. It was really good to see him. I've known him since I was nine years old.

The lighting in the place was sort of yellowish-dim. There was the smell of old wood and turpentine and sea food and steamy clam chowder. It didn't go over too well with Sheilah. She looked slightly irritated. She opened her purse and took out a pack of cigarettes, and then she struck a match and lit one, and then dropped her head back and blew a fine stream of smoke toward the ceiling. She wouldn't look at me. Then she began to light matches and drop them in the ash tray and watch them burn down. She made no effort at all to enter into light conversation. I tried to ignore it all and pretended that everything couldn't have been better. After a few minutes had passed, she reached into her purse and pulled out a pair of dark glasses and put them on—it was very Hollywood—and she put her hands on her temples, as though she were just waiting for her head to explode.

She sighed, then took off her glasses and wiped her eyes.

Branlee came by the table and said, "How are you, Mr. Lionel?" and handed us some menus, and I said, "It's good to see you, Bran. This is Miss Lorraine."

"It's nice knowing you, maam," he said, and then he went to the back again. It was interesting that he called me, 'Mr. Lionel.' I guess he was trying to help me make an impression. He normally called me 'Old John.'

I looked at the menu, then closed it and looked around the room. Although it was fairly crowded, it was rather quiet. Sheilah was being very aloof. I was a little surprised at the way she was acting, but I wasn't disappointed. I even liked the way her moods kept changing. She was far from boring. I opened the menu again, and I said, "Look, the clam chowder is fairly good here." Sheilah covered her face with her napkin—she began to laugh—then she drank some water.

I looked down at the table, took a deep breath and opened the menu again. The print ran together for a moment, and then became clear again. I concentrated on the words, 'flounder' and 'Maryland Crab.' She put her hand lightly on my arm.

"Look, don't worry," she said, smiling.

"What do you mean?" I said.

"You're a wonderful boy, that's all," she said.

I drank some water. She was treating me like her little brother. I would rather have had her call me a 'dirty old bastard' than a 'wonderful boy' any day. It was obvious she didn't think I was a person to take seriously, and it was certainly no compliment when she called me a 'wonderful boy.' Naturally I didn't let on that I was upset, and I opened my menu again like nothing at all had happened—I was fairly close to tears—and I acted as though I was even faintly amused by what was going on. I certainly wasn't going to let her know that I was upset. I studied the menu like the only thing I really cared about was having a good dinner at Harvey's.

When I looked over at Sheilah, she suddenly laughed again for no reason at all, and then she shook her head and sighed. A very slight film of perspiration was on her upper lip. It made her look dewy and fresh. I drank some water and put the glass down.

She smiled again.

"You're awfully nice," she said, nodding.

I was really surprised.

"Thanks a lot," I said. "You're fine yourself."

I just blurted it out, and when I realized what I had said, I had a brief coughing fit. I was really embarrassed. I should have just said, "Thanks a lot" with a tone of slight sarcasm, and I don't know why I had to add, "You're fine yourself." There's nothing worse than overdoing it. It was the sort of thing that Alice would do. I really hated myself.

Branlee came over, and we gave him our order. We started off with a shrimp cocktail, and Sheilah ordered a lobster for the main course. I picked the halibut. I was fairly hungry, in spite of the pea soup I'd had earlier.

After the shrimp cocktail, Sheilah lit up a cigarette. She seemed rather happy and nervous at the same time. She was what you'd call a 'high strung' girl. I'm fairly high strung myself. I suddenly felt wonderful. I sat there in my gray summer herring-bone suit feeling I was more than just fairly good. I felt I was 'a little bit of all right,' as Ewing would say. It's strange how great the right girl can make you feel. I looked at her, and for the first time noticed that her eyes were blue with little flecks of green, and she had a very smooth and nicely shaped forehead with a few freckles just below the hair line. She was so interesting looking sitting there in her blue dress, with her auburn hair falling over her shoulders. The more I looked at her, the more in love with her I became. It was a great feeling, but there was a kind of agony as well.

As she ate her lobster, she seemed to change in her attitude toward me. It wasn't just this sweet 'little brother' business, and

I could tell that she was showing me a little more respect. She didn't smile so easily, and I could tell she was having a little trouble figuring me out. When people really think they know you inside out, they take you for granted, but Sheilah was having a hard time knowing me, because while she was eating her lobster, I was fairly aloof, like I was deep in thought about something, and I never gave her a chance to settle her mind on me. I was changing every few seconds. For example, I'd smile, then suddenly look very thoughtful and absent minded and place a hand on my chin. I'd pick up a spoon and tap the glass ever so lightly, and then I'd look at Sheilah in a very strange way, like she'd just become incredibly interesting to me again, almost too interesting for words. And just when it looked like I was going to say something, I'd gaze off at the people sitting in Harvey's Restaurant. Also, I'd look over at her and smile from time to time, to let her know I hadn't completely forgotten her. I used several varieties of smiles and tried to remember which one worked best. I was so busy thinking, I was under a terrible strain, and I got a slight headache.

"John, are you all right?" she said, putting out her cigarette.

I nodded. Branlee came over and filled our glasses with water. He smiled at me and nodded.

"How are you, Bran?" I said, for about the third time.

"Barely making it," he said. "How you doing, Mr. Lionel?"

"Fine," I said.

He picked up a tray and went back to the kitchen. Sheilah was looking at me strangely, but I managed to strike what I thought was a fairly careless, indifferent pose—I leaned back in my chair, tilted my head slightly to one side and smiled. I was feeling somewhat lightheaded.

I ate some more halibut and some asparagus and a little mashed potatoes and green salad. For a moment I thought of poor Alice. I wondered how she was doing and if I'd really made her unhappy. Maybe I'm no damned good, I thought. That's what my father thinks at times, and and he lets me know it, too. He'll say, "John, you're not worth a good God damn." Well, that's his opinion, I thought. He thinks I'm selfish and inconsiderate. My mother and sister agree. They're not altogether wrong, but they're not altogether right either. I could say a lot about what's wrong with them, but why bother?

I'm rather fond of them anyway. The thought of Alice really upset me, and I tried to put her out of my mind. She wasn't going to ruin my life, I thought, looking at my plate. I concentrated on my food like a very cosmopolitan man who's been around and knows what good eating's all about. And I sort of savored it with this far off expression on my face.

When I finally looked at Sheilah, she was staring at me. It made me a little nervous.

"Well, how was the lobster?" I said, trying to be pleasant.

She shook her head and looked annoyed.

"What's wrong?" I said.

"Nothing—oh, everything. I don't like your whole attitude," she said. Her eyes were bright and shining.

"What do you mean?" I said.

"You're behaving foolishly, that's all," she said. "It's not very relaxing."

I didn't say anything.

She sighed.

"Oh, look, please don't mind me," she said, suddenly smiling. "Let's change the subject."

"Fine," I said.

We didn't say anything for a few minutes. I felt sick.

"Tell me, what have you read lately?" she said, finally.

I took a deep breath.

I told her that I was reading *Ivanhoe* by Sir Walter Scott and the stories and poems of Edgar Allan Poe and *Leaves of Grass* by Walt Whitman, which I recently checked out of the library.

"How nice," she said, with this smirk on her face.

I asked her what she was reading.

"*The Playboy of the Western World* currently—and of course, Proust."

I didn't say anything.

"Have you read him?" she said.

"Who?"

"Proust."

"Not really," I said.

"You mean, not at all," she said. "You're really so vague and indefinite, John." She laughed and lit another cigarette. I didn't say anything. The truth is, I'd never even heard of that writer. I hoped we'd get off literature. It obviously wasn't my strong subject with her, even though I'm fairly well-read for my age. I've read Robert Louis Stevenson, Mark Twain, Bret Harte, James Fenimore Cooper, Nathaniel Hawthorne, Thomas Hardy and Charles Dickens and some of Shakespeare as well as Jack London and a number of English poets. But how could I talk about literature with a girl who'd probably read nearly everything.

She drank some water and smiled.

"John, you're really amusing. I mean you're genuinely amusing."

"What do you mean?" I said.

"Well, you're rather naive and innocent, that's all."

"Oh, I don't know."

I felt myself turning red.

She laughed.

"Don't be so sensitive. It's no disgrace to be a high school boy."

I didn't say anything.

She lit another cigarette and smiled. I was really upset. I didn't like her calling me a 'high school boy.' It was the truth, but there was something sarcastic in the way she said it. Jesus, it was really a joke on me, I thought, to pick up this lovely girl in the Willard Hotel and end up in a restaurant getting criticized. This pain went all through me, and it was like a black curtain was coming down over my eyes. I didn't like the part about being 'naive and innocent' either. God knows what she meant by that. I briefly thought of Alice. Now Alice was naive and innocent. She didn't know anything, but I've certainly been around some and have had a lot of experience for someone my age. I drank some water and took a deep breath, and I felt a little better.

Branlee came over to the table and filled our water glasses. He was looking a little tired. He was wearing a white coat, and there was a napkin across his arm. While he was pouring some water in my glass, Sheilah got up and excused herself in this very cold, formal way. She was going to the ladies room. I stood up out of politeness, and then I sat down again.

"Branlee, you're looking good," I said. "You the one who

looking good," he said. "You got a pretty girl." He smiled.
"How's your daddy?"

"Fine," I said.

"Your mother and sister, they all right?"

I nodded.

"Well, tell them Branlee said hello," he said, and then he
walked back to the kitchen.

When Sheilah came back, she was smiling. She had powdered
her nose, and her lipstick was darker than it was before. Her
lips were so beautiful and inviting that I felt like kissing her
right in the restaurant. It would have shocked plenty of people,
but I'd have done it anyway, if I felt she'd have let me.

We had some coffee, and then I paid the bill—it came to
about six dollars. I said goodbye to Branlee, and then we
walked out of Harvey's.

It was about ten o'clock. We started walking south in the
general direction of the Willard Hotel. I was thinking about
taking her dancing, but I wasn't sure of the right place. I'd
never taken a girl out dancing before, except to a school affair,
but I'd been to a few Washington spots, like the Blue Room
in the Shoreham Hotel, with my parents and sister, Carol.
It didn't seem like the right place for Sheilah though. I'm not
a bad dancer. I'm fairly good at the fox trot, but I find those
latin dances fairly embarrassing. I don't know how to do them
either. I was going over this in my mind, as we just strolled
along.

She was in a much better mood now, and I was glad to see
it. I took a deep breath and stopped and looked at her—she
was so beautiful—and she turned around.

"What's wrong, John?"

"Nothing."

She laughed.

"You're being so dramatic," she said.

I felt myself turning red.

"Look, would you care to go dancing?" I said.

"Oh, I don't think so. I'm a little tired, and I have to get
up early in the morning.

It was a relief. It had suddenly occurred to me that maybe
they wouldn't let us in the Blue Room, as they served liquor
there, and I think you had to be in the company of an adult.

It was the same way all over Washington. I felt I had to ask though, as dancing was a fairly suave way to end the evening.

"Well, what would you like to do?" I said. I'd run out of ideas.

"Oh, we could take a little walk," she said.

"Fine," I said, and we started walking.

"I wish we could walk near the water," she said, as we strolled along. "Is the river far?"

"Well, we could take a cab," I said.

"Oh, let's do. That would be wonderful, John," she said, smiling. "I love the water."

So I hailed a cab and told the driver to take us to the Potomac River. He was really surprised. "Which part?" he said. I told him to go towards Haines Point. "I'll let you know when to stop," I said. I had to smile. He seemed rather confused, and I could hardly blame him. Sheilah's idea of walking along the river was certainly a novel way to spend the evening. Alice would never suggest anything like that in a thousand years. Her idea of a good time was going to a movie. Sheilah was full of surprises though. Being married to her, I thought, would no doubt make for an interesting life, with each day more exciting than the last.

I told the driver to stop near a grassy bank along the Potomac River. After I paid him, he looked at us in a rather strange way and then he drove off. It was very quiet. Some cars passed occasionally, and each time the light from the headlamps gave a glow to Sheilah's face. She was half smiling, with her teeth pressed against her lower lip. Her eyes were wide open. She kept staring at the water, her arms folded against her stomach. I wanted to say something to change the mood, but I couldn't think of anything to say.

We started walking toward the river, and when we got near the edge, Sheilah said, "I'd like to sit down here." I took off my coat and spread it out and asked her to sit on it. I sat down beside her on the ground, which was fairly wet from the dew. It was a beautiful night. There was a little breeze. The stars were out. You could see some of the constellations very clearly—the Big and Little Dippers, Orion and Ursus the Bear. The Milky Way covered the sky with a kind of powdery light. It was all so calm and pleasant. Sheilah sat cross legged on the ground. She lit a cigarette and handed me the pack. I lit a cigarette myself.

"Are you feeling all right?" I said.

She nodded.

"I guess so," she said, not looking at me.

I didn't say anything. After a while, she seemed to forget about her cigarette. It slowly burned down between the fingers of her right hand which rested on the ground. I got up and took the cigarette from her before she burned herself. Then I sat down again. She seemed in a daze. Her mouth was slightly open, and there was a strange faraway look in her eyes.

After a while, she looked over at me. She seemed a little more alert, but there was still a strange look in her eyes. I moved a little closer to her, still sitting on the ground, and then I placed a hand lightly on her shoulder—in a very casual way, as if to say, "Don't worry. You've got a friend here" —and then I slid my hand across her back, feeling a little nervous, not wanting to make a false move. I had my arm around her. She reached up and took my hand that was resting on her shoulder and held it for a few moments. Across the river, there were lights from a few small towns in Virginia. She placed her face against my shoulder, and I looked down at the top of her head, and then she slowly looked up at me. It was all so quiet and beautiful, sitting there on the grass by the river, under all those stars, and I never felt so scared and tender in my life. There was a smell of honeysuckle along with Sheilah's perfume. I placed my cheek against her cheek, and I could hear the water rippling against the bank, and I kissed her on the eyes and then on the mouth. It was a light kiss, and I was a little afraid I'd gone too far, but then she put her hand behind my head and pulled me down on her and kissed me hard on the mouth, and we just lay there in each other's arms for about two minutes on that kiss alone.

We got our breath, and then we kissed again. The second kiss lasted longer than the first, and it was all so warm and pleasant.

I looked up at the sky—there were a few fast-moving clouds

sailing through the moonlight—and then I looked down at Sheilah again. She was looking at me with a faint little smile on her face, and I thought, God, I've never been so happy in my life, and I kissed her again. When I stopped for a few seconds, she began to murmur, "I care for you, John. Do you care for me?" and "Kiss me again. Don't stop kissing me," and while I was kissing her, I put a hand on her breast just for a second but I took it right away as I was afraid I'd gone too far, and then she took my hand and put it back where I'd had it, and said, as she pressed her forehead against mine, "I'm growing rather fond of you"—God, she felt so wonderful and smelled so good—and then she slowly sat up, and she was breathing deeply and sighing with her mouth slightly open in a little smile, and she was so pleasant and natural, not at all nervous like she'd been. I was rather wild with passion, but I managed to control myself, and we both just sat there, looking in each other's eyes, and not touching one another, and then we gradually began to breathe more quietly again.

We looked at the river and the sky, at the powdery star-light and a yellow-orange three quarter moon that was reflected on the water. It was very quiet and still except for the sound of little waves lapping against the river bank and an occasional car passing on the road behind us.

"John, do you like me?" Sheilah said, suddenly.

"Well, yes," I said, a little surprised.

"Would you just do anything I asked?" she said.

"Sure."

"I bet you wouldn't."

"Sure, I would."

"Do you really like me a lot?"

"Oh God, yes," I said.

She smiled, then laughed, taking my hand and squeezing it and then letting go. She bit her lower lip and stared at me for almost half a minute. I was never so happy in my life.

"Suppose I gave you some ridiculous command," she said. "Would you obey it?"

I nodded.

"Then take a solemn oath," she said. "Say, 'I solemnly swear to do any outrageous thing Sheilah Lorraine asks me to do'."

I said it, smiling the whole time.

"Now you made an oath, John, and it's your sacred duty to perform it," she said, her eyes sparkling.

"That's right," I said, smiling.

"Then take a swim," she said, smoothing back her hair.

I wasn't expecting that. I thought it would be something fairly humorous, like "Kiss me, my fool," or "Sing a song, hopping on your left foot," and the like.

I didn't say anything.

"Are you speechless?" she said.

"No."

"You look so shocked."

"I'm not shocked."

"You are, too. Do you really like me?"

"Sure, I do."

"Then take a swim."

"But what for?"

"You promised, and I want you to."

She smiled and put her cigarette out in the grass, blowing out the smoke. She began to bite her lower lip and stare at me without blinking. I was crazy about her all right, but I didn't want to take a swim in the Potomac. What good would it do? I'd probably get typhoid or a bad case of cramps and drown. I just smiled and was very nonchalant.

"Well, are you going to do it?" she said.

"It doesn't make sense," I said.

"Stop being a little high school boy."

I went into a momentary daze and felt these pins and needles all over my face and body.

"John, do you want to be a perfectly ordinary person all your life?"

"No."

"Then don't try to make sense all the time."

I didn't say anything.

She licked her lips and smiled slightly.

"Look, can't you do something that doesn't make any sense at all? Aren't you capable of a grand gesture? I asked you to go into the river, and if you like me, you'll do it, just because I asked you."

I liked the part about it being a 'grand gesture,' like Beau Geste, and I tried to kiss her, but she pushed me away.

"What do you say, John? It's great that you don't want to do it, but would do it anyway." She suddenly gave me a quick little kiss on the mouth. I tried to kiss her back, but she pushed me away. She lit a cigarette, dropping her head back and blowing the smoke toward the sky.

The sky was a great swirl of light. I saw a shooting star. She smiled at me.

"Come on, what do you say, John? Do you like me enough?"

I felt very strange. I stood up and started walking toward the river. I prayed to God I wouldn't drown, then took off my Bostonians, then my socks. While I was taking off my shirt, Sheilah walked over and sat down at my feet. I was hoping she'd change her mind, but she just smiled up at me. The water was partly dark and partly shimmering in the moonlight. I wondered about the current. I was a good swimmer, but even the best have been pulled down by an undertow, and what about a stomach cramp? There was no defense against that. And the Potomac was one of the foulest, most polluted rivers in the world.

I tightened my belt a notch, then I stepped off the muddy bank and into the water. "Take a swim for Sheilah," I heard her say. I looked back at her. She suddenly laughed, then coughed into her hands. The water swirled around my legs. It was muddy and slippery underfoot, with small, smooth rocks on the bottom. As I moved slowly toward deeper water, I stepped on a can and a piece of glass, but fortunately I missed the sharp edges and didn't cut myself. I moved out into water up to my waist, keeping my arms straight out from my shoulders. It was a 'grand gesture' all right. I wanted to get it over with as fast as I could and get back on dry land. I waded out in the Potomac until the water was on a level with my chest. I looked back at Sheilah again. "Go on. Go on," she said. As I moved out, the current got a little swifter. The main thing I was concentrating on was to keep my mouth closed, and to keep my head above water. I didn't want to swallow any of the Potomac River. Suddenly, I couldn't touch bottom, and the current was much faster. I began to tread water, and then went into the side stroke. The water was very cold, and my pants were getting in the way. I don't know why I didn't take them off on the bank. I guess I was a little shy. It was the end of my gray herringbone, I thought. I was about forty yards off shore, and I kept doing the side stroke against the current in order to stay in one place. I looked over at Sheilah. She was waving my shirt, and she yelled, "Oh, marvelous!" I swam around a few more minutes, and then I made for shore. I would have sprinted in with the American Crawl, but I was afraid to get my face in the water.

Dripping wet, I walked the final few yards, and the way Sheilah greeted me, you'd have thought I'd swum the English Channel. She threw her arms around me, and then she began wiping my back with my shirt. It was cool with the breeze, and my teeth were chattering. "Your lips are blue," Sheilah said. I put my damp shirt on, and my coat over that, and then I put on my socks and slipped into my shoes. I felt all right, except for my legs, which were wet and very cold. I wasn't sure I smelled particularly well from the river, but Sheilah didn't seem to mind. What I could have really used was a bath and a hot cup of coffee. We sat down on the ground, and I continued to shake. Sheilah kept saying, "You did it for me." It was true. I'd done it for her all right. I sure wouldn't have done it for Alice, or any other girl I knew. Sheilah lit a cigarette, and we kept passing it back and forth.

"Would you do it again, if I asked you?" she said.

I didn't say anything.

"Well, would you?" she said, looking a little upset.

I was still shaking.

"Sure, I would," I said. "But I don't feel well right now."

She smiled. She was all aglow, just knowing that I loved her enough to do anything she wanted. In a way, I felt a little disgusted with myself, but as soon as I looked at her smiling at me, I felt all right again.

I put my arm around her and kissed her. We continued kissing for a while. I was really mad for her.

After a while, she began to cough and we stopped, and just lay on our backs and looked up at the sky. While I was lying there, I thought of poor Alice. She'd never understand why I went into the river. Why, it's really the same kind of thing I once read about in a book called Tales of Chivalry—

every knight does a task for his lady—not that I considered myself a knight or anything like that.

As I lay there on the grass, still shaking slightly, I almost wished that Sheilah would ask me to go jump in the river again.

We lay there and held hands and smoked. We talked about how fond we were growing of one another. I put my arms around her and kissed her, and she kissed me back. We lay in each other's arms for quite some time, and got rather passionate. I wanted to go further than merely kissing, but Sheilah said, "John, I think I better get back."

It was about one o'clock in the morning. There were a few thin, wispy clouds in the sky. Some birds flew low over the trees, circling and diving, then swinging high again. A breeze blew across the water, sending little rippling waves to shore, and causing the leaves to rustle and the trees to sigh and bend. It was wonderful how the grass was quivering in the breeze. Across the river, most of the lights in Virginia had gone out. I could have stayed there all night, watching the river and the sky, and kissing Sheilah, and occasionally smoking cigarettes and having these tender little conversations. But nothing lasts forever.

We started walking back to the Willard Hotel. I was feeling very light and happy. The streets were very quiet. We walked arm in arm. Every so often Sheilah would stop and look up at me, and I would kiss her standing under a tree or by a parked car. A block from the Willard Hotel, we sat on a bench in Lafayette Park, and I told her, feeling a little afraid, that I really wished we could spend the night together—it was a fairly suave thing to say, and it was the truth, too—and she said, "I wish we could, too, but perhaps not tonight—"and then she laughed, and said, "I'm going to kiss you whether you like it or not." And we kissed some more. I never really counted on spending the night in the Willard Hotel with her. In the first place, the way I looked, they'd have called the cops as soon as I walked in the lobby and had me arrested for vagrancy. Besides, my dad wouldn't quite understand my spending the night with the girl I loved. Why, if he saw my bed empty in the morning, he'd call the Missing Person's Bureau. I have to come home every night.

We sat in Lafayette Park until some policeman came by and said that we'd better be moving on. So we got up and walked the remaining block to the Willard. It was about two o'clock in the morning.

Outside the Willard Hotel, Sheilah had the most interesting expression on her face. It was a little sad and strange—and affectionate, too. I told her I'd see her in the morning.

"I'm getting an eight o'clock train to New York," she said.

"I'll take you to the station."

"Well, goodnight, John. Please kiss me goodnight."

I kissed her again, and then I said, "Sheilah, I really care for you."

"I know," she said.

It was really hard to say goodbye.

"I'll come and see you in New York," I said. "Well, goodnight."

She went up the steps and turned around and waved. "It was a lovely evening," she said, smiling. "Au revoir." And then she went inside the hotel, turned once and waved again, then disappeared. As I started walking, I felt so light and happy and pleased with the way things had gone. It didn't matter that she was eighteen. I was going on seventeen, and the important thing was how we got along.

I walked all the way home, about five miles, occasionally breaking into a run, and when I arrived at our house, I felt so wide awake that I couldn't imagine going to bed.

I sat down under a tree and thought of Sheilah. My heart was practically exploding. I must have thought of her for hours. Later on I walked around the neighborhood, and tried to calm down. I was so happy, it was slightly painful. I walked for an hour or so. It was more like floating than walking. And then I sat down again under the tree in the yard. The sky slowly turned pale, until the whole neighborhood was in gray light. About six thirty, the sun came up, and the sky turned to light blue. There was dew on the grass, and everything was fresh in the morning.

I went in the house and very quietly went up the stairs and into my room. I took off my pants—they were still damp from the river—and then, turning down the sheets of my bed, I lay down for a minute to make it seem like I'd slept there all night. Then I got undressed and took a hot shower, ending up with a cold spray. I towelled dry and put on my bathrobe. After hiding my gray summer herringbone suit behind a box in the closet, I went down to the kitchen and made some coffee. I had a cup with plenty of milk and sugar, and I smoked a Camel cigarette. It was about quarter to seven. I had to start getting ready to take Sheilah to the station. So I went upstairs to my room and changed into my other summer suit, a gray glen plaid, and put on a blue shirt along with another of my father's ties, a light green with white dots. And then I put on a pair of plain brown cordovan shoes. I went downstairs and brought in the Sunday papers from outside. I looked at them for a while. Then I had another cup of coffee. I wanted to be alert for our farewell.

Sitting in the kitchen, I wondered if she'd been able to go right to sleep, or if she'd been up thinking about me. Had she been tossing and restless and getting up and turning on the lamp? I stirred the sugar in the cup. I felt strange. I was a little delirious. Had she fallen in love with me on first sight? I wondered. It wouldn't be the first time, though usually a girl has to get to know me first. Of course, some have hated me on first sight, and even more when they got to know me, thinking I was conceited and selfish. I yawned. I was getting sleepy. I slapped myself on the face a few times to improve the circulation; then I went into the bathroom and placed a cold washcloth over my eyes.

It was about ten after seven. Wanting to make more noise than usual in leaving the house, I thumped up the stairs again, then ran down, hoping they'd hear me and know for sure I'd been home. But no one was up or stirring. I left a note on the dining room table. I said I was out taking a walk.

As I went out on the street, in the silence of the morning, and looked at all the old houses and trees, I thought of Alice. It was sad in a way. She'd been a very good friend. Standing there with the sun on my face, I lit a cigarette. I'd probably never see her again. I suddenly felt so strange and sad that I had to lean against a parked car.

I pushed off and began to walk towards Connecticut Avenue. I just wanted to be happy, I thought. I began to think about

Sheilah. At the thought of seeing her again, I felt this tremendous excitement, but then, oddly, I began to lose some of my coordination and started weaving down the street. I slowed down and leaned against a tree. In the branches were some robins and Baltimore orioles and a few bluejays. They were singing away. Listening to them, I almost felt like my old self again. I started walking, and a few minutes later, I came out on Connecticut Avenue and hailed a cab for the Willard Hotel.

All the way down in the cab, I kept yawning and growing more keyed up at the same time.

As the cab pulled into the curb in front of the entrance, I told the driver to wait, and I jumped out and went into the lobby. It was seven thirty sharp. I picked up the house phone and asked the operator to ring her room. It rang for about two minutes, and there was no answer. I flashed the operator and asked her if she was sure that she was ringing Sheilah Lorraine's room. She said that she was certain, then gave me 'information,' and the clerk said, "Miss Lorraine has checked out." I hung up. I didn't even have her address or telephone number. I slumped forward on this little ledge and covered my face with my hands. She was gone, and I'd never see her again. As I took my hands away, I saw Sheilah over at the Cashier's window, paying her bill. What a feeling! I watched her with a kind of mad happiness. She looked so neat—so fresh and cool and sophisticated, while she talked to the cashier. She was wearing a very simple and elegant green dress, and her auburn hair was hanging loosely on her back. I noticed again that she had wonderful legs—maybe the best I've ever seen. I managed to walk over to her, and then, with this great smile spreading over my face, I said, "Good morning." She seemed startled, as though she almost didn't recognize me. It was like a knife in the heart. I thought I was beyond getting all upset if she didn't look at me just right, but I was as easily hurt as ever. Sheilah smiled quickly and said, "Good morning. I'll be with you in a minute." I took a deep breath and let the air out slowly. She finished paying the cashier, then went through some things in her purse, completely ignoring me. It was very painful. She kept going through her purse. I didn't know what she was looking for. We should have kissed when we met. I believe in that, particularly when you're in love, like I thought we were.

She pulled her room key out of her purse and left it with the cashier. Then she looked over at me. I tried to look rather indifferent, but it was a terrible strain, and I suddenly thought the hell with it. All this jockeying around for an advantage, it makes you tired.

"Hello, John," she said. She smiled, but it wasn't from the heart. It was impersonal and a little cold.

"You didn't have to come," she said, hardly looking at me. "It really wasn't necessary."

I wanted to say, I know it wasn't necessary, but I just wanted to see you again. But I couldn't get it out. She was so formal. God, I thought, didn't she remember last night? She'd been so warm and passionate then. Was her caring for me all a big lie? I thought. Was it just one of those 'brief interludes' I'd read about? I picked up her suitcase, and we walked through the lobby to the cab waiting outside. I opened the door, and she got in. I put her suitcase in the front seat, and then sat down beside her in the back, and we started out for Union Station.

I wanted to talk to her, but it seemed like the wrong time and place. There was no privacy. We hardly said a word to one another. I was a little tense, but she was perfectly at ease, and acted like she never felt better. It was obvious that she wasn't sad to be leaving.

When we pulled up to the unloading platform of Union Station, I opened the door and jumped right out of the cab. I helped Sheilah out, then got her suitcase from the front seat and paid the driver.

As I started walking with Sheilah's suitcase, she said, "John, I can take that. You don't have to go in with me."

I kept walking with her suitcase, and we went into Union Station. It was about quarter to eight. There were a lot of travellers in the station, even at that hour, on a Sunday morning, sitting on the long dark wooden benches in the main waiting room. Though it was bright outside, it was dim in the station. It was like being in a great dusky cavern. There was a sound like the roar of the ocean, with sharp and muffled noises reverberating off the walls. As we walked through the waiting room toward the train gates, I suddenly stopped near the Traveller's Aid desk and put the suitcase down.

"John, what are you doing? Why are we stopping here?" Sheilah said.

"When will I see you again?" I said, feeling sick. I held on to the Traveller's Aid desk for support.

"John, I have to go."

"Will I ever see you again?" I said, looking down at the suitcase.

"I'm going to miss my train," she said.

I pulled out an old envelope from my pocket and picked up a pencil that was on the desk. "What's your address and telephone number?" I said. "I'll write. I'll come to New York. Look, I can come and visit you at Bryn Mawr in the fall."

She shook her head.

"Oh, what's the matter with you? Please. Let's go."

She looked very uncomfortable and somewhat annoyed.

I picked up her suitcase, and we went through the swinging door to the train shed, and walked toward the gate of the Morning Congressional to New York.

When we reached the gate, I wouldn't give her the suit-case.

"John, I've got to go!" she said. We stepped aside to let some people pass.

"When am I going to see you again?" I said.

"Oh, must you go on about that?" she said. "Will you give me the suitcase?"

"Not until I get an answer."

"John, I'm too old for you. Now give me the suitcase."

"Didn't you mean what you said last night?" I said, feeling sick.

She threw her head back and gave out this exasperated sigh. "We had a nice time, didn't we? Let it go at that—" She coughed. "I mean, it was amusing. Look, don't take everything so seriously, John—" She smiled in this very pained way. "Look, you're too young for me, and I'm not in love with you. Please give me my suitcase. I'll miss my train. People are looking at us."

I put the suitcase down and let her pick it up.

"Well, goodbye, John," she said.

I didn't say anything.

She went through the gate. Little eddies of steam came from under the cars and swirled around the platform. She walked down to a coach a good distance from the gate and climbed aboard. I was hoping she'd turn around, but she never looked back.

I went back inside the station, and sat down on one of the long benches. For a second, I closed my eyes. I felt myself falling to one side, and quickly sat up and opened my eyes again. I wished I'd never met her. I got up and walked a few feet to a water fountain and had a drink. Then I returned to the bench and sat down again. I was too young for her, and she wasn't in love with me. That was the truth. I was sorry I hadn't drowned in the Potomac.

I started to force myself to my feet—I was really drowsy—but then, I thought, the hell with it. I'm not going anywhere. I sat back down and folded my arms across my chest and slumped down a little lower on the bench. I dozed for a while. When I looked up, the station clock said twenty after eight. She was somewhere south of Baltimore. I began to stare at my hands. There were rows of callouses on the palms, just below the fingers. It was from swinging the bat. I suddenly thought of the Johnstown Tournament up in Pennsylvania. It was double elimination. You lose twice and you're out. We had a fairly good chance to go all the way. My eyes got very heavy. I tried to imagine Sheilah sitting on the train, but before I could see her, I fell asleep.

I had a dream. I was in a green field in Washington. It was a summer afternoon, with a nice breeze and fleecy clouds moving across a blue sky. I was walking with Alice, and she was smiling and looking at me with great affection. On the edge of the field, there was a grove of trees. Skylarks were sitting in the branches. Their singing made me very happy, and I said, "Alice, you're really a blithe spirit," and she said, "Oh, John, I'm so happy. You're the most wonderful person in the whole world." When I woke up, about an hour later, I went right to a telephone booth in Union Station and called her up. We made a date for that night.

Later that evening, having slept in the afternoon, I took her to a fairly sophisticated movie at the Loew's Palace. Sitting in the darkened theatre, I thought of all that had happened. It hardly seemed real and was more strange than the movie on the screen. I looked over at Alice. She looked so glad and innocent, and a little shy; and I thought, she's really a fine and tender girl.

Afterwards, we went out for a cup of coffee, and it was a very friendly, pleasant time. We were so relaxed, and the conversation flowed. Naturally, I did most of the talking, but Alice didn't seem to mind. I thought of Sheilah every now and then, and there was a little stabbing in the heart, but all things considered, I felt pretty good. There was no point being sad over what was gone. I stirred the sugar in my cup and drank some water, and I tried not to think of her at all.

EVELYN HARTER has written many stories about the interplay of personality and character between Americans and Indians as a result of observations made during three trips to India working as a graphic arts consultant with her husband, M. B. Glick. These stories have been published in *Southwest Review*, *Virginia Quarterly Review* and *Antioch Review* among others. Originally from Keokuk, Iowa, she now lives in Darien, Connecticut.

The Stone Lovers

The letter was from Pramila who had cooked for us for nine years, though it was written by the village scribe, vain of his flourishes.

> "Dear Mrs. Luddy Madam:
>   May God bless you. My girls and I are keeping good health. We pray that you are keeping fit too. You know, Madam, my son Das went to America after his BSc. here and became an enginner in America. Now he has asked my permission to marry American girl. I know not what to say. I have asked Das to bring her to you to request your blessing, and if you say she is good wife for Das, then it is well with me. May God keep you, Madam.
>
>   Pramila (x) her mark."

His New Jersey address was in the corner. Of course Das wanted to be an engineer, the ambitious ones did, and Das had been smart and hard-working, though if Simon hadn't taken an interest in the rascal, tutored him and helped him get into college, Das would still be in Ammapet, sitting as his father had done, cross-legged in the bazaar, trying to pick up a rupee or two each day from the sale of his little stock of knives, chains, padlocks, bottle openers.

"The Stone Lovers"—Evelyn Harter, *Southwest Review*, Copyright © 1970 by Southern Methodist University Press.

I wrote Das to come at once and bring his friend—he worked about a hundred miles away—and then I went down to the church to poke the delinquents, as it was Wednesday. When I first came to the rest home, Dr. Martin had called on me and wondered whether I might like to contribute some secretarial and bookkeeping help to the church. He smiled apologetically, saying that he himself had never been good at administrative work. Long ago someone had told him that he was a dear little boy, and he had never succeeded in being sure it wasn't so.

I knew that one, but I agreed to go down on Monday mornings to help count the Sunday collection, enter the payments made toward pledges in little white envelopes. And on Wednesday mornings I would copy tactful, dunning letters to people who were behind on their commitments. This would be a better way of spending time than endless small talk with the other inmates wanting to hear the worst I could tell them about poverty, disease, and superstition in India, and it might help keep my head clearer a little longer. Every so often the woolly whiteness would close in, first a fog and then pressing on all sides as solid as cotton batting, swathing my head.

The week after I wrote Das, he came. From the parlor I saw him walking up the steps with his girl friend, leaving at the curb a red sports car probably bought on the installment plan. Ho! If his mother could see her slender boy in a winter greatcoat, earmuffs, and galoshes, she would think he was a dancing bear. And his girl in short fur coat and stretch pants some kind of performing monkey.

"I want you to meet Dottie," he said, confident that she would seem as beautiful to everyone else as to him. There was nothing self-depreciating about Dottie as she peeled off her coat and hat, revealing her absurd, chopped-off skirt, like bathing trunks, her ratted hair and frosty lips and green eye shadow. She began talking about what Das had told her about me, no doubt to put me at my ease.

"He says people in his village still talk 'bout how you and your hubby usta walk down the road holdin' hands." They probably said more than that. Simon had been an ardent lover, sometimes too much for me. I couldn't keep up with him.

There was one night when I laughed and locked our bedroom door against him, and he pounded so hard that the servants and the neighbors heard—a scandal.

Doubtless Dottie couldn't help it that she was breathy and would get fat early. Das's mother wasn't fat; there weren't any fat villagers in Ammapet except babies while they were still draining their mothers. Or her careless English. Das spoke it better; we had taught our children pride in their speech. And he had done better than the other mission students; he had always wanted more. Most of them we taught reading and writing and a little arithmetic, enough so that they could work in the post office, or drive for the English planters, or go to the city to work in the western hotels. After they were married they brought their children to us to bless, already smeared with ashes by the Brahmin priest.

"And Das has told me how you usta sit on the steps of an ol' temple and tellim stories," Dottie said enthusiastically.

Of course I would give the girl my blessing; I had known that before she came. Pramila would probably never have to meet Dottie, for Das would send money home, he would write letters, and though he might go back for a visit himself, he probably had enough sense not to take Dottie. I would write Pramila a letter saying that her son had found himself a real American girl, and I was sure they would be happy together.

"That old temple where we used to sit, you and I and Perumal," Das said. "Perumal wrote me that he has a chance to buy it if he can raise three thousand rupees. If he can, he's going to set up a shop on the High Road and sell the sculptures. There's quite a market for those old things now, you know."

"Oh, no!" I cried out. "He can't do that! The sculpture must stay where it is. You should write him at once. Tell him not to move it."

He looked startled at my cry, at the way I jumped up.

"He mustn't sell it like knickknacks in the bazaar." Around the base of this old temple there were worn friezes of elephants holding each other by the tail, of flute-players and drummers and dancing girls, all blurred by erosion, and above were panels of lovers carved in high relief, embracing each other tenderly. There was one pair in particular, on the corner. After a thousand monsoons, a light smile still played on their lips as their eyes rested on each other from half-closed lids; they touched each other gently with the nerve ends of stone finger-tips, his hand on her breast and her hand on his hip.

"Mrs. Luddy, you know Perumal. If he sees a chance of making a rupee—" Perumal was a Chettiar, he belonged to the money-lending caste. I remembered his shy smile which was a disguise for his cleverness.

"But he ought to be able to see—If he's still your special friend, can't you write to him?" I could speak Tamil, but couldn't write it, and Perumal could understand English, but couldn't read a letter.

"Please, Mrs. Luddy!" Das suffered, confronted with his obligations to me, his elder, his teacher, his benefactor. "I can't stop him. You must know how he is. . . . The government ought to do something."

It was what the Indians were always saying, but this time it was true. The government should take over the ruins as a protected monument, should have done so long ago. It was a small, unused temple, the walls and steps of its pond fallen in; for a little while after the monsoon the pool had enough water to be used as a buffalo wallow. Weeds and saplings grew in the cracks and a few snakes lived there. Many of the stones had been carted away to be used in retaining walls or bridge abutments. During our time in Ammapet a vandal had knocked the nose off the lover on the corner, but it did not spoil his composure, and she, for her part, did not seem to mind his broken nose, but continued to look fondly at him. As Simon said, all the couples had carnal good manners; they made the *Kama Sutra* seem only a funny book. But none of the couples had as much grace as the two on the corner who were not weary after centuries of looking at each other. No after-sadness or sodden sleep. No scampering after each other on a Grecian urn.

Das frowned over his government and its neglect of ruins because he saw it was important to me, but he cared no more about the sculpture than about Grant's Tomb; he looked at his Dottie dotingly and she was already fidgeting, wanting to go.

"I shall write to your mother, Das, that I think you will be happy together. And I'll write to the Archeological Survey about the temple. And please, will you tell Perumal as strongly as you can that he should let the ruins stand, that he should make himself their protector. The temple will be an asset to the village when tourists begin coming on the new road to Tanjore."

"I'll try, Mrs. Luddy," Das said in the conscientious tone of going through motions to please me. "Now promise me that you will come and be my family at my wedding in June."

As soon as they had gone, I lay on my bed and cried as much as I needed to, thinking of the nights when Simon and I sat on the temple steps, listening to the frogs in the pool and the jackals yelping, playing like dogs in the moonlight. When the fog really moved in, I would not be able to remember the imperturable lovers, or Simon's arms around me.

"You must understand your situation, Mrs. Luddy," the doctor said when first I came. "You are an intelligent woman, a reasonable woman. Your only difficulty, you see, is that little connections in your head aren't always completed, and then you forget. Not your fault. You must expect little intervals, like checkered sun and shade, I sometimes say. Like sun and shade." The doctor was a hand-patter, which I cannot abide. "The people at the Missions Board tell me they are prepared to do anything that will make you comfortable, and you do deserve a rest. What they advise is that you sign this paper; then you can relax and enjoy life here without any worries. You'll be like a colt in clover, a colt in clover."

I understood, must have been having a spot of sun just then. He wanted me to commit myself, save everybody trouble that way. It was true, occasionally I could not remember whether I was in New Jersey, or back on the farm in Maine, or in the compound at Ammapet. Then everything was blurred, like waking up at dawn under the mosquito net.

"All right, I'll sign your paper." A rest home, as they are pleased to call it, is as good a place as any. I had my own privacy and would have more soon. "Give me a pen."

"Good girl. You'll be allowed more liberty than most of the other guests. Go downtown by yourself if you like."

After I had my cry over Perumal's letter, I wrote to the Archeological Survey in New Delhi, asking them to send a man to Ammapet to inspect the old temple, to appraise the sculpture; surely they would then agree that it deserved the status of a national treasure, that it should have watchmen to protect it from thieves who would sooner or later come in the night to chisel away the good pieces and sell them on the black market to foreigners in Bombay or Calcutta. I also wrote to AID in Washington, to the Ford Foundation, to the Asia Foundation, and even to the Board of Missions.

If I'd had money, I could have bought the temple myself. If ever I had cared about money, or saved any. But Simon cared nothing for the stuff, either. He shrugged when he was approached for an administrative job at a higher salary in Madras, said his work was cut out for him at Ammapet. We longed for home leaves, though, and on nights in Ammapet when it was 110 degrees, we lay on the roof as limp as sacks of boiled potatoes, talking about what we would do when we went home to Maine.

Simon would say the first thing he would do would be to bite into a Mac's crispness and eat it down to the last black seed. I said I wanted to stick out my tongue in falling snow, and walk crashing through the thin ice on puddles. Simon would say he wanted to make ice cream the old-fashioned way, breaking ice in a gunny sack with the flat of an ax and turning the freezer by hand. I said we'd toss a coin to see who would get to lick the dasher. Simon said we'd go bellybust on a sled together right into a blizzard. I would be flat on top and he'd look ridiculous raising his long legs so that they wouldn't drag.

But when the Mission Board offered us home leave at the time of the plague, Simon said for God's sake or for some god's sake, put the money into rat poison. The next week he was himself curled in agony, the black stream spurting from his mouth.

When I told Dr. Martin that I was in great need of $450, he was patient and kind. "Of course, if it is important to you, I will speak to the Board about it."

"It's very important."

"It would help in presenting the case if you could tell me what it is to be used for."

"It's a personal thing," I said.

"It will be hard for me to put it forcefully if I can't give grounds for the request."

"They wouldn't approve," I said. "You wouldn't either."

"Perhaps I don't have to approve. Only to know," he said gently.

"Well, if I told you that it was to buy an old temple, to save some stone figures from vandals?"

"Oh, my dear woman!" he cried. "Stone figures? You mean idols?"

It was a queer word to use and not correct, for these figures had never been worshiped in a shrine, though Simon and I had stood before them, paying our own kind of homage. "Not idols. Stone lovers."

"Lovers?" After a moment he managed. "But why do you care so much?"

"They remind me of Simon," I said, to keep it simple.

He looked apprehensive about pursuing this, but said, "Simon?"

"My husband."

"Yes, you must have faith that he is waiting for you."

But Simon had known, and I knew, that we would never be together again in the dear flesh, in our tender, strong-bodied embrace.

"I wonder, could I be given the minimum wage for my work here," I said. "In a year or two I could repay you."

"To be sure. I'll take it up with the Board, Mrs. Luddy." From the expressionless way he said it I knew I could expect nothing from *him*.

It was necessary to think up another way of getting the money, though my head felt thicker than ever when I tried; I was standing in the center of a plain under an empty white sky; the horizon gradually drew in until it was tight as a bathing cap around my head.

In a few weeks Das came again, without his girl this time, though still happy as a bird about her, bringing an answer from Perumal. It was in Tamil, which Das read to me.

"Dear Mrs. Luddy Madam:

I am well and my wife and children are keeping fit also; the gods have been good to us. Your message came from Das and I will not pull down temple if you say that is bad. I remember how you spank me once, and I deserve it because I tore page out of arithmetic book. I was honored by that spank. But I have not 3000 rupees, and man is here from Bombay, talk about buy it. I will try to get those rupees that I need. May you have many auspicious days. God bless.

Perumal"

After quite a silence Das said, "No word from the Indian government people?"

"Oh, the government!" I slapped the table top. "Of course not. Bureaucrats—they're the same in India and America." I would have liked to shake those inert shoulders, knock those bored heads together. I knew my letter would lie for a month each on six different desks and then be stuffed into a file reading "Action" which might as well be put in a time capsule.

"They have to follow their orders, Mrs. Luddy. It is their duty."

"Ah, they are like whipped pi dogs, like water buffaloes lying sick in their wallows."

"You know there are *thousands* of ruins in India. . . ."

"*Acha, cha, cha.* You don't know how rich you are." Indians, rich and poor, they would give their money to greasy little street idols, for festival processions and trips to the Ganges, to every kind of foolish godly notion, but when it came to saving something valuable from their own past—save it? They did not even look at it; they had no more interest in it than Americans had in a car graveyard.

"And the Americans, they haven't answered either?"

"They wrote. 'You can see that our priorities are for food, for family planning, for control of disease, for education.' No, nothing for old stones."

"Mm." He was pained by my pain.

"Das, it is very hard for me to say this, and I hope you won't mind, but I think you ought to buy the temple."

"Me? . . . But I'm a *Christian*, Mrs. Luddy."

"So you are."

"I—I'm going to be married. I've got a honeymoon in Nan-
tucket to pay for, and two months' rent on an apartment
and . . ."

"I know it is a bad time for you," I admitted sadly.

"But I'm an American now, Mrs. Luddy, and I don't *need* a
temple."

"Your ancestors probably helped build it." He was of an artisan
caste and his family had lived in Ammapet for generations.
They might easily have made and sharpened the tools for cutting
the stone.

"But why do *you* care so much, Mrs. Luddy?"

It wasn't possible to tell him, it was too personal. Simon used to
say that after we were gone, the stone lovers would be there for
another thousand years and maybe they would remember us.
He joked, saying that they would be our monument, a kind of
headstone. All I could say now was, "For Simon's sake. He
liked them."

"Some people think the sculpture isn't proper, Mrs. Luddy."

Of couse I knew what they said, the prudes. Shocking. Ob-
scene. And the pornies. Snicker. Jokes about the man's permanent this and the woman's granite that.

"Did you think it wasn't proper, when we used to sit on the
temple steps?"

"It didn't mean much to me then, Mrs. Luddy."

"Do you think you could borrow the money?"

Stricken with the misery of the beneficiary offered an un-
timely chance to repay, he lifted large black eyes to me. "I
guess I could raise it somehow. It is my duty."

"I wouldn't ask you if I had anyone else to turn to."

"I am honored, Mrs. Luddy. But what would my mother think
of me buying the ruins?"

That did set me back. A pile of old stones instead of what
Pramila would have wanted: dentures for herself, education for
the little girls, another room for a kitchen, some new saris. I did
not know what to say, and he took pity on me. "I will tell her
that you wish it. That will be enough."

I was sorry for him, having to do this, and sorry for myself to
have to make him. But I needed to know that the stone lovers

would go on smiling at each other after my head was nothing
but a wad of cotton batting.

"Thank you, Das. I do thank you and Simon would, too. Please
write Perumal at once, tell him to act quickly. Let him know
that you will be sending the money as soon as you can."

"Yes, I will do that," he said bravely.

"And now, what would you like me to wear at your wedding?
A pink dress, or my green sari?"

"Please, wear the sari, since you will be there as my mother."
I was certain that he answered so not because he preferred
it—he might have been more proud of having a western-looking
sponsor—but because he thought I did.

On the morning of the wedding, which was to be at Dottie's
house, he came for me in his red sports car. I wore my pink
dress. Sitting in the driver's seat, before he started the motor,
he pulled an airgram out of his breast pocket. It was from
Perumal.

> "Dear Mrs. Luddy Madam:
> I grieve to tell you, Mrs. Luddy Madam, that before letter
> came from Das, the man from Bombay bought the old temple
> and chop away some of the figures. I grieve for your pain. But
> Mrs. Luddy Madam, if bad men pay enough, they will not
> harm the stone people; if buyers spend many rupees, they will
> be careful, isn't it? May you live long and have many auspi-
> cious days. God bless,
>
> > Perumal"

Gouged out. Gone. Raw, jagged holes staring at the sun. The
lovers jolting along in a bullock cart under a load of sugarcane
on their way to Madras and then probably by truck to Bombay.

"I'm sorry," Das said, and of course he was, though he couldn't
keep the relief out of his voice at being let off. Now there was
nothing to dim his happiness over today's unique event.

I told myself that there was something in what Perumal said.
If people paid enough for the sculpture, for whatever reason,
they would value it and care for it. How Simon would roar in
laughter over that, our lovers swaddled in somebody's greenbacks! Traveling out into the world, to New York or Paris or
Helsinki, all the while looking only at each other . . . But there

could be accidents out of carelessness, or defacement out of meanness. They hadn't been safe, even at Ammapet.

Mustn't spoil the day for Das by crying. We traveled over the turnpike at sixty miles an hour, his eyes on the road ahead, but that was not what he was seeing. My own eyes opened wider, for his head was tilted sidewise, his smooth cheeks were molded upward in a half smile, his lower lip hung in that same perfect curve.

He hardly knew I was in the car with him, and so I went on looking. For one moment more, don't say anything, Das, don't move.

THOMAS PARKER worked his way through Stanford University and studied writing at San Francisco State, where he received an M.A. He is now teaching at the College of San Mateo.

Troop Withdrawal—The Initial Step

The position that Specialist 4 Wetzel had assumed in a morning formation in Southeast Asia was not one covered in Army Regulation 122–156, "Dismounted Drill," Section 2, "Inspections and Formations." It was, in fact, a position not covered in any Army Regulation and was therefore unauthorized, an infraction of the military rules for body member placement. Wetzel's legs were not shoulder-width apart "at ease," nor were they together from crotch to heel at "attention," with the toes canted outwards forming an angle of not more than forty-five degrees. Only a single leg of Wetzel's touched the ground at all, while the other was elevated flamingo-like behind him. And each time inspecting officer First Lieutenant Ernest Bauer clicked his heels in a in a left face in front of one of the men standing at "attention" in Wetzel's platoon, Wetzel clapped his hands in a short burst of praise. Men to his right and left glanced at Wetzel out of the corners of their eyes, some with disdain, others with amusement, all, however, wondering what 1st Lt Bauer's reaction would be to Wetzel's nonmilitary behavior, to such an undisguised flouting of an officer's authority by an enlisted man.

Wetzel himself wondered how Bauer would react. Along with the clapping and his lack of "attention," would Bauer also ignore the tarnished brass belt buckle, the boots that had taken on the color of the hundreds of things that Wetzel had kicked, tripped over, and stepped into since the last inspection; would Bauer, for his own sake, for his own protection, pass Wetzel by without a word? It was a fair possibility. Wetzel had calculated that, despite Bauer's learning disabilities, by this, the third week of Bauer's conditioning, he would have caught on. The officer clicked his heels in front of Wetzel, looked him over, and, with a queasy smile, clicked his heels again and went on to the next man. Wetzel was pleased; it seemed that his Pavlovian experiment with Bauer was finally succeeding.

Lately, Bauer had been struck down by an epidemic of shots. Following some reprimand to Sp4 Wetzel, who was in charge of Company Personnel, his official shot record would be lost and he would once again have to undergo the full battery of inoculations specified in AR 134–161, "Health in the Sub-Tropics." In the last month alone, Bauer had had sufficient immunization to guarantee the enduring good health of a sperm whale.

Wetzel's antagonism toward Bauer was not an immature one. It had been nurtured over the past year, growing through infancy, childhood, and adolescence, and finally reaching adulthood as their fifth month together in Vietnam was about to end. It was an antagonism which germinated from Wetzel's experiences with Bauer at Fort Polk, Louisiana, where the two of them had gone through Basic Combat Training together, forced by circumstance to be "buddies," communally eating sand and dirt, drinking rain, sleeping on rocks, and following impossible trails at double time to get to useless objectives, where, if they got there fast enough, they could take a five-minute-long "ten-minute break," to sit in the snow and smoke and fart to keep each other warm.

About three weeks into Basic, Wetzel realized with impassive understanding that he and Bauer were star-crossed. There, in an olive-drab mural of arms and legs, he among 250 men would run a hundred yards into the hand-to-hand combat sand pit, where, by the rules, the arbitrary man standing to his left would be his opponent for the lesson. Wetzel would turn and, without a single prayed-for exception, there would be Bauer glaring at him, frothing from the run, eager to try out a new twist of the rear-takedown-and-strangle. When Wetzel was the "aggressor," he took it very easy, dummying the kidney punches, letting the "enemy" fall gently to the ground, and then applying a minimum amount of pressure to the throat and larynx. But then Bauer was the aggressor, smashing his fist into Wetzel's kidneys, taking him down so Wetzel would hit the sand like a sack of ballast, and applying sufficient pressure to the throat and larynx so that Wetzel's eyes would bug, his lips would begin to turn purple and the color would disappear from beneath his fingernails.

Also, in bayonet drill, prefaced by a card shuffle of 250 men counting off, calling out numbers, where men whose numbers equaled twice plus six the square root of each other became partners, it was always Bauer's number that would fit Wetzel's equation. Wetzel, when he performed as aggressor in the   long-thrust-hold-and-parry-horizontal-butt-stroke,   thrust short, parried half-heartedly, and the horizontal swing of his weapon was a good two feet away from Bauer's head. Bauer, true to form, as aggressor, made incisions into Wetzel's web-belt, parried so zealously that Wetzel's weapon dropped from his hands to the ground, and performed a horizontal-butt-stroke with such gusto that the sand embedded in the heel of Bauer's stock would scratch Wetzel's nose.

But the greatest single contribution to Wetzel's growing antagonism toward Bauer was made by their Mexican drill instructor—a man whose name started with "F" and ended with "o," whose name no living man could pronounce, but whose name was shortened and simplified out of desperation by the men in his platoon to Sergeant Frito—who matched Bauer and Wetzel as bunkmates and buddies. It was a match that forced complete responsibility for the other man, a match which entailed making bunks together and making sure your buddy was dressed in time and wearing the right gear. It was a perverse marriage between men who never shared anything sacred in their nine weeks together other than air, water, and cigarettes and the fact that neither of them had been circumcised.

It became increasingly evident to Wetzel as Basic painfully dragged on, that Bauer had something going with Frito. Whenever anything had to be done for your buddy, Wetzel seemed to be doing it: cleaning Bauer's weapon, taking notes for classes Bauer missed, making Bauer's bunk, polishing Bauer's brass. Bauer cleaned his own weapon only once during Basic and that was in front of the entire company as a demonstration. "It was," said Sgt Frito, "the cleanest weapon in five platoons."

During range fire for record, Bauer was in sick bay, but nevertheless led the company qualifying as "expert." While it was unlikely that squinty-eyed Sgt Frito could even see as far as 350 meters, much less hit a target the size of a large man perched at that distance, it was nevertheless true, unless there was something that Frito had going with the cardboard silhouette as well.

So it seemed to Wetzel that truly, Bauer's trophy for soldier of the training cycle, Bauer's medal for M-16 firing, and Bauer's commission had been a mistake, the result of logical fallacy like so much else he knew existed in the Army. While death may have been a great leveler, leveling all men to zero, the Army leveled live men to an IQ of 85. Halfway through Basic, Wetzel resigned himself to sailing forever in Bauer's torpid wake, at least while they were both in uniform.

It came as no surprise to Wetzel then, when he was finally sent to Vietnam after two months of typing school at Fort Tara, Virginia, where, when he entered the course he could type seventy-plus words per minute and, upon leaving, was cut to a more moderate thirty-minus words per minute—under the theory that typing so fast demoralizes the other men—that he and Bauer were to be in the same company. For his efforts with Sgt Frito and whoever else's palm he greased in OCS, Private Bauer became 2nd Lt Bauer, and then miraculously, 1st Lt Bauer, stationed with a hospital company of almost a thousand men.

On the outside, Bauer had driven truck for a large fruit concern and had recently made the transition from fresh to quick-frozen produce. It was a status job, a bigger truck, ten feet longer, a foot wider, and the latest in cabin design. When he stopped at cafés with the new truck, he took little or no shit from anyone except maybe the Mayflower guys. Even then it was all in good fun, although Bauer once had his nose broken by a stainless-steel cream pitcher being used as brass knuckles by a guy with a small laundry truck who didn't seem to give a damn what anyone was driving. This code violation was a mystery to Bauer, who, without ever considering what it meant, thought that fair was only fair.

Because of his specialized background, Bauer was made Ground Transportation Officer in the company, a job that involved trucks and similar vehicles. Since the hospital was a permanent Army hospital near Saigon, the only real ground transportation that Bauer was called on to regulate was an eight-times daily bus to the city and an occasional ambulance to pick up American survivors who were injured in terrorist attacks. Usually however, the attacks were thorough and there were no survivors. At that point, the Vietnamese police would deliver to the hospital any bodies that seemed American. It was a "hands-across-the-sea" program that Bauer himself had instituted. There were only problems when it was impossible to tell whether the victims were Vietnamese or American or when they were not quite dead. Bauer, put a thirty-mile-an-hour governor on the ambulance so that it would take just about a half-hour to make it into the city, and by that time, things would have, in his own words, worked out one way or another."

All in all, Bauer didn't mind the war much. It was a way of passing the day. Enlisted men assigned under him kissed-ass and he responded by giving freely of absurdly long passes, which Wetzel, in Personnel, would find reasons to tear up and then send the men back to Bauer for others. In this way they would miss at least one bus, although sometimes Bauer would run an unscheduled charter for his men alone, which Wetzel, in Personnel, would find out about and feel obligated to mention to Colonel Schooner, who, in turn, would be duty-bound to mention it back to Lt Bauer. It was then that Bauer would mete out what he considered just punishment and Wetzel, as a result, would spend series of weekends on KP and consecutive nights as Charge of Quarters. The fabled shit rolled downhill from rank to rank until it hit Wetzel, who, in Personnel, having no one under him, did what he could for vengeance and protection, destroying Bauer's official shot record, and then, as a dutiful Sp4, notifying the proper medical authorities.

On the other hand, Wetzel *did* mind the war. Before he was drafted he had been working as an accountant in a branch bank in San Francisco, where, other than an occasional holdup which would cut into his two-hour lunch break, he led a quiet, safe, and unobtrusive life. In Vietnam, what quietness there came to him was inner, his unobtrusiveness was the result of his rank, and safety was a thing of the past.

And then there was the problem of the sounds. He had very poor filtering devices and the constant going off of claymore mines, rockets, and other forms of ammo would get on his nerves, and often, before a day would end in the building where he went over officers' and enlisted men's records, he would stutter and show other visceral signs of psychic disorder.

In his room in Saigon atop a small barbershop, Sp4 Wetzel lay on his bed listening to the rockets and claymore mines go off. It was a drag, he realized, more than a drag, a colossal mistake for him to be here. He would have to leave at the soonest time possible. Why, he wondered, didn't he leave right now? The answer he came to, he had arrived at before and before that; he lay too close to the half-inspired middle of mankind. He was neither smart enough nor stupid enough to desert; and also, he didn't have the guts.

On his bureau in olive-drab cans marked with black letters which read, "10 Weight US Army Oil," "20 Weight US Army Oil," "30 Weight US Army Oil," and "10×30 Weight US Army Multipurpose Oil," Wetzel kept his different blends of grass. The fact that he turned-on did not necessarily distinguish him from the thousands of other enlisted men in Vietnam that did also. For Wetzel though, the grass provided neither a good stoning nor an orgiastic trip. It was merely a component in his survival kit, used to abstract, to make things disappear, things which ordinarily imposed themselves on his being with the bluntness of telephone poles. It worked: it kept him from harm and didn't seem to be doing him any harm.

It was anyway only the officers, medical and otherwise, who feared the stuff and they would drink themselves into a puking stupor every day, sometimes so far gone by noon that they would disappear into their posh quarters, leaving the enlisted men in the hospital to perform reasonably delicate operations and to zip up the plastic bags which contained the newly dead patients. Wetzel could only guess how many of them weren't really dead when they were zipped. The fresh corpses simply didn't show the life-signs that the enlisted men were taught to look for: a certain level of heartbeat, breathing, pulse, the ability to cloud mirrors, etc. Zip! Off to the States, dog tags hanging from the zipper tabs on the outside, the name inked-in on the chest of the returnee. An early-out, Wetzel realized one day in the zipping room—a thought.

Wetzel, along with every other man in the entire United States Army, was allotted by Army Regulation 14-198, "The Billeting of Troops," Section 1, Paragraph 2, a minimum of 300 cubic feet of living space, which, when broken down, yielded approximately 6 feet by 6 feet by 8 feet. He did, in fact, have at least that much living space in the five-hundred-man barracks, but other than make his bunk there the first day he got to Vietnam, the 300 cubic feet went almost completely unused. Like all the other enlisted men in the company who had space allotted and a bunk assigned them in the barracks, Wetzel didn't live there. Only when it rained, when it was impossible for him to maneuver his motor scooter through the shellpocked streets from the hospital compound to Saigon, would he have to spend a night; and then it would be a night completely alone, for Wetzel was the only man not to qualify for Bauer's emergency transportation to the city. The last bus would leave Wetzel in the barracks among millions of cubic feet of space.

Appropriations for the maintenance and upkeep of the barracks, Wetzel found out one day reading Colonel Schooner's memo to First Army Command, was over $800,000 a year. This included the substantial maintenance and upkeep of Captain Ellsworth, Officer-in-charge—daily changing of sheets, Vietnamese maid service, and what seemed to Wetzel an inordinate amount (3 miles) of mosquito netting. Once a month a barracks inspection with all five hundred men present would be held and Colonel Schooner, nearly blind in both eyes but much in need of a year's active service for retirement points, would walk through followed by a retinue that included all the field-grade officers in the company along with a certain first sergeant named Horzkok.

"Horzkok," the colonel would ask, "are these men getting their sheets changed?"

"Yes, sir," Horzkok would reply, writing something down on a clipboard whose top sheet hadn't changed since Wetzel had been in the company.

"Horzkok, are the maids coming in daily?"

"Yes, sir."

"What about the netting? Do you need more netting?"

"Probably more netting, sir."

The colonel grinned and winked at Horzkok.

And so the retinue would eventually make their way past Wetzel's bunk, grown men, some of them making more than a thousand dollars a month, inspecting a barracks that no one lived in, checking to make sure that all the special niceties in these barracks for the hospital personnel, who lived twenty miles away in hovels and brothels, were being carried out.

In the beginning of his Vietnam stay, all that made life bearable for Wetzel were the menial tasks he performed while working in Company Personnel. There he could create his own order; there, all his antagonists existed only in paper files, on green and yellow cards, and on sheets of paper stapled to forms that, Wetzel realized one afternoon, in a company of a thousand men, only *he* understood. In realizing this, he realized also in a clouded way, that whatever power he as a Sp4 had, lay in this sole understanding of the forms.

In these first few months, Wetzel did little with his recognition until one night in his Saigon room after some moderate smoking, the idea came to him in a raw but almost crystalline form. As Wetzel looked up to study the contours of his thatched ceiling, Bauer appeared out of the smoke of Wetzel's burnt-down joint, the genie of Wetzel's high. But this ethereal Bauer was not the singular Bauer of the past; rather, Bauer took on the face and dimension of all the men in Wetzel's basic platoon, all the typical American fighting men that Wetzel had known. Here was Bauer with his Army sense of fairness and morality, his self-righteousness; of a certain breed of man, Bauer became their everyman. As the smoke dispersed and the ceiling came back into focus, Wetzel remembered the forms.

Why not, he wondered? Why not, if Bauer is indeed what I see him as, why not de-form him, re-form him, change his being, make him into a more agreeable human. Or why not change his duty station? But then Wetzel realized that by making small changes on Bauer's forms he would be just playing with him. It would be no different than destroying his shot record. It was in this second, as Wetzel recognized the pettiness of merely toying with Bauer's file, that the missing card meshed with the computer tabs in Wetzel's brain and lodged itself resolutely there, leaving nothing else to be considered. Why not plainly murder Bauer, eliminate him entirely, take him out of the war? After all, it would be simply a matter of form, of a form, to wound Bauer in action and have him captured, to make him a hero, a coward, to ship an unidentified body with Bauer's name on the chest along with a copy of Bauer's dog tags, which Wetzel could cut with the machine in his office, back to the States. All the Army would need would be the correct forms and the body would be buried in some military cemetery and his insurance policy paid.

What it came to with the imposition of the reality of the next morning was that Bauer was far more than just Bauer, and to eliminate him would be the initial step. It would be ample, sufficient, for Wetzel to know that while Bauer was harassing him in some formation, that the Army was concurrently paying off $10,000 to Bauer's beneficiary and inactivating his file in St. Louis—where it is said (and probably lied) that every man's record exists in duplicate.

If every day Wetzel weren't witness to the same idiocies of men whose actions were outlined by the cumbersome regulations —the brains behind the men who had given up their own—if every day he didn't feel that the Army, with him included, was digging deeper and deeper into the soggy Asian soil, if a hundred other things he had witnessed, noted, and forgotten hadn't happened, the idea would have never entered his head. But lately, as he sensed things getting worse around him, he turned-on with greater frequency and was beginning to stutter.

Somewhere also, Wetzel knew, if he kept after it, he would run down the regulation that would simply provide for his own release, the one that would send him legally back to the States. There, if things were not truly better, at least there was a semblance of order and peace and the Bauers were back on their trucks and not directly, at least, foisting their guerrilla tactics, their self-respected killer instincts, on those that had no desire for or interest in them. Wetzel didn't have it in for teamsters or even Bauer anymore, really. Only symbolically did his war concern these people.

The morning following Bauer's nocturnal visit, his tragic story began to take form. Wetzel never felt as justified, as sure, in anything else he had ever begun. Using the regulation method, he changed Bauer's record to show that the Ground Transportation Officer had orders releasing him from the hospital company and transferring him to a small infantry unit a few hundred miles north of Saigon, where daily confrontations with the enemy produced a high rate of casualties. Now it was simply a matter of how and when it would happen. Would Bauer be a hero or a coward when he died? It was a decision that Wetzel could make without any more real concern than flipping a coin. He decided to wait before he actually killed Bauer off. Let him get used to his new surroundings, he thought. Let him get the feel of his new duty station before he died defending or running away from it.

Wetzel cut a set of the phony orders on the office mimeo machine and distributed copies to all officers that were in some manner concerned, but not in any position to care or to do anything about them. One thing was definite: everyone believed printed orders, and orders anyhow, were orders. Among the recipients would be the United States Army Records Center in St. Louis, Missouri.

The hospital mail clerk hoisted the bag with the bogus orders from the office floor. It seemed to Wetzel that the first budging of the huge boulder that he himself had been called on to push was, that second, taking place. Now it was merely a matter of momentum. As in any large organization, minor errors would become major errors, would become glaring errors, would become more than errors, lofting themselves into the fields of absurdity until finally, a frantic hush-hush would become their epitaph.

Wetzel felt as he watched the mail clerk leave Personnel and make his way to Captain Ellsworth's bunker to pick up the never-existent barracks mail, that his decision to end Bauer's involvement in Vietnam, even in an advisory capacity, was doing more for his private antiwar effort than if he himself had deserted, gone on extensive AWOL, or lied his way into the hospital with phony meningitis symptoms. It was to be something finally done; in his life, something he embarked on that soon would be completed, something he could actually be proud of, Bauer's paper-death. Through his mind flashed an image of Bauer doing a short-thrust-vertical-butt-stroke. "You're a grand old flag, Bauer, but you're a big boy now."

Wetzel did wonder, weeks before and even now, who was he, Wetzel, to be deciding the number and frequency of Bauer's inoculations and now his death. His own was not a history of unblemished service in the progress of mankind. Hadn't he frittered away a quarter of a century in self-indulgent sloth and leisure? In ways, didn't he share Bauer's guilt; was there really that much difference between negative action and in-action, Wetzel wondered.

For an accountant, he had done very little accounting in his lifetime, none actually until he was hit with the reality of the sounds of mines and rockets. But Wetzel also realized the afternoon the orders were sent, his part counted for nothing. One felt experience, one significant understanding in a lifetime, sometime, and you're on your way; and all that could be said about it was, if it happened, it happened. And now Wetzel felt that he was nearing the point of its happening.

If it was Bauer who had provided the emotion for Wetzel's homicide plan, it was the zipping room that contributed reason. Whenever anyone was zipped, Wetzel had to bring down the ex-man's 201 personal file to the zipping room and check his dog tags with his file for spelling, blood type, religion, and serial number. If any one of these things was off, Wetzel would have to cut a new set, then bang them up a little for authenticity and hang them on the special hooks at the top of the zipper. Accounts checked this way: St. Louis was happy, Colonel Schooner had no reason to be unhappy. But even when things ran smoothly in the zipping room, Wetzel was unhappy about the entire situation; more than unhappy. Each trip to the room took him further and further away from believing that he actually saw what he saw. The eerie, overlit room with its plastic cleanliness and its antiseptic pink and black bodies made imperfect by bullet holes and missing chunks, became unreal to him; part of a white light-show that he was forced to participate in and then leave, spent and drawn, as if he had danced there too long. When Bauer was in the room, as he often was, overseeing a delivery, Wetzel's anxieties became directed and plain to him: clearly Bauer was in some way responsible.

The door to Personnel opened. Bauer stood in the doorway for a second, attempting, what seemed to Wetzel, a certain effect, and then walked in. Wetzel stood up, mentally discovered, his thoughts detonated and scattered. Immediately as he was faced with the man, Wetzel was sorry that he was so mercilessly, so whimsically, so self-righteously plotting his demise. It was impossible in the intimate situation of two men standing right next to each other without weapons, for Wetzel not to bridge the span between men, and, for an instant, make himself that other man. But his feeling changed the second he saw the glint in Bauer's eye. This was not the glint that would save Bauer from death. Had he come with sorrow, with reverence, with a question or a runny nose, with anything other than the look of a man thinking that what he was doing was unquestionably justified, Bauer might have been saved, Wetzel might still have relented and had him transferred back to the hospital company.

"What's this dickin' around in formation, Wetzel? I want to know about that. I let it go today. You know why?"

Sure. Wetzel knew why. It was the shots. Bauer was actually tired of the shots, the side effects, the vaccinations that must have pocked his arms like craters. Bauer had ground the gears in his sturdy but simple brain and had finally made the connection between the shots and Wetzel.

"Well, Wetzel, I'll tell you why. Your attitude here is the shits. It demoralizes, it pisses-off the men. They look at you and figure, 'Why not, if Wetzel can do it, why not me?' And when there's a war going on, there isn't any room for that sort of crap. So today I decided I wouldn't draw attention to you by yelling in front of a whole platoon, but believe me, you better change your whole way of life around here. I'm telling you that personally, here and now, so that you know I'm not just jerking you around as an example. It's you and you alone I'm going to get, unless you change that high-and-mighty garbage of yours. Believe me, Wetzel, I'll have you out of this cozy office, working your ass off permanently for me, if you don't cut the shit. Do you understand that, Wetzel? Understand?"

The man would have to die, Wetzel than decided with all

his heart. Bauer had just turned Wetzel's half-formed, fairly definite whim into an irrevocable mission. He had to see Bauer's file sent away, he had to see the look on Bauer's face on payday when he didn't get his cash to buy his prophylactics, beer, and ugly trinkets. Revenge asserted itself back into Wetzel's plan. He now knew, that in order to stay in Personnel in the weeks pending the final processes of Bauer's demise, that he would have to be careful, that he would have to stay away from Bauer's shot record altogether. It was unfortunate, but a necessity. It was something in Bauer's tone that indicated this to him, something that tipped him off to the fact that Bauer would literally kill him if there was a way of making it seem in the line of duty.

"Wetzel, I asked you a question. When an officer asks you a question, you answer. Do you understand *that*, Wetzel?"

It was then, at that very instant, the second that Wetzel was to come out with his servile apology to keep him safe in his job in Personnel, as Wetzel understood the meanness of means and the glory of ends, that the hospital compound was hit soundly, initially and accidentally by a squadron of American planes launched from the carrier *Wendell Willkie* to fly cover for some Marines about to walk into the range of at least a half-dozen machine guns guarding VC mortar implacements, a few miles from the non-city side of the hospital.

The plan to paint the roofs of the various buildings that made up the compound white with huge red crosses like the other hospitals in Southeast Asia, had failed when 1st Sgt Horzkok had ordered the wrong color paint from Supply. Colonel Schooner, in an attempt to cover up for Horzkok's error, pointed out at a high-level staff meeting that the crosses were not necessary. The hospital had excellent natural camouflage; having been built by a youthful and recently drafted group of Engineers, it was a masterpiece of integrated structure and terrain. It was impossible, the colonel assured his men, to spot the sprawling bunkers from the air or even from any distance on land. Colonel Schooner had called it right, but unfortunately the perfect camouflage was not working in his favor.

The entire out-patient clinic was destroyed with the first impact. With the second went the enlisted men's barracks. The building made a decent little puff and then, after a few seconds of limbo, burned itself to the ground; just minutes before, all the sheets had been changed. The zipping area was hit and the building in which Wetzel and Bauer stood facing each other with hate, then with questioning, and finally—and Wetzel noted it distinctly in Bauer's face—with fear, collapsed around them. Filing cabinets vomited out drawers full of papers and then the cabinets themselves fell. The wooden roof collapsed, raining down thin slats and shingling, and finally, the sides, no longer feeling any responsibility for the roof, bowed and quit. In the middle of the tangle of typewriters, paper, and Army Regulation pamphlets, Bauer and Wetzel lay pinned beneath a bookshelf, bodies crossed. Wetzel had hit the ground first, covering his head, having attended that particular class in Basic, and Bauer followed, not having attended the class but having been told about it later by buddy Wetzel.

"Get the hell off of me, Bauer." Bauer didn't respond. Wetzel heard further impacts off in the distance. Possibly by now Radio Operator Keyes, whose knowledge of international code was limited to a few words and catch phrases, would have awakened and shot a quick message to the United States Navy or the United States something to ask for a bombing halt.

"Come on, Bauer, get the hell off!" Still no answer, but then Wetzel heard a moan. Bauer was alive! Big deal. Of course Bauer was alive. All that had actually landed on him were some AR pamphlets and a bookshelf which had fallen on Wetzel a few days before when he had attempted to move it and the regulations outside the building.

Wetzel managed to crawl out from under the Ground Transportation Officer. Off in the distance he could see a fire in one of the wards, backlighting crafty Marines as they snuck up on the unsuspecting VC. There were bursts of machine-gun fire, lots of lights from flares, tracers, and flames and huge explosions from someone's heavy artillery. The war arena had invaded the sanctity of the hospital compound. Bauer pulled himself up next to Wetzel, looking out to the left and the right as he did.

"Jesus! Come on, Wetzel. We got to do something. We can't just stand here. Follow me to that fire!"

Wetzel ran behind the man. As he ran, all he felt was the movement of his legs and his face heating from the blaze he neared. Bauer spotted some men in beds behind the flames and ran through to them. Wetzel didn't have time to decide, running through a few steps behind him. If he had stopped for just a second, he would have never done it. In the pulsating orange light, he saw Bauer pick up a man from one of the beds and run out of the building with him. Wetzel looked around, picked someone up himself, felt the weight on his shoulders, ran with it, was outside, and dumped it off. He started back in after another, but this time he stopped for a second and thought. He hesitated at the edge of the flames. In the meanwhile Bauer had torn through and dumped another body.

"See what you can do for these men, Wetzel. I'm going back for another."

It was the perfect reason not even to think about going back in, realized Wetzel. Bauer had given an order and now the idiot was running back in himself. Wetzel looked down at the men on the ground in front of him; all three of them were dead. The one Bauer was running in to get would probably be dead also. But Bauer couldn't know that; he was this second too busy being a hero. Wetzel wondered, how many rights did Bauer have to do to make up for his wrongs? What went on in that plodding mind that could transform Bauer from what he ordinarily was to the man who just ran back into a burning building to save what he thought was someone's life. As Wetzel looked again at the men on the ground and heard the machine-gun fire of the Marines or the VC, he realized that it was Bauer's wrongs that, by contrast, would put him in a position to make his rights seem great. If Bauer really thought about the humanity he was lugging out of the fire, he wouldn't be here in the first place: not in this hospital, in this fire, in this war or this Army. It hit Wetzel that way, but he knew it wasn't that simple, although he wished it was.

The fire went on for most of the day and into the night before it was finally put out by equipment that Bauer, in his official capacity, commissioned from Saigon, where it was always vitally needed. The equipment was not returned the next day or the day following. Wetzel knew it would go the way of all equipment that had been borrowed by the hospital. During an inspection, Colonel Schooner would spot it, declare it obsolete, and insist it be dismantled for parts.

Personnel was rebuilt in a day. It took three days for Wetzel to straighten out all the records. In that time he re-resolved that Bauer would have to die, but it became increasingly clear, as Wetzel relived the moments of Bauer's running into the burning ward, that to have him die a coward would be a lie. It was an option that circumstance had stolen from him. It bothered him to have to admit this. What death, then, would he himself have to die? What sort of man was he, Wetzel, who would choose cowardice over almost anything else dangerous or painful? He thought and all that came to him was that the heroes must be the men who didn't attach any worth to life— what did that make them: stupid, insensitive, unappreciative, or great, vital, keyed even more to life because they were that much more closer to death? Whatever, the world needed these men; Wetzel decided that he was not one of them. Most people, though, were or wanted to be heroes.

After Bauer's file had been located and carefully arranged, Wetzel made his way to the zipping room, carrying with him the file along with a newly minted copy of Bauer's dog tags. A large hole in the room's ceiling, still not repaired from the attack, admitted the sun and rinsed everything in the room in natural light. Boxes of the zippered plastic bags sat on one side of the room on shelves labeled "small," "medium," and "large." One entire wall of the spacious chamber held the deep drawers that contained the bodies that had been recently zipped. Because the bodies would never spend more than a day in the hospital before being lifted off by helicopters to landing strips where airplanes would take them back to the States, these drawers were not refrigerated. In the latest *Army Digest*, Wetzel read in an article entitled, "The Wonders of Body Evacuation," that the body of a United States serviceman killed in Vietnam could be evacuated from a given battlefield and be back in the States in less than twenty-four hours. Implicit in the article was the message that the Army profited doubly by this efficiency: first, by not having to refrigerate the filing cabinets which held the bodies and, second, by always having empty drawers in the case of a major enemy offense.

On a smaller wall, though, there was a group of the drawers that were refrigerated. In these drawers doctors would keep such perishables as sandwiches spread with mayonnaise, beer, mixer, etc. These would usually surround the "no-names" that were also in the drawers and were bodies being held for positive identification. Occasionally, during a rush, semi-positive identifications were made by Colonel Schooner or some other high-ranking officer, and the bodies would be zipped and shipped, telegrams sent and policies paid. All in all, it was a lot cheaper than expanded refrigeration.

Wetzel opened one of these drawers. A man lay on his back in a torn and burned fatigue uniform. His face had been scarred to a charcoal anonymity and next to his left arm was some onion dip with a few pieces of potato-chip shrapnel in the center of the bowl. The no-name's uniform had no identifying patches other than the one which read "US Army," black on green so that he couldn't be spotted by the enemy during nightfall. There were no dog tags; they had probably been destroyed in the same fire that the man had died in, obliterated in the heat.

The second before he decided anything, Wetzel noticed in the sunlight how very calm the no-name looked; the pressure was off. The only thing left for him to do was to lie there and eventually decompose. Compose, decompose, he thought; no matter; there was work to be done. "Well, Bauer, it may be better than you deserve; I'm not really sure. But I'll do my best for you." He wrote Bauer's name on the man's chest with the regulation pen, zipped him in the plastic bag on which he lay, and, with his own heart beating with notable panic, transferred him to a slot in the non-refrigerated section. In less than two hours there would be another lift-off; in less than ten the body would be on its way back to the States. Bauer, as his file had indicated, had no living family, no loved ones. The beneficiary on his Army insurance policy was a Teamsters local in Detroit, who, when they found out about Brother Bauer's demise, would cancel his card, take the $10,000, and have a wake with the corpse in absentia. Wetzel affixed Bauer's dog tags to the bag.

Then he went back to Personnel and cut orders to the unit that Bauer was supposedly transferred to, to drop Bauer's name from the morning report and all other rosters. To the Army Records Center in St. Louis and to the Pentagon, Wetzel sent the following letter:

Sirs:

1st Lt. Ernest L. Bauer, 0967543, a short time in my command as Unit Transportation Officer, was fatally wounded when trying to drive a burning truck away from our ammunition dump. Through his courageous action, the lives of our entire company are in his debt.

I therefore recommend that Lt Bauer receive commendation for his valor, hopefully in the form of the Distinguished Service Cross. Lt Bauer lives in our minds as an example to us all.

WILFRED KRIEG, MAJ, INF-USRA 045328
6789th Inf Reg, Quo Hop, SEA

Major Krieg, Wetzel had learned in the *Vietnam Newsletter*, had been recently captured by the VC, so there was little or no official way to check the story out. Besides, there was no time to check stories out. In the meanwhile, Wetzel knew that with the receipt of his letter, Personnel at Quo Hop would be desperately dummying-up records to show that Bauer *had* been there. It was far better than trying to deny it. If they did, there would be investigations, the Inspector General would insist on auditing all the reports filed in the time of Bauer's supposed presence. It was better, far better, to change a few records, to forge Bauer's signature in a few places. Wetzel also sent Quo Hop a belated copy of Bauer's phony original orders, those that transferred him there in the first place. With them, Quo Hop would have nothing to worry about. It was now only a matter of hours before the Teamsters local would be notified.

With the death of Bauer completed, Wetzel who had been short of breath ever since he had lifted the no-name from the "pending" to the "out" file, sat and slowly mused over what he had done. And indeed, it had been done. In its execution, he realized its infallibility. The huge wheels, though held on by plastic cotter pins, would run true; turning and churning, they would soon eliminate a member. Somewhere in St. Louis, Bauer's duplicate file would be pulled and put into another container; somewhere in the Pentagon, the decision was being made about Bauer's decoration. Wetzel had done what the negotiators had been trying to do. And he did it without violence, without more destruction, and, the second he actually zipped the bag, without any personal hate.

He wondered; if one man could be so easily eliminated, what about a platoon of men, a company, an entire regiment? It would be a graceful and honorable withdrawal. The Army had actually provided the framework for it to be done, what with each man's complex file, the mass of orders and orders counter-manding orders, the regulations that by their mere volume would have to lead to a notable contradiction—a massive one that could bring the Leviathan crashing from the sea. He would have to study it all more carefully before he went on.

In the rearranging of the files, Wetzel did run into the regulation that earlier he had expended so much energy looking for, the one which quite clearly outlined his way back to the States. It would work if he changed a few things on his own file. Other than that, it involved having a stateside contact locate an old man dying in a hospital and having the man claim that Wetzel was his son, his only family. The Red Cross would be notified and, in turn, would notify Personnel in Southeast Asia for verification. If the stories checked, in less than twenty-four hours, Wetzel could be at the old man's bedside. And possibly the man would grab at the last of life—and the choice of the old man would have to be wisely made—leaving Wetzel at his bedside for the duration of his active obligation. It would be time well-spent, Wetzel conjectured; he would give an old man, who may well have been in a war himself, some solace by telling him that, indeed, he was dying in vain, but that we all did. "The world didn't improve between our wars, old man, it just got a little more complicated."

But Wetzel decided to forego this loophole. He was onto something bigger, something far more worthwhile. Now, as he read through the regulations to see what else there was to do, he anxiously awaited the initial correspondence that would be crossing the Personnel desk. It was inevitable that the note would come from St. Louis, a response to Bauer's urgent request. It would state as succinctly as possible, composed and typed by someone in Personnel:

Dear 1st Lt Bauer:
    The reason that you were not paid on 1Jul68 was because you were killed in action a month preceding your request. You

have been awarded the Purple Heart and the Distinguished Service Cross for your heroic service.

Further explanation of this matter will be found in AR 167-18, Sec. 3, para 4, "Payment Procedures." Any further correspondence should be taken up with:

> AM-AGAP, 67543
> APO San Francisco
> Sp5 Giles Blanchey
> Personnel Specialist

I'll Call You

Otto Ludwig, the German dramatist, in his middle age turned to a study of Shakespeare which lasted a decade and, instead of rejuvenating his artistic energy, desiccated it.

"I've spent twelve years on Ludwig, counting my thesis, and I'm dried out at forty-one."

Bea quivered as a fly settled tentatively on her shoulder-blade. Tony propped himself on an elbow to brush it away. They reclined on the balcony of Bea's apartment under the noon sun and a snowfall of tufted seeds from the cottonwood tree.

"Rub some oil on me"—her voice drowsy, almost stifled by the crumpled blanket and her careless long hair.

He dribbled lotion across her buttocks and thighs and massaged it into the chunky flesh.

"You're getting a burn."

"Why don't you scrap Ludwig?"

"The book's almost done. Another year. It's like a bad marriage, a penance."

"As if one weren't enough."

"You should know."

"Mine was six months, and no children. You're not the type. With a twenty-three-thousand-dollar townhouse. Published in all the journals."

"I'm the world's expert on an obscure Shakespeare scholar even the Shakespeare scholars don't read any more."

"Underneath all your disguises, even that one, there's the good Italian peasant blood, even from Salida, Colorado. Anyway you've got tenure."

"And you."

Haven't I? You didn't mean what you said Friday. This frivolity. 'Italian' with that inflection. 'Even.'

Not you. What are you not saying?

Two months ago you played Marge's occasional divorced sister from the biology department, as remote. Your party. Carol in bed five blocks away with her Kleenex and Coricidin. Later, how obliquely we spoke, how simply I built a fire in the grate and you cooked an omelet; and then you lay staked out on the rug like a sacrifice, all mouth and nipples, and belly tipped with damp fur, with tears in your eyes, chanting in distracted melodies and phrasing—as if hunting the perfect pitch—"I love you."

She rolled onto her side, facing him, her breasts ripe and pendant as prayers. With her index finger she traced a line from his throat to his navel.

"Your torso," she said, not specifically. "How long do you suppose Carol's known about us?"

"I doubt it. Do you think so?"

"We're not invisible. Marge sniffs something. A departmental secretary lives on being olfactory. Hell, she's known Carol since high school. We're all so chummy it's like wife-swapping."

"Carol doesn't suspect. I assure you."

I wish she did. We could stop feinting and duel.

Bea's finger resumed its path to his groin and twined a tuft of hair.

"Why are you teasing me?"

She yanked at the knot, less capricious than sadistic—lips pinched, eyes opaque—so that he jerked and said, "What's bugging you?"

"I may be leaving."

"What!"

She let go and rolled away supine. "I've applied for a grant at Cornell. If they take me, I'll go."

His heart turned, a scaffolding gave way.

"You can't."

"I'm a New York girl who despises Denver and good old rock-'em sock-'em Rocky Mountain State as heartily as you do."

Her voice was toneless as a sybil's. Her eyes looked at nothing in particular, as if through her spasm of guilty violence she had moved beyond trouble or connection.

Thou hast ravished my heart with one of thine eyes, with one chain of thy neck. Thy—your lips are—sugared, your flesh—my haven. Words wither.

She said, "I meant it the other night. About a future."

"You won't find a future independent of the present. This is it. But I won't marry you."

"I'd say no if you asked. Your class is in half an hour."

"I'll give you a ride."

"No."

Friday night, by the fire, you asked me to read aloud. So I recited Eichendorff, in German and my improvised English. "*Mein Lieb' ist verschwiegen*": "My love . . ." I could say it translated. Must I bleat it?

"No," she repeated, "we're not going to be careless." She smiled, but the spell was not broken nor its revelation of an infinite cruelty. "I brought my work home. I'll get you some coffee."

They dressed horizontally, for the balcony railing was only three feet high, and Marion Street two storeys below.

In Bea's kitchen he tried to sip the coffee; his throat would not swallow.

She said, "Don't forget Marge and Jack's tonight after the lecture."

"What lecture?"

"Europe House. The Hungarian Student."

"I forgot."

Sol co-sponsors the series; the German Department "will attend."

She kissed him, his chin, playfully goodbye.

"Cornell," he said. "You'd take the offer?"

"I've applied to Michigan, too. And UCLA."

You're not serious. You're as desperate as I. We're growing old. I missed my direction, you yours, you said so.

"You'd hate Los Angeles." He embraced her. Her skin retained the warmth of the sun, but as if for some private use. "You were nice today."

"I wasn't there. Neither were you."

"You're beautiful."

He descended the wooden fire-escape into a suicidal despair. Nor would his class dispel it: Beginning Grammar and Composition for somnolent freshmen with a "language requirement," who could scarcely survive a sentence of English.

Afterwards Herr Bridges visited his office. The boy sat hunched on the rickety chair, intimidated by the bookshelves and desk, contemplating the hands with dirty fingernails that were balled in his lap, working the chin that sprouted a blond fuzz: they were at odds, the boy and his body.

"That D on my midterm. I'm on probation. If I don't make a C in German, I can't come back fall quarter."

"What are you majoring in?"

"Pre-med."

Tony's laugh threw him on the defensive. "I got a B in trig winter quarter."

"Why medicine?"

"I've got an uncle in Pueblo, he's going to retire, he wants me to take his practice. He's in pediatrics—Dennis Bridges.

"My dad, he went to RMS. I want to transfer to CU next year. What I want to know is, if I get a C on the final, do you grade by improvement or on an average?"

"Get a B on the final and it won't make any difference."

"Yes, sir."

Herr Bridges sat quietly, then rose and left. His shadow dwindled on the mottled glass door, was transposed into the stenciled rune:

ANTHONY LUINO
Associate Professor
Modern Languages

Beatrice. Thou hast ravished my heart.

But Solomon's was a dalliance between sportive tribal wars, not an affair to match the threat of the white nuclear light that in a second may illuminate and seal our eyes forever.

Am I a hypocrite to blame that threat? Do I justify myself? Or you?

Someone knocked. The silhouette suggested Fräulein McKinney from his Classicism seminar. He waited. She knocked again and went away.

If I should, say, kill myself, Herr Bridges will be the last man to have seen and spoken to me. That will make no difference. Nor to Carol or Else, or our probable second child. But to you?

Strange there's no pain. I'm not even sad. Just suspended. This abyss: I knew you'd leave me but not that you'd leave this space.

He considered the wall map of Berlin, the push-pin apartment on Fasanenstrasse where he had lived as a proud, desolate student; and drank without sensation the dregs of a papercup of coffee.

At the drive-in bank he scribbled a savings-withdrawal slip for a thousand dollars. The solution had come that easily.

The teller blinked her charge-account eyelashes. "Are you closing your account, Mr. Luino?"

"How much do I have?"

"I'll be glad to check for you."

Shortly she returned. "You have a balance of seven hundred nineteen dollars and eighty-eight cents."

He had forgotten the new furnace. He rewrote the slip. "Make it six hundred then."

"In cash?"

"Please."

YOUR NEIGHBORLY BANK complied with blinks and a fresh-frozen smile.

"Guten Abend," Carol will say.

Guten Abend. Guten Morgen. Ich liebe dich. The little repertoire of endearments from German 103. At 24, in her pullover and shorts, she can still pass for a sophomore. Mother of one child in the equally ill-timed expectation of another.

But call her accent flat, evoke Montana, and she will say "Salida, Colorado"—as if your hometown might undo everything.

"Guten Abend." She broke eggs into a plastic bowl. There were two cans of chopped mushrooms.

"What's that?"

"Mushroom omelet."

"For dinner?"

"You said I should try it."

"I meant it would be nice for an evening supper or a Sunday breakfast."

She pushed the bowl of eggs aside, tossed her hair in a definitive, characteristic motion of defiance, and opened a cabinet above the counter.

"All right. I'll see if there's some tuna and noodles." Her voice quavered, tears betrayed the drama of martyrdom.

"I didn't mean that. An omelet is fine."

Charlie Kendrick interrupted them.

"You know what happened, Mr. Luino? After school. Elsie, she was trying to nail an airplane and a big board hit her bonk, right on the head. It had splinters in it. It was an accident. We're sorry, Mr. Luino."

"It wasn't serious," Carol said. To Charlie: "You're supposed to be home, your mother's called twice. Where's Elsie? Tell her we're going to eat."

"Her name," said Tony, "is Else, with a z sound."

"*Deine Pedanterie . . .*" Her vocabulary abandoning her, she left the accusation hanging.

With his teeth he broke the seal of a fifth of bourbon.

"There's no time for drinks. We have to pick up the Levins at quarter after seven."

He poured a double, triple shot over ice.

In the livingroom, toys and magazines and ashtrays. Bea, too, was careless, in her laboratory and her home, but she was a superb cook and in her very carelessness superbly stylish.

As for Tony, the front screen door that was to have been oiled last spring still bloodcurdlingly squealed; the new furnace and the garage.

Suddenly he thought, Six hundred dollars will hardly take us to New York, let alone Berlin. What would we do?

From the rear livingroom porch he surveyed the narrow, fenced rectangle of grass blotched with weeds and yellow patches. Instead of trees there were a rusting jungle gym, a tricycle, a swing, and the nailed crosses of two-by-four that Charlie Kendrick called airplanes.

Dusk deepened in a whorl of silence hollowed by the rattle of icecubes in a glass.

Beatrice.

"Blue?"

He jumped at Carol's voice and touch.

"Want me to have a drink with you?"

"No."

"I'll learn everything, I'll do everything for you." She rested her cheek on his shoulder. "You don't have to sacrifice everything to being a nice guy."

"The nice guy's dead. Now the pedant has to be killed off."

"We could stay home tonight."

"The Hungarian may be what I need: a last straw."

Sol introduced him as Joe Andrassy—the surname pronounced like a drunken slur of "Anderson" and the nickname an incorrect Americanization of "Lajos" which had stuck—"student, athlete, former freedom fighter in the Hungarian revolution." He was husky, swarthy, an operetta Hungarian already developing a paunch.

His subject sounded informal and innocent—"Some Hungarian Impressions of America." But between his trite, well-practiced humorous asides ("He who has a Hungarian for a friend has no need of enemies") there emerged only one, grim "impression"—of a nation being self-obliviously devoured by the communist conspiracy. Was he really exhorting his audience to complete the Hungarian revolution, ten years later, with American troops? Was he blaming or merely censuring Adlai Stevenson and Eleanor Roosevelt? His uncertain meaning was further clouded by an often impenetrable Magyar accent.

Yet he had spent four years of his young manhood in AVO jails, for a principle presumably. His ideals glowed, awakening Tony unexpectedly—the restless energy as he paced, pantherlike, back and forth before the podium, the uselessness of his courage which, through an association of ideas and insights, put the uselessness of Tony and life itself back into joint and made it not only possible but bearable.

And there is Bea, five seats away, with her head back, a faint smile on those sculptured lips. You are following, you understand it, too, how strong, how permanent we are.

Since Jack and Marge had not come, Tony accepted the duty of host to Andrassy and the others.

"You have a car? You can follow us."

Andrassy fervently crushed Tony's hand. "Oh, thank you very much."

As they drove home, Carol said, "A little while ago you were desperate to be alone and now you invite everyone to a party. I thought the lecture was terrible."

"It was, magnificently. After all the tired undergraduates and pooped professors, I'd forgotten what a healthy human being looks like. Hungary must be a stirring place."

"We'd better stop for some beer, and change to pay the babysitter."

Andrassy, however, preferred orange juice ("In the prison is damage to my liver"), and as Tony opened cupboards and cans, he heard the mixed conversation in the livingroom modulate into an impassioned baritone solo.

"They tie you up like this—" Tony entered to see Andrassy leaning forward on his chair, clasping his ankles with both hands "—with—*mit einem Stab*—"

"Staff," Sol Levin translated.

"Rod," suggested Tony simultaneously.

"With a rod, yes, here under the knees, so you are like a ball. They throw you on the floor. Then they beat with clubs. You are naked, you are helpless. They beat everywhere, the shoulders, the kidneys, even the *Geschlechtsteile*. Many were for always injured. Other things also they did, I cannot describe here."

Carol blushed and recoiled. Alma Levin wheezed with asthma while Sol stared ahead; what was a manhandled Hungarian compared to his own parents and sister and race gone up the flues of Dachau?

Bea, half reclining on the sofa, her feet tucked under her hips, listened and watched Andrassy, his muscular contortions, with wide eyes, obscurely roused. Her lips were moist.

You are no better than the AVO men who beat Andrassy, my sweet. With all your breeding and master's degree. Nor am I. To answer that look, cover you again with bruises and bliss . . .

"Why?" she asked Andrassy. "Did you have such important information?"

"No, is because they hate Hungarians. Hungarians always fight Russians, they always love freedom. You think only Hitler was bad. Lenin, Stalin, Khrushchev, they were much worse."

"At least the Soviets," said Sol laconically, "unlike the Germans, were not trying to wipe out a people."

"The Germans fought the communists! If they had help, then would be no threat of world communism today. The Soviets have said they will conquer the world." Andrassy's pitch dropped under Sol's chilling stare. "I do not say the Germans did not do bad things."

"Anyway," Tony interceded, "you had a chance to fight back."

"Even in the prison I fight. Others in the prison, they say I fight too much, is why I am always beaten and put in solitary—how do you say—?"

"Confinement."

"Thank you very much. They say I get them in trouble. When I am going to the university in Oregon two years, just before now, they say I make trouble when I say there are many teachers communists. I know the communists."

He clenched his fist.

Go on. You have possibly saved my life, you bigot. Secret police and a revolution have silhouetted your enemies on every horizon like pasteboard targets. Teach us a simpler enemy —yourself if necessary—and to fight and rejoice.

The Levins rose to depart, Alma still wheezing, Sol embarrassed and bitter, accepting Andrassy's effusive salutations and brutally conciliatory handshake with a pained smile.

Bea went to the stereo and selected a recording of Viennese waltzes.

You're ignoring me too conspicuously, getting tipsy besides. I feel your vibrations, they concur that whatever our prisons, we remain free to share each other. And tonight I'll tell you, bleating happily, that I love you.

Andrassy resumed his seat in the chair confronting Tony.

"You have been in Europe during the Hungarian revolution," he said.

"I was in Berlin. I remember the broadcasts from Budapest, with the Soviet tanks in the suburbs."

"Then you know. Radio Free Europe promised to send us arms when we fight. Why didn't America keep its promise? Why is it blind now to the conspiracy?"

"Radio Free Europe is not America, which doesn't excuse a tragically ambiguous message. But if Hitler had been thwarted at Munich, or Lenin at the Finland Station—Nietzsche's diagnosis would still hold. Anyway, Americans are too innocent and comfortable to be much good at conspiracies, as they recently learned trying to persecute one."

"You call the Americans 'they.' And your name 'Luino.' Do you come from Italy?"

"My grandparents. I was born on a Colorado farm. Never could speak Italian. I ought to change my name to 'Lewis' or something." Why not Levin?

"You were in the World War?"

"On Guam—after the war. The experience taught me nothing constructive."

"You love America."

"Not really. I love mountains; some cities, restaurants, rooms, ideas; a few people—"

Bea, listen.

"—The sea very much. Flaubert said, 'The three finest things in creation are the sea, *Hamlet*, and Mozart's *Don Giocanni*.'" He might have added, 'And a woman.'

"Coffee?" asked Carol, entering with a tray and her infallibly inept timing.

Bea declined. Andrassy took his cup with a generous addition of cream and three teaspoons of sugar.

Eat. Drink. My house is yours.

"You have many books," said Andrassy, scanning the shelves. He glimpsed the framed photograph of Else. "Your daughter?"

"Yes," said Tony.

"Very pretty. I love children. In Budapest I teach children swimming and skiing. You make sport?"

"I used to play tennis."

"I show you."

Andrassy hoisted to the coffee table and unzipped a tattered, bulging briefcase, from which pamphlets, dictionaries, testimonials and clippings unfurled like entrails:

HUNGARIAN CLAIMS
USA UNPREPARED

FREEDOM FIGHTER
SLATED FOR TALK
AT LEGION MEET

And photos: Andrassy wrestling, diving, boxing; a mettlesome teenager in soccer uniform; with chest outthrust as an Oregon gymnastics coach; on skis embracing a bosomy, heavily sweatered blonde.

"Who's that?"

Andrassy blushed. "My friend in Zell am See. You know the place?"

"Only in summer."

"Beautiful skiing. Nothing is like in Hungary. In Denver it must be wonderful, with the Rocky Mountains."

"I'm sorry," said Bea, rising suddenly, unsteadily from the sofa, "I must be going, I didn't realize how late it was. I have lab students in the morning."

Andrassy shot from his chair. Bea thanked Carol, who said, "Wish you could stay, we've hardly ever even met you. Love to Marge."

Andrassy elevated her hand as if preparing to kiss it. "It was very nice to meet you, I hope to see again."

She nodded nervously.

In the hallway Tony procured her coat, using the open closet door as a screen, slowing his movements to provide time.

"Tomorrow?"

"I'm leaving Friday for the interview at Cornell. I have a hundred things to do."

"Lunch."

She smiled half-heartedly, slipped out of his quick squeeze. "It's too late," she said. "It's dangerous."

"They can't see us, and they're talking."

"I didn't mean that," she said cryptically.

You're almost forty, too. Yet so beautiful. There's more

youth in your body than in all the nubile maidens of my
freshman class, than in my own child bride.

Were we only white birds, my beloved, buoyed out on the
foam of the sea.

"I'll call you," she said.

She was already in her car, backing down the driveway,
when he remembered what he had planned to tell her.

Andrassy repacked his briefcase, Carol feeding him the folders
and clippings consecutively.

"It's fantastic the things you've done," Carol was saying.

"Don't leave yet," Tony told him. "We'll have another beer,
or coffee."

"Thank you very much. I must go."

"Where are you staying?"

"My car."

"I mean, where in Denver?"

Andrassy fidgeted. "I sleep in my car."

"You don't have a room?"

"Is fine in the car. I sleep often. To save my money. Tomorrow
I will talk to the coach for a summer job, perhaps he knows
a fraternity who takes a foreign student."

"You're staying with us."

"Thank you very much. I can't."

"Of course. We have an extra room upstairs."

"Please," added Carol, and from a face only blurredly hers,
from some benevolent interior space, Tony caught the glint
of a possibility too simple, too daring to be contemplated
now.

"Thank you very much. If there's no trouble. You are very
nice people—Tony and Carol—and please call me Joe. I hardly
know you, and I call you by your first names. I think I'm more
American than the Americans."

Not the Hungary of Saint Stephen or Mathias Corvinus; nor
of Kossuth or Petöfi or even the battle of Temesvar. (But when
you mention the Empress Elizabeth, who was both beautiful
and Roman Catholic, Joe smiles tenderly.) To say nothing of
Kodály or Bartók. Their names rippled through his speech, and
through the little short course of Magyar history with which he

would vault into political argument, but they came from text-books; a catechism.

Joe's secular Hungary was blood red, striped by the bars of an AVO jail, and perhaps it was to escape as well as memorialize it that he became on short notice a phony Hungarian who combined a tziganer excitability with an overdone politeness, and spent the next afternoon in his host's kitchen preparing goulash with dumplings *nach echtem Rezept.*

Carol loved it, as when at breakfast he had deftly kissed her hand. She twisted her hair into an ingenious and fashionable knot, and drove Joe to the supermarket to purchase the proper cuts of beef, certain white onions and paprika. She attacked drawers and cupboards in pleasant distraction, fetching saucepans and bowls while Joe wrapped a dishtowel around his waist and thoughtfully tested knives with his thumb.

Tony imagined and found them thus when he came home from his afternoon class: Joe at the stove, Carol seated on the counter stool with her perpetual cup of coffee. Her eyes flickered over Joe's arms and back as he worked. Tony noticed her scent, her coiffure and earrings. He smiled.

"Joe's keeping his promise," she said. "You'd never dream what's gone into that goulash."

Joe spooned dumpling batter into boiling stock. A drop of sweat slipped from his brow and hissed on the burner. "Must be very hot with paprika," he said. "After we eat, we talk about politics."

Carol giggled.

I'm buying you off with Joe. It's all so convenient and symmetrical, and whose fault? that looking into your face, I see another's—who hasn't called me today or answered her own telephone.

Maybe she's punishing me, she thinks, for you. But thanks to Joe, I too have my purposes now and shall get her back as on that first night. And tonight I'm going to be a student again and get drunk on beer and argue politics till morning with a zany European.

Joe supported Else on her stomach with one splayed paw, and flew her from kitchen to livingroom and back. He had her stand with her back to him and extend her hands underneath her outstretched legs; grasping her tiny wrists, he pulled upward, flipping her over. Her long hair billowed; she landed on her feet dazed, squealing.

"Do that again, Joe."

He did, several times, until Carol announced bedtime.

"I love you, Joe," Else confided, still gasping. "Good night, Daddy." She mouthed Tony's evening stubble.

"Joe said I was a Boeing jet," she told her mother as they mounted the stairs.

While Tony opened another beer to quench his undigested and still smoldering dinner, Joe spread out again the contents of his briefcase, those papers, clippings, photos that were a substitute family, his only proof of an existence in time, of a youth and nationality.

He handed Tony a dogeared folder enclosing sheets of minuscule handwriting.

"My talk that I give. I took a speech course so I could write myself."

"It was fine, except the title's misleading; it's not 'impressions' but a political tract."

"That's the important thing, to teach about communism. The New Freedom Press of America made two thousand copies. But the English is still bad. If you would read."

"Correct it? Rewrite it?"

"If you could improve—it."

"That was a perfect slip."

"What?"

"You really meant that *I* should improve, see the light; and you use every means you can think of, even down to getting me to put words in your mouth." Tony grinned. "I'll do it for friendship's sake. But don't expect anything from my rhetorical style. The last time I gave a formal speech was in the ninth grade, when I had to welcome parents to a school assembly. It was supposed to be a funny speech, and they laughed and laughed. Afterwards I discovered my fly had been open."

Joe smiled politely, and after being enlightened, chuckled.

"For me I always have trouble with the American slang. I went to the big drugstore, where they have stationery, to buy an eraser, and I ask for a rubber. Once I tell the swimming team they must get on the balls."

Carol returned and stood ready to speak.

"Don't ask it, you're going to ask if we want some coffee, and the answer is no. Unless Joe'd like some."

"No, thank you very much."

"You shouldn't have so much coffee," Tony added to his wife.

"It's hot. I hate to waste it."

Then you can't get to sleep and toss all night, or wake up at two with a crying jag.

"If you're going to the kitchen, you could bring me another beer."

"And you shouldn't have so much beer."

With polite deafness, Joe proffered Tony another folder containing transcripts—Oregon, Arizona, Tulane . . .

"How many colleges have you been to?"

"In America eight. My cousin from Budapest teaches at Tulane, he got me a scholarship for one semester. The rest are most—mostly scholarships and jobs for sport."

"Your degree?"

"I worked for three years in Hungary for a degree in economics, the *Diplom;* then the Russians came."

"You're how old?"

Carol brought coffee and beer and sat between them with a look of self-conscious expectancy.

"39. There is a problem with credit. In America they don't give credit for Europe or other colleges."

"If you'd stay anywhere longer than a semester . . ."

"The trouble I told you about. In history the professors talk about the Soviet Union but they don't tell the truth. They give me an 'F' because they don't like that I know more than they do. At one big university is a professor who says he is an 'ideal Marxist' but thinks it was all right for Kennedy to negotiate with that criminal, Khrushchev."

I resent you, I envy you: bachelor, rabble-rouser, wanderer. Always coming upon money and friends.

"Americans are not all communists," Carol interrupted. "I mean, at the universities there may be some crackpots, but there are brilliant scholars too."

Joe smiled at her. "I am not a scholar, I am just an ignorant Hungarian orphan. But I know what is right and what is wrong."

Tony asked, "Did you talk to the coach?"

"They say next week maybe I start teaching some swimming and boxing. In fall semester I can enroll. Perhaps they will give me a room and board in the fraternity house."

"Meantime? Money, that is. I can lend you some."

"You are too kind already. I could not." But his eyes were pleading.

"Twenty? Thirty?"

"Thank you very much. To get my car fixed. Maybe I can't pay you till next week."

"That doesn't matter."

I'm buying you for myself, too. *My* Hungarian. Yet I need your friendship.

When Tony opened his wallet, he found the six hundred dollars, forgotten, that he had withdrawn the day before.

"Hungary is now a small country," Joe said. "But once it was like America, a melting pot, the meeting place between East and West. At the time of Mathias Corvinus. . . ."

It was midnight. Carol sat in bed reading *East of Eden*. With her eyeglasses, she always recalled the student he had taught beginning German five years ago. Fräulein Keller (her grandfather had come from Milwaukee) in the second row. Young, coltish, a revivifying contrast to the superweary or superintense feminine graduate students and assistants who shared his everyday circle or—rarely—his nighttime bed. The intricacies of a foreign syntax made her scowl and prettily blush. Under the C-minus on her final examination he had boldly written, "How about dinner and a movie next Friday?"

"Think you'll get your forty dollars back?" she asked.

"Joe's honest."

"Remember the twenty dollars you loaned Steve. And the Dutch boy who stole your whole set of Hebbel."

"Good riddance. What do you suddenly have against Joe?"

"Nothing. I like him. Elsie adores him. It's nice having two men around the house." Instead of none, you mean. "What were you talking about so long down there?"

Now I get it. You're jealous. Maybe that's a good sign, or am I making the wrong moves? I've had too much beer and I'm going to belch or fart or something and I hear you say, '*That* was unnecessary.'

Stifling his noises, he undressed and lay down with his back to his wife in her glasses and nightgown, thinking of another woman who slept naked but not answering her phones, not calling, leaving soon for a week, making keen torture of his love.

He heard Joe moving about the hall turning off the lights. A loud sniffling made him look over his shoulder. Carol's book had fallen to her lap, her glasses tilted askew. Beneath their rims trickled tears.

Oh God, not now.

"What's the matter?" He sat up heavily.

"Nothing. Something you forgot—yesterday."

He strove to visualize a calendar.

"I saw Dr. Whaley," she said.

"Already? I didn't realize. What did he say?"

"Yes."

"Oh, sweetheart." He was surprised by the fervor his own voice could conjure as, with a perfectly painted smile, he pivoted like a great wooden puppet to embrace her.

He shaved, bathed, ate breakfast, taught his classes in a risky stupor, as if the slightest mistake in word or gesture might incur madness. He apprehended an affinity with melancholiacs and murderers, how the accumulation of trivial irritants and large pressures may result in the intolerable shove.

He guarded carefully his external rationality.

That night Joe was invited out by a group of summer fraternity students eager to capitalize on the spreading aura of his background and various prowesses. After dinner, Tony drove to the campus.

"Evenings at the office" had been evenings at Bea's apartment. Now he was palpably here with his books and manuscripts and the telephone that purred infuriatingly when her number was dialed—and shrieked through the rooms at the other end, hunting her in every corner.

She had "checked out" of the biology department. "I don't

know," said Marge. "You've seen her more recently than I have." Her sudden curious frown blocked his pursuit of other clues.

Sunset light tinted the sorority girls at their volleyball game, a young couple like a frieze against the Gothic portal of the library.

He turned from the window to his card file and notes for the current Ludwig chapter: Musical influences on dramas—Studies with Mendelssohn—Wagner (exactly his own age)—Opera check E.T.A. Hoffmann—Elizabethan songs for Shakespeare?—Check Schoolfield.

He wrote nights the rest of the week (Friday the hardest, not knowing Bea's flight number or time or even if she was still in Denver) and into the next. He would come home when Carol was already asleep and Joe, who had betrayed them both, still abroad with his new friends and converts.

He finished the draft Wednesday night. The building was deserted, on the quadrangle no breath stirred the muggy dusk.

The bedroom will be stifling.

Joe sat at the diningtable, his bulky shoulders not quite obscuring the Department of Modern Languages stationery on which he was writing a letter, the postage stamps from Tony's desk.

"That's university letterhead," Tony said. "I can give you plenty of plain paper."

"I cross out the print! I write my aunt in Hungary. She is very sick and alone. Her son was killed in the revolution."

"All right," Tony said, laughing. "I give up. So where have you been?"

"Tomorrow I am invited with the boxing team for demonstration in Washington, D.C. The Boxing Association will pay for everything. When I come back on Sunday I move into the fraternity."

"You're leaving us."

"I don't want to. You and Carol are more kind to me than anybody. I'll call you as soon as I get back. I will miss the little Else and you and Carol. Carol seems very—sad sometimes."

And I?

"Women have their moods." Why don't I tell him she's

pregnant? Too late for everything. "I want to talk to you, Joe."

"Yes. The university pays me not until the end of August, I can't repay your kindness until then."

"To hell with that. I meant about something: my life."

"The Boxing Association pays for the trip. But I must buy some clothes."

"Some more money?"

"I have a check. If you can cash it, if there's no trouble." He uncovered a book of checks embossed with his name— Lajos Andrassy—and address—Tony's.

"Twenty dollars is all right?"

Tony shook his head. "Sure."

Carol's lamp flickered with moths. She emerged from the hallway.

"I've been up with Elsie since nine o'clock. She has a terrible cough."

"She needs the vaporizer."

"I've had it on for two nights, and poured quarts of medicine into her."

"We can call Dr. Reeves in the morning."

"Were you up talking with Joe?"

"I just came home. Finished my work."

"The book?"

"A chapter. The draft. Was Joe home tonight?"

"Not much likely."

"You mean, 'not bloody likely.'"

She shrugged. "He's never home before eleven."

"You sound like a housemother."

"The place can be empty. You at the campus. Joe out with whatever woman it is."

"Girl?"

"Woman."

"Perfume?"

"Lipstick. On his undershirt."

"He's alive."

She smiled with no trace of humor.

"What's the matter?" he prodded. "Did he make passes at you?"

"Me?" Face and voice turned to metal. "Look at me." She tossed her hair and leered. "Who'd make passes at *me*? Would *you*?"

He snorted. She slapped him hard.

"Would you?" Screaming. "Would you?"

She leaned over the dresser, beating its surface with her fists, shoulders convulsed as she sobbed.

He felt a certain thrill. His hand, raised and flattened to strike her back, curled instead toward a gesture of comfort. But she moved away.

"I saw your face," she said. "You wish he would. To get me off your hands."

Yes. No.

She said, "It's the end."

"I'll sleep on the sofa, when Joe's gone to bed. I'm leaving tomorrow."

"The very end."

"Probably not. That's what sickens me."

He moved to a motel on East Colfax Avenue, and from there a day later—appalled by the cost of food, lodgings and freedom—to the old wing of the YMCA hotel, a sunless, airless room with battered furniture, a Gideon Bible, a view of asphalt and soot-crusted sandstone, and a fire escape that might have led down two storeys to Purgatory.

He mailed money to Carol, a frantic letter to Bea's apartment with his latest telephone number. From the foreign student office he obtained the name and number of Joe's fraternity —but Joe was still on the East Coast.

Saturday night: hamburgers in a Sixteenth Street cafe, beer at a piano bar, walking, smoking, browsing through paperbacks, bourbon in the anonymity of the Hilton bar. The lights went out one by one. A whore whispered from the dim entryway of a bank. An ambulance wailed.

He lay naked on the bed, sweating into the thick night, slept, awoke to the siren of another ambulance, slept again, at six, suffocating, rose to shave.

A row of ringed washbowls, a broken toilet flushing into eternity. Here no vestige of woman's powder and perfume. Certainly no child bemused by the lather that hides my face.

Only grime and graffiti: PUSSEYS WANTED TO EAT—R &
S OKLA CITY—8 IN. HARD FOR SUCK THURS. PM;
only the hairy, rancid-smelling beast in the mirror.

Down the stone canyons of a city dawn. Banks and stores
are closed, and with them all motivation for these streets: the
shops where who will ever buy anyway the orthopedic ap-
pliances, the silverplated pickle forks, the "specially reduced"
skirts and blouses, the yellow shrinking pages of last year's
Saga?

A weary bellhop in a crumpled red uniform, a leftover
conventioneer still wearing his "Hello There I'm" badge. The
trashcans with their printed morals.

Farther down toward the old center of the city you find
doorways marbled with vomit, and now and then, in a heap,
one of the men who did it.

The rectangles continue pitiless waffle of an Assyrian ruin.

Yet there is a satisfaction, too, somewhere, in this dereliction,
this aridity.

I could get drunk on a drop of rain.

A CLEANER DENVER IS UP TO YOU.

The summer semester came to an end. In his office lay
stacks of blue books, at the hotel a sheaf of mail forwarded
by Carol: bills, a notification from the bank that Joe's check
had bounced. He could not bring himself to call either Joe or
his wife. Everything remained tentative, dependent upon another."

At last, one Sunday evening, his telephone rang, and he
clutched at it.

A man's voice, belligerent: "Tony?"

"Dad? What are you doing in town?"

"Some business for the farm. Listen, what kind of a trick
are you playing! It's terrible—just when a woman needs her
husband most."

"I didn't choose the time."

"First you renounce the mother church. Do you ever think
of your immortal soul? Now you abandon your wife and children." His father's voice dropped to a confidential pitch. "Listen, Tony, if it's another woman—I know, a man reaches a
certain age—I know . . ."

Carol's voice intruded, husky but firm: "Hello, Tony."

"Hello. How are you?"

"Fine. You?"

"Fine."

"Your father's here for the weekend. He just took us out to dinner at Trader Vic's."

"That's nice."

"We may go back with him to Salida."

"You know what living in Salida is like, not to mention my parents."

"I can't very well go back to Bozeman."

Her voice disturbed him, its steadiness, no helplessness or whine. His cheek smarted in remembrance: her slap, too, had suggested not the petulance of a child but the controlled violence of a woman. It reminded him of Bea.

"I've deposited in the account," he said, "so you can write checks."

"I know."

They were silent. There remained the coda:

She said, "If you're lonely, you know how I've lived. If you're not, you will be."

Be. Bea.

"I'll call you," he said.

Once a night he drove down Marion Street in the hope of a light in a third-floor balcony window. Mornings he checked with the secretary of the biology department, then sat in his own office preparing notes for his fall lectures.

His colleagues had gone on vacation. Two eager young fall-semester teaching assistants were moving books and bric-a-brac into their respective cubicles. They addressed him as "Herr Professor," ill concealing a certain scorn, or possible pity, for this scholar who made a career of a half-forgotten 19th-century dramatist, while they wrestled the medieval epics, the bawdy student songs and profound love lyrics that were a triumph of Western civilization.

"You're a literature man yourself, Herr Professor," said young Hemingway over coffee. "What do you think? In Middle High

German, don't you always end up studying philology instead of ideas?"

"Philology is the means to the end: literature—expression—the telegram to someone you love."

"That's what I mean. The wording of the telegram is so important."

It was Saturday morning. In front of the fraternity house, students in blue jeans, early arrivals, hosed down their cars and each other, hooting at passing coeds and menacing them with careless sprays of water. On the lawn a group of boys played touch tackle.

Joe emerged from the scrimmage in shorts and a sweat-stained RMSC tee-shirt, sucking in his gut. He crushed Tony's hand.

"Tony, good to see you! I called you but you are not at home."

"No. Never."

"I have news. Next week I go to Los Angeles. This friend of my uncle, he has a gymnasium in Santa Monica, he wants me to teach sport. I'm taking with me a wonderful new friend . . ." Joe squinted in the focus of Tony's seriousness.

"Let's go somewhere and talk."

"Come inside. I want you to meet my fraternity brothers."

"No, privately."

"If it's about the money, I'll pay you next week."

"It's not that."

They followed the path between the fraternity house and its neighbor, up the grassy knoll where right angles receded, streets and buildings obscured by pine and elm.

"You are not happy," Joe said. And then, "Do you believe in God?"

"If God's intelligent, he abandoned me years ago."

"You say, 'if he's intelligent.' You admit he's there."

"No. If he's there, we have no traffic with each other, and if this is his world, he's not to be praised. I'm sick of all this. I'm sick in love, if you want to know."

Joe eyed Tony shrewdly, but since no explanation came, he extended his arm toward the trees, snapping in a sudden gust of wind, and the western wall of the mountains, serene.

"Look, the world. How beautiful."

"I agree. But indifferent, too."

"You say you're sick with love and still the world is indifferent."

"Yes. Like that mountain wind in the leaves. Like a woman."

"Your love is not good."

"How the hell do you know?"

"Your woman is not good, if she makes you think like that."

"It's not 'my woman.' I love and I think and I despair."

"I know despair. I show. Look!"

Tony studied Joe's left hand blankly.

"The fingers."

And Tony saw that the third and fourth fingers were grotesquely disjointed.

"My eyes. I have terrible headaches. From the lights they shine, every day 24 hours. My kidneys, when the pain comes I can't stand up. My back. Look."

He yanked out his shirttail, pulled it to his shoulder. "Look!" From neck to waist his broad back was crisscrossed with puckered furrows and pale, hairless splotches.

"You think I forget?" he yelled to Tony. "You think I forget?" he yelled to the plains and the mountains.

Then self-consciously he sat down on the grass. "My eyes are weak, but I see. We fight to destroy communism in Viet Nam, and they are afraid to bomb even North Viet Nam. They can destroy Red China, but they are afraid. The students —here on this campus—march to protest, but they are afraid, the communists are working everywhere, you will see, we must destroy . . ."

Some students waved to Joe from the curb.

"I'm sorry we don't have time to talk. Before I go to Los Angeles I hope I can see you again and Carol and the little Else. You are so good to me and always my friends."

"If you want to borrow some money—"

Joe smiled. "I borrow now from my fraternity brothers."

The Saturday round: barber, cleaners, laundromat—for clothes that are fluffy and whiter than white, but not I.

Sunlight sloped against the broad staircase of the biology

department. Take them on a run, diagonally, fourth brick over on every fourth stair, and she'll be back. He missed as usual the twelfth stair.

But there she was, at her desk in the deserted laboratory, emptying drawers of books and papers into cartons.

She was shorter, stouter, more elegant and voluptuous.

She was startled. He ground his stubble into her hair, mouthed her ear, clutched her familiar contours and fragrance.

She twisted her chest backward and her thighs sideways from his body.

"The window looks out on the whole campus."

"How long have you been back?"

"Thursday."

He held her away. Her face twitched. He glanced from one to the other of her eyes, hoping for a contradiction of what her voice had implied.

"You didn't get my letter," she said.

"What letter?"

"From New York."

"I haven't been home. I've left Carol. I love you."

She shook her head and stubbed out a cigarette that she had been smoking the while. "I was stupid to think I could work it out without hurting you." She stared at his shirt pocket.

Stop.

"I'm going to Los Angeles," she said.

"New York, you mean."

"I didn't get the job at Cornell. But when I was in New York with my other sister, I got a letter from Marge—she forwarded it—from UCLA. It's a wonderful job, with magnificent research facilities. An assistant professorship. Imagine old Bea Mullen with tenure."

"I don't believe it."

"It's true nonetheless."

"You're not old, my sweet. Listen: I'll marry you. I've found an apartment, an ad in the *Post*, on Sherman Street. I haven't seen it yet, but I can get it on a discount."

She smiled ruefully.

"There's nothing wrong with me?" he said.

"No, my dear, believe me."

"Then what's in it for you in Los Angeles? You'll hate the place, I've told you. Cancel your flight ticket."

"I'm not flying, I'm going by car."

"You didn't tell me you'd bought a car. Is that on the advance from your professor's salary?"

"Joe's driving me."

"Joe who?"

"Joe Andrassy. He's going out to a job managing a gymnasium."

"I don't get it."

I do: 'I'm taking with me a wonderful new friend'—you! The night you were at my house, and Yeats. Joe living with us. Lipstick on the undershirts—yours? I'll kill him. I'll cut his balls off.

"Tell me."

She grimaced. "When I met him at your place, and seeing you and Carol for the first time together, everything, I saw I was alone . . ."

"I was there."

"You thought you were. I discovered where you had been those weeks. Not in your lovemaking; in your mind. Joe was the battery I was wired to. And then in New York he called me from Washington and came up a couple of times."

"So the two of you got to know each other, if you get what I mean."

"He may marry me."

Tony laughed. "I thought you'd learned your lesson."

"Compared to my first husband, the Marquis de Sade is every girl's dream. Joe's gentle. I love him."

"You've been plowed by a Hungarian stud."

"I've never been that way, you know it. I do like men, but I've never had it that bad."

"You like it front and back, top and bottom, any way it comes."

"What you're saying is, you like it too. Anyway, I've never slept with Joe."

"So?"

"I'll get my doctor's degree and go on smelling like chemicals. A marriage and an abortion haven't made me any lovelier, but thanks for telling me I'm not old. I'm a damned good biologist, a pretty good cook, and I should be a mother."

"Has he asked you?"

"No. But I think he will. In a few weeks. Months. He's sudden in his emotions, but in other ways really very old-fashioned, old world."

"You'll have to support him. He borrows from everybody; he owes me at least sixty dollars."

"He works hard. He's the strongest and finest man I've ever known." She smiled and added, "Single man."

"You'll have to eat his politics, too."

"I'm liberal enough. For a woman it's different."

"Does he know about us?"

"He knows I'm not—intact. I'd say he and I are equally battered, equally lonely."

"In other words, you told him you were married before."

"Do you want me to tell him about you? You're one of the few friends he has. When he says 'Tony,' that's the best."

She lighted another cigarette. Tony felt impelled to strike her, to bend her back over the desk and take her right there by privilege, without games or grease.

He said, "Do you understand I've left Carol? That for three weeks I've been calling you every hour and writing you letters and beating on your door, and nights clawing the walls of my cell?"

"I've been lonely, too, most of my life."

"You're quoting Carol. We quote each other in circles."

"Listen:—No, don't touch me—Carol is lovelier, more loveable than you let her be. More than me. God knows she's willing to serve you like no other woman I've ever even heard of."

"I don't want a waitress!"

"Have you told her? How much you hate her? A woman becomes what a man creates . . ."

Carol's face when she hit me, her voice on the telephone, yours now as you turn away from me with the sunlight on your hair and earring, squinting from your cigarette smoke and the ashes about to fall.

". . . Anyway she's, well, I suppose willing to let you play around, or even not to know about it."

"I don't 'play around.'"

"Yes. It's not your loneliness but your violence. You're infinitely more dangerous, Tony, than Joe with all his vindictive patriotism. I've had a few little scars from you. Not like Bruce was, I don't mean that. You and I, we're too civilized, all of us, dishonest."

The cigarette ash shriveled in despair and fell. Bea flicked the fragments from her breast.

"No, don't," she said.

"Let's have a drink somewhere and dinner."

"Joe's taking me out, he'll be here any minute. I have to pack. I'm going to Aspen tomorrow, the cabin, and Joe's picking me up Wednesday." She slipped from her seat on the desk.

He held her shoulder again.

"It's all over, Tony."

That's what Carol said, and I said, No, that was what sickened me.

Bea wiggled out of his embrace and existence. The door opened. It was Joe.

"Tony, what a good surprise!" He surveyed them happily. "You know we go together to Los Angeles. I'm sorry we don't have time to talk this morning. Well, it makes no difference. Let's all go out to dinner, everybody; Tony, you can bring Carol and the little Else?"

Tony's fisted arm lashed out, he saw Joe stagger back surprised, turning his face to avoid the blows which finally connected, making hard, dull reports.

Whereas in fact Joe had not moved, no time had passed, they were talking in an alien language composed of banalities about friendship and meeting again and calling on the telephone, and Tony had been trapped into the ultimate betrayal of shaking Joe's hand.

He watched television in a bar, that is, he watched Bea's apartment, the shelves and tables bare, the cottonwood seeds drifting across the unswept balcony; watched Joe displaying his scars, which she touched delicately—motels in New Mexico and Arizona with Joe's Chevrolet parked in front—another apartment in Beverly Hills and her breasts rising and falling under a thin sheet, while curtains bellied in the Pacific wind.

"Two o'clock!" said the bartender, and added confidentially, unwittingly. "Think you can make it, Joe?"

The hangover came, but in the afternoon he read a detective novel and ate a sandwich, and in the evening he drove to the campus to walk in the shade of the elms.

Time stifles me. Yet I understand that I am paroled, that this passion and disarray will recur, until I am an old man with bony neck, dangling paps, scrotum shriveled to a dry pod.

That you will grow old, in a distant city.

I curse the dusk.

The house was chill. On the floor beside the sofa, in the beam of the lamp, Carol had read a magazine and fallen asleep, her head against the cushion. Her feet were tucked under her thighs, her mouth had fallen open in a wordless song of weariness.

Somewhere in the pile of letters on the table lay one, postmarked New York, whose message he would save.

"Tony?" She raised her head, blinking into the light. "Where have you been?"

"Having a little love affair."

She swallowed, licked her lips, wiped her eyes and in the same movement brushed her hair from her forehead, each gesture pitifully, painfully familiar.

"I was afraid you wouldn't come back."

He lowered himself on one knee beside her. Her face was flushed, forehead moist.

"Tony, I was so afraid. I'll learn everything, do everything for you." Her face fell against his chest.

Carefully he lifted his wife from the floor and carried her up to that more precarious, more necessary haven where, in the lengthening nights of autumn, he would unleash his hatred.

JOSEPHINE JACOBSEN lives in Baltimore and spends her summers in Whitefield, New Hampshire. Her most recent book of poems is *The Animal Inside*, and her most recent book of criticism, with William R. Mueller, is *Genet and Ionesco: Playwrights of Silence*. Her story "On the Island" appeared in *Fifty Years of the American Short Story*, a collection of stories selected from the O. Henry Awards.

The Jungle of Lord Lion

It was on the morning of the sprinkler debacle that Mrs. Pomeroy remembered that she had first noticed Mrs. Chubb—truly noticed her—over the matter of Lord Lion, a matter as small as Lord Lion himself.

Lord Lion's baptismal name was Hubert, and his feral quality would have struck no one. Indeed, Mrs. Pomeroy would never have known he *was* Lord Lion, had Mighty Vampire not sung *Island In The Sun* and *Yellow Bird* to their group, stopping as he trudged down the blazing beach toward the cruise ship floating white and racy on the blue water of St. Jude's harbor. Mighty Vampire had tramped off, followed moments later by two small donkeys with rope halters and swags of crimson bougainvillea around their necks, each donkey ridden, just over the tail, by a long-legged Boudinian; just behind them a tall, sooty, handsome girl, reared back with a slow swagger, toiled by in the soft sand with a basket on her head from which acid-green bananas, breadfruit and a springing swatch of gaudy croton sprouted.

Now, looking extra-small, as he especially did when driving, Lord Lion sat with his patient paws on the wheel. There was always the air of an admirable trick about his chauffeuring, as of a small monkey taking his pony through a paper hoop. When he had arrived at the beach-house, the Marmows and

Mrs. Pomeroy had been ready. They had accumulated everything, and they stood in the frond-shade where Lord Lion had
stopped the Morne Jaune's station wagon. They waited for
Mrs. Chubb, who was still concerned about her ant-bites, as
was, necessarily, Miss Gilse.

"Yes," said Lord Lion to Mrs. Marmow. "I know the Mighty
Vam-pah, and so." His forehead, always wrinkled as in distress,
contracted further. "He sings songs by others, and like that.
I sing My Own Compositions. I am the Lord Lion. I sing My
Own Compositions. *Beautiful Boudina,* and *So Darling Come
Shift,* and *Boudina Jump-Up.* All my own."

As Miss Gilse patted Mrs. Chubb with a bathtowel and the
palms slightly made their raining sound, Lord Lion amplified:
he did not batten; he created. Every night he practised. Eventually he hoped to go to Trinidad. The Mighty Sparrow had
come from a small island, Grenada. Lord Melody—

Here came Mrs. Chubb, refraining from scratching; hot with
the cross of self-discipline, she climbed in back. Miss Gilse followed with the thermos, towels, bronzite and the plastic head-
rest, and Mrs. Pomeroy joined them. Mr. and Mrs. Marmow
rounded the car and climbed in beside Lord Lion.

Suddenly Mrs. Chubb said clearly, "Wouldn't they like to get
back here? Couldn't we squeeze them in back here?" She addressed Mrs. Pomeroy, who stared. Mrs. Marmow, a small quick
woman, looked nervously over her shoulder. "This is fine," she
said in her muffled English voice. Mr. Marmow, elbow to elbow
with Lord Lion, looked studiously ahead.

"That's why I like to have someone with me over here,"
said Mrs. Chubb, speaking to Mrs. Pomeroy over Miss Gilse's
head. "In these islands. When you're one alone, they take
advantage of it, and they put you in front. Right next to the
driver." Her small unsagacious eyes rayed significance at Mrs.
Pomeroy. No one said anything at all. They sped around a
curve, a girl in a red dress leaped up the bank. A goat sprang
away, chickens scattered. Here they were already. The kindly
gates, dripping coralita, swallowed them and Lord Lion, much
more cautiously, curved under the green fountain of the mango
tree and stopped.

Mrs. Heatherby stood on the steps. She always looked as
though she had been carved and, with fortunate taste, set down

where she stood. She was a beautiful, tall woman. Her skin was a lustrous gold and she had ripe, cleanly-shaped lips. Her hair, iridescent as feathers, gleamed black in a tower on her head, and she wore Chinese blouses and tailored silk shirts. The good modeling of her long narrow feet was interrupted only by the sandalthong between her toes. She was a recent widow with three children; two pale tall girls in a convent in Trinidad. Mrs. Pomeroy had seen their pictures, pleated skirts and Peter Pan collars. There was a little boy, Patrick, almost black, finely-boned and thin, only four. Mrs. Pomeroy could see him now, dragging his wagon across the lawn toward the lily-pond. Cynthia, the Marmows' blond fat six-year-old, trailed behind him.

"Hubert, go and get the ice," said Mrs. Heatherby to Lord Lion, and she smiled slightly as her guests straggled past her to their rooms.

After lunch, Mrs. Pomeroy, who every day now was really feeling much better, decided that as soon as she had spoken to Mrs. Heatherby about her breakfast trays, she would go to her room and lie down until the cool of the late afternoon. She felt that she had been unreasonably put out by Mrs. Chubb's stupidity; her own intense reaction had seemed more like the raw-nerve vulnerability of her last two weeks in New York than like a part of the extraordinary fragrant peace that seemed to have descended on her as silently as dew in these days on Boudina. She understood that if she were not to ruin everything, she must take her fellow guests as they came, especially in so small a guesthouse as Morne Jaune. After all, the taking could be very minor—a few minutes en route to the beach; passing a table, the civility of a breakfast greeting. If she thought about Lord Lion, driving them so wildly well, incandescent with his Own Compositions, spattered by Mrs. Chubb's arrogant idiocy, it was possible to get angry; but Lord Lion must long ago have devised his defenses. He had a good place to live, she thought coming down the steps from the vine-hung concrete porch into the dazed, spicy, glittering air. Even the blackbirds were quiet in the heat. The African tulip-trees near the gate blazed away, and as her foot touched the ground, one of the smaller gold and turquoise lizards flashed past her toe into the grass soaked by the sprinkler. "Lord Lion's jungle . . ." she thought. And then she thought, *They say the lion and the lizard keep/ The courts* . . . and laughed quite happily to herself. She went along as far as the little conical dinner pavillion and hesitated. Mrs. Heatherby was nowhere in sight. She was almost always about, strolling quietly and terribly here and there. Everyone said that was why the place was so marvelously well-run. Since Mrs. Pomeroy had decided that having breakfast in bed was to be part of her program of self-indulgence, she might as well say so now. She stepped under the shade of the roof and sat down in one of the deep cane chairs. It was very quiet. Down the slope of the lawn toward the sea was another sprinkler, and in it Patrick, in vestigial shorts, and Cynthia, in a red polka-dot bathing suit, jumped back and forth with faint shrieks of pleasure.

Just as quickly as her doctor would allow her to travel after the operation, Mrs. Pomeroy had come to Boudina. It was a long-held ambition and, amazingly, Boudina had disappointed in no detail. In fact, the special quality of its light, that light which seemed to live inside its flora and fauna, radiating from the great ragged banana leaves, the huge golden calyxes of the *coupe d'or*, the black gleaming skin of the fishermen moving over the turquoise and lilac sea, seemed to reveal to her not an island, but a planet, as though the plane from Kennedy Airport had never come back to earth at all. She was sometimes aware that this had to do with her uncertainty in regard to her going on living; security might have dulled it, or a definitive sentence have set it small and implacable before her. Whereas the uncertainty of her relations with life, like those of a passionate but insecure love affair, lit everything—was perhaps itself the Boudina light. She was happy as she had never been happy after her husband's death quite a long time ago. Waking each morning, in the smallest, cheapest room, to the bowing of fronds a few feet beyond the open glass louvers, to the languid explosions of the waves on the rocks below, she would move her hand, turn her head, prop herself on her elbow to stare more fully at the new day, one of an endless file which as yet there was no need to count. This holiday, extravagant but not ruinous (in case the news should turn out to be good), would not end for three and a half months; over fourteen weeks, over ninety-eight mornings. She had been delighted to find that she need spend virtually nothing, beyond payment of her weekly bill. On what would she spend it? Lord Lion took them to the beach in the Inn's car. Certainly she had no desire for the boutiques and festivities of the two beach hotels. So that breakfast trays would be perfectly feasible.

There was a louder shriek from the lawn. Cynthia had sat down on the sprinkler; strangled, it jetted feebly in place, prickling her hair and water-speckled face. Elated, Patrick danced wetly about her; suddenly, unable to sit, too, on the sprinkler, he sat in her lap. A small local rainbow shimmered over them; they were bathed in bands of peacock blue and jonquil. Something in Mrs. Pomeroy's wrists and breast gave a queer lift. It was as though just there shone all beginnings.

"It is a calm day at sea today," announced a voice, and there was Mrs. Chubb, right beside her. For a minute Mrs. Pomeroy, gazing at her, thought she had come out with some pigmented and loathsome disease, the outward and visible sign of an inward and spiritual splotching. She looked like a nasty sea-monster, all blubber and malignancy. "Violet Gentian," she said in her fat voice, noting Mrs. Pomeroy's dismayed fascination. Those bites are poisonous, if untreated. I am waiting for my Captain." Mrs. Chubb was either unaware of Mrs. Pomeroy's sentiments in regard to her, or indifferent to them. She went on to explain. Two couples, friends of Mrs. Chubb's from New York, were arriving next week. They were, all five, chartering a yacht, and would take trips, cruising through the Antilles. Miss Gilse would stay here. Miss Gilse was a bad sailor, and indeed preferred her native Toronto to the slack air of the Caribbean. Mrs. Chubb did not bother to explain what Miss Gilse was doing here at all, in that case, and Mrs. Pomeroy considered it unnecessary. As the only iguana on the property suddenly emerged from a tree trunk behind Mrs. Chubb's head and flowed over the railing and down the lawn, Mrs. Pomeroy said to herself that if she ever had seen a dogsbody, born, it was Miss Gilse. As though she were a thought-reader, Mrs. Chubb now said that Miss Gilse would remain here, and, very kindly, attend to any important mail. They would all, of course, keep their rooms between trips; the Morne Jaune was not yet full, but it would be, all ten rooms of it. "Will you be here long?" she suddenly asked Mrs. Pomeroy. "Oh yes," said Mrs. Pomeroy luxuriously, "until May."

"It is a sixteen-foot ketch," said Mrs. Chubb in answer to this. "But the Captain should be here now. It sleeps eight, and that means that five of us will be comfortable."

Still Mrs. Heatherby did not appear. At this moment, Mrs. Pomeroy had an intuition for escape. Exactly as she had it, Mrs. Chubb cried, "Look at that!"

The iguana had run up the little mariposa tree; its head stuck out, lifted from the bark, still as porphyry. Mrs. Pomeroy would never have seen it but by following the children's gaze. Ravished, immobilized, they crowded over each other, transfixed as the reptile itself.

"Doesn't it look old?" said Mrs. Pomeroy. But Mrs. Chubb, her voice slightly expanded by the intensity of her feelings, said, "This is a perfectly disgusting sight. It is cheap, and demoralizing, and it cannot—it *cannot* be tolerated." She was gazing, rigid as a pointer, to where the soaked and shining children clutched each other, motionless.

Just once in her life, Mrs. Pomeroy had been caught by a serious undertow, and now with a lurch of apprehension she recognized the violence and rapidity of what was pulling her: she knew also that it was the ricochet from something that had shone with life. But she could not stop. "What is cheap?" she said.

"You cannot have a white little girl and a black boy playing together half naked, unless you are a fool," said Mrs. Chubb. "If Patrick doesn't know his place he'll only be unhappier. Mrs. Heatherby must know that. She's intelligent. It's her white blood. Patrick is black, and she can't pretend anything else. She should have thought of that—it's too late now. In a place such as this you can't have niggers playing with the guests' children. She'll *lose* her guests, if she isn't careful."

With the awful detachment of a bystander, Mrs. Pomeroy heard herself speak. "I can't imagine," she said, "why *anyone* would want such a ridiculous and unpleasant person as yourself, anywhere at all."

As she turned, Mrs. Heatherby, materialized from the middle air, stood behind her. In her quiet sandals she stood a foot away; on her arm was a wicker basket of bougainvillea, and from her long fingers hung bright shears. She was looking past Mrs. Pomeroy at Mrs. Chubb, and even in her red-hot exaltation Mrs. Pomeroy gave a small shiver.

From the blazing blue water at the foot of the slope the conch sounded its hoarse breathy bellow.

"That's our fisherman," said Mrs. Heatherby, as Victoria emerged from the kitchen door, a basket on her head.

Nearly at sunset, Mrs. Pomeroy went down to the little ridge just over the tide. It was large enough to establish one chair. She had carried one of the feather-light aluminum and plastic affairs there last week and it had not been replaced on its proper stone terrace, so her habit seemed established. It was five minutes to six.

The sun, a large flame-colored disk, was just off the pure bare curve of the sea. Mrs. Pomeroy walked down slowly, in the curious leveling light. In the islands, sunset, rather than announcing the end of something, had the quality of an introduction. And like that of all introductions, its intimation was still undefined. Mrs. Pomeroy sat down gingerly; there was really very little room. Below her the tide plunged raggedly toward the rocks, broke with a seething hush, leaped up and fled back. The straight great palm to her left at the rim of the bank had lost its glitter; it darkened instant by instant. Warblers in very rapid flight darted erratically through the air, into which darkness seemed to be visibly filtering. The sea, almost totally gold and lilac, darkened, too. The disk was in the water. On the little mariposa tree clutching the ledge beside her, the leaves had folded thinly shut, thinned as the closed wings of butterflies. Once in the daytime she had tried to shut them by hand—they sprang open, of course; and once at night she had lightly forced one apart. With a delicate shrinking it had reclosed.

A deep rose, mixed with darkness, fumed into the sky in silence; it struck Mrs. Pomeroy that all this was going on in silence. In silence a steel-sharp star pierced the last stain of color and in the instant the lighthouse at Pointe Orage flashed. It flashed again, vanished as the ray pivoted, recurred. The darkness, rather than quenching, seemed to have gathered into itself all the detailed brilliance, the coarse rich blossoms, the sea's last stains of lilac, the folded mariposa leaves. Suddenly, as though since last night it had never stopped, the liquid, high sweet pulse of the tree-frogs, directionless in the dark, flooded the air. I am absolutely happy, thought Mrs. Pomeroy.

When this relief from fear, sharp as a starved appetite gratified, had first stung her, she had been differently frightened; it was almost an hallucination. The words . . . a terrible beauty is born . . . recurred insistently, to her embarrassment. There was something shaming in the equating of her precarious glance at life, with great words. But the words were as true as bone, and finally she understood that it had nothing to do with herself—it was life held up like a transparency to the blaze of loss.

Sitting on the ledge, she had not mislaid her knowledge of realities, it had only been assimilated. She tried now to exercise this knowledge of the unforgiving mechanism, and gradually, with effort, it became real to her. The birds, zigzagging a moment ago through the melting color, flew to hunt, they were death on the wing. Under the hyacinth surface, pop, lidless eyes cruised in a permanence of ravening. In the hills the mongooses had rabies; there were poisoned baits out for their hunger in the dark. And the cane-field rats could choose between bait and mongoose. But she might have been reciting a geometry formula. Knowing all this, she was now permitted to accept it. It was assimilated effortlessly into the scented dark in which at the core of the glassgreen leaves the green throats of the tree-frogs, compelled to exult, brimmed the night. The stars had all come out.

At dinner Mrs. Pomeroy found to her amazement that she was not in the least distressed or embarrassed by the thought of her unique, her unpardonable outburst. Even Mrs. Heatherby's outrage, the warning of her eyes on Mrs. Chubb's face in the pavilion, she recognized as something amply provided for in that lady's beauty and pride. She did wonder if her own serenity could be a token of the setting-in of isolation, but she felt only cheerful, and faintly curious as to whether Mrs. Chubb would remain cheek-by-jowl with a guest whom she must regard as a madwoman. After that look of Mrs. Heatherby's, a look whose grimness did faintly trouble Mrs. Pomeroy's vision, surely no one could stay. But then, she realized instantly,

how could she assess the look seen through Mrs. Chubb's eyes?
Could Mrs. Heatherby simply demand that Mrs. Chubb leave?
She supposed not, and yet there was a dignity of toughness, of
the ability to move, in Mrs. Heatherby which showed in her
walk, in the strong turn of her superb neck. Just suppose Mrs.
Heatherby *should* move, thought Mrs. Pomeroy; how bright
would the lighthouse be then. She felt no qualm of mercy for
Mrs. Chubb. Obviously she could manage either of the beach
hotels without a quaver; it must have been some obscure thirst
for pre-eminence that had led her to the economy of Morne
Jaune in the first place. Mrs. Pomeroy guessed that Mrs. Heatherby *would* move, but not precipitately or naively.

Mrs. Pomeroy's book was exciting. By dessert at her little
table, spooning her sour-sop ice cream unseeingly, she had
only two chapters left, and the odds were beautifully balanced.
The denouement would take place in bed—Mrs. Pomeroy's bed.
After the last mouthful of coffee, she went out the screen door
and, by the help of the light-bulb lashed to the mango, along
the side of the house toward the small separate square of her
room. But she almost stopped dead, and had consciously to
push forward. The open window of Mrs. Heatherby's office was
lit. She sat at her desk, erect and absolutely implacable, and
across from her stood an agitated Mrs. Chubb. Mrs. Pomeroy's
heart rose in a pure and ferocious joy. She understood that this
vindicated every blade, every frond and petal; the island, as
though fed by an infusion, shone glosser in the dark.

Mrs. Pomeroy went softly along and into her room, and as
she closed the door the rain struck. It fell, not as at home in a
strident whisper, but straight, furiously, with a glorious din. In
the dark she leaned against the single window's open louvers.
Spray fumed in her face, the thick flowering bushes gave off a
noise like drums; the palms streamed and strained. It kept on
for almost a quarter of an hour. In her nightgown Mrs. Pomeroy
brushed her hair. Abruptly, the rain diminished; but it was still
dropping noisily when there was a light quick knock on Mrs.
Pomeroy's door. She opened it, and there was Mrs. Heatherby.

Suddenly Mrs. Pomeroy knew that at the moment there were
things she could, and things she could not, handle, and that
Mrs. Heatherby's frank appreciation might be one of the latter.
"Mrs. Heatherby! Come in," she said.

Mrs. Heatherby, a light raincoat over her shoulders, was gleaming with drops.

"Do sit down," said Mrs. Pomeroy.

"No, thank you," said Mrs. Heatherby, and her rich voice sounded fainter in the noise of all the drops falling and dripping. "I must tell you our trouble, Mrs. Pomeroy," she said, and she smiled without agitation.

"I know," said Mrs. Pomeroy, more impulsively than she had intended. "I'm extremely sorry. But it isn't really *important*, is it?" she said hopefully.

"Mrs. Pomeroy," said Mrs. Heatherby, "we are having some work done here—there is a threat of termites."

Mrs. Pomeroy stared, confused. "I'm sorry," she said again. "About the termites, I mean."

"Yes," said Mrs. Heatherby. "It is most unfortunate. I'm afraid the workmen must take over this room."

The sound of drops had stopped and in the stillness Mrs. Pomeroy said, with a slight sinking of the heart, "I shall have to move to another room?" She thought rapidly: But the others are all more expensive. . . . But perhaps as it isn't my fault. . . . "Well, of course," she said. "How soon?"

"But this is the unfortunate part," said Mrs. Heatherby. Her face, in the lamplight, looked paler than Mrs. Pomeroy remembered it. "There are no other rooms, except the rooms which must be worked on. We are completely booked."

The two women stood there looking at each other. Then Mrs. Heatherby's gaze moved to the window. "I'm afraid your blanket got damp," she said. "These storms are brief, but so violent."

Mrs. Pomeroy had risen above nothing. Panic, fury, and a total, childish grief raged in her chest, so that for what seemed a long pause she could not speak. Then she heard her voice from a sickening distance. "Of course, I see. When do you need the room?"

Mrs. Heatherby's eyes reached past her to the dark outside the window. "Tomorrow, if that's possible," she said pleasantly. "If not, of course the next day will be perfectly satisfactory."

"I see," said Mrs. Pomeroy again.

Mrs. Heatherby with a quick motion almost like anger slipped her coat from her shoulders. She flung it over her arm; bright drops flew to the straw rug. She looked directly at Mrs. Pomeroy with a curious urgency, like that of an accomplice telegraphing a hopeless message.

"Thank you, then," she said. At the door she turned. "It's been a pleasure to have you here," she said. She went out, closing the door lightly and surely behind her, and Mrs. Pomeroy could hear her quick heels receding on the wet flagstones.

Mrs. Pomeroy went to the window. The clouds were tearing apart in rapid silence; a star, three stars appeared swinging toward her through thinning vapor. Then as the wind shook a small storm of raindrops from the heavy banana leaves, the whole golden configuration was framed again in her window.

Mrs. Pomeroy stood looking at it; and she remembered it. She had seen it from the ledge. It stood over the jungle, and contained it, as the jungle, wet and glittering in the dark breeze, contained tiny Lord Lion and beautiful Mrs. Heatherby, and the tentative future of her own body.

She could not remember her own anger or fear, though they were there, somewhere within her knowledge. She had understood the terrible components of joy. Alive, and breathing, Mrs. Pomeroy stood there in the wet soft air, looking into the darkness.

JOYCE CAROL OATES has written many short stories, poems and several novels, her most recent of which, *them*, won the National Book Award for Fiction in 1970. Her latest book, *The Wheel of Love*, is a collection of short stories several of which have appeared in earlier O. Henry Award volumes.

The Children

This is not really a story about children, or even about a marriage, though a marriage is at its center. It is not even a story about a "husband" and a "wife," for the two never thought of themselves in those terms. They were married in their mid-twenties; they had been doing chemical research, and the match was considered a sensible, attractive one. It had the flavor of graduate student romances—a premature camaraderie about it, difficult to explain. Consider Ronald and Ginny: serious and intelligent, a little nervous, uncertain of themselves, but very good people; in short a sensible, attractive match. The story is about the girl, Ginny, revealed to her through children. All her life she had been fascinated and a little frightened of children, and of the thought of having children of her own, as if she might somehow not be worthy of them.

When they married her career passed from her and left her relieved. Beneath her fastidiousness was a peculiar laziness, a desire to be left alone and to watch others. She liked to read, idly. She liked to listen to Ronald's ideas, it was perhaps her notion of marriage—the young wife listening to her husband quietly, agreeing with him, not allowing her mind to jump ahead in an attempt to outguess him. That sort of thing was over now that she was married. So her career passed away from her and her husband concentrated on his work, with enough energy for both of them. He soon moved beyond her, and this too was a kind of relief for her; she was finished with that sort of thing, the competition and the uneasiness.

While he was still at the university they had their first child, a girl. It had been a difficult pregnancy and Ginny felt a firm, stubborn satisfaction in the baby, which had caused her so much suffering. At that time they lived in a one-room apartment. She felt harassed and a little wild, with so much pressure upon her, so much work that had to be done—unlike her husband's work in the laboratory, which could wait. She thought of his life as infinitely easier than hers. She was anxious about the baby, always thinking about its future—what if it were retarded? What if she failed as a mother? She never really slept for months after the birth, lying in a daze of lukewarm sleep as if she were lying just below the surface of a body of water, waiting in suspense for something to happen. Many things happened but they were all minor. The "something" never happened.

Ronald said to her often, "You're an excellent mother. Where did you learn all these things?"

She blushed at this and could think of no reply. For they were not easy, open people, either of them. Ronald worked too hard, studied too much, stayed far too long in the laboratory. It was difficult to say whether he loved his work; he would have said that, himself. Instead, he seemed to be "in" his work all the time, never out of it. He thought about it all the time and it was colored by his mood, it never caused his mood. He had a reputation for being brilliant. He was twenty-seven when they married, a tall, thin, easily-embarrassed young man with a wedge-shaped face and hair that was already thinning; he looked at once older and younger than twenty-seven.

Ginny was as tall as he, the kind of intelligent, shapeless girl one often sees late in the afternoon in university buildings—dark-rimmed glasses, a distracted, vaguely startled look, intelligence marring her forehead with tiny heartbreaking lines. She was twenty-five but looked older, perhaps. She wore dark, quiet colors, and her feet were long and narrow and a source of embarrassment to her. Marriage welded her to a boy as serious as she, and his seriousness was a kind of drain for hers. After the marriage she let her hair grow out. She had worn it cut short for years, she was tired of that style. It was as if she were discovering girlhood, which she had scrupulously bypassed; she let her hair grow long, she put away her chemistry books and read the new, important books in sociology and psychology that all their friends read, and in a while she was pregnant.

They were both guiltily proud of what they had accomplished. It had nothing to do with their parents' pride—that was an embarrassment. It was instead a kind of secret, astonished pride in the discovery of themselves, in the discovery of their bodies. Ginny felt that her baby girl was an extension of her own body, an innocent being linked mysteriously to her and through her to Ronald, binding them all together. It was a mystery that bewildered her. She sometimes sat for hours staring into the crib, alone with the baby in their apartment. But of course she never thought of herself as alone. At these times her mind seemed to pass out of her and she had no "ideas" at all. She was baffled by the mystery of life, her having accomplished—what? She had passed over the boundary into another life, the world of adults who have secrets, who cannot be mastered. Was she now an adult? What had happened to her?

They were very happy together.

But beneath their enchantment they were still serious and intelligent, very intelligent. Ronald finished his studies and was offered a good job in a midwestern city. And they accepted this, too, eagerly, as a sign of their being adults—what did it matter if, at the very center of their being, there was a kind of doubt, of wonder? Ronald kept saying, pleased with himself and with everything, "She's going to bring us good luck." The "she" was Rachel; she was one year old when they moved.

They lived in an apartment for some time, and Ronald began his career. Ginny, left to herself and the baby, scuffed around in bedroom slippers, began to gain weight, took to standing at the window with the baby, in a kind of wistful happy daze. It was difficult for her to understand that she was an adult, that she was married and had a baby. Rachel seemed to her a delicate, exquisite creature—really an amazing creature. There were times when Ginny felt inert and ugly beside her own child, though of course this was nonsense. She liked to read stories to the child. Rachel, naturally, was advanced for her age. They believed she could distinguish between different types of music, preferring baroque. . . . It was one of their fables, but they took it seriously.

New acquaintances in this city congratulated them on their child. "It's such a relief to see a really pretty baby, not to have to lie about it," one girl told them. They were very pleased to hear this. Ronald was a fine person but he was not handsome, not at all; there was something gently perplexed about him, as if a thought were working its way to the surface of his mind, upsetting him. And Ginny with her thin, severe face, her rather lifeless hair . . . no, she had never been pretty, exactly. So it pleased them to have a child other people considered pretty.

They lived in that apartment for two years, and then Ronald was taken on by another company. He had an excellent salary now for a man of thirty. So they bought a house some distance out of the city, in a new subdivision called Fox Hollow.

"Because of the children," Ginny was going to say, when their acquaintances asked why they had moved so far out. The "children"—she was pregnant again and quite satisfied. She was proud of Rachel and of her husband and of the new house, and of her new pregnancy. Most of all, perhaps, she was proud of her satisfaction, for she was the kind of woman one might have thought terrified of childbirth: that long, lean, offended body, that overscrupulous gaze. . . . But if she was terrified she never allowed herself to think about it. She thought instead of how normal she was, of how she had crossed over into the world of adulthood and taken up greedily all its symbols, without hesitation. The house was another symbol. It was a colonial, rather box-like, "economical," located on an unpaved road called "Glen Lane."

They moved into the house in spring, and already the neighboring lots were being levelled. New houses were going up everywhere. All day long they heard the screech of trees being cut down, which upset Ronald but which Ginny accepted with a kind of ferocity as another sign of her being in the real world—not hiding in an apartment, afraid to grow up. She thought with scorn of their friends, childless and city-bred, who had not really considered this move to the suburbs wise. "But the suburbs?" The suburbs? they said. Ginny thought of them with scorn, pitying them.

One morning on her walk back from the mailboxes she

was absurdly pleased by this event: a young woman in a yellow sunsuit, whom she had often heard scolding her two boys, crossed the street to say hello to her. Ginny stopped and the two of them talked, with the rapid, gushing relief of young mothers who have located each other. "Just what do you think about that mud? Isn't that a *crime?*" the girl said. She had an animated, enthusiastic face, a faint odor of milk about her, and front teeth flecked with curious white spots. Her sunsuit was rather soiled. "My husband has an hour drive and he's pretty crabby on bad days—what about yours?"

"It takes him an hour too," Ginny said.

"I think they should pave these streets," said the girl. She spoke with the sort of delicious, rushed anger Ginny had often heard in the young mothers who met out on the sidewalk. One of her boys was tugging at her wrist, but she brushed him away without seeming to notice him. She smiled at Ginny and showed her big frank teeth, speckled with tiny cords of white. "Hey, my name is Louise! Louise Schultz!" she said, as if she had just thought of this.

"My name is Ginny. . . ."

It was absurd, to be pleased about this. Ginny seemed to move away from herself and watch in amazement the two young mothers chatting over their children's heads, animated and oddly pleased with themselves, as if intoxicated. What intoxicated them? They were sisters, they recognized each other. They were alike. It was good to complain like this, with such proud, self-righteous anger—about the mailboxes all in a group down at the road, and the mud puddle around them, and the unpaved lanes ("Spruce Way," "Willow Pass"), and their husbands' long drives into the city. "But of course this is the only place to live, with children," Ginny's new friend said. A patch of freckles on her cheeks and nose seemed to darken with the wisdom of this remark.

Their children made friends. One of Louise's boys was Rachel's age, exactly. The other boy was five. "Oh, they're lots of trouble, they're regular pests. Aren't you pests?" Louise cried happily at her boys.

The next day, Ginny met Louise and another girl, in a green sunsuit. They chatted. They chatted for two hours. Ginny once again seemed to hear them from a distance, marvelling at herself, at the way in which she agreed with these women and seemed a sister to them; it was all so strange! And when one of them said, "You know that was just a rumor about a nigger moving in?" Ginny not only showed no surprise but felt none. Some change worked upon her in the presence of these women.

She told Ronald that she had made some friends. "And Rachel has too. It's good for her to have someone to play with." Ronald thought this was good, but he did not ask much about Ginny's friends. Ginny resented this. Heavy and warm, she spent hours sitting out back on their "patio"—a nine-foot square slab of concrete, unshaded—watching Rachel play with her little friends, sipping coffee with Louise and the other girl. Sometimes she watched the children alone, happy to take care of the other mothers' children for them. She was anxious to see how Rachel talked to other children—she wanted to see if the girl was more popular than she, Ginny, had been as a child. She hoped desperately that this would be so. So she stayed home and watched them, slow, happy, lazy, her dark-rimmed glasses sliding slowly down her perspiring nose.

The children were so delicate—two girls and two boys—they played in the sandbox, they played with dolls and toy automobiles and shovels, they were marvelous creatures and Ginny felt that the other mothers did not know enough to appreciate them. Swollen with her second pregnancy she felt overcome by the mystery of birth, in a kind of trance with the very promise of physical suffering. The other women were too simple to understand this.

One day Ginny looked out her patio window to check on the children, and she saw an older boy with them. He was a stranger, about seven. He had thin, bony shoulders, and a small head, and his clothes were filthy. She saw him squat down in the midst of the smaller children and distend his mouth in a peculiar way, so that his tongue appeared between his teeth like an animal slyly peeking out. Ginny went to the door, trembling. "What do you want?" she said. The boy's head jerked up and he got to his feet, not frightened but cunning. He ran around the side of the house. "Who was that?" Ginny said.

One of Louise's boys said, "That's Goober"—or "Gomber"—a strange name Ginny could not make out. "Does he live around here?" she asked. The children seemed not to know, or not to understand.

But the boy returned that afternoon. Ginny actually saw him coming, through the living room window. She was frightened by the urgent, foolish shape of his head—it reminded her of an ant's head, set forward and slightly crooked on his neck—and by his filthy clothes, as if these were symbols she somehow recognized but did not want to admit. He ran around the house and, before she could get out there, he had trampled on the smaller children's toys. With a high inhuman shriek he ran around the other side of the house again. The children began to cry, terrified. Rachel cried convulsively, gasping for breath, and Ginny was filled with a terrible anguish. She knelt to embrace the child. "It's all right, darling. It's all right," she whispered. Sobs shook Rachel's body and Ginny was overcome by a sense of the child's vulnerability; it was a terrible thing for her to understand.

That week, Ronald had a fence installed around the house. "It was about time, really. Most of the other houses have fences," he said, trying to make little out of the incident. He was rather upset by Ginny's strange, fierce stare. She kept saying, "That little bastard, if that little bastard comes back here. . . ." and he heard in her voice a sound he'd never heard in it before.

It was a relief to him when the new baby was born. That birth was more trouble, even, than the first, and when Ginny returned it was as if she were coming to a new house, to a new family. She seemed more intense, concentrated upon herself more, very serious about her motherhood. She had a queenly air about her even when she was dressed in her old, sloppy clothes. What made her happy was the other mothers' attention turned upon her—they were so generous, so helpful! When she was recovered enough to go out she began to go to their houses for coffee, taking Rachel and the baby along. They all spent hours together, every day. These young mothers were not sloppy but they had no "pretensions," as they put it, and Ginny agreed. "There was one girl here was real pretentious, she had napkins and silver stuff—Christ! We all came in our shorts and she was dressed up, what a nut. They finally moved out," Louise said in her rush of chatty, amazed anger. Ginny felt very comfortable with them, like a new person. She seemed indeed to be a new person. She could almost feel her face grow slack, the very muscles in her body sagging with comfort. They all talked about such easy, simple things—they were going to vote Republican—they were all putting a little extra on their mortgage when they could afford it, "that really cuts down on the interest,"— they were interested in recipes, complaints about in-laws, their husbands' jobs. One day Thelma, who was a very short, plump girl with bleached hair, pointed out the front window and cried: "That's that Gower, look at him! I thought he was put away!"

They crowded around to look, and it was the boy who had run through Ginny's yard a few weeks ago. Ginny asked about him. She was told that he was a devil, wouldn't mind anyone, "mentally nuts if you ask me," and he was small for his age— he was almost ten. Ginny felt a stab of fear. "But can't his parents do anything about him?—for him?" she asked.

"Oh, they're nuts too," Thelma said in disgust.

"Not nuts *exactly*," Katie Farmalow said.

"Nuts is nuts, don't tell me," Thelma said. "That kid is going to kill somebody someday, and it hadn't better be my kid."

Ginny looked at her. "Are you serious about that?"

"Sure I'm serious."

"But—why would he do that?"

"Because he's nuts."

As time went on she noticed the other children, the small children, speaking of someone named "Bambah." They played noisily out back of her house, and she sometimes hid behind the patio door to listen to them. Now that Rachel was older she was less quiet. She was in excellent health. One day Ginny said, coming outside with the baby, "Who's this Bambah you're talking about?"

A little boy snickered. Rachel had to answer, since this woman was her mother. "Oh, nobody," she said.

"Is it a friend of yours?"

"Nobody, I guess."

"Somebody you made up? Did you make him up?"

"Nobody."

And another time, seeing a dead squirrel in the street as she drove home, she heard Rachel beside her blurt out with a a kind of shocked, astonished delight: "Bambah!"

"But what do you mean by that, honey?" Ginny asked.

"Oh, nothing."

"Who is Bambah? What's that?"

"Nothing."

So the children had a language of their own, and Ginny could not understand it.

She spent most of her time with the baby, of course. She fed him, and put him to bed, and while he napped she waited for him to wake again; and when he did not wake for several hours she woke him herself, a little impatiently. He was her best baby, her darling. She lifted him from the crib that had been Rachel's and carried him down into the kitchen and set him into the high chair. It was warm still and Rachel was playing outside, next door. When she paused she could hear the sound of the children playing, and Rachel's clear high laughter. It pleased her to think that Rachel could assert herself, as a child, while Ginny could not remember having had a self to assert until her marriage. It was strange, how that child had come from her and Ronald, and had a life now of her own, a nature that was totally her own.

Ginny liked to lift the baby in and out of the high chair, in and out of the crib. There was something about his warm squirming weight that pleased her. He was able to smile at his mother, knowing who she was. It was time to eat. She opened a jar of baby food, pressing it against her hip as she twisted the cap, and she noticed that on her bathrobe was a red stain from an earlier jar of baby food—beets. She fed the baby. Outside an automobile passed, older children on bicycles rode shouting by, but inside the house everything was under control. It was hers. It was comfortable and safe here, with the baby who could not yet speak, and she felt an odd disappointment when the feeding time was over. So close to this baby, as if she and the baby were somehow one person, she thought with a remote bewilderment about her other child and about her husband, as if uncertain of their relationship to her.

Rachel was a healthy girl with fair, curly hair, who liked to dart about like a delighted little animal. In fact, she looked always as if she were about to jump up and dash away and hide. She was so pretty! She sang little songs at the top of her voice, nonsense words and chants, she rocked from one side to the other so that the room shook, she was able to wrestle her father off-balance at times. She had too much energy, Ginny complained happily to the other mothers. She was so healthy, growing so well, she liked to eat and there was certainly no problem about getting food down her—but there was one problem, which she did not mention.

If she wasn't watched closely she would tease her baby brother. Ginny noticed her tickling him one day, much too roughly, and as a final parting gesture she jabbed her fingers into his stomach—that startled Ginny, who was not quite sure of what she had seen. This was important, a very important thing, so Ginny came to Rachel and said carefully, "Rachel? Why did you do that?" Rachel said she was sorry.

But still, she did it if she wasn't watched. It was a strange thing. Ginny never became angry but instead knelt down to look into Rachel's small flushed face. "Honey, you don't want to hurt Baby Brother, do you? He isn't big and strong like you."

Rachel looked guiltily at the floor.

"He's just a baby, so you should take care of him, shouldn't you?"

Rachel shook her head, yes.

And while there was no problem exactly about her eating, there was another problem at the supper table. Rachel jiggled the table while Ginny fed the baby, anything to get attention away from the baby and onto herself. She pounded with her little fists and laughed feverishly, especially when the baby drooled or spat out food. "Lookit the pig! Little piggy!" she cried. When they calmed her they felt how hot her skin was, really hot to the touch. She sometimes distorted her face and rolled her eyes crazily, to make them laugh; this was a trick she had picked up from that boy Gower. Ginny was a little alarmed to see the real violence, the intense, crazy violence Rachel showed, just in screwing up her own face like that and rolling her eyes. It was as if she were trying to break her face into pieces, or trying to break by some confused magic the face of the baby who was gaping at her.

This sign of an outside force, some demented force of disorder and brutality, frightened Ginny. She remembered the small children playing and the boy Gower trampling their toys, ruining the peace of that summer afternoon with no fear, no regret, hardly any effort. . . . It was so very vulnerable, so very easily ruined. And she had no idea what she could do about it.

But the time just before bed was the nicest time: they had special little games involving pieces of furniture, a game invented by Rachel and Ronald. At these times Rachel showed a delicate, feverish joy of life that Ginny loved, and there was no sign of any outside world; nothing but their own world. When Rachel ran from one piece of furniture to another, in a hectic game, Ginny watched the little girl closely and thought that she did love her. She loved her very much. And yet her mind detached itself from the cramped living room, moving spaciously into the distance. She seemed at such times to be awaiting a certain understanding of herself. What were these children, after all, but a part of herself? And yet the understanding did not come. Surely some vision lay at the very center of her life . . . ? She summoned up intelligently the differences that lay between her and the woman she had become, this rather slovenly mother with nondescript hair and a fretful, maternal frown, a husband who never quite looked at her and did not need to look at her. Yes, there was a difference. It seemed to her that everyone else moved without defenses and without disguise, while she was never quite herself, always harassed or taken off guard.

Rachel lay on her back one night and shrieked with laughter, kicking the floor with her heels. Ginny said, "Rachel, be quiet!" because the baby was upstairs, sleeping. Rachel paid no attention; she simply did not hear her. "The baby is trying to sleep," Ginny said helplessly.

"I don't like him," Rachel said.

"What, you what?" Ronald cried, in mock surprise, not seeing or not caring to see that Rachel was serious, and he scooped her up in his arms and swung her up toward the ceiling. . . .

It was in such ways that she was taken off guard; she was never really herself. What would her real self have said to that flushed, spiteful child?

At another time Rachel said, close to tears because of some mishap: "You're a bad mommy and I hate you."

"Well, that's too bad."

"You're a bad mommy."

"You're a bad little girl."

"No, I'm not," Rachel said loudly. She was sucking her thumb because she knew Ginny disliked this. "But you are too a bad mommy."

"Who says so, you?"

Ginny was trying to keep her anger and nervousness down, wiping the counter in her kitchen.

"Reeny's mother says so. She says so."

Reeny's mother was Thelma. "Reeny's mother does not say so," Ginny said.

"She does too. Says you're a bad mother."

Ginny made a derisive snorting noise and did not reply. But Rachel's use of the word "mother" was strange, for it was a word Rachel did not ordinarily use. Ginny kept on wiping the counter, busy. She felt so weak, so strangely vulnerable herself, that it occurred to her suddenly that a life of this kind was no good, not worth living. How could she endure being always open to hurt? Like the children themselves, she was open to any sudden attack, any spurt of senseless aggression, and she could not defend herself. . . .

But in the next instant Rachel no longer "hated" her; she loved her Mommy, yes, it was all forgotten. And it was truly forgotten. Ginny read her a story, Rachel clambered up onto her lap, the whole strange incident passed away.

Ginny thought of her life in two parts: she had been a girl, and now she was a woman. Her identity, when it did not detach itself from her, was confused with the two children, meshed in with their two quite different personalities. She liked to spend time with them, alone with them. She really did like the rainy days when Rachel had to stay inside, despite Rachel's fretfulness, and she felt a violent dislike for the mothers who suggested that all the children get together in someone's house. "They get in my hair, these two," Louise complained, "couldn't we herd them all together somewhere?" This was over the telephone and so Ginny could keep Rachel from hearing. The little girl always tugged at her skirt when she talked on the phone, as if certain that the message was really for her and Ginny was keeping it from her. But Ginny said, "Not today, Louise. It's a good idea, though." So she stayed with them, close to the baby as if guarding him, and her life was certainly

united with theirs. And yet there had been another life, before
these children. She could not quite remember it. Had she ever
been a child, herself? For some reason it frightened her to
think so.

Because there was so much danger in that world: consider
the Farmalow boy. With a toy rake he had scratched the face
of Thelma's littlest girl, in a scuffle over someone's tricycle. It
had happened suddenly, though Thelma had been nearby,
and who could have prevented it? Everyone said, "What if
it had been her eye . . . ?" And the Farmalow boy was forbid-
den to play with their children, and nothing Katie Farmalow
could do would change their minds. "He's as bad as Gower,"
Louise said angrily.

Gower was still with them, too. Ginny met his mother one
day in the supermarket, by accident. They met in the baby
food aisle and could hardly have avoided each other, though
the other woman was slouched over her shopping cart as if she
needed it to support her. She was peering at the labels with a
scrupulous, exaggerated concern, knowing that Ginny had seen
her. Though they had never been introduced they knew each
other, everyone knew one another. "Hello," said Ginny. "Hello,"
said the woman. Ginny understood bitterly that while she and
her husband had bought a house well within their income,
everyone else in Fox Hollow had mortgaged and borrowed
themselves to the limit, to buy houses they could not really
afford. That was the kind of people Ginny and Ronald were
neighbors with.

The woman was in her mid-thirties. She had a seedy, slightly
criminal, apologetic look, not just because of her clothes—pink
pedal pushers and a too-sheer blouse—but because of her face
and body themselves. Her eyes protruded slightly, as if forced
out of her skull by some profound mysterious pressure inside.
Her lips did not quite close. Her body was thin and alert, her
shoulders terribly slouched.

She and Ginny passed each other politely. But then, in order
to avoid another encounter, both skipped the next aisle and
started down the cereal aisle, Ginny at one end and the
woman at the other. So of course they could not back out again.

This time they stopped to chat, it was the only thing to do.
The woman was chewing gum. A little girl appeared alongside

her, whining, "Mummy, Mummy," but did not expect to be noticed. The girl had come out of nowhere. As they talked this little girl gaped up at Ginny, and Ginny felt a cold sensation of revulsion. She forced herself to pay attention to the woman's chatter: "I saw your little girl and she's real cute, wish this one had hair like that. . . ." "So I said, I know he's bad but I can't help it. How can I help it? Little Gower was always like that, he always had so much energy. I know he's bad," she said, turning the palm of one hand up in a frank gesture. "The principal said he'd have to stay home, but I said don't we pay taxes? Anyway, how can I help it, I said—how can I help it?"

"I don't know," Ginny said uneasily.

"I mean, what can I do about it? Kill him?" The woman was leaning over her shopping cart again, staring earnestly into Ginny's face. Ginny could smell the oddly fresh, fruity odor of her gum. The woman's eyes were yellowish and unclear, the irises looked enlarged. "He's just got a mind of his own," she said.

Ginny said slowly, "I heard he pushed a little boy out into the road. That could be dangerous."

"Oh, I know, I know," the woman said at once, "I know that. And he did something in someone's house—I don't know them. He did something nasty in there, right on the rug. Everybody tells me. But what can I do about it? He always had a mind of his own, right in the crib."

On television that evening there was a news photograph of a man injured in a gunfight with police, and Rachel blurted out: "Bambah!" Ronald said, "What was that?" but Rachel wouldn't tell. She chortled secretively, quite pleased.

"Oh, she won't tell. She never tells," Ginny said, making light of it. "It's just something she made up."

"It is not," Rachel said.

"What is it, then, Honey?" said Ronald.

It irritated Ginny to see how Rachel preferred her father, but she never let this irritation show. Rachel said in a high, lilting voice, "That's what he's gonna do."

"Who?"

"Bwa-wah," she said. It was baby talk of some kind.

"Who is that?" said Ronald.

"Bow-wah."

Ginny, across the room from them, said suddenly: "Gower?"

Rachel laughed. She shook her head and would not answer.

"Are you talking about Gower? What about him?" Ginny said.

Rachel giggled but would not answer.

"Is that the boy who's always in trouble?" Ronald said.

Ginny and Rachel ignored him, he was so foolish, far from their own world! "Did Gower do something bad?" Ginny said.

"I don't know."

"What did he do?"

"I don't know."

"Did he kill something?"

Silence. Rachel stared at a spot on the floor, her cheeks flushed.

"Did he kill an animal, or what?"

Ronald interrupted uneasily, saying, "Ginny, really—"

"This is none of your business, Ronald," Ginny said.

"It certainly is my business. You're frightening her."

"I'm not frightening her!" Ginny cried. She wanted to laugh, he was so stupid. Imagine looking at that flushed, pleased face and thinking the child was afraid! "Rachel, tell me what it means. Did Gower kill something? Is he going to kill something —what is it?"

"I don't know."

"Rachel, you'd better tell me."

"No, it's a secrud."

"What do you mean, a secret?"

"We can't—we're not spost to—" She fell silent and the corners of her damp little mouth turned up, as if by themselves. "It's a secrud."

"Rachel, come over here."

"No. I don't like you."

"Rachel—"

"I don't like you. You're a bad mommy."

And so Ginny had to let her go, could not push in any further. The blood pulsed violently in her body. She felt as if she were in the presence of a terrible danger, almost a kind of corruption. It was as if the boy, Gower, were in the room with them.

That night Ronald tried to console her but she said slowly, "You don't understand. You don't know what it means." And

Rachel, the next morning, flew about the house impatiently because it was drizzling, as if she could not bear to stay cooped up with her mother and baby brother: she was such a healthy, busy child! Ginny wondered why it was so hard for her now, to love her daughter. Why couldn't she love her? Rachel must have guessed. She came over to where mother and infant sat, on the sofa, and rocked from side to side in imitation of something, and rolled her eyes wildly in her head, and made a high, ear-splitting noise. "Don't scare Baby Brother, now," Ginny said. In immediate response to this Rachel's fist jerked out and she struck the baby on the chest.

It was a hard, sharp blow, and the baby gasped at once and began to bellow.

"What did you do? What did you do?" Ginny cried.

She was shaking, she could not control herself. She banished Rachel upstairs, to bed. Muttering, she held the baby in her arms and tried to calm it, to restore that sleepy blank contentment; the room was now pierced with the baby's screams. Her brain throbbed with this sound and with a rage she could hardly understand. The word "Bambah, Bambah," kept running through her mind.

When the weather cleared that afternoon she let Rachel out. The child was sleepy with having cried so long, her eyes reddened, her playsuit soiled. She stared up at Ginny, shyly. Ginny moved in a kind of trance, hardly seeing her. "Go outside and play. Go outside now," Ginny said. Rachel waited, waiting to be told to play in the back yard, or next door, or waiting to be scolded again; but Ginny said nothing. She was holding the baby, on her way to the bedroom. She seemed hardly to notice Rachel.

When the baby slept that afternoon Ginny slept with him. Rachel had gone and they were alone, she had pulled the crib up beside the bed. She slept heavily. She had a confusing dream, a nightmare, about a pack of wild dogs breaking loose upon her and her children . . . barking, yipping, the wild dogs rushed upon them and tore Rachel from her arms, and were about to seize the baby when Ginny woke, terrified. The dream had been so real that she could not get the terror out of her for some minutes.

But the baby slept peacefully in his crib. Outside, a dog was barking. It had a forlorn furious bark. Ginny got up and at once her head ached; it was as if the dream she had had was somehow still present in her brain. The dream pained her. She felt overwhelmed with a terrible burden, a kind of guilt. Another dog joined in and the two yipped, whined, barked sharply at each other. . . . Ginny went downstairs to make dinner. She opened cans and dumped their contents into a casserole dish, wearing her bathrobe, groggy and apprehensive. She heard a siren in the distance. The noise meant nothing to her, where once it would have signalled danger—for Rachel was still outside—but there were so many noises in the neighborhood, too many noises. No one could hear them all. Dogs, chain-saws, automobiles, children. . . . She realized groggily that Rachel had not come back yet, and in a minute she would go to the door and call. Her head ached under the pressure of that mysterious dream.

It was about five-thirty when Rachel returned, by herself. She was very dirty. She creeped in around the screen door and said, "Mommy?" Ginny looked at her. "Mommy it's nice out now," the little girl said. She had a sweet, clear voice. Her eyes were very blue and her hair light, almost blond. Ginny stared at her and felt the same feeling, sudden and unmistakable, that she had felt about the little girl in the supermarket. She stared. "It isn't wet out now, it's nice," Rachel said, rubbing her hands together to get the mud off, awkward and fetching. Ginny understood that the child had secrets, terrible secrets. The children had a language of their own and secrets of their own. Once they had played near her, with no secrets, but now they ran like wild creatures down the block and through everyone's front lawns, screeching and stopping for nothing, just like wild creatures.

"You wanted to hurt your brother," Ginny said suddenly. "What, Mommy?"

She stared down at Rachel, half-turned from the stove. The sun in the west was dazzling in this part of the house. It was somehow mixed up with her vision of Rachel, of the terrible secrets the girl had and of the hurt she had wanted to do to her brother. A nerve moved frantically in Ginny's brain and she reached out for Rachel, who instinctively leapt back. But Ginny grabbed her and began spanking her. She

woke up, now, to this spanking; she had not really been awake
before. Rachel cried at once, exaggerating her surprise and
pain. How she cried! It was terrible to hear her cry, and
maddening, because it was so exaggerated. Ginny pulled down
the little girl's panties to spank her harder. Rachel pushed at
her mother. Ginny, grunting, bending over her, wrestled with
the strong, furious little body, and, to keep it still, began
striking her anywhere—on her back, her chest, her shoulders.
The girl's body was so delicate. She could feel her bones
beneath her skin, fine delicate bones that were an outrage to
Ginny, so perfect were they, so finely structured to last that
lifetime, a lifetime that had taken itself out of Ginny and would
run and run away from her and never come back, stinking
with the mud of great distances and beyond all the range of
Ginny's voice. "A bad girl, you're a bad girl!" she cried. Rachel
screeched; the sound was shrill and crazy, an animal's sound.
She was like a crazed little animal twisting and jerking in her
mother's embrace.

"A bad girl! A bad girl!"

Ginny reached around blindly, into the dazzling sunshine,
and took something from the counter—a big metal spoon with
a wooden handle. She beat the child with this, she could
swing it with great strength and rapidity, every instant waking
to what she was doing, shaking off the lethargy of sleep; the
very feel of the handle encouraged her, sending strange waves
of strength up into her arm. She screamed, "A bad girl! A
bad girl!" Then time must have jumped, or perhaps did not
jump at all, and her husband was in the kitchen trying to
stop her. He was a terrified man with glasses, still holding
a newspaper. He snatched the bloody spoon from her and with
a groan of hatred she pushed him away, both hands against
his chest. She cried impatiently, as if speaking to a child,
"Oh, *you* don't know! What do *you* know about it? What do
you know?"

ELDRIDGE CLEAVER, the author of *Soul on Ice*, is at present living in Algiers.

The Flashlight

From each obstacle encountered and conquered, Stacy sapped fresh strength with which to confront the next; and from that next conquest, his depleted drive was again restored and poised to meet the latest oncoming task. Life to him was an endless series of regularly spaced hurdles he had to leap over. This was the form of his imagination—not that he was in any big hurry to reach some particular goal in life. But life was motion and motion required a direction and Stacy was young and saw the years stretched out before him as he sprinted down the track of his days. He hated dead ends and stagnation and wanted always to see ahead ample room for maneuver. He thought of himself as having no fear, as a strong, rough cat who would become even more so, because in the world he knew, strength seemed to have the edge.

He was lord of his gang and his word was law. He was light and quick on his feet, and a fierce, turbulent spirit drove him on, like a dynamo imprisoned in the blood, flesh and bone of his body. He set the pace. It was not that his gang did only the things Stacy did best but that everything they did he seemed to do better. The others deferred to him as though he were a prince among them, with mysterious powers of a higher caliber than theirs, as if somehow he was born with a built-in gun and they with built-in knives. They did not question or resent this. To them, it was life, nature. They were glad to have Stacy as one of their own and they followed his lead.

Stacy was conscious of the role he played, but he did not prance before the grandstands. It could be said that he was humble in his way and bowed low before the others even as he bullied them about, because there was always absent from this bullying that ultimate hostility of which they all knew he was so capable when up against cats from other neighborhoods. Among them, there was knowledge of each other, the thick glue of the brotherhood of youth, of their separate selves bound into one. If Stacy made a decision, it was only the summation of their interests as a whole, because as far as they wanted anything, they all wanted the same things. He was the repository of their youthful collective sovereignty. Perhaps, then, it is incorrect to say that Stacy's word was law. Their law was that of a roving band owing allegiance to itself alone. Stacy occupied his peculiar place among them precisely because he knew the restraints and sanctions implicit in the mechanics and spirit of a functioning gang. Had he been less skillful in his choices, less willing to risk all on the curve of his instincts, it would have been their loss as much as his. Together they formed a unit, clinging to one another for support. What he had he gave to them and the others did the same. There was nothing premeditated about it. It just happened that Stacy had the power of the endearing smile, the rebuking frown, the assenting nod, the admonitory shake of the head.

Of late, however, Stacy was growing friendlily disgusted with the others, primarily because they seemed content to continue in the same rut. He was beginning to feel miserably trapped and hemmed in by the thick futility of the very things he had loved and pursued with satisfaction and a sense of fulfillment. Only a few weeks ago, he could still draw delight and deep contentment from the raids they threw on El Serrano, from kicking in a window and ransacking a store, from stripping the hubcaps, wheels and accessories from cars, from stealing the clothing from clotheslines or from breaking into a restaurant or café after it had closed and eating up as much food as they could hold in their guts and taking away with them all they could carry. These things no longer filled him with a warm glow after they were all over; rather, he would feel dejected and somehow disappointed in himself and the others, as if it all had been a big waste of time. When he went on a raid now, it was only because he knew the others depended upon him and that they would be angry and confused if he refused to go with them. Besides, he did not have anything else in mind to do, and he was not the type to enjoy doing nothing.

Stacy liked the money and the extra clothes that thievery brought him, but he was burned out on the ritual of these raids. As far back as he could remember, they had been a part of his life, and he knew from neighborhood lore that the practice of the raids existed as a tradition in Crescent Heights long before he or the others came along. It seemed natural for the youth of Crescent Heights to steal whatever they could from the white people of El Serrano. At this time in Stacy's life, Crescent Heights was separated from El Serrano by two miles of unimproved vacant lots that ran up to the top of a hill, so that from Crescent Heights, El Serrano could not even be seen. The long slope of the hill was a wall between the Negroes and Mexicans who lived in Crescent Heights and the whites of El Serrano.

On a clear night, the lights of El Serrano could be seen against the sky from Crescent Heights; but from El Serrano, the sky over Crescent Heights looked black and unbroken, even by the moon and stars. Stacy was fascinated by this contrast. Many times, either when setting out on a raid or on his way back, Stacy would pause at the top of the hill and brood over it. The darkness in which Crescent Heights was wrapped seemed familiar and safe to him, warm and protecting, while the lights of El Serrano held both a fascination and a terror for him. He was principally aware of the lights because they were central to the ritual of the raids. It was a maxim to his gang that "where there is light there is wealth." They often repeated this to each other when searching through El Serrano for things to steal.

Each neighborhood had its own school. The police station and fire department servicing both areas were located in El

Serrano. El Serrano was a thriving community with a frisky business section, while Crescent Heights was a residential slum devoid of any business except for a few corner grocery stores, liquor stores, gas stations and beer joints.

The only swimming pool and motion-picture theater in the region were in El Serrano, and during the summer, the kids from Crescent Heights hiked over the steep hill, paid their money and went in for a swim. On Saturday and Sunday, they'd go to the movies and, on their way home, fan out through El Serrano, looking for loot. By bedtime, the wealth of Crescent Heights was certain to have increased in proportion to a corresponding decrease in that of El Serrano's. Stacy's gang not only picked up things on the way back from the swimming pool or movies but two or three times each week, they'd wait for nightfall and then trek over the hill to throw a raid.

All this seemed so futile to Stacy now. He could feel that a change had to be made—just what, he could not tell. But he knew that something would happen and a way would open up for him. In the meantime, he continued to lead the raids and, although he would be just as systematic and cautious as ever, it was no longer a pleasure. It was a task.

Stacy loved Crescent Heights. He did not feel comfortable or secure anywhere else. When he ventured out of the neighborhood, on infrequent trips downtown or to the East Side or to Watts, he was always relieved when the trip was over and he was back among the familiar sights and sounds of Crescent Heights. Even school was still far enough away from his part of Crescent Heights that he felt alien and uncomfortable until he was away from the school and back on his own stamping grounds. He hated the teachers at Crescent Heights School for their way of talking down to the Negro and Mexican students and the superior attitude he saw reflected in them. He hated most of all the discipline they imposed upon him, the authority they tried to assert over him, to which they wanted him willingly to submit but which he resisted and rebelled against. The school seemed to him more like a prison than a school, the teachers seemed more like custodial guards than instructors and the atmosphere seemed more like that of a battlefield than of a place of learning. Stacy never got into fights with the teachers, as some of the others did, but he let it be known that if any of the teachers ever hit him—if the boys' vice-principal, for example, ever took him into his office and tried to force him to bend over and look at the rainbow colors drawn on the lower part of the wall, while the v.p. swatted him on his ass with his huge perforated paddle, as he did some of the others—there would be blood. Understanding this, the teachers would turn their heads from certain infractions when committed by Stacy, while they would pounce on other students for precisely the same transgressions. Sometimes, in the dreams of his heart, Stacy longed for one of the teachers to lay a hand on him, so that he could work him over. In his mind, he saw himself grabbing a teacher and beating him down to a bloody pulp. The teachers, sensing something of this desire in him, left him alone.

Stacy loved the freedom he found in Crescent Heights. He felt he was losing it each time he set foot on the school grounds. It was not that he found the schoolwork difficult—he found it easy and was quick to catch on—but the whole situation repelled him. He felt that books and the knowledge in them were part of a world that was against him, a world to which he did not belong and which he did not want to enter, the world of which the hateful teachers were representatives and symbols. After school each day, it took several blocks of walking before he was free of its field of force. Then he blossomed, felt himself. His pace quickened and became his own again.

Stacy's loyalty went to Crescent Heights. To him, his neighborhood was the center of the world. Isolated somewhat from the rest of Los Angeles, in the way that each part of that scattered metropolis is isolated from every other, Crescent Heights was a refuge. If Stacy had been captured by beings from another planet, who cast him into a prison filled with inhabitants from all the planets, and if he were asked by the others where he lived, he would have said:

"I'm Stacy Mims from Crescent Heights."

"Crescent Heights?" they would ask, puzzled.

"Oh," Stacy would remember, "Crescent Heights is the name

of my neighborhood. I'm from Planet Earth. Crescent Heights is on Earth. It's in the United States of America, in the state of California."

The nucleus of the neighborhood was the Crescent Heights housing project, a low-rent complex of 100 units, laid out in long rows. They looked like two-story elongated boxcars painted a pale yellow or a weak pink, the colors alternating row by row. At the center of the project was the administration building and in back of it was a large playground. Behind the playground was a huge incinerator with a chimney that towered high above the buildings of Crescent Heights. Tenants from all over the project brought their trash to the incinerator to burn. The project sat down in sort of a valley formed by hills on three sides, with the fourth side wide open and leading down to Los Angeles. All traffic entered Crescent Heights through this side. As one traveled farther up into the valley, the streets ran out of pavement and asphalt and became dirt roads. The dirt roads turned into well-worn footpaths; the paths tapered into intermittent trails; the trails evaporated into the rolling hills, which the people of Crescent Heights regarded with a peculiar love. And while the county of Los Angeles had built the housing project with its drawn-to-scale playground laid out scientifically—basketball court here, volleyball court there, horseshoe pits here, swings there, slide over there, monkey bars and ladder here, tetherball there, hopscotch here—Stacy's playground and that of the members of his gang had always been the hills of Crescent Heights.

Scattered throughout the hills surrounding the project were the ramshackle houses of the old families, the houses Stacy and his gang grew up in. There was a subtle distinction between the old families, who lived in the hills, and the inhabitants of the project. It was not that the houses in the hills had been there long years before the project; there had been similar houses on the site where the project now stood. The owners of those houses had been evicted by the county and state authorities after a bitter fight, which was lost by the homeowners before it ever began. The memory of it was still fresh, and there was a lingering undercurrent of resentment at this encroachment. The project itself was a symbol of the forces that

had gutted the old neighborhood against the will and desire
of the people, breaking up lifelong friendships and alliances,
demolishing the familiar environment and substituting a new
one. Although this prejudice was not as strong as in former
times, it lingered on in the lore of the people.

The major point of difference was that most of the inhabitants of the project were women with small children, women
who had not grown up in Crescent Heights but who had come
there from other areas of Los Angeles, whose ties were with
friends and relations who were strangers to the people who
had lived in Crescent Heights all their lives. The names of
these women had popped up on the Housing Authority's long
waiting list downtown and, eager to get the apartment for
which they might have been waiting for a year or more,
they accepted a vacancy in Crescent Heights, sight unseen.
These were unwed mothers on state aid, divorcees, women
who had been abandoned by their men and the waiting wives,
living on allotment checks, of Servicemen stationed always
somewhere far away. The turnover was rapid among residents
of the project; someone always seemed to be moving in or
out. But no one ever moved out of the surrounding hills.
There, whole families lived. Most of them, like Stacy's family,
owned the little plots of ground on which they lived.

After school each day, and after they had eaten their evening
meals and performed whatever chores they had to do, Stacy's
gang used to meet at the playground in the project, pouring
down from the hills, drawn there like moths to a light. On
weekends and holidays, they usually hiked deep into the hills.
They would take along their slingshots to shoot at the doves,
pigeons and quail, which were plentiful in those hills. Sometimes they would return home in the evening with fowl for
their mothers to cook. Or they would give the birds to women
in the project, who always received them gladly, sometimes
giving the boys some small change in return. In season, they
would collect wild walnuts from the trees, and there were wild
peaches, apricots, pears, figs, loquats and quince. Wild berries
grew in patches here and there. Old Mexican men plowed
sections of the hills and sowed them with corn, squash and
sugar cane. There was always plenty for all who took the

trouble to help themselves. Stacy and the others would some-times harvest large quantities of this corn and sell it to the women of the project.

Those hills were the soul of Crescent Heights. Old-timers spun out legends concerning them. They told how somewhere in those hills was hidden an ancient Indian burial ground and that the graves were filled with priceless treasures. There was gold, intricately worked by artisans and set with splendid jewels, goblets encrusted with precious stones. The old-timers would talk and the youngsters would listen. A curse would fall on anyone who went looking for the treasures; to reach them, one had to disturb the sleep of the dead. It was said that many people had gone into those hills and were never seen or heard from again. Under this ominous cloud, Stacy and the others would test their courage by roaming deep into the hills, their eyes peeled for signs of an Indian grave, half expecting to be pounced upon by supernatural guardians of the dead, deliciously savoring the sweet taste of fear defied. With a gentle breeze waving the tall grass, they walked barefooted under the sun, drawing strength from each kiss of the soil on the soles of their feet.

Once in a while, shepherds from out of nowhere would appear, bringing huge herds of sheep to pasture and graze there for a few months. From his house, Stacy sometimes looked out to see the dark, undulating mass of shaggy creatures sweep-ing in a rolling wave across the hills, the bells tinkling round the necks of the leaders and the sheep dogs running back and forth, keeping the strays in line. The shepherds would be seen with long sticks, trudging along with their flocks. It always reminded Stacy of scenes from the Bible. Only the style of clothes had changed.

During summer, when the grass on the hills dried out, some-times it would catch on fire, by the working of the sun through the prism of a broken wine bottle. Sometimes Stacy and the others grew impatient with the sun and would, out of sight of everyone, toss a match or two and wait for the fire trucks to come racing over from El Serrano. They would hear the sirens screaming in the distance, listening tensely as they came closer and closer, until finally the huge red engines would swing into sight and the firemen would go into action. With guilty knowledge or not, Stacy and the others would watch the firemen and sometimes would even help them. Sometimes to avoid inconvenient surprises and possible disasters, the county would send out crews and deliberately set a fire and control it, burning all the grass near the houses and back for about a mile into the hills as a safety measure. The whole neighborhood would turn out to watch a fire, to see the flames walk across those hills, leaving a black sheet of ash in its wake. It was always something of a shock to Stacy to see those hills transformed in an instant from tall grass to burned-out cinders. Black and barren, the hills were no good for walking barefooted, and there was no hope of finding any fowl concealed in a clump of grass. The youngsters of Crescent Heights did not enjoy the hills when the grass had burned. Fortunately for them, the fires never succeeded in burning all the grass, and they could always go deep into the hills until they found a point to which the flames had not penetrated.

One time the hills were so burned out that the gang had to hike a long way before reaching the green grass. Mitch, characteristically, set the grass on fire to spoil their day. Helplessly, Stacy and the others watched as the fowl took to the air. Turning on Mitch, they punched and kicked him until he cried. Stacy did not tell them to stop. Mitch was mean as a dog. From him, the others learned early that a human being is full of surprises and capable of evil improvisations.

Mitch was full of peevish taciturnity. He was sullen and vicious. The others watched him, waiting for each new manifestation of his scurviness. Many times, Stacy had sat mystified in Mitch's back yard and listened with astonishment as he cursed out his mother. He would hurl at her the most vile names, in English and Spanish and combinations of both languages, and his mother, who seemed not at all surprised or shocked, would never raise her voice. She would ask him, in very gentle tones, how he could talk to his own mother that way, inspiring an infuriated Mitch to a new torrent of epithets. She would stand there, at the top of the stairs, gently, calmly drying her hands on her apron, waiting for him to finish, never interrupting him. If she had started to speak and he cut her off, she would stop in midsentence, half apologetically, and let him finish; then she would start again, very slowly, cautiously, kindly.

"I'm your own mother," she would say to him in Spanish, or: "Come inside and talk to me, son; you can bring Stacy with you, too, if you like."

Mitch would only curse her more.

After a while, Stacy, unable to stand it longer, would make Mitch come away with him. Stacy liked Mitch's mother. He saw her as a sweet old woman who always gave the neighborhood kids little Mexican goodies to eat, which she made up and kept on hand for when they came around. Big and fat, she went to Mass every Sunday morning, rain or shine, with a black shawl over her head and shoulders, her small children trailing behind her. These small children were one of the mysteries of Crescent Heights and the subject of endless rumors. Mrs. Chapultapec had children who were over 40 years old, while Mitch was 14. There were always new children being added to the household. Around the yard, they followed her like tiny shadows. Nobody seemed to know just which of the children were her own or, in fact, if any of them were actually hers. If asked, she would only smile and say that all the children in the world were her own, and refuse to discuss it further. The older people understood that she had had, all her life, a great love and tenderness for children, and she would take in anybody's unwanted child and raise him as her own. Nobody knew how many children she had actually raised. Some she would keep for a few years, then their parents would come and take them back. At the bottom of Mitch's rage lay the fact that he did not know who his parents were, because he did not believe anything Mrs. Chapultapec told him.

Once, a new little face showed up in the house, and it so happened that Mitch knew that the little boy belonged to one of the women who lived in the project. Overhearing Mrs. Chapultapec telling someone, in her way, that the little boy was her own, Mitch was suddenly blasted by a vision that Mrs. Chapultapec was not really his own mother and that he did not know who his real mother was. When he asked Mrs. Chapultapec about it, she just told him that he was her very own. He accused her of being a notorious liar.

Mitch used to threaten to kill his father, or, rather, Mr.

Chapultapec, whom Mitch always had believed to be his father but whom he later "disowned." A small, stooped, white-haired old man with quick, birdlike movements, he would never scold or correct the children. He was terrified of them. He would go straight to work and come straight home in the evening, except on Friday evening, when he would stop off at the Cozy Corner Café, down a few beers with the old-timers and listen to a few Spanish records on the jukebox. Tipsy from the beers, his spirits charged from the music and the few moments spent in the company of the gents he had known all his life, he would walk crisply home, speaking to all he met.

"*Buenas noches, Señor Chapultapec,*" Stacy and the others would say to him on Friday evenings.

"*Salud, muchachos,*" he'd answer with extreme good feeling.

If Mitch was there, he would hurl a curse at the old man, who would cast a frightened look Mitch's way and continue on without a pause.

On Sunday evenings, Mr. Chapultapec could be found down at the Catholic church across the street from the project, sitting in the little area set aside for *fiestas,* sanctioned by the Church, which were held several times each year. There were booths set up where bingo was played; where darts three for a dime were tossed at balloons to win a Kewpie doll or a piggy bank; where washing machines and sets of silverware were raffled off; where kids, their eyes blindfolded, took turns trying to burst the *piñata* with a stick, then scrambled over the ground to retrieve the prizes that had been inside. At *fiesta* time, the whole neighborhood would turn out, drop by the church to look, to be seen, to participate. And although the church belonged more to the people of the hills than to those of the project —most of whom seemed to be Protestants or atheists or people who did not belong to anything—they, too, came round.

But on these Sunday evenings, the churchyard would be quiet; and while Mr. Chapultapec sat outside with one or two old men, watching the cars going up and down Mercury Avenue, watching the people passing by, Mrs. Chapultapec would be in the little kitchen in the back of the church with four or five other old women. They would make *tacos, tamales, burritos* and chili with fried beans, which they sold over a counter through a slitted window, like tellers in banks. The customers would mostly take their purchases with them to eat from paper napkins like hot dogs; but if they chose, as often happened if a fellow had a girl with him, they spread their orders on a table in the yard and enjoyed the serene atmosphere. Stacy could recall that when he was very little, he and the others would go to the window and the old women would give them a *taco* or a *tamale* free, with a kind word and a smile. After he was older and had the money, Stacy would still drop by Sunday evenings to purchase these warm goodies. He loved these old women and their quiet Mexican dignity. They asked no questions and condemned no one and seemed always to have their inner eyes fixed on a distant star.

It was from these old ladies that Stacy first heard the legend of the *Llorona*. He had been younger and the story fascinated him. In the long, long ago, the old women had said, in a small village deep in old Mexico, a wicked woman murdered her three children in a jealous rage, to get revenge on her unfaithful husband, who had run off with a beautiful *señorita*. She hid their tiny bodies so well that even she could not find where she had hidden them. Sometime later, an angel from God visited her to deliver a divine sentence. Until she found the bodies of her children and took them to the priest for a proper burial, she would know no peace. The wicked woman searched all over but could never find her little ones. Her doom was to wander the world over—in vain!—searching for her lost *niños*. When the wind, blowing down from the hills, whistled through the trees, or when a coyote or a dog howled mournfully, or when there was any other strange noise in the night, it was said to be the *Llorona* crying for her lost *niños* and for mercy from God. The mothers of Crescent Heights kept their kids in line by saying that if they were bad, the *Llorona* would come carry them away. That was why, when Mitch cursed Mrs. Chapultapec, sometimes he would put in, "Fuck the *Llorona* up her ass!" At this, Stacy would feel a chill down his back. One day, Mitch screamed at Mrs. Chapultapec:

"You're the *Llorona!*"

Stacy's would be the last generation to grow up in the old Crescent Heights, the Crescent Heights of the hills. They sort of felt that. They felt themselves to be part of something that was passing away. The world of the housing project would conquer in the end. Along with the houses, which were succumbing to decay, Crescent Heights was dying. An image of its death was reflected in the decaying bodies of the old men and women. The younger people were moving deeper into the central city, drawn from the outskirts of town to the inner core by the same forces that attracted other generations of Americans into the new cities from off the farms and out of the countryside. Like all those other great neighborhoods of Los Angeles of the first half of the 20th Century, Crescent Heights had commanded a fierce tribal loyalty from its inhabitants and, along with Maravilla, Flats, Temple, Clanton, The Avenues, Hazard, Happy Valley, Alpine and Rose Hill, it had achieved a greatness and a notoriety in the folklore of Los Angeles. But the glory of these neighborhoods was of a genre alien to that inscribed in the official histories of the city. These were outlaw neighborhoods inhabited by Negroes and Mexicans, viewed by the whites in the core of the city as a ring of barbarians around their Rome, a plague of sunburned devils raging against the city gates. But the people of these neighborhoods had their lives to live. They were born and they died, they loved and they hated, they danced and mated with each other and fought against each other and won their reputations by day and by night.

A clue to the unimportance with which the city fathers regarded Crescent Heights is the fact that during election campaigns, the candidates never bothered to visit there in search of votes. They neither needed nor wanted those tainted votes. In turn, the people of areas such as this viewed the metropolis with distrust and hostility, if not hatred and scorn. Their sons were inducted into its Army and were locked into its jails and were channeled, along with their daughters, into its factories. But it could not claim, nor did it seem to want, their loyalty and respect. The metropolis asked no such tender sentiments of the peripheral neighborhoods: It asked only for their sons and daughters.

After the heart had been cut out of Crescent Heights and the housing project built in its place, the inhabitants of the old neighborhood, or what was left of it, lived on in an uncertain wind, under the threat that at any moment, county and state authorities would take over their land, invoking eminent domain. There were all kinds of rumors, inspired by uncertainty and the memory of how suddenly and without warning the other homes had been condemned. One would hear of secret plans to build a country club and golf course in the hills, that the hills would be the site of a huge new campus of the University of California, that the Brooklyn Dodgers were coming to L.A. to build a stadium in the hills or that the Housing Authority would extend the project, covering vast areas of the hills with concrete, with the pink and yellow rows of apartments designed to official specifications. The only sure thing about these rumors was their effect on the people. No one bothered to lay plans, because they might be forced to move at any moment. No one bothered to improve or repair their houses and land, because they did not want to go to the trouble and expense, only to see their work rolled down the hills by bulldozers—just as they had seen the other houses and dreams demolished to make way for the project. All that was left of the old Crescent Heights were the old people and the last of their children. And in the new, the Crescent Heights of the project, there were only the women with their fatherless children—and the Marijuanos.

In that underground world, psychologically as far beneath the consciousness of a city's solid citizens as a city's sewerage system is beneath its streets, in the subterranean realm of narcotics peddlers and users, marijuana peddlers, gamblers, pimps, prostitutes, the thugs and the cutthroats, the burglars and the robbers, and the police—Crescent Heights had long been known as the marijuana capital of Los Angeles. If the old Crescent Heights was dying, the marijuana traffic did not feel the sting of its death, and it was not the odor of decay that the marijuana pushers smelled but the aroma of folding greenbacks. Even before the project, there was marijuana in Crescent Heights, grown in the hills in modest quantities. But the demand so vastly exceeded the supply that could be cultivated with safety in the hills that of the tons of marijuana flowing into Los Angeles from Mexico, hundreds of pounds of the weed found their way to Crescent Heights. The project became the base of operation, and the weed was controlled by the outlaws of old Crescent Heights, known by the local people as the Marijuanos. They were the alienated sons, in their 20s, of the people of the hills, those sons whom the metropolis had found indigestible. They had criminal records or had dropped out of school without acquiring any skills to fit into the economy. And they were either unfit or disinclined to enter the Armed Forces. They had fallen back on the skill of the hills, the knack of eluding the police while trafficking in contraband.

While he was very young, Stacy had the exciting experience of knowing a neighborhood hero who happened also to be one of Mitch's older "brothers." Known as Flamingo, his heroism consisted of the fact that he was the first guy from Crescent Heights to go to San Quentin. Surprised in the act of robbing a liquor store in El Serrano, he was wounded in a blazing gun fight with police. His crime partner was shot dead. When, years later, he got out of prison, Flamingo joined the Marijuanos and started dealing in weed. Soon, however, he disappeared from the scene. No one seemed to know where he had gone, but it was said, with knowing winks, that he had gone to Mexico and bought a fabulous hacienda from which he directed the flow of marijuana into Crescent Heights.

In Stacy and his gang, the Marijuanos inspired a romantic apprehension just short of fear. Not that they had anything to fear from the Marijuanos, whom they had known all their lives and to whom they were connected by memories and, in some cases, by blood. But the presence of the Marijuanos infused Crescent Heights with an aura of danger and mystery. At night, while Stacy and the others would be down at the playground, loafing, they would see the strangers who came to Crescent Heights furtively, after dark, and who would sometimes ask them:

"Are any of the guys around?"

Stacy had directed many an inquirer to the spot where the Marijuanos might be. But if, when out at night, Stacy's gang was always aware of the whereabouts of the Marijuanos, it was more for the purpose of keeping out of their way than anything else. If the Marijuanos came too near, Stacy and his gang, with the excited feeling of being brushed by danger, would run away to another part of the project. But the Marijuanos kept generally to the darker sections of the project and Stacy and the others had the playground and other lighted areas to themselves. It was commonly known that the Marijuanos sometimes knocked out street lights to make it darker in certain favored spots; it would be a couple of months before the county sent someone around to fix them.

If Stacy or the others ever saw a policeman, they'd run tell the Marijuanos. "The narcs are over there," they'd say, and the Marijuanos would melt away into the shadows. But every so often, Stacy would hear that one of them had gotten caught by the narcs and was put in jail.

Stacy wanted something to happen. The gang was beginning to seem like a prison and, although he continued to play his role, he went through the steps mechanically, his mind drifting, looking for somewhere to lodge. He had toyed with the idea of quitting school to look for a job somewhere, but it did not occur to him that he would really do this; it was more or less his way of threatening himself. He did want profoundly for his life to change. He felt that he could no longer endure school, the gang and the endless round of throwing raids on El Serrano. Now, when he burglarized a building, he would come away feeling disappointed, no matter what the haul. He no longer had the patience to search out all the hiding places, and so if things were not left out in plain sight, he would miss them. And this had been Stacy's main function in the gang. He was known to have a nose for sniffing out the valuables hidden by the owners in some secret cranny. Now he could feel a growing dissatisfaction among the others and, although no one criticized him, he knew they were watching him, wondering. How could he explain to them what was going on inside himself, when he himself didn't know? How could he explain that his pride was offended by what they were doing? How could he make them understand that if they carried off everything in El Serrano, it would not be enough to satisfy what he was beginning to feel inside?

He did not voice these questions; they were the ghosts behind his changed attitude toward the others. It began to bother him that when they burglarized a place, he was always the first one to go in, to look around and make sure it was safe before the others entered. If he didn't go in first, they'd just stand there and scare each other, and the fear would travel round the circle until panic set in. But even after he had crawled through the window, searched the whole place for hidden danger—a night watchman, a dog—they were still afraid, it seemed to him, of the dark, of what they could not see in the dark if something were there. It was easy for them to imagine anything being there: a squad of policemen crouching in the corner, waiting until they were all inside, before switching on the lights to mow them down with shotguns or to capture them and take them to Juvenile Hall; or a pack of menacing Doberman pinschers or German shepherds too cool to bark that would leap on them from behind and rip their flesh to shreds. This fear had always been with them and, in the past, they all used to laugh at it. But now it seemed totally unacceptable to Stacy.

Mitch, though, was never afraid. The danger with him was that, spurred on by his total contempt for everything, he would crawl through a window as if he owned the place and, once inside, while shaking it down to see if it was safe, would growl viciously to attract any dogs, kick over packing crates, upset tables and chairs, in an effort to smoke out something. He'd open closets and storerooms. Unable to see in the dark, he would not hesitate to yell into the void:

"Hey, you in there, I see you! Get the fuck out of there!"

The first time he did that, pandemonium broke loose among the others and they took off, running. Stacy had to run after them, overtake them, shake some sense into them before they could understand that it was only Mitch who had shouted. It had been a hard job persuading them to go back with him and impossible to get them to crawl through the window into the dark room, because Mitch, when Stacy called to him to prove to the others that it was safe, refused to answer. Stacy pictured him, leering at them through the dark, that sullen, scornful scowl on his face. In that moment, Stacy wanted to kick that face. He knew that Mitch was probably looking right at them, at the window that was a patch of light silhouetted against the night sky, but would not answer.

"You lousy bastard, Mitch!" Stacy said into the dark window.

But in another sense, Stacy thought it was beautiful of Mitch not to answer, especially at a time like this, when he himself was absolutely serious and the others were afraid and they all were a long way from home and in danger of being shot or taken to jail. It took real dedication for Mitch to remain perverse in such circumstances. The others refused to precede Stacy through the window.

"Well, fuck all of you, then," he said, exasperated, and went swiftly through the window.

The others hesitated at first, decided all at the same time that they'd rather be inside than out, and they all tried to squeeze through the window at once, making a ton of racket, cursing and scratching each other as they fought to get through.

Then Mitch, somewhere in the darkness, hissed at them, "Shut the fuck up!"

Guided by his voice, Stacy caught Mitch in the dark and, bringing up his knee with just slightly less than hostile force, he shook Mitch up and shoved him to the floor. "Next time, you better answer me, you stupid shit!" he said. And, extending his foot in the dark, he made contact with Mitch, jarring him with a stiff thrust. It felt like he got him in the side.

Now that they were inside, Stacy could hear the others as they scuffled about in the dark, searching for objects of value with which to fill their gunny sacks. Stacy did not even unroll his sack. He leaned against a wall and let his mind drift as he waited for the others to finish. He was thinking of what had happened the previous week, when he had first made up his mind that this could not go on, that something had to change, that he had to find himself a new life.

The thought had come to him during a raid on a school cafeteria a week before. After eating all they could hold and filling their sacks, they had thrown all the other food on the floor, gutted the refrigerator, smashed all the cups, salt and pepper shakers and glasses, scattered the silverware, bent the trays out of shape and overturned the tables.

"Stacy, make Mitch stop!" Turtle said.

Mitch had turned all the jets of the gas range up full blast. Flames leaped at the ceiling. Shoving Mitch aside, Stacy began spinning the knobs to shut off the flow of gas. Screaming, Mitch came at him with a fork. Stacy feinted at him and, when Mitch slashed at him with the fork, Stacy stepped back and caught his arm, twisting it behind his back.

"Drop it!" Stacy demanded, applying pressure.

"You cocksucker!" hissed Mitch, defeated, holding the fork just long enough to register his defiance.

Stacy turned all the burners down.

"Let's burn this motherfucker down!" Mitch pleaded. "Then the *gavachos* won't have a school to go to!"

"That's going too far," the others protested in a chorus.

That did it. That nauseated Stacy. *That's going too far.* The words burned into his mind. What did they mean by that? That's when Stacy really knew that he was finished, that he had to cut all this loose. Like a sailor locking the hatches on a submarine, he twirled the knobs, opening all the jets all the way, and the range burst into flames again.

"Let's go!" he shouted. He helped the others out the window. Looking around, he saw Mitch in front of the range, jumping up and down, laughing hysterically and cursing the flames in Spanish. Stacy rushed back and dragged him away by his belt.

"Leave go! Leave go!" Mitch yelled, as he struggled to free himself, straining toward the flames.

The building was mostly of wood and in a minute it would be one raging inferno. Stacy, seeing that Mitch would not relent in his efforts to return to the fire, hit him in his gut and shoved him up and out through the window. As Stacy came through the window, just as he expected, Mitch tried to kick him in the face to knock him back into the burning room. Catching Mitch's foot in the air, Stacy hurled him backward into the dark night air, landing him on his ass; and as Stacy ran past Mitch, he was very careful not to miss stepping on him. He heard curses behind him in the night as he ran to catch up with the others.

The idea, voiced by the others, that Mitch had been "going too far," bothered Stacy. It sounded like the belief that if one sailed far enough over the open seas, one would eventually sail off the edge of the world. He found solace in repeating to himself: The world is round; you can sail on and on and end up where you started. It was as if the others were saying to him that the world is flat. His mind seized upon this incident to justify breaking with his gang. He was only waiting for the right moment.

The next time the others asked him to go on a raid, Stacy said no. After the others resigned themselves to inactivity for the night, Mitch and he stole away from them, leaving them sitting around the playground looking dejected, and the two of them headed for El Serrano by themselves. They prowled around for hours, without spotting anything worth while. It was Saturday night and every house seemed occupied; every business establishment, though they saw some that were obviously deserted and closed down for the weekend, seemed strangely forbidding and whispering of threat, crawling with hidden danger. They both felt this, without speaking about it, tacitly deciding there was no chance for action that night. Walking through alleys, down dark streets, always in the shadows, cutting back, zigzagging, to avoid the glow of street lights, they trekked to the heart of El Serrano. They knew they could not afford to be seen by anyone, because only whites lived there and one look at them and it would be all over. If a car headed their way, they scrambled for cover, crouching behind parked cars, lying flat behind trees, kneeling down in the shrubbery near houses. The police would know, upon seeing them, that their only business there was to steal. El Serrano was their happy hunting ground. They had been hunting there for years, and for as long as he had been doing it, not one of his gang had got caught. The cops would lie in wait for them, leaving a bait of valuables out in clear sight, but they always passed it up. "That's a fishhook," they'd whisper to each other in the dark, gliding through the shadows. Sometimes they'd sneak noiselessly right past the cops sitting in their patrol car parked in the shadows. Once, Mitch had crawled up to their car on his belly, like a commando, and removed the valve from a rear tire. By the time the cops detected the flat, Mitch was well away.

"Let's hit a few cars, if nothing else," Stacy said to Mitch, as they crept silently down an alley.

"OK," Mitch said.

With their screwdrivers, they jimmied the vent windows on

the passenger side of a few cars, sticking in an arm to roll down the window, then shoving their heads through the window to look around inside the car. It was their habit to take anything of value. They'd take coats, binoculars, guns, tools, radios, groceries, anything they could use or sell. Most of their loot they sold to the people of the project at cheap prices. They didn't care; all they wanted was a little something to keep them going from day to day. Goods in hand, they'd go from door to door and show what they had. The people would jokingly call them bad boys, but they were always glad to see them. They'd let them in, pull the curtains and examine the display. Clothes for their children, for themselves, cooking utensils, lamps, clocks, radios—everything went. If they could not sell something, the gang would give it away. If nobody wanted it, they'd throw it away. But most of the time, if they had something that wouldn't sell, they'd let Mitch keep it. His cellar contained a wealth of worthless loot.

Their pockets and sacks filled, Stacy and Mitch had almost called it quits when Stacy saw another car that seemed to beckon to him. That car, he was to think later, communicated with him. He had already got himself a nice leather jacket that, because he was big for his age, was not a bad fit. He got to the car and opened the window. On the front seat was the long, snaky body of a five-battery flashlight and a fifth of whiskey in a bag. Good for a few bucks, Stacy thought. He fell in with Mitch and they headed for home.

As soon as they were a safe distance away, Stacy tested the flashlight, playing it down a pitch-black alley, fascinated by its powerful beam.

"Put out that fucking light, man!" Mitch growled curtly. "You trying to signal to the cops where we are, or something?"

Stacy shined the light in Mitch's face. Mitch tried to stare the beam down, but it wounded his eyes, forcing him to turn his head.

"You crazy fucker," he said in disgust.

Stacy felt giddy about the flashlight, his new possession. Its properties he seemed to appropriate and incorporate into his own being. The light, he felt, was a powerful extension of himself.

The next night, when they all met at the playground, Stacy took his flashlight with him. It was an instrument that had to be used, a charge that by its potency refused to lie idle. As he left his room, it all but leaped into his hand, guiding itself into his palm. He had taken it completely apart several times, feeling a flush of triumph each time he reassembled it, flicked the button and saw the bulb glow. It seemed to him that when he assembled the parts, he was creating the light. And he had the strange feeling that this light would be the instrument by which great change would come into his life.

He loved his light. When he broke it down, he would caress the five batteries with his fingers, and the bulb, the gaskets, the spring in the cap. So closely did he examine each part that he had no doubt that out of a mountain of similar parts, he could easily select his own.

He would use the power of the batteries sparingly. As they all lay on the grass of the playground, the others kept urging him to turn it on, to show them how powerful was its beam. Stacy stood up and cast the beam into the hills, and a patch of light could be seen dimly sweeping the surface of the hills at a great distance. The others were impressed. Stacy lay on the lawn, fondling the metallic tube that held the mysteries of his future.

"Where did you score it?" asked one of the others.

"El Serrano," Stacy answered.

"When?"

"Last night."

"Last night?" Turtle perked up. "I thought you said last night you weren't going?"

Stacy made no reply. A heavy silence ensued. The others, not looking directly at Stacy, were nevertheless watching him closely, waiting for an answer to clarify what looked now like a betrayal.

Stacy said nothing.

A few minutes passed in this silence.

Then Mitch said, "Don't you punks know when you're not wanted along? Can't you take a hint?" Mitch spoke in a harsh, contemptuous tone, which was not directed to Turtle alone but to all the others. "Me and Stacy ducked you suckers last night and we scored heavy by ourselves. I got myself a flashlight, too, just like that one." After a significant pause, he added, "Who needs you guys with them? All you ever do is make noise."

Stacy was embarrassed, for he could feel himself how Mitch's words were hurting the others. He smothered an impulse to smash Mitch's face, to make him shut up, to make him retract that lie about his own flashlight—but he held back. Inside, he was glad that Mitch had spoken these things, for now something was done that could never be undone, and he had the intimation that Mitch was setting him free. Then he said, "You've got a big, dumb mouth, Mitch."

"It's my mouth," Mitch snapped back, "big or not."

Suddenly, Stacy felt a deep loathing for the position he was in. He hated the necessity of giving them an explanation. If he acknowledged that he owed them an explanation, he would be sucked back in and lose this chance. Jumping up, he kicked Mitch in his side, and as he ran off into the night, he could hear Mitch's laughter following him.

He ran until he was exhausted, then walked until he found himself at the other end of the project. Around him, it was quiet and dark. The apartment windows were yellow squares where the shades stopped the light. He sat down on the lawn, propped himself up against a tree and closed his eyes. His heart still raced in his chest from running. He clung to his flashlight, glad to be alone.

Sometime later, he became aware of the sound of movement near him; he heard the muffled rustling of paper. Opening his eyes, at first he could make out nothing, then just below him, where the lawn on which he sat sloped down to meet the sidewalk, he saw a shadowy form kneeling and reaching into the hedge next to Mrs. Chapman's front door. Stacy realized it was a Marijuano, but he couldn't make out which one. As he sat there, watching, it seemed to him that he was becoming aware of the Marijuanos for the first time. Then he wondered, what would the Marijuano do if he shined the flashlight on him? This thought, this possibility of making something happen, already had fastened upon his imagination; and even as he hesitated, he knew that he would end by doing it. He perceived, in a flash, that such a step would set in motion forces of which he was not even aware. What will happen? he wondered. Am I afraid to do it? By putting the question to himself in terms of his courage, he knew that he had to do it.

Silently, he got to his feet and squatted on his haunches. Aiming his flashlight at the phantom, he savored the keen edge of the moment before the action, anticipating it with sharp exhilaration. Then he pressed the button. It was Chango! Chango froze, all lit up, his face contorted, eyes wide with panic. For the briefest moment, Chango remained motionless, his arm buried in the hedge up to his shoulder. Then he exploded, scooting backward on his knees, stumbling to his feet, tripping, falling down, crawling, looking over his shoulder to see if he was being chased, his face hysterical. Stacy kept the light on him till he turned the corner on the hump, then he flicked off the light and ran toward the playground. When he came to another dark spot, he fell onto the lawn and laughed till he could hardly breathe, rolling on the ground. The way Chango had looked when the beam first split his face, how he had flown! For long after, just the thought of it would send him chuckling.

That night, he dreamed that the world was inside a box with steep sides and no top, like the walls of a frontier fort, and the sun was a huge flashlight of a billion batteries with a tube so long it never ended; and some kid in the sky watching the people groping in darkness below pressed the button and the people said "Day" and he released the button and the people said "Night." Stacy woke up in a sweat, clutching his flashlight, keenly appreciative of the powers of light.

The next day, time seemed to slow down on purpose to torture him. It was with a keen foretaste of pleasure that he awaited the setting of the sun. All during school, he could think of nothing but his flashlight, the Marijuanos and how he would terrorize them again tonight. He saw himself chasing them all over the project. They would be there tonight, he had not the slightest doubt. They were always there. When it rained, they donned heavy coats and plastic slickers and did business as usual. The only time the Marijuanos would leave was when the cops came; and when the cops went away, the Marijuanos reappeared, like air drawn into a vacuum. That evening, Stacy hid in the bushes around the square at the end of the row of apartments in which Mrs. Chapman lived, not far from the spot where he had surprised Chango. The square was one of several located at strategic intervals throughout the project, placed there by the architects to add beauty to public housing. It was a concrete-covered clearing 30 feet by 40 feet, surrounded with hedges and flowers and shaded by a tall tree. The tree's rich foliage hung over the square like a giant umbrella. It could actually stop rain. On each side of the square were four cement benches of the type often seen in public parks: a flat slab resting on two upright stays. During the daylight hours, the little kids scampered and romped in the square, riding in their wagons and on tricycles, catching and bouncing big rubber balls, jumping rope, playing jacks and hopscotch. At night, the Marijuanos took it over, using it to contact customers who came to Crescent Heights from all over Los Angeles to score their weed.

Stacy waited for the right moment. Hidden in the shadows of the square, the Marijuanos were smoking weed and making transactions. The acrid aroma tantalized Stacy's nostrils. He had smelled burning marijuana before, but never from so close. He knew that what he was doing was very dangerous and this knowledge, coupled with the intrigue of the night, the smell of the burning marijuana and the sight of men moving back and forth, talking in low voices and laughing now and then, gave it all a touch of adventure. Stacy felt keenly alive. He was doing something not often done, something he had never done before, something none of the others had ever dreamed of doing. He knew also that if a bush moved, the Marijuanos noticed it. Like him, they were all neighborhood boys who had spent their entire lives in the immediate area. They knew every tree, every hole in the ground, every rock, every bush and everybody. They could feel a cop coming. No cop could have snuck up on them as Stacy had done. It would not have been natural. But Stacy, who knew and loved every inch of the earth of Crescent Heights, had crept right up on the Marijuanos. With a little effort, he could have reached out and touched them. When he could bear it no longer, Stacy aimed his flashlight into the square. Before pressing the button, he gave the bushes a violent shake, drawing the Marijuanos' attention to him, then let go with the light. The Marijuanos gave up the square in a mad stampede, crashing through the bushes and running over each other. Stacy then dashed off in the direction the Marijuanos were least likely to take: He sprinted to the well-lit playground.

Three days later, at school, Mitch said, "The Marijuanos are after you."

"After me for what?" Stacy asked, a look of surprise on his face.

"You know for what," Mitch said curtly. "You and that flashlight, that's what."

"What about my flashlight?" Stacy asked, hungrily wanting to hear any details.

"You won't be playing dumb when they catch you," said Mitch. "Cutie, Chico and Chango said they're going to catch you and fuck you up. You know better than to fool around with those guys."

Stacy had not expected the Marijuanos to send him congratulations, but he did not really feel in danger; just as when he went on raids to El Serrano, he had not regarded the dangers as real. They were part of a game, like a penalty in football. If one made no mistakes, it was as if the penalties did not even exist.

"Fuck the Marijuanos," Stacy said.

"That's easy to say," said Mitch, "but wait till they get their hands on you. The Marijuanos don't play around when they mean business."

Stacy had assumed that each time he turned on his light, the Marijuanos would automatically react the same way—run. But now that they knew it was he and not the cops, he knew their reaction would change. Whereas their main purpose had been to flee from a cop, it was now an angry desire to extinguish Stacy's light.

"The Marijuanos said you're putting the heat on them," Mitch had said.

"Later for them," Stacy said. But he was jolted by that charge. In Crescent Heights, only a rat would knowingly put the heat on someone. And a known rat couldn't last five minutes in Crescent Heights. It was unheard of. Stacy had not expected such a charge. He threw it from his mind as too absurd and unpleasant to think abut. He continued to creep up on the Marijuanos and flash his light on them. And when he did, it was

he who had to take off, running, because the Marijuanos would
be right on his heels. It was easy for Stacy to outdistance them.
They laid traps for him. Some of them hid in the bushes while
the others tried to sucker him in. They laid up a store of bricks,
bottles and beer cans. Once, they hid near Stacy's home to
ambush him on his way home. Stacy laughed at them and out-
flanked their every maneuver. Their battle, the Marijuanos'
efforts to catch Stacy and his efforts to escape, became notorious
in Crescent Heights. Everybody knew they were after him.
Everyone waited for news that Stacy had at last been caught.
Eluding the Marijuanos became his fulltime occupation. He
defied them with pride.

But underneath it all, Stacy had some regrets that the feud
had ever gotten started. He would have liked nothing better
than to be out of the spot he was in, which was becoming
more difficult to occupy. He wished that he could just leave
them alone and drop the whole thing, to be done with the
whole affair, to be free from worrying about how to get away
from the Marijuanos in a given situation. But he continued to
force the issue, convinced that he would somehow come through
it all unscathed. The Marijuanos became marksmen with bricks
and bottles and it took some prize footwork by Stacy to keep
from getting his brains knocked out. Even so, they hit him in
the side once with a heavy rock that took the wind out of him,
and the only thing that kept him from collapsing on the spot
was the sure knowledge of what they would do to him if they
caught him.

The Marijuanos sent people to talk to Stacy, but he refused to
listen. They repeated that he was ruining their business.

Stacy's mother said to him: "Son, you better mind your Ps and
Qs. I know what you been doing and you'd better stop it."

"I know what I'm doing," Stacy said.

Now the other members of the gang shied away from Stacy.
They said he had gone crazy and they saw nothing positive
in his keen thrill of excitement in outwitting the Marijuanos.
They didn't know how it felt to be hunted by them, to elude
their traps, to spring out of the bushes unannounced with
a blazing torch and scare the pants off of the Marijuanos. The
Marijuanos were all in their 20s and Stacy, who felt neither old
nor young, enjoyed this relationship with individuals already

grown. He was a factor in their existence, whether they liked it or not. He had chosen them, like some gadfly in a dangerous game. They were stuck with Stacy and it was up to them to solve the problem. For his part, Stacy's course was clear. He would continue to bug them with his light.

One night, he climbed up a tree and from his perch saw Polio, a fat, phlegmatic Mexican, hide a little bag behind a bush. Several times, Polio returned to the bush, extracted from the bag, replaced it and went away. Stacy shinnied down the tree and chose a spot ten feet away from Polio's stash. The next time Polio came back, Stacy waited until he had gotten the bag and stuck his hand into it, then he hit him in the face with the blinding beam of the light. Dropping the bag, Polio uttered a cry and was in full flight before he realized it was Stacy, him-self already running through the night in the opposite direction. He had scored again. It was coups like that that egged him on.

The Marijuanos tried a new trick. As Stacy walked home from school with the others one evening, two cars, one in front of him and one behind, pulled sharply into the curb and out poured the Marijuanos. They had not, however, counted on the speed of Stacy's legs. Stacy leaped over a fence into some-one's yard and, before the startled dog in the yard realized what was happening, ran out the back way, was over the back fence and cutting out up the hill. Looking back, he saw the Marijuanos pile into their cars, burning rubber getting out of there. The stakes were going up. Such desperation!

When Stacy was in his classrooms, he was careful to sit near a window, in case the Marijuanos burst in to trap him. He suffered through his third-period class, because it was on the second floor and there was no ledge outside the windows. He felt trapped in that room. He fully expected the Marijuanos to know all about this particular room, and he would not have been suprised to look up one day and find them there. He watched for them in the halls, on the stairways, in the schoolyard, be-hind lockers in the gymnasium. During lunch hour, he often saw the Marijuanos drive by the school, their faces sweeping the crowd with Stacy-seeking eyes.

One day, the Marijuanos stopped chasing him and they stopped throwing things at him. When he crept up on them and flashed his light, they'd just look at him, in his direction. Stacy couldn't figure it out, but he didn't hang around waiting for answers. He ran away, as usual. One evening, Stacy was down at the playground, loafing, with his flashlight stuck in his belt like a knife or a gun. Turtle walked up to him.

"Chico wants to talk to you," Turtle said, pointing to another part of the playground, where, dressed in blue demins and wearing dark glasses, Chico stood waiting on the other side of the Cyclone fence. Warily, Stacy walked over, staying on his side of the fence, continually looking over his shoulder to see if the other Marijuanos were sneaking up on him while Chico held his attention.

"What do you want?" Stacy asked, mistrustfully.

"Say, Stacy," Chico began, "this shit has got to stop, man."

Stacy could see that Chico was burning with anger but trying also to conceal it. It shone like flaming coals in his black eyes. His mouth was set in a fixed, down-thrusting scowl. Through the fence, Stacy got the same feeling he had had when, at the Griffith Park Zoo, he had stood outside the cage of a lion and stared into its huge cat eyes. He was thankful for the fence between them. He said nothing, only stared into Chico's dark glasses, at the fire in those eyes, and he saw something there besides anger and hatred, something that surprised him: He saw the embryo of a smile.

"I want to make a deal with you," Chico said.

"What kind of a deal?" Stacy asked, regarding Chico narrowly. His anxiety was that the other Marijuanos were sure to try something.

"Here," Chico said, and he shoved a ten-dollar bill into a square of the fence. Stacy let it lie there, wedged in the wire.

"What's that for?" asked Stacy.

"For your flashlight," Chico said.

"For ten dollars, you can buy three or four like this one," Stacy said, patting his flashlight on his side.

"I want yours," said Chico.

The flashlight weighed heavily on Stacy's side. The full realization of what a burden it had become flowed in upon him. He wanted with all his heart to be rid of it.

"Listen to me, Stacy," Chico said. "You're a young cat and you don't realize what's going on. But you'd better think fast, because you don't have much time left. You know what the other guys want to do? Look." He lifted the corner of his shirt and showed Stacy the handle of a pistol stuck in his belt. "They want to just kill you. Because you're ranking our play. You're messing with our bread and butter, man."

Strangely, Stacy was not afraid. But he felt a knot in his chest, to think that the Marijuanos had been discussing his death.

"Listen, man," Chico went on. "We could kill you and bury you up on Walnut Hill and nobody would ever find your body. It would be no trouble at all. The cops wouldn't even look for you. You're just another nigger to them and they don't give a fuck about you. You know why we haven't done you up?"

Stacy stared at him impassively, not trusting himself to ask why, for not wanting to sound too urgent.

"Because you're one of us. You're from Crescent Heights." Chico paused. "So we decided to give you the respect of letting you make a choice. But maybe you're too fucking wild to see what's happening. We never like to fight with each other in Crescent Heights, Stacy, you know that. Because by sticking together, we can all make it, maybe. At least better than by fighting ourselves. At least we'll have a better chance. I'm a married man and I have my family to look out for. I don't have time to fuck around with you or anybody else. This is strictly business with me. If I get caught, I'm going to the can, and I don't look forward to that. I'm going to do everything in my power to see to it that I never get caught. Right now"—Chico paused, then went on—"right now, you are more of a problem than the narcs. So we've got to settle this right now. Right now. You know what, Stacy?" Chico looked at him and seemed to be measuring him. "You're getting to be about the age. . . . Do you get high? Do you blow weed?"

"No," Stacy said.

"Well, pretty soon. . . ." he paused. "It won't be long before you're going to get tired of running around in a pair of dirty Levis, fucking off your time with those other young cats. I've dug you and I know that you've got something on the ball. Pretty soon, you're going to want some nice clothes and some money in your pocket, some of that folding money, and you're going to want a little car of your own to ride around in with the bitches. But then you're going to find out the world is not a"—he broke off, looking around him, and swept the area with his arm —"a playground. You're going to find out the world is not a merry-go-round. It's hard, hard, Stacy. But we've got a good thing going for us here in Crescent Heights, and we intend to keep it working for us. You guys call us Marijuanos. . . . Yeah, we're Marijuanos, all right. But there are lots more Marijuanos in L.A., and lots of them come to us to score their jive. And you, with your flashlight, are fucking with all of that. I used to think like you and act like you. You know my brother Black Jack, don't you?"

"Yeah," Stacy said. "Everybody knows Black Jack."

"He used to control the action in Crescent Heights," Chico went on. "And he used to try getting me interested, but my mind was locked somewhere else. I was about your age and I used to call him Marijuano. Now I've got the bag and you're calling me Marijuano. It goes around and comes around; you take it a little way and then pass it on. Pretty soon, the little kids will be calling you Marijuano and, someday, kids that are not even born yet will be calling them Marijuanos. It will never end. But it's going to end for you unless you straighten up your hand.

"Take the money," Chico said, "and we'll forget the whole thing. We'll forget it all happened."

Stacy hesitated for a long moment, then said, "What about the others?"

"Same with them," Chico said. "Nobody will bother you. I give you my word. But you have to give me your word that you won't fool around anymore. I'm not giving you the money to buy you off. I'm giving it to you to wake you up."

"What good is your word?" Stacy asked. "How do I know you're not just setting me up?"

Chico looked at Stacy fiercely. "I never break my word when I give it like this. If I say I won't bother you, I won't. If I say I'm going to kill you, you're as good as dead."

Stacy walked down to the end of the fence, where it was lower. As he jumped over, he saw Mitch and the others watching. He walked up to Chico and handed him the flashlight. Chico pulled the ten-dollar bill from the fence and placed it in Stacy's hand.

"Play it cool," Chico said and walked away.

Stacy did not turn around to look after Chico. It felt good. It was a relief not to have to look over his shoulder anymore. The others walked over to Stacy. They all understood what had happened. There were all glad it was over. They all laughed and punched each other lightly to the body.

"You punks are crazy," said Mitch, off to the side.

"Let's throw a raid on El Serrano tonight," Turtle suggested.

"Count me out," Stacy said with mock astonishment, "I might find another flashlight!"

That night, Stacy walked into the square. When they saw who it was, the Marijuanos quickly surrounded him. There was murder in the intense way they crowded him.

"What the fuck you want?" Cutie snapped, fuming, his voice menacing, with overtones of blood.

"Nothing," Stacy said. He felt crushed, confused.

"Leave him alone," Chico spoke up. "Forget about it. I gave him my word that it was all over."

"You gave him your word," said Cutie, "but I didn't give him mine."

Stacy heard the click of Cutie's knife as it sprang open, although he couldn't see it in the darkness. He was afraid. Cutie was breathing in his face. The others stepped back. Stacy calculated his chances of running. All Cutie had to do was thrust upward with the blade to do damage.

"When I gave him my word, I gave him yours," Chico said. "And nobody's going to make me out a liar. Leave him alone, Cutie." Chico spoke with force and authority and he added, lowering his voice ominously: "Or are you going to make me out a liar?"

Cutie stepped back from Stacy and put his knife up. Tension evaporated from the square. The Marijuanos lit up joints of the weed.

Chico offered Stacy a joint.

"Never mind," Stacy said halfheartedly.

Chico fumbled with the joint and then lit it from the one being smoked by Gato. After he had taken a couple of drags, he passed it to Stacy.

"Here," he said.

Stacy took the joint between his fingers and raised it to his mouth, puffing in and immediately coughing out the acrid smoke. It felt like breathing over a burning rag. He was amazed at how the others could be smoking it if it tasted so bad.

"Do it like this," Chico said, taking the joint from Stacy. Chico took a long, powerful drag. Stacy watched the coal of fire travel up the joint as Chico consumed about half of it in that one drag. "Take it down into your lungs and hold it," he said. "You'll get used to it. The main thing is to hold it in your lungs as long as you can."

Stacy struggled over the remainder of the joint, coughing and choking occasionally, his throat getting raw, his eyes running, his heart racing. He was confused and a little apprehensive but continued to inhale the weed and hold in the smoke until his lungs expelled it. Then it was as if he ceased to exist. He was confronting a stranger in a body he recognized as his own but with which he was out of touch. His former state was now a memory; his new state was a soft, jet-smooth present fact. He had the sensation of being two disembodied beings fighting to inhabit one yielding body. His body, offering no resistance, became a battlefield on which two rival armies contended. The pitch of the war escalated as he took in more marijuana from the joints being passed around the circle of Marijuanos. Stacy accepted every one offered to him, and once he ended up with a lit reefer in each hand, puffing first one and then the other. He no longer cared or tried to keep track of how the war inside him was progressing. No matter which way it went, he thought, he'd still be the winner. He lost track of time. Everything seemed to occur without sequence, as if it was all happening simultaneously and spontaneously, separated rather by space than by time. He was dimly aware of people furtively entering the square, engaging one or another of the Marijuanos in short, snappy conversation. He watched as the Marijuanos collected money and disappeared from the square for a few moments, to return and hand something to the customer. These furtive shadows would brace up and, in a moment, fade from the square into the vast Los Angeles night.

Stacy was so high off the weed that the center of his vision was blotted out, although he could see perfectly well around the edges; and through these clear edges, he was trying to see into the center, around the dark spot. He had the impression that someone had taken a bottle of liquid shoe polish and, using the dauber, painted his eyeballs down the center. He did not notice that everyone was leaving, had drifted out of the square and gone for the night—except Chico, who was talking. At first, Stacy could make no sense of what he was saying.

"What? What?" Stacy kept asking him, over and over again.

"Go home, Stacy."

"What?"

"Go to your pad, man. I'm going to split."

"What?"

"It's one o'clock, man. You got too high."

Chico was laughing in Stacy's face. He was really having a big laugh. Stacy laughed, too. His face felt like rubber and he couldn't control his expression, though it was very dark in the square and Chico could not tell. Stacy's face seemed to be sagging and he was flexing his facial muscles to hold it in place, but it kept sliding down again. "I'm not high," he said.

"No, you're not high," Chico said, laughing. "You're wasted!"

Stacy was laughing, too.

"Do you think you can find your way to your pad?" Chico asked.

"Sure," Stacy said. "Who could forget that?" Even as he spoke, he experienced the panic of having no idea where he lived. "Where are we right now?" he asked Chico.

Chico knew that, although it was funny, it was also a serious phase Stacy was going through; and if he had not been there, Stacy might have wandered around Crescent Heights all night, looking for his house.

"We're in the square by Mrs. Chapman's house," Chico said.

"Where is Mrs. Chapman's house?" Stacy asked.

Chico turned Stacy to his right and he recognized Mrs. Chapman's apartment at the end of the row. From there, traveling like a beam of light, his mind raced off into infinity, reconstructing that portion of the universe of which he was aware. . . . There is Mrs. Chapman's pad, this is the square, the playground is down there, that's Boundary Avenue up there, Florizel Street over there, Mercury Avenue over there, downtown L.A. is that way, Pasadena is that way, Lincoln Heights is over there, El Serrano and Alhambra are over there—I live down that way. Stacy felt serene, lucid, triumphant, peculiarly masterful and at peace.

"I'm going home," he said to Chico.

"Think you can make it?"

"Sure," he said. "Ain't nothing to it."

"I'll see you around," Chico said.

Stacy had started to walk in the direction of home when he missed something. He stopped, wondering what it was he was forgetting. Then he remembered the flashlight and laughed to himself. He did not know yet whether a Marijuano had any use for a flashlight. As he walked dreamily home, he had no doubt that he would soon find out.

ELEANOR ROSS TAYLOR is a North Carolinian living in Charlottesville, Virginia, where her husband, Peter Taylor, teaches at the University of Virginia. Her book of poems, *Wilderness of Ladies*, was published in 1960.

Jujitsu

It was the best of June days. They drove up early, he in white shirt and tie, his speech in his brief case, she in jeans and scarf, for she planned to stop off at the cabin and spend the day in idle solitude.

"I wish you were going with me."

Fifi, asleep on her lap, stirred irritably.

The cabin appeared in a hole in the valley, a well of morning sun. (Turn up refrig. Fill kettles. Open windows. Check garden.)

The lettuce was up, the squash sprouted. Up on the hill shone glossy laurel clumps with clusters of pale buds. Fifi snorted among the bushes by the creek. Rabbits, groundhogs, skunks. Perhaps a deer. Or a bear.

He kissed her goodbye; then, his hand on the car door, turned back.

"Sure you won't just change and come with me?"

"Not on your life!"

Now it was all hers. Jubilate. Spirit, dominate.

She made for the rock. But when she left the meadow and began the hill, she turned, her eyes narrowed in a sort of ecstasy, to look at the unfortified cabin on its marshy nest, to take in the sheltering rhododendron along the creek. Up on the rock she would watch for the green heron. And perhaps it would be her day to see a deer.

A cardinal, thinner, wilder, and less brilliant than those that came to her feeder at home, fidgeted in the alders. She willed him hers for his wildness, his fugitive nature.

Halfway up the hill she stopped to behold a Michaux's lily, a gemini. It was exceedingly rich, black-peppered blood-orange. The petals were voluptuously extended, overlapping behind the blossom face. She did not touch it, but knelt and partook paganly, her face to its divided face, its pendant bosom. Only in a nunnery, such purity.

On the rock, big as a porch, she stood a moment scanning the world, valley from north to south, mountain facing her, loving its stature, its bones, its pine whiskers. Then she sat down on the moss-scabbed rock and put the binoculars to her eyes.

She found the heron. He was stationed stiffly, below the bushes at the edge of the pond. He was hunting. And he was on the lookout for other hunters. She was too late to see him circling and hear his cries over the meadow. But when they were there overnight Richard was always clipping things, driving places, calling her, as if they were still on Globe Street, so that even then the heron, the hedgehog, all the wild things abandoned them early. Small wonder Richard marvelled at her observations.

Why had she never seen a deer? They were known to be in the valley. Mr. Otterbein had seen a doe with two fawns in front of their cabin last week. She settled, knees up, searching with the field glasses. What size would it be? Small, she reminded herself. Smaller than a horse, larger than a dog. Of course, this was the day she really should go to see Mrs. Otterbein . . . downright un-Christian not to make yourself known to any of your neighbors.

Something unbending in the list of the rhododendrons before the wind attracted her. A groundhog was standing up, his nose to the wind, his Oriental eye on the meadow. He dropped fluidly to the ground and disappeared. She found his hole and his bare doorstep among the rhododendron roots. She was alone, human-being-among-the-creatures. My spiritual refill, she said wryly to herself.

She returned to the groundhog during the morning and closing her eyes in the sunlight imagined his underground quarters, the dirt corridors where there was still enough light for casting small shadows. Once she thought she made out dirt on the end of his nose. He listened long before any move, smelling out mysteries. Had he had a brush with violence? The final expectation of a wild thing was ambush, murder, fatal error—to be by natural weakness annihilated. And of every civilized thing? It lived by inner strength—if one had the solitude, the time to draw on it.

She tramped her paths. She greeted with passionate eyes the ferns, the brambles, the ground lichens. She crouched in the under-pines dens covered with needles. She left the garden for last, to ease the transition. Perhaps, sometime—in the future —one could stay up here. *From this dark world I would draw thee apart.*

Solitude is strength. Spirit, dominate. There was no joy in giving birth; it was painful and degrading. Though she loved her children, there was no joy in nursing one's babies; it was an animal dependence. Defecating, urinating, menstruating, eating—why had these ignominies been inflicted on human beings? She hated her heartbeat when she sat still, her pulse when she lay quietly at night; when she was aware of her breathing it annoyed her, sometimes almost maddened her. Coupling was the only acceptable human office, the one inseparable from spirit. And of the senses, hearing was a doubtful blessing, touch useful. Smell was so of the mind and so untranscribable as to be almost spiritual—the hair-splitting spectrum of smell—is it a lilac or a narcissus? The pepper of one rose and the musk of another. Peach, cantaloupe, or apple? . . . But seeing was life, was light, was truly understanding.

The sun had warmed the rock like the top of a cake-baking oven. There suddenly came, like the pain in her side, the thought of Richard, of where he was. Richard was on the platform. Alone, he was alone. Strange, she had always thought of his audience as being part of him. But there he was, in need of support. It was not one of the old days or nights when she had sat waiting for the car that would bring him from the party. The same party, the same friends, the same struggle between them. . . . But she had been strong enough to bear it, to bear it all alone.

She squatted, pulling up carefully with two fingers the tiny weed plants among the lettuce seedlings.

The wind creaked a locust branch. She looked up. For a moment in a vision there were, around her, playground swings, chains creaking, and slides, her grandchildren laughing the already artificial laughter of the social group. Yet her neck held inclined, waiting for their soft, sweatered arms.

Fifi came wet from the cold creek and ran wildly around the grass and naughtily through the garden. She ran with Fifi around the cabin.

When she had raked the spot where the tomatoes would go and put the rake back into the shed, it was five.

She began expecting Richard. The grosbeaks were making a last food round-up. The light was going. She locked the windows, covered the tables, turned down the refrigerator.

At five-thirty she went to the window. Bridge and road were empty. A car tore by on the highway. It was an isolated spot. Sometimes when they came there were hunters' footprints, horses' hoofmarks, by the pond.

She settled in the rattan chaise by the window and watched the bridge. The sun was set. The green heron flapped across high over the meadow. Her intent ears caught that dull ringing of absolute silence like the grinding of the universe. Was it really only the blood pulsing in the ears? How *like it*, to be just that. Nothing still, on the bridge, nothing coming down their own little road. Everything was graying out.

But beyond the bridge there was something, or somebody, under the apple tree. She leaned forward and searched into the dusk. A large animal was surveying the cabin.

She took the binoculars to the window. A dog, a German Shepherd lightly colored like the twilight, sat on the threshold of the bridge watching the cabin intently. He was bigger than a dog; he looked big as a man. Why should he be watching from so far? He knew she was here. Did he come with some trespasser when the cabin was empty? She did not like the look of him. She called Fifi, who had been ranging near the foot of the big rock, and latched the screen door. Perhaps it had been a mistake not to have a telephone. What would she do if something had kept Richard overnight? Not spend the night here alone.

She had forgotten to put foil over the kettle spouts.

When she looked back the dog had stationed himself closer. Through the glasses his eyes, in spite of the dusk, were bright. The contradiction of his immobility and his advance was eerie. Fifi put her forepaws on the window sill and looked toward him, but did not bark or growl. In comparison to him Fifi was hardly a dog.

It was suddenly night. An inexplicable uneasiness filled her. After all, it was only a dog. He would go away. She checked the supplies. There were some cans of soup. After nine the place on the highway closed. Could that unnatural dog ambush Richard? No, again some chill in her extremities insisted—it was after her.

Had it got cold with dark? Silly. She went again to the window. Was he gone? Where was he?

She was too late. He had moved around the cabin to the garden. Now he could be seen without the binoculars, just presenting himself in the edge of the porch light. It was uncanny how he moved behind her back. As if an image in the eye shifted with the eye's glance from place to place. His posture was unchanged, his eager eyes had the same glitter, but now his tongue panted out. Did dogs really crash through windows? This dog had the look of a killer. Fifi was growling now, and staring as if hypnotized. She called her into the cabin—the porch was an unsubstantial structure—and thought to lock the door. But as she did so, Fifi, still growling to herself, lunged with a ghastly force through the rotting screen door and streaked into the dark toward the enemy.

She slammed the door, trembling, and snapped off the light. Slipping close along the wall to the window, she saw the dog still sitting in the yard gazing soulfully toward her. There was no sign of Fifi, no sound. All was silence. All was gray and dreamlike. She pushed the table against the door, slid the chairs next to it.

The rifle. Then she stopped, her foot on the loft ladder, for her impulse had been to point it not at that decoy, but at herself for the *coup de grâce.*

She felt tears. What was this beast? What did it stand for? She only knew Richard and Fifi were gone. Except for this strange adversary she was alone.

She expected it through the back door, and stood with her hand on the front doorknob, ready to play a last desperate game for salvation. When the moment came, and that horror stormed her barricade, at that moment she threw herself out the front door, slamming it to behind her. But she slipped, on the great stone step, on Fifi's blood, and her head cracked, with a sound like target practice, on the rock.

She lay dazed, arms flung outward. The rock's paralyzing magnetism seeped through her slowly. She did not try to move. She was sure she could never move again.

The headlights wheeled their twin rays over the valley as the car turned at the bridge. The doe, munching an alder sprout, looked up and, taking no chances, stepped down the bank and splashed delicately downstream; and the heron, his eyes blinded, spread his wings angrily in his secret nest.

PHILIP L. GREENE was born in New York, attended Lowell Technological Institute and New York University. He is an Associate Professor of English at Adelpi University and was Associate Editor of *Venture* magazine from 1953–59. His first novel will be published this year.

The Dichotomy

They were discussing the dichotomy between the essentialists and the existentialists just after the two o'clock class. Sucking on a cigarette Rollie turned in his swivel chair and searched for the right phrase. "What the Platonic world ignores is the . . . human condition. Rudebager in Wisconsin, when I was out there, held that *angst*-less belief is basically a failure of moral nerve. The dichotomy . . ."

"Yes," Malcolm cut in softly, "I see what you mean. I have a very nice student, doing A- work actually, who is very excited about the dichotomy. But the boys in my classes don't seem to be interested in that sort of thing. All they want to do is play."

Rollie snickered and swiveled back to his tea. He had to be cautious not to injure Malcolm. Rollie's favorite students confided that Malcolm was a very sweet man, well-prepared and all, but he was so square, he would never talk about sex or anything. They complained that Mr. Duckworth was always talking about image patterns, word clusters and syntactical strategies.

"In my eleven o'clock," Rollie said, "we were discussing the on-going dialogue between Nietzschean *Gott ist todt* and Buber's I-Thou relationship."

"What were you applying it to?"

"We're doing *Catcher in the Rye*. I was comparing Holden's journey with Odysseus's quest. They lit up when I mentioned alienated man. Holden is very Buberesque. But most of the class think he's sick. We got on to psychic disorder. They like Holden, but they want him to cool it. They're all involved in cool form. Anybody who plays it straight is a 'cop-out.' So I said 'I dig' and they all laughed at me. Anyway, one girl, maybe you know her, Marvena Portney, sandy hair, big breasts, skinny legs, eyes dilating all the time, a speech and drama major, Marvena shot up out of her chair and ran out of the room holding back the tears."

"What happened?"

"I don't know. She'll be in soon for a conference."

"Yes, it is difficult," Malcolm said with concern. "I never knew what to do with crying students. I usually offer them a clean handkerchief, but they always reach for the kleenex in their bags. They carry everything in those bags. I have a weakness for crying girls with big bags."

"I wonder what they carry in there," Rollie said, slyly.

"Ha, ha," Malcolm said.

"There aren't many virgins left."

"Ha, ha," Malcolm said.

"Do you think there are any virgins left?"

"Some, I guess." Malcolm's voice dropped a bit.

"Do you think they use the pill?"

"The pill? I think not. I don't think they use anything."

"They don't?" Rollie swiveled with the tea cup in his hand.

"The boys probably use something, you know, in the old-fashioned way."

"I hear they use Saran Wrap."

"Saran Wrap?"

"They buy it in the supermarket. No problem with drugstores."

Malcolm shook his head.

"It might be fun," Rollie said.

"Ha, ha," Malcolm said.

Rollie watched Malcolm walk out of the room with a manila folder tucked under his arm, his face composed for official business. He loved to play secret agent. Last year it was a confidential report on the revamped Freshman Contemporary Civilization program. Rollie had talked his way into seeing the report by goading Malcolm into defending the Aristotelian categories by which he was setting up the course. With some

delicate maneuvering Rollie managed to show Malcolm that the
act-agency formula, good for drama perhaps, would foul itself
as an analogue for the literary history of civilization. This year
Malcolm was iron-lipped, friendly but alert, jocular but cautious,
blue eyes slit with razor-edge awareness. It was already late
November and Rollie had not had an inkling of what the
top secret file held. Yesterday evening, after everyone had gone,
and the secretary had marched down the hall to powder up,
he made a hasty survey of her desk, and came upon a note
informing the tenured department members to report at three
the next day for a meeting. Sly old Malcolm Duckworth.

Marvena Portney appeared at the door carrying a big, saggy,
leather shoulder bag. She was dressed in bohemian black. Rollie
swiveled to the girl and motioned her to the conference chair.
He clicked on the small desk lamp, lit another cigarette and
slid into his favorite ankles-crossed, hands-clasped-on-stomach
position. Voices of students on the walk drifted in on the
afternoon light.

"Now," Rollie said comfortingly, and waited.

Marvena held her bag in her lap and waited.

"Is it the dichotomy?"

"What?"

"You ran out of the room. Did I say something?" Rollie watched
Marvena reach in her bag for a lavender tissue.

"It's nothing."

"Do you usually cry over nothing?"

"Sometimes. I don't know. I'm just blue."

"Does Holden have anything to do with it?"

"Well, like you said, there was this dichotomy."

"Yes." For some years now he had understood the meaning
of restraint.

"I was thinking of the I-Thou relationship. I have it here
in my notes." She reached into her bag and pulled out a
notebook. She read: "'Holden's spiritual intercourse with the
adult world and its system of values has been short-circuited.
In a world without meaning he finds himself pinned to a rock,
with the vulture Society pecking away at his heart. The mad
world is a ravenous beast bent on devouring its young.' That's
just wonderful, Mr. Mergenthaler."

"But it makes you blue." Rollie sat back and mulled his

words. He remembered pausing in class before coming out with "spiritual intercourse."

Marvena put her bag on the floor and shifted to a slouch position. In the fading day a small circle of light from the desk lamp glowed brightly. The two faces, hidden in the darkness on either side of the lamp, eased into anonymity. The voices floated over the bridge of light.

"If two people want to relate to each other," Marvena said, "there must be some kind of connection. Isn't Holden kind of disconnected?"

"Yes, but that's what makes him whole. That is the ironic paradox. The existential coming-into-being is a result of this self-confrontation. That is why I used the Prometheus image."

"Isn't the book about love?"

Rollie uncrossed his legs and leaned forward. "That is the dichotomy. How can you love in a loveless world. The ultimate meaning of love is self-love."

"All by yourself?"

"I don't mean you shouldn't have someone. There must always be someone."

"Is that what you call spiritual intercourse?"

"There are many kinds," Rollie said. It was rolling now. Marvena reached in her bag for another tissue and clenched it in her fist. She wore her hair in the new manner, soft, falling over the eyes. In the lamplight she looked chaste and sensuous. She smiled at him and waited.

"You know the line from Shakespeare," Rollie said, " 'Let me not to the marriage of true minds admit impediments'?"

"It's a poem about true love."

"Ah, yes, true love," Rollie said. He thought of himself and Bonnie at Wisconsin in his little cubby-hole office and her pleading little grey eyes blinking true love like a pinball machine. That was the door-opener, but he had difficulty remembering what the heat had been all about. He leaned over to put out his cigarette and brushed against Marvena's hand. She looked up and away quickly.

"The act of love," Rollie said, shifting to a tone of wise counsel, "is a spiritual, you could even call it a religious, encounter. That is probably the underlying meaning of the I-Thou relationship."

"The act of love?" Marvena looked puzzled.

"Making love." The words buzzed across the light. Rollie saw himself and the girl as two poles of a battery with the current sent across the invisible wire of sound. No one had ever clinically pursued the dynamics of the interview situation. There were absolutely no theorists in this field. They had turned a deaf ear on him in Wisconsin when he tried to explain his conference with Clarissa. There had been some bad moments with Bonnie over that.

"The sexual act is a pure thing. It is a form of spiritual intercourse." Rollie swiveled away from Marvena and stared out the window. He wanted her to consult her feelings privately. He turned back quickly with another thought. He was strong now, sure of his way. "Physical union was the price the two in the garden paid for disobeying God. But God meant that carnal knowledge would be a way, a long, suffering, but ultimately beautiful way, back into spiritual identity with God. You see, when Nietzsche said God is dead he meant that the orgasm had been separated from its purpose. In existential terms, man has lost contact with the original, spiritual purpose of sexual life. He has lost touch with himself."

Marvena, her lipstick caked on her parted mouth, uttered a small, bewildered sigh. "I never thought of that."

"What do you think?"

"About what?"

"About that."

"You mean that."

"Well, that's what we have been talking about, isn't it?" Rollie believed in listening to his inner ear, the timing mechanism which announced that the moment of truth was at hand. He remembered the time Susan, a black-eyed Economics major, a type he had not encountered, and the premature timing, the inner ear warning him, but he had jumped the gun, and the whole construction, every brick of irrefutable logic, crumbling like sand. He had tried Krafft-Ebing on her, she was very bright. Marvena needed different tactics. She was very good in class, but she had a book mind.

"I have a girl friend," Marvena said, "she's pinned to this fellow in Law School. We have discussions about this. Aileen says she couldn't walk down the aisle if she knew she had done anything. So, I asked her if Fred is just a soul mate. They've been going together for a year. She says Fred believes a woman should be put on a pedestal, but I know Fred, I used to go out with him, and every once in a while you have to get off the pedestal. I don't mean they should go the limit, although a lot of girls around here do. I know a girl I won't mention her name, but everybody on the campus knows about her. Who's going to marry her? She is soiled linen, a tramp. But if there is real love, maybe something like what you say, a kind of spiritual thing, people who have lots of personality and they like the same things, then I don't think it's so terrible if they fool around a little. Do you know what I mean, Mr. Mergenthaler?"

Rollie looked at the black mesh stockings with flecks of skin showing through her crossed legs. The holes were too big, the skin chalky and flat. Her nostrils flared too much. Her arms showing through her sleeveless black sweater were freckled with large greenish spots. Her eyes had the look of burnt bacon. She was a petting-to-the-climax specialist, a manipulator of small triumphs out of which one manages to fashion major spiritual defeats. Rollie abhorred the sexual Philistine.

He leaned over and patted her once, then again, letting his hand linger an instant longer on the black mesh. He felt the leprous, corroding flesh turn to flame at his touch. "I think women got off the pedestal a long time ago," he said. He thought of Melanie Armbruster, who had tricked him into agreeing that yes love was a many splendored thing and the heart has its reasons and how do I count the ways. And here was Marvena Portney, the Eastern archetype, *la femme moyenne sensuelle*, the back-seat sensualist with a front-seat philosophy.

Marvena rose suddenly and apologized to Mr. Mergenthaler, she had car-pool responsibilities, three other kids were waiting for her. Could she see him next week about her paper? Rollie watched her skitter down the hall, hair bouncing gently, buttocks jiggling confidently, flying to join the pedestal-burners.

The phone call home was tender, conciliatory. Did Bonnie have a good day with the kids? It is rough not having a girl coming in. They would drum up the money to put Jessica into nursery school. Next semester he would definitely ask for no night classes. They never get to see each other. When tenure came things would change. No more hopping around from school to school. Was Rollie having a conference? Please dear, couldn't he cut down on the conferences, for a little while? She shouldn't worry, he keeps the door open and the conferences short. What else could he do? They come after him.

As Rollie hung up Malcolm came in and slipped his folder into the desk drawer. Malcolm had the mysterious document look about him, the neck sitting stiffly on the porcine shoulders, the faded blue eyes tilting left and right in search of rats in the corner, the girlish hands furtive and nervous, dancing over the papers on his desk. Rollie shopped around for a vulnerable point of entry. Some time ago he had discovered Malcolm's weakness for Lewis Carroll and J. M. Barrie, and the Milne stuff, things Malcolm finally confessed in absolute confidence that he read at night instead of detective stories. Malcolm had shown him his Beerbohmish parodies of the children's classics, fey, sparkling little things, colored by cute adult sexual innuendos.

"I'm absolutely washed out," Malcolm said, paving the way.

"Must have been a rough meeting."

"Nasty."

Rollie didn't want to push. Malcolm was a liberal humanist. If there had been injury at the meeting he would talk. He recalled Malcolm standing up at a faculty meeting, his voice shrill with passion, to defend on principle the hearing rights of a dismissed instructor. The weak, the lame, the halt, the unprotected brought Malcolm to the ramparts.

"There was a heated discussion," Malcolm said, after a while.

"Yes." Rollie grouped factions quickly. He was sure of at least three people. But there was Buckley and his Renaissance Puritanism, a cold, murderously isolated man who despised students.

"Well, I might as well tell you." Malcolm clasped and unclasped his hands.

"Buckley wants us to sign a Code of Ethics, something like a loyalty oath. I think teachers have an important function. *In loco parentis* has been a motto of mine. But this has the odor of McCarthyism."

"What does he want?"

"I'm not at liberty to say just yet. But I can tell you this. He feels tenure should not be given if the candidate doesn't measure up to the code. My goodness, right now I'm committing a terrible breach of ethics."

"What are you not at liberty to say?"

"Well, you know."

"What do I know?"

"I can't say."

"The idea of an ethics code has merit," Rollie said, lighting up a cigarette and swiveling in a wide slow turn. "As a department of Civilization we should be committed to a philosophy. Heidegger's *Dasein*, his being-in-the-worldness is a form of action ethics, a restoration of a condition upset by the Cartesian dichotomy. The mind-body split disappears. To shift the image, Nietzschean Apollonian—Dionysianism is part of the picture. A modern ethics which addressed itself to a pure existence philosophy, a naked facing of the what-isness of the human condition, this would be a great thing. I suppose Buckley didn't have this in mind."

"Well, I don't think so." Malcolm's eyes were glazed.

"I've always held for a *modus vivendi* that would satisfy our need for identity."

"I think Buckley had something else in mind."

"What did he have in mind?"

"I really can't say."

"Is he after me?"

"Not exactly."

"What is he after exactly?"

"More basic considerations." Malcolm patted his forehead with a handkerchief.

"Like what?"

"Oh, you know, the public image."

"Yes, of course, I can understand that." Rollie had meant to get rid of his old sharkskin suit, the blue-grey one with the bus driver's shine in the seat. "How is mine?"

"You talk in the dark."

"You mean in conference?"

"With female students."

"That's a bad image."

"You could put on the light."

"I have to find out what is hurting. It's better in the dark. Do they hate me for that?"

"Nobody hates you."

"They don't love me."

"Ah, well."

Maclolm had to dash home to feed Archimedes, his dog. On the way out he handed Rollie his folder. "I'm violating a confidence, but if you keep it to yourself . . . this is strictly *entre nous.*"

After Malcolm had gone Rollie went down the hall to the hot plate and poured a cup of tea. The day people had gone and the night people had not yet arrived. The hallway was quiet except for the scraping of the porter's trash barrel at the other end. To Rollie the twilight hour was a time when naked hallway bulbs and impassive porters with noisy barrels struck the right note of portent. What concatenation of events would express exactly the terrors of the dark night of the soul?

He closed his door, sat down, blew on his tea, lit a cigarette, sipped and read Buckley's proposal, a series of Mosaic commandments, which warned the instructor that thou shalt not dress unseemly, thou shalt not be late for class, thou shalt not hunger after popularity, thou shalt not serve Mammon, thou shalt not turn out the lights in the office, thou shalt not covet students in conference. Above all, thou shalt not commit Conference Ambience, a configuration of conferences which create an atmosphere of provocative intimacy. Malcolm's spider script followed the injunction with the minutes of further discussion about the aims and goals of the department that must fulfill the needs and wants of students. Orientation toward ethical attitudes is a primary aspect of the harmonious adjustment of the staff-student relationship. Undoubtedly, the educational values which are in reality the target-goal, should be fostered, if not indeed enhanced, by a code of ethics which announces boldly principles of belief in the inherent dignity of the experiential validity of college life.

The committee voted unanimously to form a committee that would investigate the procedural matters involved in the final wording of a Code of Ethics for the Department of Civilization. Malcolm's note at the bottom read: "See RM about conference ambience."

Rollie closed the folder, put out the light and turned his chair toward the window. He watched the cars of the evening students stream into the parking lot. Tonight he would deliver Montaigne on friendship and love to the tired, blank, sullen faces. He would administer the alchemist's potion and see the dull stirrings of their thick blood spirit them into new being. They would pummel at the door of his sensibility and shout to be let into the secret chambers of consciousness. "Mr. Mergenthaler, I never knew I could feel," "Mr. Mergenthaler, I understand now," "Mr. Mergenthaler, you have given me a new. . . ." Falling to their knees, they would touch the hem of his cloak, and he would console. In the Judaic-Christian heritage man was conceived as tragic, suffering, alien, estranged from the body of the world, estranged from the godhead within. Embrace the stranger in you, make love to the enemy within. Find in yourself your existence. Bind the dichotomy, make a knot of the graceful and the grotesque. Deliver yourself out of bondage to Egypt in you. Restore yourself to the terrible freedom of the self. Tear down the walls of the temple.

Rollie put his head down on the desk over his folded arms and waited for the burning hum in his eyes to stop. Buckley would bury him. He was the spokesman for the ethical head-hunters, those cannibals of heart who cowered behind their forms, as if they had no secret life. Had he not told them all that man trembles at the abyss of freedom when he discovers the body is not a cage for the spirit? Let the bird of joy and love out and plunge full-plumed into the dark, liberating waters below. The smirky smiles, the frozen pieties carved in their cheeks, the drip and dribble of their rational sensibilities were everywhere. Even poor, sweet Malcolm minced along, delivering his tepid bromides, tuning in surreptitiously to Rollie's conferences, licking his thin, vicarious lips wth salacious hunger.

Rollie rose and went to Malcolm's desk and file cabinet. Hidden somewhere in the years of departmental espionage was a secret hoard, Rollie didn't know what, some evidence perhaps of a former colleague's demise, and ugly truth scavenged on the endless hunt for the enemy. He tried Malcolm's closet, and pulled out several cartons of old texts, term papers, departmental memos, flyers from book companies, notes and plans and pamphlets—a junk yard of educational debris, stored and treasured, a legacy of a lifetime of service to the institution. Methodically, Rollie stripped each carton, book by book, paper by paper, until, at last, in a sturdy carton marked Seagram's V-O he came upon a bulky manila envelope tied with string. He untied the string carefully and slipped out the contents onto the desk. Eight-by-ten photographs, two or three dozen, sparkled in the reflected light of his desk lamp. Oiled young gods in loin cloths with pouting stoic faces glared up at him, flexing bulging biceps and staunch thighs, swarthy Latin Adonises and sunburned Teutons, firm-jawed sculptures in flesh, mindless beauty fixed in time and space, a small army of heroes of the body poised in triumphant vanity. Malcolm's lovers cached away in the bottom of a whiskey carton. How many times had Malcolm tied and untied that string? How many times had he run his puffy, docile hands over the glossy bodies? How many times had he dreamed of being locked in lubricous arms?

A soft knock on the door broke his reveries. Rollie hurriedly tied the envelope, replaced it in the carton and pushed it back into the closet. He opened the door and ushered in his conferee, Sherry, a twenty-one-year-old divorcée majoring in Civilization at night. Her first paper on love among the Medici had shown astonishing insight, written in a kind of serene prose, disengaged, without nervous tics and cute defenses of the average paper. She said she wouldn't dream of writing a paper without first freeing herself, and Mr. Mergenthaler could free himself too. She would help him if he was interested.

"I brought the stuff," she said, as she took Marvena's seat.

Rollie liked to work his way into a subject. Her abruptness disturbed him.

"What stuff?"

"I told you I would turn you on."

"I have a class in an hour."

"We can share a joint. You'll teach up a storm." She reached into her bag and took out a cigarette, loosely wrapped, with the paper twisted at one end.

"Doesn't it make you kind of free, sexually, that is?" Rollie asked, looking at the cigarette.

"You know it," she said. She took out a pack of matches and started to strike one.

"Wait a minute," Rollie said. "I want to talk about this a little more. I don't know what I'm supposed to feel. Do you get high, like with liquor? Is there a big release?"

Sherry leaned back in her chair and sighed. "Larry, my ex-husband, he asked me the same thing. What does it feel like? Will I get hooked? He was afraid he would lose his substitute teacher's license."

"Malraux had an opium smoker in his book, *Man's Fate*. He tries to show a spiritual nirvana, a lucid self-awareness as a result of the drug. I was wondering whether marijuana might not combine spirit and sense in a meaningful way, so that the essential I-Thouness could be achieved. You know, a short cut from the meditative procedure recommended by ecclesiasts."

Sherry looked at him for a moment and lit the cigarette. "Here, you have got to take in air, a lot, as you puff. There's a lot of I-Thouness in every puff. There is probably even some you-meness too."

Rollie puffed and Sherry puffed and an acrid haze hung thinly in the room. They talked through the haze:

SHERRY: Cool, isn't it?

ROLLIE: I don't feel anything.

SHERRY: Time wounds all heels.

ROLLIE: I expected *Walpurgisnacht*.

SHERRY: You know it.

ROLLIE: What am I supposed to feel?

SHERRY: It'll come.

ROLLIE: I believe in feeling.

SHERRY: It's the only thing.

ROLLIE: I could run on that platform.

SHERRY: You're the most.

ROLLIE: I think I hear something in my head.

SHERRY: You are getting there.

ROLLIE: Should it buzz or hum?

SHERRY: Just let it come.

ROLLIE: I lost it.

SHERRY: I got my own problems.

ROLLIE: I think I ought to do something. Maybe it's happening.

SHERRY: It's a happening.

ROLLIE: Maybe there should be a click or something. I believe there should be a click.

SHERRY: Cool it, baby.

ROLLIE: Why do you keep saying that? I want to hot it.

SHERRY: Stay loose.

Rollie got up, reached over and put his hand on Sherry's breast. She was wearing a sweater. Sherry looked up at him. "What's your problem?"

"I always start with the breast," Rollie said.

"Oh, all right."

Rollie put his other hand on the other breast. He stood over her with two hands on her two breasts. "I may lose my job. I'm up for tenure," he said.

"Huh?"

"Your breasts are soft and warm. Mushy." She didn't answer. "I'm dying of a fatal disease," he offered.

"Cancer."

"Conference Ambience." He let go and slumped into his seat. The back of his head felt thick, knotted. The girl's intolerable eyes, blistered and porous, were fixed on the book shelf on Malcolm's wall. She seemed to be reading the Handbook and Rhetoric section with fierce concentration.

"You poor kid," she said without interest.

"Without a goal-oriented philosophy where can you go?"

"I'm stoned."

"I look at your hair, your face. You have a disaffiliated face. Centuries of disaster have emptied you of meaning. A little Zoroastrian pot to make the world go round. Sherry, a tragedy." He leaned over and tried the breast again.

"Two for a quarter," she said.

The door opened and the porter with his big trash barrel stood with immigrant servility. "Excuse," he said and trudged in to empty the waste baskets. Slowly, Rollie took his hand away and sank back in his chair. After emptying the baskets the porter worked his push broom around their chairs excusing himself with garlic grunts. Rollie swiveled himself across to Malcolm's side of the room, the casters squeaking loudly against the floor. The porter bent under Rollie's desk and the broom whisked out one of Malcolm's glossy heroes that had slipped from the desk. "Pretty man," the porter said as he handed it to Rollie. At the

doorway he turned back and smiled. Rollie caught the tender
curve of his mouth and felt his heart give a frightened leap.
Sherry got up and took the photograph from Rollie's slack hand
and held it under the desk light.

"Oobie doo."

Rollie pressed his hands over the bridge of his nose and
listened to the sound of the porter's barrel down the hall. The
cigarette had left a dry, papery taste in his mouth. He took the
photograph from Sherry and put it in his drawer.

"Oobie doo to you too," he said.

On his way home after class in his station wagon he thought of
something he had said to Malcolm earlier about satisfying his
need for identity. The porter's grainy face and quick smile
flickered in front of him. Ooobie doo, Sherry had said. He turned
the car around, went back to the darkened office, pulled out
the body folder and drove over to Malcolm's house. Malcolm
answered the door in a Chinese robe and big, furry slippers.
He offered Rollie a glass of port and set out on a Delft dish
some Huntley and Palmer biscuits.

"My aunt sends me a package every year from London. Like
Girl Scout cookies," he said, taking a chair opposite the couch
Rollie had slumped in. Malcolm crossed his legs and pulled
the silky robe over his knees. His hairless calves stuck out from
beneath the robe.

"I would like to try your bar bells," Rollie said.

"Bar bells?"

"Your weights. You use weights, don't you?" Rollie's voice
cracked. He sipped some wine and twisted the stem of the glass
in his fingers.

Malcolm crossed his legs and smoothed the robe again. "I
have an exercise bicycle in the cellar. You are welcome to it."

"Is that what you use? Let me ask you something. Do you
believe in original sin? I'm sure you think about things like
that. The redemptive theory. How do you buy back what you
have lost? How does one redeem oneself?"

"You could save enough S & H Green Stamps. I'd say I'm
worth about one and a half books."

"Do you keep oil? I might like to try the oil."

"What oil?" Malcolm's tone was pitched a bit higher.

"Body oil. After the weights."

"What are you after?" Malcolm was tense, hostile. His white, beardless face showed patches of red under the cheekbones.

"What I'm after. What I'm after." Rollie shrugged and drained his glass. "I'll confess. I'm after the Redemptive Principle. Man is alone confronting the void. No original sin. Martin Buber says . . . Never mind. The agony of self knowledge. Who are you? Who speaks for man?" He paused and turned on Malcolm. "Where do you keep your weights?"

"I'm really very tired."

"Here's something to perk you up." Rollie opened his briefcase and took out Malcolm's envelope. He untied the string and shook the photographs out on the couch. "Pretty men," he said, trying on the porter's smile.

Malcolm stood over the pictures, rubbing his sweating palms. The big, furry slippers held up pelican ankles. He picked up one of the photographs with listless fingers.

"I'm all alone in this thing," Rollie went on. "Everywhere I go it's the same. What have I done to deserve such despise? I need some more wine."

Malcolm waved in the direction of the decanter, picked up the rest of the pictures and sat down, dealing them in his lap. The robe had slipped from his thighs, exposing clean milk-white flesh. Rollie filled his glass and paced the floor, sipping and waving as he walked. "I know this may hurt you, but I see it as an act of compassion. The right hand feeds the left, or something like that. I mean there is nothing *wrong* in this." He took the pictures from Malcolm's lap. "But do you think they would understand? I saw Buckley's Proposal. You and me, Malcolm, they are after us. The bearers of light. Prometheans. That's what we are." He dropped the pictures into Malcolm's lap. Malcolm leaned his head against the high back of the Queen Anne chair with green and blue paisley slipcovers.

"As a child I was the marble's champion of my street," Malcolm said, shuffling the pictures. "Mary Lee Danforth and I would play doctor. Once I stuck my finger in her vagina for five marbles. She didn't care. She was a terrible tomboy. All she wanted was the marbles championship. When I was thirteen I offered Mary Lee my marble collection. She asked me what I wanted for it. She would have done anything, I guess. She didn't want the marbles anymore. She was smoking by that time. I told her it was a gift. I wanted nothing. Mary Lee ran off with a Mexican trumpet player when she was fifteen. It was this finger." Malcolm lifted the index finger of his left hand.

"I use the middle finger," Rollie said.

"Yes," Malcolm said absently.

"I didn't mean anything," Rollie said.

"I want to show you something." Malcolm shuffled to the closet in the foyer and took down a square tin canister from the shelf. He held it in his upturned palms, bearing it like a precious gift. "I've kept it all these years. Would do like to have it?"

Rollie hesitated, and then reached for the canister. As he offered the gift, Malcolm shuddered, his hand jerked back. Rollie flinched and the canister fell to the floor, the lid popped off and the marbles spilled to the floor. As they reached the end of the rug the marbles clattered on to the wood.

Malcolm dropped to his knees and scurried along the rug. "My marbles. I lost my marbles," he called out to no one in particular.

"I'll help you," Rollie said, and he fell to his knees, and with swift, precise sweeps of his hand he gathered marbles. Together they popped the marbles back into the canister.

"Would you like to play a game?" Malcolm asked, as he held the canister in his arms. He explained that he had become a champion by playing for hours on the Oriental rug, not nearly as good as the Kerman on the floor now, but also full of intricate patterns, with many targets that required control and patience. "Do you see the fleur-de-lis in the center of the rug? You shoot for that. Shall we start?"

They reached into the canister for shooting marbles. Rollie selected a clear glass marble with light sweeping wisps of clouds. Malcolm chose a yellow and blue swirl with a roughened surface, his favorite shooter. Rollie held the marble in his warm palm and felt a hollowness in his head. The port and the marijuana were probably working their way in. He knew he should call Bonnie and tell her not to worry, that he would be late playing marbles with his friend Malcolm, but she might try to reason with him and he didn't want that.

"You know," he said, quickly, with a tone of candor that

promised a revelation, "this afternoon when I was discussing the dichotomy . . ."

"Oh, that old thing," Malcolm said. "Come on, let's play."

"O.K.," Rollie said, ballooning out a gust of stale breath. He looked at Malcolm on his knees, marble in hand, with his Chinese kimono and his furry slippers, and wondered what it was all about.

"Shoot," Rollie said, feeling a catch in his throat, as he cast his first marble.

STEPHEN MINOT was born in Boston and received degrees from Harvard College and Johns Hopkins University. His stories have appeared in *The Atlantic Monthly, Harper's, Kenyon Review* and *Carleton Miscellany* among others. He is currently working on a critical anthology of modern fiction which will be published next year. He is a professor at Trinity College, Hartford, Connecticut, where he teaches the Fiction Workshop and Advanced Literary Writing as well as a Senior Seminar in the Creative Process.

Mars Revisited

"Like I'm telling you," the sergeant said, "th' kid could be anywhere. But he's not here. So if you want to keep looking, go with the patrolman over there."

Frank Badger turned to see a patrolman elbowing his way through the crowded Headquarters, heading for the door, apparently in a hurry. But Frank hesitated. He wanted to ask the sergeant at the desk *why* he was supposed to follow the patrolman and what the man's name was and where he was being sent. He didn't like the idea of nodding or saluting or doffing his cap and running to do what he was told. At forty-two he'd outgrown all that.

But the sergeant had turned to argue with three men in dark suits—detectives or perhaps suspects—and already the patrol-man had made it out into the street, so Frank didn't really have much choice.

He had to hurry to catch up. It wasn't easy. The room swirled with activity. He squeezed by a desk where two reporters were questioning a man in a pinstriped suit who might have been an alderman or a prisoner; he pressed himself against the wall to let a handcuffed pair go by; behind him in the next room three policemen were talking with a long-haired creature of undetermined sex. He found himself staring at everyone, a bewildered Adam trying to find names for each new object he saw. But that was nonsense. He wasn't a part of all this. It wasn't as if he'd been arrested. He hadn't even been asked to appear. He was only a father looking for his son. He was just following up a rumor that the boy was being held by the police in this city.

The uncertainty of it all had left him unsettled. He had spent three hours in a jet and was dizzy from two changes in time zone, from four shifts in altitude, from the jarring contrast between the sweet-talking stewardesses and the surly Desk Sergeant, whose language, he recalled now after so many years, was the language of all sergeants everywhere. And now the patrolman he was to follow had disappeared through the door out into the night and he, Frank, had better get his ass out of there. . . .

The walls spread to the size of a warehouse and the blues of the uniforms faded to khaki. It was brutally hot and humid. He could smell the greasy dubbing which they had smeared over their new boots and the sweat of a thousand inductees being herded. They had been lined up by barking sergeants whose voices echoed up to the steel rafters and back, and now they were told to lay out their gear—all their belongings which had been carefully packed into duffel bags at four that same morning. And when they had spread out every last thing—every sock, belt, shirt, underpant, photo, toothbrush, condom, book, packet of letters—all of it lined up neatly on the sooty, paper-littered floor, they stood at attention for an hour for an inspection which never came.

And of course when the order was given to pack up again, they were to do it "on the double," they were to "get the lead out of their ass," they were to "look alive" as they stood alphabetically in groups of fifty for another half hour, this time "at ease," speculating to themselves and in undertones to each other where they might be going. That was all more than twenty years ago, and Frank couldn't remember what city that warehouse had been in, but he could feel with right-now clarity how the sweat ran steadily down his neck, shoulders, and back, tickling as it plowed little furrows through the film of coal-dust which clung to his skin.

He was out in the street now, looking for the patrolman. A squad car was coming in with lights flashing and a number of pedestrians stood about—the same kind of crowd that gathers for accidents. The patrolman was getting into a second car parked further down the street. Frank ran and opened the back door just as the motor started.

"The Desk Sergeant said for me to go with you."

He paused as if by some reflex he was asking for permission.

"Well, get in then," the patrolman said.

"Front or back?"

"Jesus, will you hurry up?"

Since it was the back door he had opened, he got in that one moving awkwardly and stumbling, half falling, over two civilians already sitting there.

"Sorry," he said, and immediately wished he hadn't. He would have to watch out for all those little phrases of accommodation with which the civil world oils its conversations. He would have to tighten up again.

They drove through an endless slum, an uncomfortable section in a strange city. The summer's heat had squeezed all the residents from their apartments down onto the steps and out to the sidewalks. The patrolman drove at a moderate speed and used no siren, but the red roof light was on and in response to it every face in every group revolved slowly, without expression, following the car as it passed.

The two passengers beside him paid no attention to the street scene. They were preoccupied in a silent search for cigarettes and matches. It was complicated by the fact that the left wrist of one was handcuffed to the right wrist of the other. It was impossible to tell which was the prisoner and which was the captor.

Finally the one whose right hand was free found a crumpled pack in the other's shirt pocket and a Zippo from his own and placed a bent cigarette in the mouth of the other and lit it. Frank could remember placing a cigarette in his wife's mouth some twenty years earlier when they were first living together, seizing time on furloughs and treasuring the nuances of intimacy.

He wished he had made it clear when he first got in that he hadn't been told where he was being sent. It seemed ridiculous to admit at this point that he didn't have the slightest idea where he was going or even where he was. As a civil engineer specializing in bridges and aerial expressways it was his job to deal in facts. Mystery or even uncertainty was at best unprofessional. It would never occur to him to spend a summer's afternoon exploring back roads without a destination; nor would he normally be willing to follow the orders of someone he didn't know and travel with strangers who wouldn't say where they were going.

Closing his eyes he could hear the endless "click-it-ti/click-click-click-it-ti/click" of that old troop train, the creak of its wooden sides, the muffled mutterings of poker players in the aisle, a harmonica somewhere, distant snoring. A night and a day and another night without the slightest idea whether they were headed southwest to Texas ("that's where they do desert-survival training—no canteens") or south to Georgia "they make 'em swim across swamps at night") or west to the Rockies ("Arctic survival—I hear two out of ten die in basic").

At night they tried to read their directions from the stars, peering upward through the filthy windows, but there wasn't a man there who could tell north from south in that way. And by morning it was drizzling so that the sun was no help. At some point that day the train waited for an hour in a sodden wasteland of stubbled, burned-over fields and red clay. No cattle grazed here and no cars moved along the puddled dirt road. But from somewhere came a tattered delegation of black children, rain-streaked and unnaturally solemn.

Frank and all the others leaned out the windows and shouted "Where are we? Hey kids, where are we? What state?"

But the children didn't understand and held out their hands saying, "Mon-ey? Penn-y. Gimmie penn-y."

The soldiers, mostly Northerners, were incredulous. "Jesus," one of them said, "they've drove us clear to North Africa." They all laughed and started pitching pennies, watching the children scramble for them in the puddles. This was even funnier. Frank pulled back from the window, brooding about where these children were, where they all were, and where in hell they were going.

"Where are we going?" Frank asked abruptly.

"Never mind about that," the patrolman said.

It seemed needlessly hostile until he realized that the driver may have assumed that it was the prisoner who spoke.

"Look," Frank said, "you don't have to talk to me like I was under arrest. I'm just looking for my son and they told me to go with you. They didn't tell me where we were going."

"We can't talk with a suspect in the car. Regulations."

His tone was neither reprimanding nor friendly. It was devoid of human emotion. "Besides," he added in the same voice, "if you'd kept your boy home he wouldn't be in trouble."

Bastard, he muttered in silence. If it weren't for that uniform. . . .

He had almost forgotten what it had been like to be hemmed in by uniforms. Below him, the old sergeants, leftovers from the peacetime army, their minds addled by military life, yet still ready to discredit the young officers over them. And, worse, the deal-making colonels who knew they had to make good before some idiot stopped the war. And those earnest captains, one notch above Frank, insisting on the rights of elder sons because they had entered the war just one year earlier—the incredible subtleties of rank.

He was startled by the siren. It was not a wail but just a low growl, the sound of a large and threatening dog. The streets were almost devoid of traffic, but they were more crowded with pedestrians; and almost as if by reaction to it the driver was going faster.

It was a mixed neighborhood and the headlights picked up white shirts against black bodies and some whitely bare chests. No one ran from the path of the car; they merely walked with insulting lack of concern until they were just barely out of range. Occasionally one would raise a fist or a finger. Frank wondered whether they viewed him personally as a friend of the police or as a prisoner. But how could they tell when he wasn't sure himself?

They paused at a cross street while four fire trucks passed by, wailing. And then patrol cars. When they started up again they turned and followed in the same general direction but not as fast. And in four blocks they had apparently arrived somewhere.

The driver parked on a side street together with an array of squad cars, patrol wagons, and a couple of ambulances. The crowd in the street, a mixture of races and ages, was scattered and calm, but the mystery of its presence—its mere existence—struck Frank as ominous. It was like the armored half-track parked under the streetlight, motionless but as arresting as if it had been an enormous armadillo. Police floodlights lit the entire area with sharp contrasts, making the scene into a moonscape.

The driver got out and opened the door for the two handcuffed civilians who emerged awkwardly. The three of them headed up the steps of a many-storied, rambling brick building which could have been an old hospital or an enormous city high school. Every window was lit.

Again he hesitated. It seemed impossible that this slum-castle would have anything to do with his son, and it seemed outrageous that the driver expected him to trot along obediently like some jeep orderly. Back in the real world Frank had thirteen draftsmen and a secretary under his command and he had forgotten what it was to be treated like a recruit.

But it was clear that if he stood there much longer he would be demoted to just another onlooker. He'd get nowhere that way. So he ran, once again, to catch up.

An adolescent-looking guardsman—a boy soldier—blocked the door with a bayoneted carbine held diagonally before him. His head was too small for his helmet and his Adam-appled neck too scrawny to fill his collar. He was the original cartoon of a hayseed recruit, the model for Sad Sack, a joke; he also held his bayoneted carbine with shocking self-assurance.

"D'you have a pass?" the boy asked.

"I'm with the patrolman."

"What patrolman?"

"The one who just came in with the suspects."

"You on the force?"

"I'm a witness. They need me in there." He tried to muscle by, but in an instantaneous, perfectly executed movement, the soldier spun his rifle to the horizontal position where, chest high, it was poised to send the intruder hurtling down the stone steps to the sidewalk below. And it was entirely clear to Frank that the soldier would do just that if he had to, not in anger or fear but in the line of duty the way a meatpacker slings a side of beef.

"Look," Frank said, trying a new approach. "I think my boy is being held there."

"I'm not allowed. . . ."

"He's about your age. I don't know what he's done, but I want to get to him. Just let me look and then I'll get out."

"We got orders," the boy said, but all self-assurance was lost.

"Could you check with someone?"

"Well, wait here a moment."

Incredibly, the boy soldier was gone and Frank walked directly into the large foyer, moving fast. He expected a heavy hand on his shoulder at any moment.

Almost at once he was in an enormous room—some kind of armory or exhibition hall—in which hundreds of people were working with intensity. The place hummed like a nest of hornets. A semblance of order had been attempted by walling off sections of floor space with Street Department barriers; desks had been improvised by laying doors across saw horses; crude signs had been scratched out in magic marker with titles such as MEDI-CAL AID, INTERROGATION, SURVEILLANCE, and AR-RAIGNED. Directly in front of him was a real desk—ancient, scarred, and official. It was covered with scattered documents, typed lists of names, and empty coffee cups. The sign, written on the back of a torn placard, read CHIEF EXPEDITER, and beside it was a small American flag on a lead base. The swivel chair which was behind the desk was empty.

Frank waited there, letting waves of busy people ebb and flow around him. He wanted to stop someone, anyone, and ask him what in hell was going on. It seemed incredible that all these people—police, detectives, soldiers, students, blacks and whites in the street—knew perfectly well what was happening and that he, Frank, was still in the dark. It wasn't as if he were uninformed. He read two newspapers and three periodicals of assorted political hues. He would have known if this city had ever been characterized as "racially torn" or prone to student strife. No, it was just another city and all of this had been going on behind his back. It chilled him to think that perhaps this scene was being repeated in cities all over the country.

Suddenly he wished he hadn't come. It was a slim lead anyway—just a phone call from an adenoidal young man saying that Francis was being held by the police in this city. But why on earth here? It was miles from the boy's college. And it seemed impossible that a student with such good grades could be deeply involved in anything political.

At his wife's suggestion, Frank had brought along the boy's college transcript. It would, they thought, serve as evidence of good character. Remembering this now, he was startled at how naïve he had been before he stepped off that plane into all this. But how could he have known? He recalled for the first time in years a "V-mail" letter from his mother which had arrived after the three-week nightmare in the foothills of Anzio. She was an unusually well-informed and intelligent woman who followed the war day by day in the newspapers and by radio, and she showed her concern by serving on the Rationing Board without pay, yet she was capable of urging him to instruct the drivers in his unit to make greater savings in gasoline by avoiding quick starts and by coasting down hills. It seemed to him then that the wall between him and the civilians back home was more impregnable than that between him and the enemy.

It was no use waiting for the Chief Expediter. Perhaps he didn't really exist. So he went over to INTERROGATION where men in civilian clothes, usually in pairs, were questioning suspects. There were ten or twelve such groups going on in the little corral. The prisoners were mostly college-aged but highly varied in appearance. From where he stood he could only see two who had the traditional long hair and beads. The others could have been pulled from the ranks of inductees—some black, some tan, and a majority white; some in torn T shirts, some in sleeveless denim jackets, one in a rumpled suit, several in polo shirts. One had a filthy rag tied around his forehead and another held a handkerchief to a cut on the side of his neck; but the rest were uninjured.

Frank stared at this group longer than it would take to determine that his son was not among them. He began to understand, quite slowly at first, that his son *could* be among them. One of the boys looked past his interrogator at Frank and his expression was derisive. His son had given him that look from time to time. But he checked his own thoughts, remembering that the boy's name was Francis and that he hated to be called Son or, worse, Boy. Francis. He deserved to be called that. It would be a hell of a thing to act out the fantasy he had on the plane while still 60,000 feet above all this, a scene in which he walked down the long, sterile corridor of a model penitentiary to the designated cell and to greet the prisoner with, "Well, Son, how did all this come about?"

The plainclothesmen were through with that student and had him sign something and sent him over to the other side of the pen where fingerprints were taken. Frank could hear one of them say ". . . over to SURVEILLANCE," and as the boy started to leave the officer added, "So don't try anything funny because you can't get out of here without a pass."

This reached Frank like the "thunk" of a slide-bolt. Intuitively he looked around for windows and saw none.

"Hey," he said to the boy as he passed. "I'm looking for someone. Maybe you know him." He paused, but got no encouragement from the boy. "His name is Francis. Francis Badger."

"Like if I knew, Dad, I wouldn't tell you."

And he was gone. Frank's hands curled up into fists but there was no one to hit.

He went over to ARRAIGNED, wondering if at this point he would recognize his Francis. Perhaps someone would have to introduce them as, in fact, they had to when he finally came home from Bremerhaven at the end of the war. "This is Francis," someone had said, and all the adults there laughed uneasily as the father picked up his perfectly strange son, two years old already, and held him awkwardly, the two of them solemn and uncertain.

ARRAIGNED was a larger pen than the others, and was furnished with greater sophistication—it had benches. The prisoners lolled, half-reclining. Some dozed. They appeared to be as unconcerned as sunbathers at the beach. But as soon as Frank reached the barrier (Road Closed, P.D.) they all turned to him as if he had orders for their disposition.

The watchdog was a first sergeant, National Guard, who must have weighed 250 pounds and flaunted his girth with a tieless khaki shirt which strained every button. His face was red, round, and sequined with beads of sweat.

"*Yes* sir," he said, Amos and Andy style, taking Frank as a plainclothesman.

"I have a boy here who. . . ."

"You're the father?"

"Yes, his name is. . . ."

"How th' hell did you get in here? You can't be here. You're outside, Mac. You can't be in here."

"But I *am* here." Frank was not certain.

"You're not on the force and you're not being held, so there's no way you could get in."

A Regular Army major came up, talking fast. "What th' hell is this? Don't block the passageway. What's going on here?" And to Frank, "You authorized?" And to the sergeant, "Who is this guy anyhow?" He looked like a welter-weight boxer who was about to take on two opponents at the same time.

"Man says he looking for his son."

"Can't be. No relatives in here."

"That's what I told him. 'No relatives in here.' I told him that."

"I mean, we can't let just any sonofabitch in off the street."

"I told him. He can't be in here."

"Then tell him to get the hell out," the major said.

"He's got no pass. He can't leave."

"Give the sonofabitch a pass, then."

"How can I? He's unauthorized."

There was a momentary pause which was broken by a third man, a tall, angular civilian with a gray suit and a face to match. The two soldiers stepped back for him like well-behaved boys.

"You have a son who might be here," the man said, reviewing the case. "You have reason to believe he might be here?"

"Well, I just got this telephone call and. . . ."

The gray man simply led Frank into the pen and sat him down on a low stool. The three of them stood in a semicircle around him. It was as if the door he had been pushing against had suddenly opened and sent him tumbling into something he wasn't prepared for.

"Have a cigarette," the government man said. Frank took one even though he had given them up two years earlier. The major lit it for him. The National Guardsman with the straining buttons stood there with his thumbs under his belt, exuding sweat. His stomach was twelve inches from Frank's left cheek.

"Nice kids can get mixed up with the wrong crowd," the government man said. "You see it all the time. Nice families.

Nice kids. Sometimes it's drugs. You wouldn't believe some of the things we see. Then it's politics. You know, leftists, anarchists, hard-core stuff. Parents lose contact. They just don't know. They'd help if they could, but they just don't know what kind of trouble the kid is in. So that's where our job begins. We try to pick them up and set them straight."

Frank, in spite of himself, nodded. In spite of himself? Hell, it was all reasonable enough. It was what a neighbor might say. It was what *he* had said from time to time. After all, wasn't that why he was here? If the boy was in trouble, it was Frank's job to set him straight.

Yet somehow, sitting there on the dunce's stool, walled in by various authorities, he wasn't sure. The simple alliances of the past weren't holding as they should. If the four adults here were on the same side, why was one of them on a stool looking up at the other three? And why was he scared?

"So maybe there came a time," the government man said, "when your boy went along with the crowd for kicks. And then he found himself in trouble. Real trouble." For some reason, this prompted his first smile. But it vanished almost at once and he pulled a spiral notebook from his pocket. "Your son's name, age, and address, please."

Frank paused. The three of them waited. The sounds of the armory blurred to a distant, rising wind. The unaccustomed cigarette made him dizzy, and he could feel his loyalties shift and heave under him. He was for a moment back at that mill in northern France, the windy night hissing through the charred trees and empty windows. The foot-by-foot advance through Italy had recently become a crazy rush of 60 and 100 kilometers a day and his group, demolition experts, was well beyond the advance lines defusing the explosives with which the Germans had so thoroughly mined each bridge. And somehow, almost unintentionally, his special detachment of eighteen men had ended up with five prisoners—not men but kids, end-of-the-road Nazis, not one of them eighteen yet, two still smooth-cheeked, all hungry-eyed and lice-ridden. They were a pain in the ass for a unit that was supposed to move fast. So the next morning Frank was waked with a cheerful shout, "Hey, who wants to go shoot the Krauts?" The shouter, a captain in command, had adopted the voice of the recreation director at a borsht-circuit resort.

Frank, a mere lieutenant, said, "Are you kidding? Execution? Those kids? You want me to include that in our next report?" *No, no,* that was *not* what he had said. He had said, "Count me out." That's exactly what he had said. Then. The other answer was the one he had said a hundred times in daydreams. But the kids were dead and not even buried. Thrown in a farmer's well. And he had said, his exact words, "Count me out."

"So what's his name?" the government man asked again. "Once we get him on the list, we'll straighten him out."

Twice in one lifetime? Frank thought. It was not courage that drove him but the horror of recriminating daydreams.

"John Doe," he said.

"No jokes now. This isn't a Mickey Mouse show, you know."

"I don't know what you're talking about. My name is Doe. Jack Doe. My son is John."

The gray man's pencil stub paused over the clipboard caught between trust and fury. He looked questioningly at the other two. The sweating sergeant was given courage.

"It can't be John Doe," he said. "That's everyone. He can't be John Doe."

And in their moment of indecision, Frank sprang up and jumped over the police barrier. Running, he heard a police whistle and a shout behind him. He felt an exhilaration sweep through him, flushing two decades of bad dreams.

He ran through MEDICAL AID, stumbling over stretcher cases, and headed for the stairs which led up. They were roped off with a sign which said "No Passing," but he cleared it with a good jump. He thought he heard angry voices behind him, but he couldn't afford to look back and the air was filled with the sound of his own feet pounding against the old metal stairs. He took two or three flights and then instinctively shifted his course and headed down a corridor of offices. All the doors were shut and locked against him except for the men's room.

He had just bolted the door behind him when he heard shouting and the sound of feet in the hallway. They passed, rattling doors, and then returned. By that time Frank had the window open—filthy opaque glass—and was out on a fire escape. He closed the window behind him, surprised at his own logic. It had been years since he had experienced fear and he had forgotten that clear-headed energy which glands can produce.

Out there in the dark he was abruptly aware that he was high above the avenue. He must have climbed more flights than he had thought. Below him, police floodlights swept the streets. The crowds, more active now, moved in long ripples across the black river. Soundlessly a red fist leapt up and he could see that a car had been rolled over and set afire. Sirens came to him like wind sighing through the rubble of a gutted city. And a strange combination of smells—the iron of the railing he was gripping, oily smoke, and the faint acidity of teargas which reached him through the open spaces of time from basic training at. . . . Odd how the name had escaped him while the smell lingered.

And now from down there the sound of firecrackers, a happy celebration, kids having fun, the family gathered as a clan for Independence Day. *Crack!* and the sound snapped into focus and he dropped to his stomach, feeling naked without a carbine in his hands.

It shouldn't, he told himself, faze him. He'd spent time behind enemy lines before. He had lived through a two-or-three-day nightmare trying to get back across an unfixed line of demarcation, trying to identify his own side, avoiding fire from his own unit, clawing to get out of a dream which was contained within a dream within a dream so that hour by hour and day by day he only moved from one box to the next, never quite catching sight of reality. But that was another life, a kind of group memory for him and his generation.

No, this shouldn't faze him—except for the fact that he had spent twenty years proving, year by year, that those nightmares had never occurred, that he had never reeked with fear, had never been propositioned by death, had never fired blindly and watched shadows of himself falling, had never struck a skull with his carbine butt because the man was flipping like a fresh-caught fish and was making sounds no human could be expected to tolerate.

For two and a half decades he had commuted between a muted family and an orderly office, creating life to replace that which he had taken, designing spans for the smooth flow of traffic, willingly washing in and out from work with the tide of his generation, sweeping with daily strokes like a hand over a blackboard, erasing, erasing.

Which is the lie? he thought. Which is the lie? For a moment an imagininary part of him walked down that fire escape, untouched by that which simply could not be happening, and turned to a friendly cop, smiling, and asked where he might find a cab which would take him to the airport. Surely he was a neutral in a foreign land; surely they would respect his passport and lead him through chaos to the Airlines desk, there to be treated as an adult whose credit rating gleamed golden like the eagles of a major general.

Was he out of his mind? He'd be shot, going down there, slithering down a dark fire escape like a sniper. Killed. No metaphor. Dead. Never mind the goddamned issues, he told himself. Leave that to the civies. Let the commentators wax eloquent over what builds the fighting spirit. In the now and here he was lying on his stomach on the metal grate, his brow pressed against the iron, his body unprotected.

And in instant confirmation, a spotlight dashed his eyes like spray. He could see nothing but a milk-white glare. He was on his feet at once and racing up the fire-escape flights, the light losing him and then catching him, raking him like a cat's claw.

Above him was the parapet. Along it were three or four heads like pumpkins. They urged him on, identifying themselves not with uniforms but by tone. And when he reached the top, he wondered if he had strength to climb over. But a clutter of arms seized him by the jacket, arms, shirtfront, and hauled him roughly, lovingly over the edge. He collapsed in the welcome dark and heard someone say, "Let him catch his breath. I'll stay with him here. The rest of you go two buildings over. Make noises."

Frank breathed deeply, aware that he was now back with his own detachment. The great booming, buzzing confusion of the conflict hushed. Years ago he had learned that in times of crisis, all loyalties and all logic shrunk finally to the level of the squad.

He lay back, still gasping for air. Above him, way above, he could see the green wingtip light and the blinking white taillight of an airliner. It seemed preposterous that a hundred or so people could be settling down to an evening highball, copies of *Time*, *Look*, and *Fortune*, soothed by the familiarity of Howard-Johnson décor, Muzak, and the cooings of stewardesses. Only that morning he had been doing just that. He was reading a "literary" best seller which described in intricate detail—like an elaborate etching—the lives of bored New Englanders who had turned to sex for therapy. Flying at 60,000 feet, the work seemed at least possibly relevant and vaguely stimulating. Now it reminded him of the early Fitzgerald novels which he had skimmed with derision in the Army hospital outside Milan. No wonder he had left it in his seat.

From the corner of his eyes he could see the bearded form who had elected to remain with him. He sat with his elbows on his knees, methodically chewing gum. He could have been some French resistance fighter. He could have been his son, Francis. Francis who had insisted on his full name ever since he read about the saint. Yes, this could be Saint Francis responding not to the birds but the killers of birds. Can there, he wondered, be love without a corresponding rage?

There was no answer but the catcalls and obscenities shouted from a distant roof, delivered for Frank's protection.

"I got involved," Frank said with difficulty, still sucking in air, "looking for my son. Francis Badger."

"I know him," the bearded one said.

"Is he all right? Arrested?"

"He was. But he got out. Same way you did."

"He's up here?" It seemed impossible.

"The other side. He got down and across. He's O.K."

"How do I get up there?"

The boy didn't answer for a while. He picked up gravel from the roof and rattled it around in his hand like ideas. Then he said, "Don't go up there. It's not your thing. We'll get you back."

Frank nodded. Of course he would go back, perhaps even looking much the same. Still, it seemed terrible, that black river that flowed between himself and Francis.

"Suppose you'll be seeing him?" he asked.

"Sure. I'll tell him you were up here looking for him." Then he laughed—a kind of quick snort like a poker player who is caught off balance by a good card. "That's something," he said. "That's pretty good. I'll tell him you gave a damn."

And then they were off over the roof tops, heading back to the homefront where the civilians—even his best friends—would listen carefully but with little comprehension to his account of the war.

CHARLES R. LARSON was raised in Colorado and received his Ph.D. from Indiana University. His numerous stories and articles have appeared in magazines like *Saturday Review, The New Republic, The Nation, Africa Report* and *Africa Today.* He edited the book *African Short Stories* and a new book, *Prejudice: Twenty Tales of Oppression and Liberation,* which has just been published. He currently teaches in the Department of English at American University in Washington, D.C.

Up from Slavery

The Reverend Chuka Asimutu was praying in his bed: crouched on all fours, quadruped-like, limbs drawn inward like the petals of a morning glory closed by darkness, bright red scarf wrapped round his neck, ends tucked into a yellowed suit of woolen underwear which clashed with his scarf—preparation for the English winter, he had said, though outside it was still the West-African rainy season. The cabin was air-conditioned, and from the upper bunk on the other side of the tiny space Peter could hear an occasional mutter break through Reverend Asimutu's prayer, a few words of Yoruba, a language he did not understand. Reverend Asimutu had remained in his cowered position for more than ten minues; Peter had timed him when he had entered into his third religious prostration of the day, the prayer before his afternoon siesta. Underneath him, in the lower bunk, Peter could hear the rasping nasalization of the Reverend Obi Okonkwo whose bronchial problems were only beginning to be realized by the poor man who hadn't slept a minute the four days since they had left Nigeria.

The first night out of Lagos, the entire cabin had vibrated, and Peter had felt entombed with a pregnant elephant in the last hours of labor—imagined the very walls of the cabin moving an inch or two every time Reverend Okonkwo inhaled and exhaled. That night had been so difficult to get used to—the initial shock coming from the realization that there were two African priests as his cabin mates (not because they were Africans, but because they were men of God). Sometime after 3.00 o'clock, when he had tried to sneak out of the cabin in order to take a walk on the deck, he had been afraid Reverend Okonkwo would ask him if he was keeping him awake. It would have embarrassed Peter to say yes. But he wasn't asked, and up on the deck had come to the realization that second class was distinguished from first by more than mere ethnic background—not only was Peter the only non-African in second class, but he had been the only second-class passenger to stay up on deck that first night past 11.00 o'clock (when the bar closed). When he went up the second time at 3.00, after lying there listening to the Reverend Okonkwo's rasping breathing, he was completely alone for a second time. Or so it appeared, the contrast being the noise coming from the first-class area which was still quite awake, at least the first-class whites; first- and second-class Africans having retired at the same approximate time: the one trait they shared in common.

About 4.00 o'clock that night he returned to the cabin. When the breakfast bell rang a few hours later, his initial reaction had been to continue sleeping, but a second's reflection reminded him that the best way to stay well on ship was to keep a full stomach. Though breakfast had never been his favorite meal—especially British breakfast—he knew he needed to put something into his belly or he would become not only tired but seasick. So he got up with the reverends, or rather, watched in horror as the two men crouched in their beds, praying, while he washed, shaved, and dressed as nonchalantly as possible. When he opened the door to the hallway to go downstairs to breakfast, his cabin mates were just beginning to roll themselves out of their beds, wrapped like mummies in wool swaddling cloth. "Good morning," Peter mumbled, closing the door behind him.

The dining hall had been nearly empty. No one was at Peter's table, and since specified seats had been assigned to all passengers it was impossible for him to eat his breakfast with anyone else—the pretty Ibo girl at table seven, for instance, who was going to London to learn sewing. So he ate in silence, waiting for one of his table companions to appear, but no one showed up.

(The two reverends eventually appeared, but they had been assigned to another table.) And when he finished, there was nothing to do but leave the dining room and return to the cabin where he thought he would be able to sleep in peace.

The cabin was empty, of course, and smelled of talcum powder and the African foods the Reverends Asimutu and Okonkwo had stored under their beds in anticipation of the day the ship would stop serving African "chop." (Peter imagined their trunks in the storage room chucked full of yams and garri, dried fish and peppers.) He stripped to his shorts and slipped back into the upper bunk. His eyes caught a glance of his towel over the sink and he noticed several dark, purple streaks, and he lay there wondering if it really was his towel which had the purple marks on it, or someone else's. Then he sat up in his bed and looked at the towel again, only to realize for certain that it was his, indeed—the one he had used not more than forty-five minutes earlier when he'd wiped the traces of lather off his face after he'd finished shaving.

An hour and a half later, he was awakened by the steward, who was obviously embarrassed at having interrupted a white man in his sleep. "It's all right," Peter told him, climbing down from the bunk. "Come on in. Just a minute." He dressed as quickly as he could while the steward puttered around the sink, making a rather dainty attempt at scouring it.

When he finished dressing, Peter pointed to his towel and said to the steward as unconcerned as possible, "Someone seems to have used my towel. Do you suppose you could get me another?"

The steward, who was obviously Nigerian—Peter could tell by the tribal markings on his face—scrutinized Peter's face, stared at the towel, and answered with a tone of disgust, "These bush people. They don't know no better." His arm reached up to the rack, removed the towel, and flung it to the floor. "Anything you want, just ring for service," he grinned, showing a toothless mouth, and Peter knew he was talking to a man old enough to be his grandfather.

"Thanks," Peter replied, "I'll remember that," and he left the cabin door open behind him.

Now, four days later, Peter lay in his bed watching the Reverend Chuka Asimutu, still on all fours. He looked at his wrist watch which told him that Reverend Asimutu had endured his position for thirteen-and-a-half minutes. Some kind of world's record, Peter thought to himself, watching the man's strong body tilt back and forth with the gentle rocking of the ship. How much longer is he going to keep that up? He tried to decide whether he should wait until Reverend Asimutu had completed his prayer or climb down from his bunk, get dressed, and go up on deck. He didn't know quite how to act around his cabin mates—they were the Christians, and Peter was nothing, though he had frequently listed "fallen Methodist" on various application forms before he had joined the Peace Corps. (On Sunday, the second day on the ship, Peter was certain his cabin mates had noticed that he hadn't dressed for any religious service.) They must think I'm some kind of heathen, he thought, wondering if he could go up on deck without disturbing them. It was obvious he was not going to get any sleep in the cabin.

He glanced over at Reverend Asimutu again, and then at his watch. The Reverend Asimutu had endured his position for nearly sixteen minutes. Maybe he's fallen asleep, Peter thought; maybe he isn't praying at all. But a moment later, when Peter climbed down from his bunk, Reverend Asimutu rolled over on his side, opened two bleary eyes, and looked at Peter for a minute before closing them again.

Peter didn't know what to do. He dressed—shoes and socks were all he'd taken off—and felt a sudden tilt of the ship. "It's a little rough," he said, glancing back at Reverend Asimutu. There was no reply, and Peter thought maybe he'd fallen asleep. Quietly, he closed the door behind him.

Up on deck there seemed to be a fervor of excitement. People were standing near the rails looking into the sea. The ship hardly appeared to be rocking at all. Maybe it was only down below that the roll could be felt. He looked into the water but saw nothing; recognized Mr. Babili, the man from the Cameroons whom he had talked to the afternoon before, crossed over to him, and asked what was the cause of the excitement.

"Fish," Mr. Babili replied, pointing his finger at the mildly choppy sea. But Peter saw nothing. "Big fish"—looking back into the sea. Peter scanned the water again, patiently waited until he saw what had been the cause of the initial excitement.

"Porpoises," Peter said, spotting what the others had already seen. "Not fish, mammals."

"Fish," Mr. Babili repeated, walking away from Peter to another part of the deck. A cry of exultation rose from the crowd of watchers as a school of porpoises darted in and out of the water, parallel to the ship. Some looked as if they were diving under the ship, only to be replaced by still others who seemed to be coming from the farther side.

Then they disappeared as quickly as they'd appeared, and after it became obvious that they were not going to return a second time the crowd dispersed, Mr. Babili walking away with the Ibo girl who sat at table seven. (Miss Egusi, she'd told Peter when he'd introduced himself the first day.)

He decided to go into the library. There didn't seem to be anything else to do. It bothered him that Mr. Babili had paid him so little attention, that the Cameroonian had walked away when Peter most needed someone to talk to. During the four days on ship, Mr. Babili had been the only person Peter had been able to talk to, and he worried, too, over the fact that after two years in Africa he still found it almost impossible to carry on a conversation with an African which lasted more than five minutes. There never seemed to be anything to talk about. With Mr. Babili he hoped it would be different. He had been chosen by his company—one of the largest banking chains in West Africa—to study accounting in London, and Peter thought they might get to know each other well enough so they'd be able to do things together once they got there. Peter had spent six months in London the year he'd graduated from college, and he was excited about getting back to a place where he wouldn't be a stranger. It delighted him to think that he could show Mr. Babili a world he was not already familiar with.

The library was empty. All the books were locked in glass cases which looked as if they hadn't been opened since the ship was christened. At least, no one had bothered to unlock them the first four days of the voyage, and it was rather unlikely anyone would because of the ominous sign stating that a ten-shilling deposit was required before any book could be borrowed. So Peter sat at one of the desks, instead, and thought about writing a letter to his parents. But there was little to say. After two years in Africa, he no longer believed in writing letters simply for the sake of writing. That stage had passed long ago, shortly after the Peace Corps dumped him at his school; shortly after the initial excitement had changed to boredom and frustration. There was no reason to worry the people at home or make them believe he'd be returning immediately. At least, not until Christmas, and that was five months away. First he had to rediscover Europe—the colder world.

Through the library window, in the niche under the stairway leading to the upper deck, Peter saw a young woman holding her baby nuzzled in her arms. He recognized her as the girl he had talked to for a few minutes the first day while he was waiting outside the Bursar's office to change some money. She had told him she was going to England to meet her husband, who had gone there to study physics the year before. Now she looked as if she were staying on deck to see if the porpoises would return. Perhaps she was with someone else, but it was difficult to tell because the window was so small that he could see only a few feet of the deck.

Then, while he watched her without her realizing it, she loosened her wrapper and exposed one beautiful, rounded breast and cuddled the baby's head to it until it began to suck. He watched her in a kind of trance, noticing her every move— the expression of love on her face. She handled the child as if it were made of blown glass. And Peter was caught in a spell, until they moved from the view commanded by his window. Then he looked at one of the bookcases.

"Exterminate all the brutes!" Kurtz had said. Peter's eyes focused on a copy of *Heart of Darkness,* and he wondered what idiot had put that book in the ship's library. The jacket looked new. Perhaps no one had ever borrowed it. Certainly not the passengers on this voyage. Second class was composed almost entirely of young men and women going to England for school, albeit not to take a degree—those like the Ibo girl, who said she wanted to learn dressmaking, though Mr. Babili had told Peter her real reason was to be a prostitute. When they returned with their training two or three years later, they would be first-class passengers, and he was certain the library on that side of the ship was different. By then they would be much more critical of their colonial upbringing. And of Joseph Conrad.

By the time the bell rang for dinner, Peter had read most of a three-week-old issue of *Time* he had spotted on one of the chairs in the library. He was beginning to be bored again and looked forward to the next day when there would be a four-hour stop in Freetown. New passengers, and a few hours ashore in another port, one of the cities he had reserved for the trip home, though he knew four hours wouldn't be time to see much.

At dinner he tried to bring up a subject which would draw some conversation out of his two table companions: Miss Sohinka, a Yoruba girl who was going to Liverpool to study journalism, and Mr. Chikudi, who was Ibo and going to London simply to see what it looked like. The first day at lunch Mr. Chikudi told Peter he was a trader and had been saving money for seven years for a three-month vacation in the "mother country, your country," he had said, though Peter had told him he was American. Peter imagined he was nearly seventy years old, though he knew he could never be certain with Africans. Mr. Chikudi had an uncanny knack for disappearing between meals. Peter couldn't remember having seen him outside the dining room a single time except during the first day's deck exercises in case of shipwreck.

But the conversation ended after they discussed the weather and the menu, Mr. Chikudi expressing his concern that he wouldn't be able to buy African chop once he got to Liverpool, and Peter trying to assure him that he would soon learn to like European food. Miss Sohinka began her meal with a dish of ice cream, which was the last thing on the menu, and when she had finished she ordered a bowl of *jollif* rice, followed by another dish of ice cream. Mr. Chikudi stuck to African food, though Peter suggested he might want to add a few European dishes to his diet so he wouldn't suddenly be confronted with an entire meal of non-African foods. Peter wondered if they would acquire any more table companions the next day in Sierra Leone. After dinner, Mr. Chikudi disappeared into his cabin, and Miss Sohinka joined the Ibo girl who was going to study sewing.

The four hours in Freetown the next day improved Peter's spirits. Already the trip was beginning to get him down—and there were still another nine days until they would reach Liverpool.

Freetown was sweating in the midday heat, but the taxi he'd rented moved quickly from sight to sight, and when he returned to the ship it was time for the daily bath which he'd signed up for his first day. After that, he felt quite refreshed, and he went up to the second-class bar and talked to Mr. Babili, who seemed to have forgotten the incident with the porpoises the day before. Mr. Babili said he was anxious to get to Las Palamas—the next stop. Then they'd be away from Africa. But that was still another four days.

At dinner, there was a new face, a Miss Morgan, who had been conveniently seated at Peter's table, a pharmacist who was returning to her home in England after eight years in Sierra Leone. "Anxious to get home?" Peter asked her, judging her age to be about forty, a good ten years older than he.

"Not that much. It won't really be home any more. It's been too long." She rambled on into something about how excited daddy and mummy were that she'd finally decided to return to England for good. "I've been at the Anglican mission in Lombarto," she told him, "waiting the past two years for a replacement."

"Did they send one?"

"Not yet, but he's supposed to be on his way."

"Eight years is a long time to be away from home," Peter said, wondering if she was a virgin. He guessed she was; certainly she wasn't anything to look at.

"Oh, I've been home," Miss Morgan informed him, "twice. Once in '58 and again in '61."

"Oh," Peter said, trying to sound responsive. But he'd given up interest once he'd decided she was too old for him. Not much shape either, though she reminded him of what another Volunteer had said about sleeping with white women again. But Miss Morgan was definitely out, and that left only the Africans, and an arrangement would be rather difficult with the two reverends as his cabin mates. It appeared as if a shipboard romance was definitely out, unless they picked up some Spanish wench in Las Palamas.

That night, after the Bursar's attempted bingo game had fizzled out (none of the Africans knew how to play), Miss Morgan sat down at the piano and collected a coterie of singers around her as she banged through her repertoire of religious hymns. Slow, dragged out tunes which reminded Peter of the few church services he had attended in Nigeria. It wasn't the sermons which had bothered him so much, but rather the singing of the Psalms, the emphasis on each article and preposition, the excruciatingly painful music which made it almost impossible for him to sit through an African religious service. Miss Morgan tromped away on the piano, which obviously hadn't been tuned in several years, and even Peter's two cabin mates entered into the revival. The Reverend Okonkwo didn't seem to be having his usual breathing problems. He had been much better the last twenty-four hours, since the doctor had given him some medicine, and as long as he was up on deck, away from the air-conditioning, he breathed almost normally. There was still the continued snoring throughout the night, but Peter had discovered that if he drank two or three bottles of Guinness just before retiring it didn't matter how heavily Reverend Okonkwo breathed. Peter sat on one of the stools in the bar listening to the lilt of the hymns burst through the second-class lounge doors. Every once and a while he caught a blast of Miss Morgan's shrill English voice, and he knew she obviously had never been the object of any romance.

The bar was only half busy. Two or three Nigerians were passionately discussing something in Yoruba, and occasionally Peter caught a word or two of English. Bursar, captain, or bloody bastard; the sequence didn't seem to make much difference. Mr. Babili had been in the bar earlier with the Ibo girl who was going to learn sewing, Miss Egusi, but they had left about forty-five minutes earlier amid chuckles and catcalls from some of the single men. Slowly, the singing was drawing all the Africans from the bar, and Peter knew he would soon be alone—unless Mr. Babili returned for a nightcap as he frequently did at 11.00, just before the bar closed.

"Why don't you go over to the first-class bar?" the bartender asked him, making a gesture at the emptiness of the room. "No one cares."

"Maybe later," Peter said, "after you're closed. This is fine."

"Any night after 11.00," the bartender replied.

Peter looked into his glass of Guinness—beautiful ebony. It reminded him of the skin of Africa, the ebony continent. He

wondered how he would ever be able to get used to whiteness again.

At ten minutes before 11.00, when Peter was finishing his
third Guinness, Mr. Babili returned to the bar. The lounge was
silent; Miss Morgan having finished her recital, nearly everyone
had gone to bed.

"You didn't enter in the singing," Mr. Babili said after he'd
ordered a large bottle of Heineken's.

"No, I'm not much for music," Peter lied. He loved music;
just not bastardized hymns.

"That's something we have difficulty understanding about
you," Mr. Babili told him, putting a shilling and nine pence on
the counter for the bottle of beer.

"Who—me? What do you mean?"

"Those of you who come to Africa. The second, third, or
maybe even fourth generations—especially Americans."

"Why?"

"You never go to church. You bring your religion—*your* religion—spend years and years trying to convert us to something
you regard as better than our own indigenous religions, and
soon as you've got us to the point where a village is no longer
split because of its internal problems—when it's being torn apart
because of the two factions of an imported religion—Catholic
and Protestant, for instance—then just as soon as this happens,
all the expatriates with no religion at all turn up. How do you
explain that?"

"Very easy. The first people who came here were missionaries. When they stopped coming—and they haven't actually
stopped, you know—then the others came. The businessmen,
technicians, and the scientists . . ."

"And the Peace Corps Volunteers," Mr. Babili interrupted.

"And the Peace Corps Volunteers," Peter repeated.

"Who seem to have no religion at all."

"That's not true. It's simply that in most cases all the foreigners who've come to your schools have been missionaries
whether they were ordained or not, or at least they've generally
been of the same faith as the school they were sent to. And
the Peace Corps Volunteers haven't. You can't expect a Catholic

Volunteer at a Baptist school to lead the Sunday-morning prayers."

"They could send them to the right schools in the first place," Mr. Babili ventured.

"They try to do that, but it doesn't always work." Peter realized he had lost the argument. The bartender told them he was closing, so Peter bought another Guinness and a bottle of Heineken's for Mr. Babili.

"You know what I think?" Mr. Babili asked a minute or so after the bartender had closed the window.

"What?"

"I think in another 100 years or so, your religions will be completely forgotten by Africans. We'll go back to our own."

"I don't know. They're not that easy to forget." He was having trouble thinking. He knew he'd had too many bottles of Guinness.

"Or else we'll be sending missionaries to America." Mr. Babili laughed. "I wonder how that would work—missionaries for America. Our own Peace Corps." He pronounced the word "corpse."

Neither spoke. Peter looked at the trace of laughter which remained on Mr. Babili's face.

"Now you've a companion," he muttered a few minutes later.

"Who?" Peter was having trouble following Mr. Babili's conversation.

"The white woman."

"Oh, her . . ." He grinned.

"Not so good, is she? You'll have to find an African girl— perhaps your last."

"When we get to London, I'd like to show you around," Peter told him, ignoring what Mr. Babili had said.

"Why?" Mr. Babili asked.

"You said you've never been there. I have. I can show you places you'd never find by yourself."

Mr. Babili looked at him suspiciously. "Are you sure that's all?"

"What do you mean?"

"You'll be different. We'll both be different. For the first time in two years you'll be part of a majority. For two years you've been having to place yourself on a level with Africans, and now you'll be able to place yourself above them. I don't know whether I'd like that."

"That's ridiculous. London's not my home any more than it's yours. All I want to do is show you what the place is like. It's beautiful—especially this time of year."

"We'll see. But things will be different. You think you're going to be a different person when you get back to your home. Equal rights or whatever your government calls it— democracy for all. And you'll be doing all you can for the underdeveloped races: speeches, lectures, telling your people about Africa. But it'll soon finish—in a short time things will be back where they were before you came here. You'll no longer stand up when you see a female come in the room, if she's black. You'll forget your campaigning for equal rights and begin to look at Africans as a lower race. It's all a matter of time. Oh, I know your intentions are fine and you'll deny me to the end of your life, but you wait, you'll see."

"You're wrong," Peter said. "I won't forget any more than you'll forget England when you go back home. It's with you forever. It'll always be there. I'll probably be coming back."

"When?"

"I don't know, but I will come back."

They talked together almost every night—usually after Mr. Babili spent some time with the girl who was to study sewing in London. Sometimes they disagreed, argued, as they had the first time, but Peter began to respect Mr. Babili unlike any African he had known before. They could talk together, carry on a prolonged conversation on a variety of subjects, and Peter knew they regarded each other as people—not a white man and a black man as it had always been previously. Color seemed to disappear. And when they were through with their nightly debates, sometimes with a row of empty beer bottles lined up on the floor next to them or on one of the tables in the lounge, they would sneak down to their cabins in the early part of the morning after having experienced the privacy of the entire second-class lounge to themselves.

One night Mr. Babili told him that the thing he needed most for the rest of the voyage was an African woman. Peter was stung by the comment, yet he could see the beauty of it, too.

When Mr. Babili made the suggestion, there was that element of African-white man, *not one of us,* creeping into his voice, but Peter knew that this was not the way Mr. Babili intended him to feel. And the next night when Mr. Babili's girl brought along another young girl who was also going to London under the façade of being a seamstress, Peter felt a biting return to his loins. Again he wondered how he would ever adjust to whiteness. The four of them sat in the bar drinking beer and Guinness mixed with lemonade until the bar closed, and then they danced highlife to some records which had been left on the gramophone from a dance earlier in the evening. It was shortly after 12.00 when they broke apart; Mr. Babili and Miss Egusi returned to her cabin, and Peter and Miss Ogene walked around the deck, shocking two English ladies when they passed the first-class lounge. Then they returned to the second-class lounge because there was no other place to go.

It was empty, of course, enclosed in a film of semi-darkness, and they sat on a sofa and talked about London, Peter telling Miss Ogene about things she would have to adapt to. He held Miss Ogene's hand, and he even kissed her once or twice, conscious of the responsiveness of her body; but it ended there. Miss Ogene asked Peter if there was anything wrong, and he knew he couldn't explain. Then they just sat there for a few minutes—and Peter was conscious again of not knowing how to talk to an African.

A little later Miss Ogene went down to her cabin, and Mr. Babili came up to the lounge.

"I have a confession," Mr. Babili told him.

"You have a confession?" Peter asked him, wanting badly to say, I'm the one with the confession.

"You know what I was doing in Las Palamas?"

"No, what did you do?" Peter said, waiting patiently for Mr. Babili to tell him what was on his mind. He remembered that Mr. Babili and several other young African males had rented a taxi together. Peter had "done" the city with Miss Morgan, whom he'd decided was not so bad when she wasn't talking about the Anglican Church.

"I had a white woman." He pulled his chair a little closer to Peter's.

"You what?" Peter asked him, a montage of distorted images

running through his head. Had Mr. Babili said what he thought he'd said?

"I had a white woman in Las Palamas," Mr. Babili confessed, obviously embarrassed. He laughed a little, and Peter tried to put his statement into some logical context. Here was something he had not thought about before, for while it was obviously suitable for a white man to go to a black prostitute his mind had never considered the possibility of the opposite. It seemed distinctly disturbing. His mind visualized a white whorehouse with a line of little black Africans leading up to the front of it, each waiting his turn to enter the bleached establishment. Perhaps this is what really makes a black man see the white world for the first time. Was it so awfully different from a white man sleeping with a black girl? He knew there were several female Volunteers who were said to have been sleeping around with Africans. One had even married an African. Obviously this was something he would have to think about. It was more than a mere confession that Mr. Babili had had carnal knowledge of a white woman.

Mr. Babili sat looking at him as if he were afraid their relationship would immediately end. "You are surprised?" he asked Peter.

"I guess I am," Peter confessed, wondering if honesty would destroy their friendship. "I guess it's something I'd never thought about. When you didn't want to go with me, I was upset. Now I understand. I thought you were visiting churches or something. Guess I'd forgotten about white prostitute houses." And finally, "How was it?"

"Expensive. Two pounds."

"Yes, I'd say so"—recalling the price he knew he could have a girl for in the bush: five or ten shillings. God, why did he have to tell me this?

"You wish I hadn't told you?" Mr. Babili asked, seriousness circling his face.

"No, I don't think so. I'm glad you did. I think you should have, but why did you wait? That was three days ago." In another four days they would be in Liverpool, and these last days were so vitally important. He felt as if each one drained a little more blood from his veins. It was the sudden realization that he didn't want to leave Africa. Something elementary was happening to him: he was afraid, afraid of what the other world had become in the two years he had been removed from it.

"I didn't know how to tell you. Tonight, when you were with Miss Ogene, I thought it would be all right."

"I'm afraid nothing happened with us," Peter said, changing the subject. "There isn't much that can be done. I mean, I couldn't take her to my cabin—what of the two reverend fathers?"

"The lounge was empty," Mr. Babili said, a warm glow radiating from his face. "That's why we went downstairs." Peter wondered where Mr. Babili and Miss Egusi always went. He'd never thought about it before, but they obviously had to go somewhere. Either his cabin or hers, which meant there was always someone else present. Making love with someone else in the same room. The idea made him ill; he felt as if it wouldn't be difficult to upchuck all the beer he had drunk throughout the evening.

"I'm afraid it would have to be in a cabin," Peter said. "It would have to be in a cabin, without the reverend fathers—and that's just about an impossibility."

"Miss Ogene says you can come to her cabin."

"That won't work either," Peter said, "unless we're alone."

"Maybe it'll have to wait until you get to London," Mr. Babili suggested, making it sound as if Peter were the only one going to that strange town.

And then she'll want money, Peter thought, realizing that after they got off the ship the situation would be changed. It was just as Mr. Babili said: once he was in Europe, he would be in the majority and his relationship with Africans was bound to change. I've got to prove to him it won't. "That's probably the best idea. I'll be there at least three weeks before I go to the Continent."

The remaining days were the same: in the mornings Peter spent his time in the library reading magazines or writing an occasional letter. The Reverend Chuka Asimutu crouched in his bed; the closer they got to Liverpool, the more frequently he prayed. It was difficult for Peter to go into the cabin without finding the man in his animal-like position, mumbling away to his God. The Reverend Obi Okonkwo snored heavily, sleeping day and night and leaving the cabin only for meals and the bathroom. The purple streaks continued to appear on Peter's towels, though the steward gave him a fresh one every day. The woman outside the library window went on feeding her child in the niche under the stairs. Mr. Babili spent some time with Miss Egusi in her cabin each night. Miss Ogene was seen with Peter Chadwick by more white passengers during their nightly walks around the deck. Messrs. Babili and Chadwick frequently returned to their cabins arm in arm, down the stairs, slightly tipsy.

"Why did you take second-class passage?" Mr. Babili asked him the evening prior to their arrival in Liverpool. Earlier, there had been the Captain's Banquet, which was followed by a dance in the second-class lounge. The bar had stayed open an hour later than usual—until 12.00—but shortly after that almost everyone had gone down to his cabin, including Miss Ogene, who had remained with Peter throughout most of the evening. Now it was after 12.00 and a few second-class passengers were still on the deck waiting to see if there were any lights visible along the English coastline. Peter and Mr. Babili were sitting in the empty bar, talking, smoking cigarettes, drinking the beer they'd bought just before the bar closed.

During the afternoon, when Peter had been talking to Miss Morgan in the library, he had looked out the window for a moment and noticed the young girl who always stood under the stairs feeding her child. And then, a little later, when he looked at her again, she was against the rail and the baby was gone, and he thought he had seen a rapid movement of her arms. But he couldn't be sure, for a scream followed, and minutes later there was a commotion on the deck and in the ship which shook him to the depths of his heart. The woman, it seemed, had somehow lost control of her child, and it had fallen overboard. There was the formality of stopping the ship and looking for the baby, and several hours were lost—during which time first- and second-class passengers intermingled with each other for the only time on the voyage. Everyone knew the search was useless.

"Why did I take second class?" Peter asked him. "It's very simple. I wanted to. I couldn't afford anything else."

"I don't believe that," Mr. Babili answered, taking a swallow of his beer. Peter was afraid this was one night he definitely would be ill. Earlier he'd been drinking Scotch and then gin. And now Guinness and beer. It would only be a matter of time—thank God all one had to do was run to the rail. Not that he hadn't learned to control his liquor—it was this mixing that his stomach had never been able to take. How the Africans could do it had puzzled him for two years.

"It was as simple as that," Peter told his friend. "First class was thirty-five pounds more. I couldn't afford that."

"Are you sure? We thought you had another reason." Peter didn't like the look on Mr. Babili's face.

"What other reason could there be?"

"Maybe you wanted everyone to think you'd become an African."

"Who's 'everyone'?" Peter asked, wondering what he meant.

"Everyone in second class."

"I don't know what you mean."

"We think you wanted us to feel that you're one of us. That's why you did it, isn't it? I mean, that's why you really took second class. So we would be thinking different of you —not that you actually wanted to travel this way. Maybe so you could sleep with African women."

"What the devil are you talking about?" Peter asked, his voice noticeably higher.

"What I just said—so you could be one of us."

"That's ridiculous. Who was it tried to get me to run around with an African girl? You, not me. I didn't ask you to go around procuring for me. You offered out of the goodness of your heart. Or maybe you've forgotten."

"Miss Ogene says you've been sleeping with her."

"That's crazy. Where?"

"Up here in the lounge. She says she's met you up here several nights after we've all gone below."

"That's not true and you know it. Even if it were, what difference would it make? You're the one who introduced me to her in the first place." Peter wondered what Mr. Babili was building up to. He knew this certainly wasn't Miss Ogene's idea. Earlier in the evening she'd given him her London address and although Peter knew he would never call her he'd written it down in his address book and assured her that he would just as soon as he'd found a place to stay. But Mr. Babili said nothing. All he did was to look at Peter and then at his drink.

"Why have you become so critical all at once? So over-sensitive of my whiteness. Maybe you've forgotten what you told me about Las Palamas."

"There's a difference."

"What difference? I sure don't see any."

"I paid for mine. Miss Ogene says you haven't given her any money."

"Of course I haven't given her any money. We haven't done anything."

"We think you came second class so you could sleep with African women for free."

"Who's 'we'?"

"All of us—everyone in second class."

"Including Miss Morgan?"

Mr. Babili ignored Peter's question. "Miss Ogene says you owe her some money."

"Jesus Christ, are you dreaming or something? You've got something all mixed up. She didn't tell you anything like that and you know it."

"Miss Ogene wants ten pounds. I said I'd get it for her."

"That's crazy," Peter told him, "absolutely crazy. She hasn't said anything like that and you know it." He was having trouble thinking. He had had too much to drink.

"You wait. You'll see. Tomorrow morning she'll ask you. Tomorrow after breakfast—ten pounds for the trip. This is no joking matter."

"I don't understand how you can say this. After all these nights we've been sitting here in the bar drinking together. I don't understand how you can ask such a thing. It doesn't make any sense."

"You think perhaps I am joking?" Mr. Babili asked him, the earlier, innocent expression gone from his face.

"I don't know. I don't . . . understand you."

"Of course you don't. You can't. You're not an African—you can't be expected to."

"That's ridiculous and you know it. You're talking nonsense." Peter was beginning to wonder if Mr. Babili was right.

"You know what I'm saying is true. You know whatever we do, you can never understand all of it."

"Like that woman throwing her baby overboard," Peter said, almost incoherently. "I suppose there's an explanation for that, too?"

"Of course. Her husband didn't know she'd had a child, so she had to do something with it."

It all seemed so simple. So taken for granted. He remembered the cries that had reverberated from the woman's cabin the rest of the afternoon, but he had been aware, too, of her appearance at the Captain's Banquet. And she had been in the lounge during the evening, though she hadn't been dancing. Strangely, Peter knew she would go free—was already free. The baby had simply wriggled out of her arms, and that was that. As Mr. Babili had said, her husband didn't know about the child, so it had to be disposed of.

He suddenly wanted to talk to someone white—even Miss Morgan. He believed she was the only person who would understand the way he felt. He wanted to tell her what Mr. Babili had told him, but Miss Morgan, he knew, had already gone down to her cabin. He pondered the possibility of crossing over to first class.

"Do you really expect that I'm going to give Miss Ogene ten pounds? If you think that, you're certainly mistaken. Even if I did, it would be to her and not to you."

There was no reply. He hadn't expected any. It had stung him to the quick that Mr. Babili should mention this in the first place—that their relationship should be reduced to this. Had Mr. Babili cherished ulterior motives from the first? Peter didn't want to think about it—it bothered him too much. He wished he were away from the ship, wished it were twenty-four hours later and he safely in his hotel room in London. If they gained the time they'd lost searching for the baby, they would be in Liverpool by early morning, and that meant he could still get an afternoon train to London. God, how he wanted to be alone in his own hotel room—away from everyone else, no one snoring or muttering in another bed.

Mr. Babili finished his beer and got up from his chair. There seemed nothing for Peter to do but follow. There was nothing else that needed to be said. Obviously, Mr. Babili realized he could not force Peter to give him the money, so they both started downstairs together as they had done many previous nights. But it was still early, much earlier than they were used to retiring, and Peter decided he would take a walk around the deck and clear his head. There was still plenty of noise coming from first class. He knew he wouldn't feel much like sleeping by the time he got to his cabin, though he'd had plenty to drink, and that might help to some extent. Oddly enough, he had not been sick as he thought he might be when Mr. Babili had started his ridiculous conversation.

He left Mr. Babili at the top of the stairs. Neither said anything, and Peter felt a particular sadness when he thought of a time several nights before when the two of them had nearly fallen down the stairs, singing, "Ho, ho, ho and a bottle of rum!" Tonight there was no singing.

The deck was empty, and the air had a pleasant chilliness about it. Almost cold, Peter thought. In two or three more months it would be fall, then winter. He knew he was going to enjoy the winter especially. He walked slowly around the deck, noticing the place where the woman had always stood feeding her baby. He wondered if she had been debating the problem every time he'd seen her through the library window. No doubt she didn't realize she could be observed by anyone from within—because of the curve of the ship, the area itself was well-secluded from both ends of the deck.

Noise blasted out of the first-class lounge; there was a band —not the phonograph records relegated to the second-class passengers—and the music was decidedly Western. No highlife. Through the windows he saw a dozen couples stumbling ineptly around the dance floor and an African couple in Western dress doing a very staid waltz. The bar was lined two and three deep, and many of the tables were filled with passengers dressed in their best woolen clothes. Here and there was a table composed of a few Africans, though most of them had gone down to their cabins.

When he finished his walk and got back to the second-class section of the ship, he made one last search for a light—something which would indicate the nearness of land. But nothing offered any clue. So difficult to tell they were actually in Europe. So difficult to tell they were fully away from Africa.

As he descended the stairs to the hull of the ship, he had a strange feeling that Mr. Babili was waiting for him at his cabin—perhaps with three or four other Africans who would demand that he give Miss Ogene some money. He wondered if he should return to the cabin—it was still so early. He could stay up on deck and watch the shore for a light. But he continued the rest of the way downstairs, through the empty corridors, noting the stillness of the ship.

When he opened the door to his cabin, the key fumbling in his hand, he thought he heard a noise. Then he turned on the light and saw the Reverend Asimutu, crouched in his bed. Underneath him was an African woman.

He spent the rest of the night drinking Scotch in the first-class bar, wondering why he had never gone there earlier in the voyage. No one asked him who he was or where he'd come from. The bar remained open until 4.00, when the last of the dancers stumbled out of the lounge and down the stairs to their cabins. And then he had to run to the rail, but by that time he didn't mind, for leaning over the edge, rasping away his insides, he saw the lights blinking in the distance and he knew they would soon be one vast blaze of whiteness.

LEONARD MICHAELS is presently the holder of a Guggenheim Fellowship while he is working on a novel. His first book, *Going Places,* was nominated for a National Book Award, and his stories have appeared in *Partisan Review, Paris Review, Transatlantic Review* and *Esquire* among others. He lives in Berkeley, California, with his wife and two children.

Robinson Crusoe Liebowitz

Mandell asked if she had ever been celebrated.

She said, "Celebrated?"

"I mean your body, has your body ever been celebrated?" Then, as if to refine the question: "I mean like has your body like been celebrated?"

"My body has never been celebrated."

She laughed politely. A laugh qualified by her sense of Liebowitz in the bedroom. She was polite to both of them and good to neither. Certainly not to Liebowitz who, after all, wanted Mandell out of the apartment. But did she care what he wanted? He was her past, a whimsical recrudescence, trapped in her bedroom. He had waited in there for an hour. He could wait another hour. As far as she knew he had cigarettes. But, in that hour, says Liebowitz, his bladder had become a cantaloupe. He strained against the window. The more he strained the more he felt his need.

"I mean really celebrated," said Mandell, as if she had answered nothing.

Perhaps, somehow, she urged him to go on; perhaps she wanted Liebowitz to hear Mandell's lovemaking. Liebowitz says her motives were irrelevant to him. His last cigarette was smoked. He wanted to hear nothing. He wanted to piss. He drew the point of a nail file down the sides of the window, trailing a thin peel, a tiny scream in the paint. Again he strained. The window wouldn't budge. And again. Nothing doing. At that moment, says Liebowitz, he noticed wall-to-wall carpeting. Why did he notice? Because he couldn't piss on it. "Amazing," he says, "how we perceive the world. Stand on a mountain and you think it's remarkable that you can't jump off." In our firm Liebowitz is considered brilliant. He should have done better in life. But there is no justice. He continues:

"My body," said Mandell, "has been celebrated."

Had that been his point all along? Liebowitz wondered why he hadn't been more direct, ripping off his shirt, flashing tits in her face: "Let's celebrate!" She was going to marry a feeb, but that wasn't his business. He had to piss, he had no other business.

"I mean, you know, like my body, like, has been celebrated," said Mandell, again refining his idea. It was impossible for Liebowitz, despite his pain, not to listen—the sniveling syntax, the whining diction—Liebowitz says he tasted every word, and, in that hour, while he increasingly had to piss, he came to know Mandell, through the wall, palpably and spiritually to know him: "Some smell reached me, some look, even something about the way he combed his hair. . . . I'd never seen him, but I knew he had bad blood."

As for Joyce, a shoe, on its side, in the middle of the carpet—scuffed, bent, softened by the weight of her uncelebrated body—suffused the bedroom with her presence. He could see the walking foot, the strong, well-shaped ankle, peasant hips, elegant neck, and fleshy, boneless, Semitic face. A warm, receptive face until she spoke. Then she had personality. It made her seem taller, more robust. She was robust, heavy bones, big head, with dense yellow-brown hair, and her voice was a flying bird of personality. Years had passed. Seeing the hair again, and Joyce still fallow beneath it, saddened Liebowitz. But here was Mandell. There'd be time for them.

"Has it been five years?" asked Liebowitz, figuring seven. "You sound wonderful." She said he sounded "good." He regretted "wonderful," but noticed no other reserve in her voice, and, just as he remembered, she seemed to love telephone, to come at him much the thing, no later than yesterday.

"The thing," says Liebowitz, quoting one of his favorite authors, "is the thing that implies the greatest number of other things." If Liebowitz had finished his dissertation he'd have a Ph.D. He had too much to say, he says. Years ago his candidacy lapsed.

When his other phone rang he didn't reach for it, thus letting her understand how complete was his attention. She understood. She went on about some restaurant, insisting let's eat there. He didn't consider not. She had said, almost immediately, she was getting married to Hyam T. Mandell, "a professor."

Did Liebowitz feel jealousy? He didn't ask professor of what or where does he teach. Perhaps he felt jealousy, but, listening to her and nodding his compliments at the wall, he listened, he thinks, less to what she said than to how she spoke in echoes. Not of former times, but, approximately these things, in approximately the same way, he felt, had been said in grand rooms, by wonderful people. She brought him the authority of echoes, just the thing; and she delivered herself too, a hundred thirty-five pounds of shank and dazzle. Even in her questions: "Have you seen. . . . ?" "Have you heard. . . . ?" About plays, movies, restaurants, Jacqueline Kennedy; nothing about his wife, child, job, or spirits. Was she indifferent? embarrassed? a little hostile? In any case he liked her impetuosity. She poked, checked his senses. He liked her, Joyce Wolf, on the telephone; and he remembered that waiters and cabbies liked her, that she could make fast personal jokes with policemen and bellhops, that she tipped big, that a hundred nobodies knew her name, her style. Always *en passant*, very much here and not here at all. He liked her tremendously, he felt revived; not reliving a memory of younger days, but right now, on the phone, living a particular moment among them. For the first time, as it were, that he didn't have to live it. She has magic, he thought, art. She called him back to herself. Despite his grip on the phone, knees under the desk, feet on the floor, he was like a man slipping from a height, deliciously. He would meet her uptown in forty minutes. Did he once live this way? Liebowitz shakes his head. He smirks. He used to be crazy, he thinks.

On his desk lay a manuscript that had to be proofread, and a contract he had to work on; there was also an appointment

with an author . . . but, in the toilet with electric razor and
toothbrush, Liebowitz was purging his face and shortly there-
after he walked into a Hungarian restaurant on the East Side.
She arrived twenty minutes later in a black, sleeveless dress;
very smart. He felt flattered. He took her hands. She squeezed
his hands. He kissed her cheek, he said, "Joyce." The hair, the
stretch of white smile, the hips . . . he remembered, he looked,
looked and said, "It was good of you, so good of you to call
me." And he looked into his head. She was there too. Joyce.
Joyce Wolf who got them to the front of lines, to seats when the
show was sold out, to tables, to tables near windows, to parties. . . . Sold out you say? At the box office, in her name,
two tickets were waiting. But Liebowitz remembers, once, for
a ballet, she failed to do better than standing room. "I didn't
really want to go. I certainly didn't want to stand," he says.
"Neither did she. But the tickets were sold out. Thousands
wanted to go." She scratched phone numbers till her fingernail
bled. That evening they stood with pelvises against a velvet
rope and hundreds stood on either side and behind them,
jammed into a narrow aisle. The effluvia of a dozen alimentary
canals hung about their heads. Blindfolded, required to guess,
Liebowitz would have sworn they were in a delicatessen. Lights
dimmed. There was a sudden, thrilling hush. Joyce whispered,
"How in God's name can anyone live outside New York?"
She nudged him and pointed at a figure seated in the audience.
He looked, nodding his head to show appreciation for her
excitement and her ability to recognize anyone in New York
in almost total darkness. "See! See!" He nodded greedily, his
soul pouring toward a glint of skull floating among a thousand
skulls, and he begged, "Who? Who is it?" He felt on the
verge of extraordinary illumination when a voice wailed into
his back: "I can't see. All year I waited for this performance
and I can't see. I can*not* see." Liebowitz twisted about and
glanced down. A short lady, staring up at him, pleaded with
her whole face. He twisted frontward and said, "Move a little,
Joyce. Let her up against the rope." Joyce whispered, "This is
the jungle, schmuck. Tell her to grow another head." He was
impressed, says Liebowitz. During the ballet he stood with
the velvet rope in his fists, the face between his shoulder
blades. And now, going uptown in the cab, his mouth was so

dry he couldn't smoke. After all these years, he was still impressed. Joyce got them tickets. She knew, she got what she wanted. Him, for example, virtually a bum in those days, but nice-looking, moody, a complement, he supposes, to her, though he doesn't really know why she cared for him. He was always miserable. "Perhaps a girl with so much needs a little misery." Not that she was entirely without it. She worked as private secretary to an investment broker, a shrewd, ugly Russian with a hunchback and a limp who wanted a "Collich girl" to kiss his ass. "Hey, Collich, make me a lousy phone call." After work, she used to meet Liebowitz and, hunching, dragging a foot, she would shout, "Hey, Collich. Hey, Collich." They laughed with relief and malice, but sometimes she met Liebowitz in tears. Her boss once slapped her across the mouth. "In a Longchamps. During lunch hour," she said, then screamed at Liebowitz, "Even if there had been a reason." Liebowitz stopped trying to justify such horror. He raged. The next morning he would go punch the man. The next morning, in chic Italian sunglasses, she left for the office. Alone. Five foot seven, she walked seven foot five, a Jewish girl passing for Jewish in tough financial circles. Liebowitz points out, "She made two hundred fifty a week in salary, and with insults and slaps, the Russian gave tips on the market." He, Liebowitz, then salesman in a shoe store, made eighty a week hunkering over corns. He had only rotten moods, a lapsed candidacy for the Ph.D. in philosophy, and her, a girl with access to the pleasures of Manhattan. Her chief pleasure was moody Liebowitz. She was twenty-four years old, a virgin when she met Liebowitz who took her, and what she represented to him, on their first date. "I don't know how it happened," she said. "Two minutes ago I was a virgin." Liebowitz coolly replied, "Normal." She had been surprised, confused. He had been merely cool, like a vulgar hoodlum. "Where's your shower?" he asked. Now he wonders if he hadn't been mean to her. He makes big eyes, he holds his palms up like a man asking for apples. "I had certain needs." The gesture is rabbinical, ancient, carried in his genes. "I descend," says Liebowitz, "from rabbis, deep readers of the Talmud and life." He had been mean, yet she was always good to him and, decently, had called him to announce her forthcoming marriage and ask him out to dinner. Walking into the restaurant Liebowitz acknowledges an erection, but, he asks, can that explain why he ran uptown with a dry mouth to meet her; then went strolling in the park, he asks; then went up to her apartment for a drink, he asks. Life is mystery, thinks Liebowitz. After the drink he was considering a hand on her knee, he says, to reach for solutions, when the doorbell rang. "Don't answer," he said. She pleaded the sweetness of Mandell, his wit, his conversational power. "Don't answer," said Liebowitz. "Maybe it's someone else," she said. It wasn't. Liebowitz opted for the bedroom, the shut door; finally, himself tearing at the window, wild to piss.

"Didn't you say you were going to work this evening?"

"Did I say that?"

Mandell had had a whimsy impulse. Here he was, body freak, father of her unborn children. She could have done better, thought Liebowitz. Consider himself, Liebowitz, for example. Seven years had passed, a girl begins to feel desperate, but still—her style, her hips—she could have done better than Mandell, he thinks, despite her strong conviction—in fact her boast—that Mandell wasn't just any professor of rhetoric. "He loves teaching—speech, creative writing, anything—and every summer at Fire Island he writes a novel of ideas. None are published yet, but Hyam doesn't care about publication. People say his novels are very good. I couldn't say, but he talks about his writing all the time, and he really cares about it."

"I can see Mandell," says Liebowitz, "curled over his typewriter. His forehead presses the keys. Sweat fills his bathing-suit jock. It's summertime at Fire Island. He is having an idea so he can stick it in one of his novels." To Joyce, Liebowitz said, "I wish our firm published novels. You know of course we only do textbooks." She said she knew, yet looked surprised and changed the subject. "He is terribly jealous of you. It was long ago, I was a kid, he wasn't even in the picture. But Hyam is the kind of man who wonders about a girl's former lovers. Not that he's weird or anything, just social. He's terrific in bed."

"Does he know I'm seeing you tonight?" His hand ached for her knee. It was getting late. Her voice had begun to cause brain damage, says Liebowitz; it had to be stopped. She laughed again. Marvelous sound, thought Liebowitz, just like laughter; and he was nearly convinced she deserved Mandell. But why didn't she send him away? Because Liebowitz's firm didn't do novels? Was he supposed to listen? to burn with jealousy? He burned to piss.

"Is something wrong, Joycie?"

Mandell didn't understand. Did she seem forbidding, too polite? Did she laugh too much?

"I wanted to talk to you about my writing, but, really Joycie, is there something like wrong?"

Liebowitz realized that Mandell was embarrassed, unable to leave. Of course. How could he leave with her behaving that way? He was just as trapped as Liebowitz, who, bent and drooling, gaped at a shoe, a dressing table, combs, brushes, cosmetics, a roll of insulation tape . . . and, says Liebowitz with rabbinical fire in his eyes, before he knew what he had in mind, he had seized the tape. He laid two strips, in an X, across a windowpane, smacked the nail file into the heart of the X, and, gently, pulled away the tape, carrying off sections of broken glass. Thus, a big, jagged hole in the pane.

"I was another Robinson Crusoe. Trapped, isolated, and yet I could make myself comfortable."

He felt proud. Mainly, he felt a searing release. Liebowitz pissed. Through the hole, across an echoing air shaft, a long, shining line. He listened to his flow—burning, arcing, resonant —as he listened to Mandell's. "I have a friend who says my novels are like writing, dig? He means they are *like* writing, but not real writing, you get it?" Liebowitz shook his head, thinking, "Some friend," as he splashed brick wall and a window on the other side of the air shaft, and, though he heard yelling, he heard nothing relevant to Robinson Crusoe, and, though he saw a man's face, he saw nothing relevant to his personal comfort, though he pissed on the man's face yelling from the window on the opposite side of the air shaft into which he pissed, says Liebowitz, as if it were his traditional and sovereign privilege to piss on the man's face.

"A very good neighborhood," says Liebowitz, with an appreciative mouth, puckered in the middle, curled down in the corners. "East Seventies, near the river. First-rate. The police wouldn't take long." He wondered what to say, how to say it, and he zipped up carefully. In the dressing-table mirror he saw a face bloated by pressure, trying not to cry. "According to my face," says Liebowitz, "a life was at stake." His life was at stake and he couldn't grab a cab. Mandell still whined about his writing. "Joyce couldn't interrupt and say go home. Writers are touchy. He might have gotten mad and called off the marriage." Liebowitz had no choice but to prepare a statement. "My name, officers, is Liebowitz." Thus, he planned to begin. Not brilliant. Appropriate. He'd chuckle perhaps in a jolly, personable way, like a regular fellow, not a drunk or a maniac. Mandell, meanwhile, was shrill and peevish: "Look here, look here, look here. My name is Hyam T. Mandell. I'm a professor of rhetoric at Bronx Community Institute, Moshalu Circle Campus. And a novelist. This is extremely ironic, but it is only a matter of circumstances and I have no idea what it means."

A strange voice said, "Don't worry, professor, we'll explain later."

Joyce said, "This is a silly mistake. I'm sure you chaps have a lot to do. . . ."

Mandell cut in, "Take your hands off me. And you shut up, Joyce. I've had enough of this crap. Like show me the lousy warrant or like get the hell out. No Nazis push me around. Joyce, call someone. I'm not without friends. Call someone."

Someone fell down. The strange voice said, "Hold the creep."

With something like hatred Mandell was now screaming, "No, no, no, don't come with me. I don't want you to come with me, you stupid bitch. Call someone. Get help." The hall door slammed shut. The bedroom door, suddenly, was open and Joyce was in it: "You hear what happened? Did you? How can you sit and stare at me? I've never felt this way in my life. Look at you. Lepers could be screwing at your feet. Do you actually realize what happened?"

Liebowitz shrugged yes mixed a little with no. "I never felt such clarity in her before," he says. He himself, he thinks, looked pale, sick with feeling. She said, "I see, I see. You're angry. You're furious because you had to sit in here. Well what could I do? What could I say? You're angry as hell, aren't you?" Liebowitz didn't answer. He felt a bitter strength

in his position. She began pinching her thighs to express suffering and, unable to deal with herself alone, across the room
from him, she came closer to the bed. "Are you angry? Do
you know what just happened in that room?" Liebowitz said,
"The cops took the putz away." His tone allowed her to sit
down beside him. "It's horrible, it's humiliating," she said. "They
think he pissed out the window." Then, "He called me a
stupid bitch." Liebowitz said, "Joyce, you might be a stupid
bitch, but I believe you look as good to me now as years
ago. In some ways, better." He put his hand on her knee.
It seemed to him a big hand, full of genius and goodness
and power. Her mouth and eyes grew slow, as if the girl behind
them stopped jumping. She glanced at his hand. "I must make
a call," she said softly, a little urgently, and started to rise.
Liebowitz pressed down. She sat. "It wouldn't be right," she
said, and then, imploring, "Would you like to smoke a joint
with me?"

"No."

She has middle-class habits, he thinks, a part of her style. "It
wouldn't be right," she said, as if to remind him of the point,
not to insist on it. But what's right, what's wrong to a genius?
Liebowitz, forty years old, screwed her like a nineteen-year-old
genius.

"My adventure," says Liebowitz, "gives me an idea for a novel.
The theme is cloacal. A novel in the first person. For example:
'I was trapped in the bedroom. I had to piss.' How intimate. How
immediate. Just like writing. But my trouble is I have no feeling
for adventure. I was once the willing fool of chance, but now I
despise adventure. It means chaos, evil. I'm a married man, I
have a little child. I swim happily in the banal quotidian. I
live in the West Nineties, I own a Dodge, a lot of furniture.
Steal the Dodge, burn the furniture, give me skin disease. So?
So I'm insured, mother, inside and out. Have you read the
Book of Job? It's not about me. My name is Liebowitz," he
says. "Liebowitz."

EDWARD HOAGLAND is a New Yorker who now lives with his wife and child in Barton, Vermont. He has published three novels, including *Cat Man* and *The Circle Home*, a journal of interviews with frontiersmen in British Columbia called *Notes from the Century Before*, and a collection of essays, *The Courage of Turtles*. He has taught at Sarah Lawrence and Rutgers and has won both a Guggenheim and a fellowship of the American Academy of Arts and Letters.

The Final Fate of the Alligators

In such a crowded, busy world the service each man performs is necessarily a small one. Arnie Bush's was no exception. He was living in the Chelsea district of Manhattan at this time, although he had lived in central California on several occasions, as well as Chicago and Crisfield, Maryland, and had put in four years or more in Galveston, Texas, at a point when he was married to a woman who lived there. He'd thought of it as her home rather than his; all of her husbands, as far as he knew, had left Galveston after their marriages to her ended. She owned a laundromat and barbershop, attached, which he had helped her manage. She was a cheerful, practical woman, Ellen, and they'd lived with her two sons in the cottage and patio area behind the business establishments. When he met her, he was a merchant seaman on leave from the sea, rooming in Galveston and hanging around the parks and bars, though he already knew the trade of barbering also. He'd given her a daughter, as a matter of fact—her only daughter—whom he kept in touch with at Christmastime. The girl, whose name was Jo-ann, had grown out of her teens by now, and he was hoping she would visit him if she came North. He hadn't seen her since babyhood, but when he thought of her he imagined that she looked like her mother. Ellen was a smally built, active woman with a bumpy complexion, a pretty figure, black, scalloped hair, and masculine blue eyes. She carped and bitched a bit too much but not so much you couldn't stand it, and since she wasn't as bossy in business hours as she was at home, and since the inescapably boring chores were handled by two colored employees of long standing, he had not found that the setup interrupted his independence. Instead, he'd liked being married to a businesswoman; it furnished him with the chance to operate a going concern without the ball-and-chain aspects of owning property. He hadn't married her for money reasons, however (at least, he didn't recognize the motive if he had), but for the special, jumping, bodily impetuosity between them, never equalled for him with another woman, which really never had turned sour. Just the degree of intimacy and understanding they had reached was unforgettable; he hadn't lived four years with anyone else, or given way so much, opened himself. He'd known what she was thinking when she didn't say anything, and known that underneath the peremptory manner she was a homekeeping woman as well, who didn't want to bitch at him if she did bitch, who disliked her own bossiness and wanted peace and a simple household.

He had appreciated her youthful bottom, her mother's bosom, and the way she gathered her hair at the nape of her neck. They went to Matamoros together on a week's trip, leaving the kids with the woman who cooked. They dressed in sombreros and paper shirts and saw a cockfight and a festival street dance, and in his memory this trip pretty well represented what a marriage ought to be like. He had delighted in the period when she was pregnant, too, partly because his own gravity had pleased him. But Ellen had slowed down—that ambitious, scrimping fussing—had leaned on him and showed a dreamy side, as he considered, like his. More than at the chance to run the business as he wanted, he'd been happy to see her soften, see her resemble him. And the whole weighty buildup to the baby's arrival—the hydraulics, the clocking of it—had seemed the marvel that it ought to be; and then the hump under the blanket and the red head and skin, the sleeping and the sucking, the rooting, the tunnelling, the reaching up, the funny-looking undershirt. He'd called her Milkmouse. He'd hung over the crib; he'd brought home cotton lambs and rubber fish, full of a welling gentleness that mixed with the detachment that was native to him and easily passed for gentleness.

There were certain moments in the routines he detested—at breakfast, for example, which they hurried through. When they were about to get up from the table, she'd mention whatever was on her mind, speaking rapidly and sharply after the silence of the meal. "I want the garbage men to clean up all that stuff they're chucking on the ground; I want you to call them about it. They can't just drive away and leave a mess like that around. And the Bendix people were supposed to be here yesterday. He knows we have two machines out. They were supposed to service us on Monday and they didn't." Sometimes she felt cornered, she said, by the need to hammer at these guys and hold her own, making them do right, though she was thankful to have Bush taking over the worst of it. She wrangled with him at breakfast to get him started strong.

When she was with her kids, she didn't hold out areas of private reserve, but, having been somebody's wife already twice before, with Arnie she was a pensive, smiling chum at best, a speedy co-worker rather than the kind of ultimate companion he'd thought a wife would be. He resented it that what was a climax for him—his marriage—should be her third, and that she didn't flare up angrily, for instance, when a lady called her Mrs. Westrom, which was her previous husband's name. It reminded him of shacking up, or of an ordinary, carnally enlivened partnership, and he was disappointed, if this was marriage, even more than he admitted. He wasn't one to raise a stew about it, however; he was a quiet, self-contained fellow. Probably he paid more attention to the females in pearly slacks who huffed and puffed about the laundromat, eating weight-saver cookies and drinking coffee from the vending machines, and remembered the sea, of course, with intensifying nostalgia. He thought of his teens in Bakersfield and of the many memories of his twenties, when he had gone to sea and knocked around the world—afterward, he'd fought in Italy as an artilleryman. Except for Ellen, the baby, and his two stepsons, he had no ties to anyone, but he discovered that these ties were not indissoluble, either. The boys were runabouts, aged eight and nine, not lovey or fazed at all, and Jo-ann was mostly Ellen's baby, or the cook's. Ellen's preoccupations were with the normalities of mealtimes, meeting the mortgage bills, preserving her neighborly relationships, and seeing the children grow, whoever her husband happened to be; this was his impression anyway. She may have supposed that no husband could be held for long. She kept a bunch of photographs of herself on the coffee table and the chests of drawers to give the kids an atmosphere of family, she said. Bush, who got awfully tired of looking at them, told her she ought to go into show biz.

He was living well but was annoyed a lot. Being a believer in the rule book, a sentimentalist, he didn't like to hear her joke about their having met on the marina, as if it had been just a sort of pickup and as if she were lucky to have gotten married to the man, finally, instead of raped by him. Best were their evenings in bed, lying against the puffed pillows watching television after the kids had gone to sleep, then half an hour's succulence after lights-out, and being a person of substance the next day. He was reasonable by nature; he didn't fume and fight as his restlessness increased. But it was really not a man's life there, putting in the bluing, making change. Ellen was defeatist when they quarrelled. If she let her confusion show, he was touched; if she was apprehensive, so was he; but she was unrelenting too. In the morning, she would tell him what she wanted done in the same remote, peevish tones, her face assuming the fat expression of someone drawing on inner resources. It was as if he'd as good as left her already and she had her children and friends to fall back on. Apparently, she thought her marriages were a sort of constitutional folly. She said her friends told her she was lucky to get off so lightly each time. Who these friends were Bush didn't know; he only saw a bunch of business friends—the liquor man, the electrician. He didn't think her marriage to him had been foolish, but if that was her attitude what could he do?

He signed on the Esso Chile at last, and went off to Bahrein and Maracaibo. He was a wiper in the engine room, on other ships sometimes a steward. Actually, he wasn't on the sea for many years during this second stint before the grittiness and bleakness of the life drove him to land again; yet he did love the ocean and continued to talk about it wherever he was. In his own mind he was a seaman—a seaman ashore. He was nearly as lonely ashore and often thought of Ellen, suspecting, indeed, that leaving had been a mistake. He knew her show of indifference had not been real. She hadn't wanted him to go, but he'd let her pretend she didn't care. They'd been afraid; they'd both pretended it was a matter of small importance—he would go back into the merchant marine, she'd live just as before and maybe marry again. So the proof that he had made a mistake was that he hadn't stayed on the sea long. Every man made his share of mistakes. He missed being part of a household and painted her in pastel colors when he was disheartened, but he decided that it wasn't the mistakes that mattered so crucially as where you were at the end of them all.

Bush was doing fairly well. Stocky and aging, he had crewcut gray hair and a mustache and lived off Ninth Avenue, close to the harbor, keeping up with a few old nautical jokers who patronized the bars he went to. Like them, he hadn't seen much of the ocean from day to day, being hard at work or belowdecks in his off-hours, but what he remembered was the massive accumulation of what he'd seen. It overshadowed the other job surroundings of his young years, just as his one marriage dominated the memories he had of other periods spent with women who for a while had supplied him with housing and with sex. He was a sailor, he told the neighbors, and at night or on his lunch hour when he took a stroll he remembered the ocean's agitated sheen, like nobbled tin, and the majestic, chastening pitch of the water when the wind blew, the ship's joints creaking, the heavily bumbering engines, the waves thudding, making a bass hiss against the hull. His apartment, although a walkup, wasn't too grim. One window faced the south, and the sunlight wasn't impeded because the adjacent block of tenements had been torn down—a process that he knew might pose a problem for him eventually, but in the meantime his rent was low. He had a barbering position in an uptown office building, and managed to live on his salary, saving his tips.

The alligator, like an overgrown brown invalid confined to bed, lived in the big bathtub. If an outsider had been invited in to look at it, he would have gaped, because this was no ten-inch plaything but an animal of barrel-like girth, with a rakish, pitiless mouth as long as a man's forearm and a tail as long as his legs. The cut of the mouth, however, was no clue to the alligator's mood, since, like the crocodile mask that a child wears in a school play, it was vivid but never changed. The eyes, eel-gray with vertical pupils, were not as static. They seemed to have a light source within them, and the great body, scummed slightly with algae, was a battlefield shade, the shade of mud. The last time Bush had tried to determine its weight, he borrowed a slaughterhouse scale, fixed a sling, and hung the scale from a ladder, and struggled to heft the animal into place, but he couldn't get its hind end off the ground. Even so, the scale read a hundred and thirty-some pounds. He didn't name the alligator, because it wasn't human; in no way was it human. Like Headley, the fellow who had left it with him years before, he never lit on a name that sounded appropriate—not the Trinkas and Sams that apply easily to dogs. "Alligator" did very well for nomenclature, being a title that loomed in the mind, and "you" served for talking to it.

On arrival, it had still been of a size to permit it to go through the motions of swimming, drawing its arms alongside its trunk and wriggling abruptly downward in the tub until its belly brushed the bottom and its blunt snout bumped the front. It had been four feet long then, and Headley and he had carried it up to the apartment wrapped in a blanket against the cold. The fellow, who was a barfly, a lathe operator, was going South to Gainesville, Georgia, to visit his brother and wanted Bush to take care of the creature until after the holidays. He kept saying that, as big as it had grown since he had bought it—a small water lizard in a pet store—it must be worth lots of money. But he didn't show up again.

Bush laid a plank on the toilet seat and sat in the bathroom watching his new companion porpoise and wallow for exercise as best it could. Once he realized that Headley wasn't coming back, he bought a jumbo junk bathtub from a wrecking company, paying eighty-five dollars, including the delivery charge. He could shower at work, and so the inconvenience of keeping the animal was slight. Furthermore, he soon entered into what he considered an intimacy with it, so that he wouldn't have wanted to give it up. While he knew very well that alligators inhabit fresh water, having it in the apartment, he found a great many of his seaman's memories springing alive with a clarity even surpassing the clarity of life. The smoldering waves, the

sharks and whales, the dull-colored, impassive seas on a smoky
day—these sailors' sights and many more churned in the roil
along with the alligator, who smelled, in fact, quite like the sea.
He fed it on chunks of stew meat twice a week, not a demanding chore, and opened the window when the weather was warm
to let in the sunlight direct.

At the public library, Bush read that alligators were mild-
tempered compared to their crocodile relatives—that a man
could swim in a slough populated with alligators without the
likelihood of being attacked. He read that they preyed on
waterfowl, muskrats, and slow-swimming fish, and he fed it a
fryer chicken once in a while, bones included and the feathers
left on. He fed it fish, too, always heedful enough in his over-
tures to its mouth end not to provoke an incident. The furor of
feeding time was the main danger, when the alligator, after
wringing a slab of meat like a rabbit, threw it up into the air for
the pleasure of catching it deep in its throat when it came down,
gargling the beef like a strong syrup. Splashing, galloping in
place, it chomped and worried the meal, and Bush was touched
because, after all, in such scanty quarters there weren't many
satisfactions available to it. On less frenzied occasions, it liked
to feel its throat rubbed, including the gums of its eighty teeth—
just as long as he kept his hands off its muzzle, where the
nostrils were, and away from its blistering, satin-gray eyes. The
eyes sat on top of its head like two midget riders, and the
nostrils collapsed and blew open like a horse's nostrils when it
ducked under water.

Though the books gave a vague set of criteria, he couldn't
figure out the sex of his animal. He did learn that at only five
years an alligator may already be sixty-six inches, which put
into perspective Headley's brief role in its life; he would have
been jealous to think Headley had had it longer.

Except to run water into the tub, Bush often left it to its
own devices. It produced a clacking sound by chopping its
teeth and at eating times it grunted, too, which he assumed
was some kind of adolescent version of the drumming, reverberating boom with which full-grown alligators shook the bayous.
The grunt, faintly explosive, contained an animal resonance as
well—a *waw*. At the zoo, an attendant told him that alligators
rarely bred in captivity, and what he observed of conditions

there assured him that he wasn't unkind to keep his at home. Like an eccentric, he didn't even regard the arrangement as strange. He was a dignified man, with a serious nose, his mustache fluffy as a Russian's, and when he got a little bit drunk nobody handled him roughly. Cutting hair every day in the week but Sunday and drinking draught beer in the evening on Twenty-third Street, he had no trouble making ends meet; and he didn't acknowledge his birthdays as landmarks at all, tucking the crimping sensation of being in his sixties into his well-knit walk. He didn't resent the gator's composure, since he himself was self-sufficient.

The alligator slipped imperceptibly toward adulthood, as befitted an animal that was created to live for a century. Its corrugated back was patterned with gray diamonds, although blurred, olive-drab colors overlaid that—not like the bright baby checks Bush saw on the specimens in the pet stores. They were yellow and black and had tiny bills, with a Donald Duck ski-jump effect at the end; their tails, though, were crenellated already and their eyes, tinted cinnamon-sulphur, were gay, iridescent, and savage.

Like a runner running a treadmill, his big friend surged in the tub, as if a birler were birling. Sometimes it inflated its lungs and then would deliberately try to submerge, swimming against its own buoyancy, until with sensuous relish it released the air and sank down. Another exercise was to seesaw, lifting and lowering its tail, making its hind legs the fulcrum—legs like afterthoughts that were tacked on. Its tail, of course, was the motive force when it swam—a walloping paddle of muscle, which the saurians of the Everglades, three times the size of his monster, swung so powerfully when they hunted at night that they could knock a drinking doe into deep water and seize her. Limber as hide, it whacked up over the edge of the tub and against the wall when the alligator wanted the sting of the blow. The tail seemed to lead a life of its own, twitching quite independently, motorized separately, and when the body moved forward, the tail, which followed after a short delay, was what lent its progress the appearance of irresistibility and crisis.

Bush provided big roasting cuts of meat now, and real mama hens. He found he was trusted more, and he could stroke the nostrils, opening and closing under his hands, or reach behind the ungainly legs to the tender, piegon-colored armpit skin. He loved the apartment's sea smell, stong as it was, and knew that in possessing such a remarkable prize he was erasing all of that bulk of his life when he'd stayed ashore as a dreamer, working in lumberyards and snipping people's hair.

Reptile leather in the handbag shops began to be labelled "caiman," the South American relative of the alligator. Then it was gavial skin, and the baby alligators also were unobtainable; he was told they weren't being shipped any more, though his own animal, continuing to grow, seemed prepared to live on forever on behalf of the species, linked back to the dinosaur dynasty. As its girth increased, the grin on its jaws became more theoretical, as if it were pulling the wings off a barfly in its mind's eyes, while in actuality it lived like a very fat fellow, whitening like ash gradually, its eyes a white furnace. The grin wasn't precisely gloating, however, because the two corners sliced back to the very roots of its head—there was more grin, perhaps, than the gator wanted—a grin of chagrin, a grin like that worn by a man whom events have let down and who, grinning to cover the fact, betrays the bad taste at the back of his mouth.

Bush, too, grew grizzled. He read the newspapers and kept up in a less hectored fashion by hearing the headlines read on the radio—the violent malaise of the sixties, the fads and bizarreries. There was a spate of suicides in the neighborhood, and people signalled with mirrors from their bedrooms, or blinked their lights. The streets were tight with pedestrians. He made his home his castle and used binoculars to keep in touch with his neighbors, though he was not himself overswept by the claustrophobia abroad in the world, being accustomed to shipboard conditions. He watched the buildings smoking, and then when the city stopped them from smoking for the sake of the air, that in a way was eerie, too, because so much was going on inside you knew they ought to be smoking.

The alligator had been ill only twice, when it seemed unable to open its eyes and the eyelids turned blue. It lay with its long maw closed, and a fixed vaudeville smile, propping its head on the side of the tub so that it needn't come up for air. Bush poured bouillon into its mouth through a tube and furnished heaters, and for the time that the illness lasted he didn't attempt to exercise it. Ordinarily, hauling, assisting, he got it out onto the floor every couple of days for a walk and to let it dry thoroughly—let it lie flat, sparwling its arms, while he cleaned the interstices of its skin where fungi might gather. The logistics were not ideal, but the business was very brotherly—the struggle, shoulder to shoulder, to jimmy the heavy body out of the tub—and he didn't get tired of rubbing his hands across the rich hide. On both occasions, the alligator got well in a week or so. There were some gradual changes, though. Whereas before when he watched the beast's clumsy galumphing he had imagined the alligators in the swamps in their glory, now he began to see his friend just trying to stay alive. The alligator stared at him through its imprisoning mask, a pleasure-pain mask, although its cruel pupils contained all the harshness of millenniums past— he wasn't so sure it was going to outlive him. A man downstairs kept fish, and Bush arranged that if he should die this person would telephone the zoo and get them to take the alligator safely. Since *he* wasn't made to last for a century, he hadn't expected that he might outlive his friend.

Besides the problem of fresh air and space, there was the elaborate question of diet. How could he duplicate the crunchy, glittery nutrients of a jungle river? Of course finally he couldn't —not with powdered Vitamin D and not with steer beef. Sometimes the alligator loped like an otter with constipation, humped awkwardly, and when that happened his own belly ached. These seizures disturbed him dreadfully, especially when he decided they were the result of a deficiency, and one he couldn't correct. Dancing like a bear that had burned its feet, the creature suffered sadly, though its mask was still heavy and comic and rigid. Great gouts of gas came up in bubbles, released from the alligator's digestive tract after much lurching and shuffling. It craned its neck to persuade them to come, after doing an agonized gandy dance, or a dance of death.

During the night one weekend, at last, it died. Bush didn't discover the fact until midmorning, because its position underwater was painless-looking and natural, the head floating just in the attitude of an alligator at peace with itself; he only noticed that it was dead when he saw that it didn't come up to breathe. However, the expression was a terrible one. The expression was like the Angel of Death's, if, as seemed likely, an alligator confronts the Angel of Death with the expression of the Angel of Death. And all of those aeons were etched on the mask—all of the meals in the bubbling mud, the procession of species extinguished, the mountain-building, the flooding seas and the baking sun. The framework of daily courtesies was over between them, and the fury and barbarism photographed on the face were alive like a flame.

He might have called in the leather-toolers, but didn't. He and his neighbor who kept fish got help and carried the alligator down to the street late Sunday night, leaving it stretched in solitary magnificence across the sidewalk for the city to figure out what to do with.

He had these three memories, then: the sea, the few years in Texas, and the years on Twenty-first Street, with the mumbo-jumbo that filled in between.

MAGAZINES CONSULTED

American Weave—23728 Glenhill Drive, Cleveland, Ohio 44121
Ann Arbor Review—115 Allen Drive, Ann Arbor, Mich. 48103
Antioch Review—212 Xenia Avenue, Yellow Springs, Ohio 45387
Aphra—Box 3551, Springtown, Penn. 18081
Ararat—Armenian General Benevolent Union of America, 109 East 40th Street, New York, N.Y. 10016
Arizona Quarterly—University of Arizona, Tucson, Ariz. 85721
Arx—12109 Bell Ave., Austin, Texas 78759
The Atlantic Monthly—8 Arlington Street, Boston, Mass. 02116
Ave Maria—National Catholic Weekly, Congregation of Holy Cross, Notre Dame, Ind. 46556
Carleton Miscellany—Carleton College, Northfield, Minn. 55057
Carolina Quarterly—Box 1117, Chapel Hill, N.C. 27515
Chelsea—Box 242, Old Chelsea Station, New York, N.Y. 10011
Chicago Review—University of Chicago, Chicago, Ill. 60637
Colorado Quarterly—Hellums 118, University of Colorado, Boulder, Colo. 80304
The Colorado State Review—360 Liberal Arts, Colorado State University, Fort Collins, Colo. 80521
Commentary—165 East 56th Street, New York, N.Y. 10022
Cosmopolitan—1775 Broadway, New York, N.Y. 10019
The Critic—180 N. Wabash Avenue, Chicago, Ill. 60601
December—P.O. Box 274, Western Springs, Ill. 60558
The Denver Quarterly—Denver, Colo. 80210
Epoch—159 Goldwin Smith Hall, Cornell University, Ithaca, N.Y. 14850
Esprit—University of Scranton, Scranton, Pa. 18510
Esquire—488 Madison Avenue, New York, N.Y. 10022
Evergreen Review—64 University Place, New York, N.Y. 10003
Extensions—855 West End Ave., New York, N.Y. 10025
Fantasy and Science Fiction—347 East 53rd Street, New York, N.Y. 10022
For Now—Box 375, Cathedral Station, New York, N.Y. 10025
Forum—University of Houston, Houston, Tex. 77004
Four Quarters—La Salle College, Philadelphia, Pa. 19141

Generation, the Inter-arts Magazine—University of Michigan, 420
   Maynard, Ann Arbor, Mich. 48103

Georgia Review—University of Georgia, Athens, Ga. 30601

Good Housekeeping—959 Eighth Avenue, New York, N.Y. 10019

Green River Review—Box 594, Owensboro, Ky. 42301

The Greensboro Review—University of North Carolina, Greensboro,
   N.C. 27412

Harper's Bazaar—572 Madison Avenue, New York, N.Y. 10022

Harper's—2 Park Avenue, New York, N.Y. 10016

Hudson Review—65 East 55th Street, New York, N.Y. 10022

Impulse—Rockland Community College, Suffern, N.Y. 10901

Intro—Bantam Books, Inc., 271 Madison Avenue, New York, N.Y.
   10016

Kansas Quarterly—Dept. of English, Kansas State University, Manhattan, Kans. 66502

Kenyon Review—Kenyon College, Gambier, Ohio 43022

Ladies' Home Journal—641 Lexington Avenue, New York, N.Y. 10022

The Laurel Review—West Virginia Wesleyan College, Buckhannon,
   W. Va. 26201

The Literary Review—Fairleigh Dickinson University, Teaneck, N.J.
   07666

The Little Magazine—P.O. Box 207, Cathedral Station, New York,
   N.Y. 10025

Mademoiselle—420 Lexington Avenue, New York, N.Y. 10022

The Massachusetts Review—University of Massachusetts, Amherst,
   Mass. 01003

McCall's—230 Park Avenue, New York, N.Y. 10017

Midstream—515 Park Avenue, New York, N.Y. 10022

Mill Mountain Review—Box 2212, Roanoke, Virginia 24009

The Minnesota Review—Box 4068, University Station, Minneapolis,
   Minn. 55455

The Moonlight Review—P.O. Box 1686, Brooklyn, N.Y. 11202

Mundus Artium—Dept. of English, Ellis Hall, Box 89, Ohio University, Athens, Ohio 45701

New American Review—1301 Avenue of the Americas, New York,
   N.Y. 10019

The New Mexico Quarterly—University of New Mexico Press, Mar-
   ron Hall, Albuquerque, N. Mex. 87106

The New Renaissance—9 Heath Road, Arlington, Mass. 02174

The New Yorker—25 West 43rd Street, New York, N.Y. 10036

North American Review—Cornell College, Mount Vernon, Iowa 52314

Northwest Review—129 French Hall, University of Oregon, Eugene,
   Ore. 97403

Occident—Eshleman Hall, University of California, Berkeley, Calif. 94720

Panache—153 East 84th Street, New York, N.Y. 10028

The Paris Review—45-39, 171 Place, Flushing, N.Y. 11358

Partisan Review—Rutgers University, New Brunswick, N.J. 08903

Perspective—Washington University, St. Louis, Mo. 63105

Phylon—223 Chestnut Street, S.W., Atlanta, Ga. 30314

Playboy—232 East Ohio Street, Chicago, Ill. 60611

Prairie Schooner—Andrews Hall, University of Nebraska, Lincoln, Nebr. 68508

Quarterly Review of Literature—26 Haslet Avenue, Princeton, N.J. 08540

Quartet—346 Sylvia Street, W., Lafayette, Ind. 47906

Ramparts—1182 Chestnut Street, Menlo Park, Calif. 94027

Readers & Writers—130-21 224th Street, Jamaica, N.Y. 11413

Redbook—230 Park Avenue, New York, N.Y. 10017

Shenandoah—Box 722, Lexington, Va. 24450

The Sewanee Review—University of the South, Sewanee, Tenn. 37375

The South Carolina Review—Dept. of English, Box 28661, Furman University, Greenville, S.C. 29613

The South Dakota Review—University of South Dakota, Vermilion, S.D. 57069

Southern Review—Drawer D, University Station, Baton Rouge, La. 70803

Southwest Review—Southern Methodist University Press, Dallas, Tex. 75222

The Tamarack Review—Box 159, Postal Station K, Toronto, Ontario, Canada

The Texas Quarterly—Box 7527, University of Texas, Austin, Tex. 78712

Trace—P.O. Box 1068, Hollywood, Calif. 90028

Transatlantic Review—Box 3348, Grand Central P.O., New York, N.Y. 10017

Trans Pacific—P.O. Box 486, Laporte, Colorado 80535

Tri-Quarterly—University Hall 101, Northwestern University, Evanston, Ill. 60201

The University Review—University of Kansas City, 51 Street & Rockhill Road, Kansas City, Mo. 64110

Venture (for Junior High)—910 Witherspoon Bldg. Philadelphia, Pa. 19107

The Virginia Quarterly Review—University of Virginia, 1 West Range, Charlottesville, Va. 22903

Vogue—420 Lexington Avenue, New York, N.Y. 10017

Washington Square Review—New York University, 737 East Bldg., New York, N.Y. 10003

Western Humanities Review—Bldg. 41, University of Utah, Salt Lake City, Utah 84112

Woman's Day—67 West 44th Street, New York, N.Y. 10036

Yale Review—26 Hillhouse Avenue, New Haven, Conn. 06520